The Attachés

Major General (Retired)

Charles Francis "Chuck" Scanlon

IM Press, Inc.

Fairfax Station, VA, 1997

Please direct all correspondence and book orders to:
IM Press, Inc.
P.O. Box 377
Fairfax Station, VA 22039-0377

Library of Congress Catalog Card Number 97-74248
ISBN 0-9660137-0-0

Published for IM Press, Inc. by
Gateway Press, Inc.
1001 N. Calvert Street
Baltimore, MD 21202

Printed in the United States of America

DEDICATION

Dedicated to those brave and often courageous men and women of the United States Armed Forces who tirelessly serve their country as military attachés. In countless foreign countries throughout the world, they are always vigilant, always on watch.

FOREWORD

The Attachés is an international adventure. The time of the book is the mid-1980s when the United States and the Soviet Union and their allies were inextricably bound in the deadly struggle between communism and the free world—the ideological struggle of the Cold War. The times were electric; no one knew when or how the confrontation would end, or if it ever would.

The Attachés is the story of one, not so well known, arm of the U.S. Military and Government that is engaged heavily in the Cold War and its many international by-products: wars, regional conflicts, terrorism, weapons proliferation, illegal drugs and espionage. This is the story of the Defense Attaché Service (DAS) and the selfless men and women who carry out its strategic missions around the world. The story is told through the eyes, voice and thoughts of the DAS commander, Major General Barton Lowe.

The DAS, like the story, is fictional, fashioned after the real world men and women who are part of an organization of military attachés existing within the U.S. Defense Department. The characters, events and locations used in the story are fictional, although inspired by similar events that occurred during the times of the novel. I have tried to be true to the history of the times, fictionally portraying as accurately as possible the kind of life and sometimes death adventures real military attachés experience around the world. Let's hope I have succeeded.

Washington, D.C.

ACKNOWLEDGMENTS

I am grateful for the encouragement and help from so many family members, friends, and professional associates.

All of my children, Teri, Brett, Ashlyn and Kellie and my wife B.J.—the real B.J., assisted in the preparation of the early drafts. Teri was my principal typist and devil's advocate.

The manuscript was read and critiqued by Major Generals Stan Hyman and Al Wheeler, Colonels Stu Herrington, George Malesish, Dick Powers, Nick Quinterelli, Jim Richey, Navy Captains Mike Messman, Walt Thomas, and Professors Richard Powers, Thomas Hines, CIA's Robert Davine, and historian Dean Allan. My best editorial advice came from Dr. Fred Kiley, Walt Thomas and Ann Hughes of Gateway Press and my tireless typesetter Rose Marie Dorer.

I am indebted to all of these professionals for their editorial assistance and thought provoking comments and suggestions. And a special thanks to Montie Sells and Frank Sullivan for providing me a quiet place to work in Florida where most of the book was written.

Finally, a special thanks to author Tom Clancy who inspired and encouraged me to write a novel.

CHAPTER 1

THE MIDDLE EAST - 1988

Colonel William Kennedy's alarm clock shattered the night. Startled, Paula, his wife, bolted upright in bed. "My God Bill, it can't be morning already."

"Shhh, go back to sleep. I'm going into the embassy early," Kennedy whispered.

"Early I can understand. But 2:00 a.m.? On a Saturday? What is it, another special mission?" she groaned.

Kennedy was already slipping into the hot shower, preparing for the demanding day ahead. He was a capable soldier-diplomat, but he had no idea how challenging the next 36 hours would be.

Kennedy had been accredited to the Syrian General Staff as the U.S. Defense and Army Attaché, or DATT, in Damascus, Syria for the past two and a half years. His military boss was Major General Barton Lowe, the demanding head of the Defense Attaché Service (DAS) in Washington. It was General Lowe's "TOP SECRET / EYES ONLY / IMMEDIATE ACTION" cable that Kennedy pondered driving through the still deserted streets of Damascus.

Eyes Only
MG Lowe sends for Col Kennedy info Ambassador Kizirian
Subject: New Terrorist Base Camp. Interagency information available here indicates probability of a new terrorist training base located approx 46 kilometers southeast of Damascus near Avon village. Coordinates 88754369. As in past any Syrian complicity will be denied unless we have further compelling evidence. You are directed to conduct a ground recon of the area ASAP during hours of darkness with the objective of photographing the suspected compound with

infrared. The operation must be free of Syrian surveillance. Abort the operation immediately if you or your personnel are in imminent danger. White House, Defense, JCS, CIA, FBI have all coordinated this action. Good luck and very best regards. - Bart Lowe - Eyes Only.

Kennedy, a 45-year-old, six foot, sandyhaired airborne ranger had conducted a number of special missions during the past two years. His remarkable success enabled the United States to minimize Syria's covert support of many terrorist groups operating in the Mid-East. But this remarkable success also worried Kennedy and his assistant attachés. Call it what you like, law of averages, Murphy's Law, whatever; Kennedy thought he might be overdrawn on his luck.

At 3:15 a.m. Kennedy walked through the U.S. Embassy entrance. He returned the salute of the surprised U.S. Marine on duty. Marine guards were used to seeing attachés occasionally appear at odd hours, but Kennedy was the fourth member to arrive within ten minutes.

As he opened the electronic security gate to admit Colonel Kennedy, the Lance Corporal guessed something really hot must be going on in Washington.

Once inside the Attaché office, Kennedy said, "Let's grab a cup of coffee and slip into the security conference room to cover the final details."

He had assembled Lieutenant Colonel Bob Taylor, the Air Attaché, Major Gordon Rumpner, one of the two Assistant Army Attachés and Marine Gunnery Sergeant Alvin Smith, the Operations Coordinator.

Kennedy's reconnaissance plan was a simple one. He was counting on the Syrian vehicle surveillance teams that regularly followed the attachés everywhere to conclude that this unusual assembly of the attachés in the middle of the night was due to some military alert in Washington. Each attaché and Gunny Sergeant Smith had driven his vehicle into the embassy garage because Kennedy had decided that no official vehicles would be used for this operation.

At precisely 4:00 a.m., the three attachés would leave the embassy and return to their quarters in the diplomatic section, a mile and a half from the embassy. The Syrian surveillance teams would follow and verify their return. Gunny Smith, according to normal habit, would stay behind to secure the Defense Attaché Office and its communications. Approximately 30 minutes later, Sergeant Smith would leave the embassy garage in his old VW van and, as usual, find that the Syrian surveillance teams paid no attention to him. This was a familiar scenario. The difference this time would be that instead of Colonel Kennedy driving his Lincoln Town car, it would be Gunny Smith who would drive the colonel's Lincoln, and remain in the car in the colonel's garage until Kennedy joined him with Smith's VW van just before daylight. If the ruse succeeded, it would appear to the morning Syrian surveillance team at Colonel Kennedy's quarters that Smith was probably dropping by some early cable traffic for the Colonel to review.

When Lieutenant Colonel Taylor and Major Rumpner learned that Colonel Kennedy intended to take on this important mission, they both protested, volunteering to go in his stead. But because of his army training and experience with night vision devices and equipment, Kennedy considered himself the best qualified man for the mission.

At 4:30 a.m. Kennedy drove away from the U.S. Embassy in Gunny Smith's VW van, attracting no attention from the Syrian security guards and surveillance teams. He started along the normally traveled route through the predominately residential neighborhood that led to the attaché living quarters. After six blocks and no sign of surveillance, he turned the van south toward the village of Avon.

Kennedy calculated the drive along Highway 6 from the embassy to Avon would take approximately 45 minutes; traffic was light at this time of the morning. In Avon he would need 15 minutes to locate his target and decide on the best vantage points for his reconnaissance and photography. Upon completing the mission, it would take one hour for the return drive to his quarters in Damascus. Highway 6 was a good road; one of the major arteries crossing Syria.

As he drove, Kennedy reviewed the contents of the briefcase beside him. He had 7X50 power binoculars with night vision attachments, two normal looking 35mm hand-held cameras with telephoto lenses, one primary and one for backup. Both cameras were loaded with infrared heat film designed to penetrate the darkness. He hoped they would reveal evidence of sophisticated weapons or devices the terrorists might be concealing in or around the compound. Several books and maps highlighting the cultural and religious histories of the Avon area covered the photographic equipment. They would serve as Kennedy's basis for plausible denial if he were stopped and questioned about why he was in Avon. Finally, Kennedy patted, for the fifth or sixth time, the official diplomatic ID in his left shirt pocket that identified him as a U.S. Military Attaché with diplomatic immunity issued by the Syrian Ministry of Foreign Affairs. He was ready for his mission.

Arriving in Avon at 5:15, he began his reconnaissance of the village. A few lights and candles were beginning to appear in windows, and some of the farm goats were stirring. Kennedy saw no police or security personnel and easily identified his target on the high ground behind the village water tank. The aerial photography provided to him by the Defense Intelligence Agency outlined the Avon area and the layout of the suspected terrorist compound.

His night vision binoculars revealed a dirt road that ran the entire distance along the high ground around the suspected terrorist compound. The compound was situated on 10 acres of rolling terrain with olive trees, and consisted of one main two-story house, a larger barn-like structure and six smaller one-story stone buildings of various shapes and sizes. Kennedy counted 10 vehicles parked by the house and barn. No guard post or individuals were outside the buildings. The entire compound was surrounded by a low, walled fence.

Kennedy thought he could photograph some of the buildings from the side streets and roads leading up to the compound. The best vantage point overlooking the compound was on the dirt road running around it. However, it also was the most risky: Kennedy saw no exits from that single road circling the compound. Once he entered the road, Kennedy could be trapped from either end.

But, the clock was running. He had to decide. Quickly he took several panoramic shots from the streets below the compound. Then he decided to take the risk. He turned in and drove slowly along the dirt road, with his lights off, snapping photos as he went. He detected no movement from the compound as he steered the van with one hand, slowing to about 10 mph, snapping the camera at each of the darkened buildings as they came into his line of sight.

Sweat covered Kennedy's body. His heartbeat was so loud it sounded like a tom-tom. He was about two-thirds of the way around the dirt road, thinking that the mission was going to be a success, when suddenly a light came on in the main house. Grabbing his night vision binoculars he saw a dozen armed individuals in dark clothing running out of the building toward two trucks. Concerned that he had been discovered, but not wanting to make his location obvious, Kennedy held his speed at 10 mph and continued to watch the compound in his binoculars. Reaching the trucks, the figures split into two groups, some in the truck cabs and the rest in the truck beds. The trucks quickly moved, heading with increasing speed toward the front gate of the compound. Kennedy knew he had been spotted. His actions now depended on what those trucks did as they reached the front gate of the compound.

Kennedy watched some of the men dismount, throw open the compound gate, remount, and head directly for the two ends of the dirt road. Kennedy quickly calculated the situation. The individuals in the trucks pursuing him were the very terrorists he had been tasked to identify. His only chance for escape was to beat the onrushing truck to the intersection where the dirt road around the compound ended. He tromped on the accelerator and the VW van lurched forward, mushrooming dust in its wake as he raced toward the road's end about a quarter of a mile away. It was going to be close. He reached the intersection first, and the truck arrived just a split second behind clipping the rear of his van with its front bumper.

He managed to keep control as the van veered into the streets of Avon. Unconcerned now about waking the villagers, he pressed for speed. Momentarily heartened by the view in the rear mirror, his celebration was short-lived. The collision had caused the truck to spin out of control and it was taking considerable time to turn about and resume its pursuit.

Anticipating that Kennedy might beat the first truck to the intersection, the second truck had gone to the key intersection in Avon that led back to the main highway. Numbingly, Kennedy looked ahead and saw the second truck blocking the road. The truck's headlights illuminated a half dozen men brandishing automatic weapons and rifles. Too late Kennedy saw the first truck closing fast from the rear, cutting off any escape. He eased the van to a halt.

Colonel William Kennedy followed the only course of action left—the standard instructions given to U.S. Military Attachés in difficulty in a foreign country.

"Remain in the vehicle with the doors locked. Open the window only enough to permit communication. Show diplomatic ID. Demand that the Syrian police and military authorities be summoned."

Six men from the first truck ran to the van where they were joined by six others from the second truck. They were relatively young males, bearded, and dressed in a variety of baggy pants, long shirts, vests and head wraps. They started beating on the van with their weapons. Peering into the van windows they could see Kennedy was alone.

Although Kennedy spoke educated Arabic, he could only pick up a few words of the odd dialect of the angry young men. Their group didn't seem to have a leader. All attempts to communicate with any single individual or to have anyone acknowledge his diplomatic credentials failed. He desperately hoped that the noise would wake some of the nearby villagers and cause them to call the police. Finally one of the youths with his face pressed against the van's front windshield, shouted "Out, Out, Out! You American dog. Out, or we will shoot you where you sit!"

Several men started firing at the tires of the van and began breaking the window glass with their weapons. Kennedy knew rescue or diplomatic recognition was hopeless. Reluctantly, he opened the locked door and gave himself over to the clutching hands of the frenzied group of terrorists, hoping to buy precious time for survival.

The next conscious thing Kennedy remembered was lying face down on the metal floor of a moving vehicle. Feet were on his head and across his entire body. He was covered with some coarse burlap material that smelled of animals and urine. His head throbbed from what must have been a blow from a gun butt. Exactly what happened when he was pulled from the van was not clear, but in the shadows of his mind the kicks and punches stood out. His hands were bound behind him and they ached from the wire cutting into his wrists.

When the vehicle stopped, his captors uncovered him, and dragged him from the truck that had carried him to the compound. Although it was still dark, Kennedy recognized they were in front of the main building of the compound he had been photographing. Kennedy was carried and pulled toward the building with all his captors striking out, trying to get a piece of him. They were like a pack of hounds wanting to share in the capture of the fox.

Once inside, Kennedy was pushed through what appeared to be several classrooms with tables, chairs, and small desks, to the rear of the building, past a storage room filled with military equipment. He was taken up two flights of steep wooden stairs to a large dormitory-like room containing 20 or more rumpled cots. He was pushed through the room and into a foul smelling, rusty piped, water-leaking latrine, and thrown on a filthy tile floor. The entrance door was locked, but Kennedy could hear angry loud voices on the other side. He was dripping with sweat, breathing heavily, and frightened. It was obvious the compound was being used as a terrorist training center.

As the shock of capture and the brutal blows began wearing off, he was able to right himself and crawl to the nearby wall. A cursory look around the room told him there was no chance of escape from the latrine. The locked door leading to the dormitory was the only egress. Now once again alert, he strained to interpret what was being said in the next room.

He was chilled to the bone when he understood, through the broken Arabic, that a debate was taking place over whether he should be killed immediately or his death delayed until someone named Ahmed returned the next day. Most of the voices in the other room roared for his immediate death. Only two or three of the individuals were arguing against execution. Their arguments sounded more procedural than humane. Someone named Omar was evidently a senior member of the compound's cadre. He argued that none of the "trainees" had the authority to order the American's death, and insisted Kennedy's disposition could only be decided by Ahmed upon his return tomorrow. Saturday was evidently a day when most of the teaching staff was elsewhere and Omar had been left in charge. From the heated discussions taking place in the next room, it was also clear to Kennedy that Omar's position of authority was somewhat tenuous. Kennedy was scared shitless.

Omar, however, proved to be a tenacious shouter and his logic won out. A delay until Ahmed returned was agreed upon. Soon thereafter Omar came into the latrine with a fat, surly looking assistant armed with an automatic rifle. Omar, a thin, middle-aged man, dressed simply in matching shirt and trousers, explained in broken English that he and his assistant, similarly dressed, were there to collect Kennedy's clothes and secure him until the return of Ahmed. The baling wire used to bind his hands and arms was removed; he was told to strip to his undershorts. Kennedy began to protest as Omar replaced the wire with handcuffs and a two-foot long chain; he quickly concluded Omar was not interested in diplomatic protocol, and the best his protests would produce would be another butt from the rifle. Despite his broken English, Omar made it crystal clear that death would definitely be forthcoming tomorrow when Ahmed returned. Omar left Kennedy, chained, near naked, feeling helpless and utterly alone.

At 7:00 a.m., as the first light streaked over the mosques, Gunny Smith, still sitting in Colonel Kennedy's Lincoln, waited in vain for his VW van.

"Holy shit," Smith thought. "It's not like the colonel to be late returning from a mission."

By 7:45 a.m. Smith knew something had gone wrong. He left the garage and went across the embassy quarters courtyard to the home of Lieutenant Colonel Bob Taylor. His first knock brought Taylor out. He, too, was concerned that Colonel Kennedy had not returned. After a brief phone call to Major Rumpner, the Assistant Army Attaché, he joined Smith and they all returned to the DAO. Finding no communication from Colonel Kennedy, Taylor called the ambassador to inform him of the situation.

"Good morning, Ambassador Kizirian. This is Lieutenant Colonel Bob Taylor. Sorry to disturb you so early on a Saturday morning, but I have some information that I'd like to give you on the secure telephone."

"Just a minute, let me switch over," replied the ambassador, punching the secure mode. "I'm ready. Go Bob."

"We executed our special mission early this morning to reconnoiter and photograph the suspected terrorist compound in Avon. Colonel Kennedy is now more than two hours overdue."

"What about car trouble?"

"If anything like that had occurred I'm sure he would have found a way to notify us. Something went wrong at the terrorist compound. If you agree, I intend to send Major Rumpner out to Avon in an official car to look around to see if we can determine what happened. I believe it would be prudent to alert our folks in Washington that we may have a problem."

Ambassador Kizirian agreed. "All right. Make sure your folks in Washington also inform the CIA and State Department.

Let me know the minute you hear anything from Rumpner. I want to meet here at the residence with you, the CIA Station Chief, and my Regional Security Officer at eleven o'clock. Will that give Rumpner time enough to report back to you on what he finds?"

"Yes, sir. I'll be in touch the moment I know something else and I'll see you at eleven."

Taylor, with more than 5,000 hours in the Air Force's FB-111 fighter bombers, was not unfamiliar with stress or danger, but his gut told him that his boss and friend was in a critical situation. He was not looking forward to calling Bill's wife, Paula.

It was seven hours earlier and still the middle of the night in Washington D.C. The clock radio in Major General Bart Lowe's bedroom at his quarters at Fort Myer, Virginia flashed 2:39 a.m. As he awoke, he estimated the secure phone had already rung two or three times.

"Lowe here."

"Sorry to wake you, General, but it looks like we have a hot one in Syria."

The caller was Air Force Colonel George Martin, General Lowe's Executive Officer. Martin, a bachelor like the General, always screened Lowe's after-duty hour calls to avoid awakening him unnecessarily.

"The duty officer received an "immediate" cable for you from the Air Attaché in Damascus reporting that the Defense Attaché, Colonel Bill Kennedy, is more than two hours overdue in returning from a special mission. The Air Attaché in Damascus has informed the ambassador and sent the Assistant Army Attaché into the area to see what he can find out. They don't expect to know any more before 0500 hours, Washington time."

"Doesn't sound good, George. Tell the Duty Officer to inform the Defense Intelligence Director. I am sure he'll want to let the Chairman, JCS, and SecDef's staff know. Also tell him to call the State and CIA operations centers and keep them in the loop. I'll call my friend, Ambassador Ross. Finally, George, let me know the minute we receive the next update from Damascus."

"Roger that; I'll be back to you as soon as anything breaks," Martin ended.

"Thank God for George Martin," Lowe thought. "I don't know what I'd do without him." Martin had been with him for the two years Lowe had been in charge of the Defense Attaché Service, routinely handling thousands of administrative details. He was the best time manager the general had encountered in any military service.

A sleepy voiced B.J. Ross, Assistant Secretary of State at the State Department's Intelligence and Research Bureau or INR, as it was known, finally answered after 9 or 10 rings on her secure phone. Lowe had known Ambassador Ross, a career Foreign Service Officer, for almost 10 years. They first met when she was the Deputy Chief of Mission at the U.S. Embassy in Bonn, Germany when Lowe had been a brigade commander. Over the years they had become best friends, and when their demanding careers would allow, occasional lovers.

"B.J., this is Bart. I regret the hour, but I need to let you know that our special terrorist mission in Syria may have been compromised."

"Oh no." B.J. was now fully awake.

"Our guy, Colonel Bill Kennedy hasn't returned from the special mission. I fear the worst. If he doesn't turn up quickly, what will our action and position be with the Syrians? You know how important the first few hours are in these situations. How do you rate your man in Damascus? I don't know him, and I haven't been out there since he became ambassador."

"He is a stand-up guy, very talented and most effective with the Syrians. Have you talked with him yet?" B.J. asked.

"No, but I intend to as soon as we receive the next update, which should be about 5:00 a.m. Washington time," Bart replied.

"I'll make sure our Syrian desk people are on top of this right away. I assume your guys informed our operations center?

Most likely we'll all spend Saturday on this. Thanks for the wake up call." B.J. sighed as she hung up the phone.

Lowe's phone rang again at 4:30 a.m. It was Colonel Martin.

"General, I have Lieutenant Colonel Taylor's latest message. Taylor says Major Rumpner's search of Avon met with negative results. No trace of Colonel Kennedy or the vehicle he used. Both Taylor and Rumpner suspect Kennedy was discovered and taken inside the compound. Rumpner reported that the fenced compound has armed guards at the front entrance. Rumpner will remain in the vicinity of Avon to watch for any sign of Kennedy or the van. Taylor is currently meeting with the ambassador and other embassy officials to determine what to do next."

"Got it, George. I'll get dressed and be in the office in thirty minutes," Lowe acknowledged.

Bart shaved, showered and pulled on his Army green trousers and pale green short-sleeved shirt with the two star black tabs. Twenty minutes later he hurried out the back door of his quarters to the garage where he slid into his 1975 Corvette. He had left the t-tops off the Corvette the previous evening, and decided not to take the time to put them on. He passed quickly through the rear gate of Fort Myer and turned onto the road running beside Arlington Cemetery. The fresh early breeze helped clear his mind so he could focus on the actions in the critical hours ahead.

At 7:30 a.m. Washington time, General Lowe was seated at the small conference table in his 11th floor office in the Stowe Building in Rosslyn. Around the table with him were Bill Libowitz, a civilian specialist who served as Division Chief for the Middle East; Colonel Mark Lender, USA, a former attaché to Syria; Bart's XO, George Martin and the State Department, DIA, and CIA liaison officers.

Lowe gestured to Libowitz with coffee mug in hand and said, "Okay Bill, where do we stand?"

"General, as you know, most of the country desk officers, here and at State, DOD, DIA, and CIA have been working together on this since the situation broke. State Department has the lead with us and other agencies in support. I'm told that the President has been informed and has stated, and I am quoting: 'The United States will not tolerate another incident like Lebanon.' You know he means the kidnapping and murder of Marine Lieutenant Colonel Higgins. The game plan is to lean on the Syrians. All here are in agreement that Kennedy is most likely being held in the terrorist compound. The thinking is that his captors have not had time to move Kennedy to another location and dispose of his vehicle. If we are wrong on this, our problem is much greater and we may never recover Kennedy. Assuming we are correct, the Syrians, if they choose to cooperate, can obtain his release. The terrorists are operating in Syria at the pleasure of the Syrian Government. They are paying dearly for Syrian support and will not want to offend their hosts. Such is the Arab world. The U.S. Ambassador will contact the Foreign Minister, demand an immediate personal meeting and insist that the Syrians go to the terrorist compound, locate and release Colonel Kennedy."

"Don't the Syrians already know that Kennedy is missing?" Lowe asked.

"Yes, Lieutenant Colonel Taylor reported it to his contact at the Syrian General Staff as soon as Major Rumpner had completed his search at Avon. We had to tip our hand, of course, concerning our information on the terrorist location because of the danger to Kennedy and so that the Syrians wouldn't try to fart it off as a routine matter."

"Also, do we know what, if any, leverage the ambassador will have in his pocket to use on the Syrians?" Lowe added.

"That's not clear yet. Diplomatic actions are being considered, but, I wouldn't be surprised to see JCS begin to run up some contingency strike options depending on how the situation develops. Bottom line, General, we're applying diplomatic pressure to see if we can get the Syrians to blink!"

Lowe looked around the table at the other agencies' liaison officers, "I've been in touch with your chiefs and I believe we're working this together as well as possible. Please pass my thanks along to your folks for their help."

Turning to Colonel Mark Lender, General Lowe directed, "Mark, I have spoken on the phone with Paula Kennedy. She is not doing too well. I know that you and Jean know Paula. It may help if you call her."

Then, standing to signify the end of the meeting, Lowe said, "Say a prayer for Bill Kennedy. He's going to need all the help he can get."

Ten minutes later, General Lowe was on the secure phone with Ambassador David Kizirian. "Mr. Ambassador, I regret that our first conversation since you visited the DAS in Washington before your confirmation has to be on such a critical matter."

"General, I want you to know that Bill Kennedy is one of the most valued members of our country team and I'm going to do everything in my power to prevent any harm from coming to him. I hope our efforts will be in time. As you may already know, the Department, the Secretary and even the President have all been very supportive and have lent considerable strength to the demands I've put to the Syrians. The problem is Foreign Minister Beiz won't agree to see me until 3:30 this afternoon. His assistants swear he's not available until then. The Syrians are obviously buying time to make their own assessments and review their options. On my instructions Lieutenant Colonel Taylor has been pressuring the Syrian General Staff to send a unit to the compound in Avon to search for Colonel Kennedy. Unfortunately, there's no movement on that front yet. General, it's about time for me to leave for the Foreign Ministry. I appreciate the call. We will be in touch with any progress," responded the Ambassador.

"Very best of luck Ambassador," Lowe said, returning the phone to its cradle.

Sixteen hours later the morning sun was warming the rural compound in Avon, where Bill Kennedy was held captive, still chained and handcuffed to a pipe between a smelly floor-level urinal and a dirty wash basin. His tether was short to prevent him from standing. His awkward position and the chill of the concrete floor had caused numbness across his lower body. The lack of circulation in his hands and wrists, caused cramping and severe discomfort up and down his arms. Without his watch he did not know how long he had been in the little room but estimatcd morc than 24 hours. No one had returned to the latrine. The angry young men who had captured him and had been shouting earlier in the adjoining room must have left. The latrine seemed well insulated from the rest of the building; he had heard no voice for hours. He had attempted several times to pull the pipe away from the wall, but to no avail. For the hundredth time he racked his brain for any possible way to escape, but nothing came to mind. Once more he mentally reviewed what he would say if and when the terrorist leader, Ahmed, showed up.

Finally, a tall, thin, tanned Arab man, surprisingly well dressed in a western suit and tie, stepped through the doorway accompanied by Omar and the rifle-toting assistant. The man held Colonel Kennedy's diplomatic pass in his hand, raised it up to compare the likeness of the photo on the ID with Kennedy's face, then said, in perfect English, "Colonel, I am Ahmed. You have presented us with quite a problem."

Kennedy immediately began, "Mr. Ahmed, as you can see from my credential I am a U.S. Diplomat accredited to the Government of Syria. People from this compound have illegally and forcefully kidnapped me. I've been held against my will. I demand that you contact the Syrian Foreign Office..."

"Colonel, don't insult my intelligence," Ahmed interrupted. "We know why you are here. You are a professional spy. Surely you considered the risk before you came snooping around here in the middle of the night. You can thank your God or my timid assistant that you picked a time when I was away. If I had been present at the time of your arrival, you may be assured that you would have been long gone from this place, probably never to be heard from again. You should consider yourself doubly fortunate that my young warriors didn't beat or kick you to death just for the training experience. Be that as it may, Inshallah, we must always deal with things as they are, rather than as they should be. What is clear to me now is that you have ruined everything for us. Evidently," he continued, "your government has told the Syrians you are here and is bullying the Syrian government to do something about it. The Syrians have, of course, been in touch with my superiors and my instructions are to wait until a mutual decision is reached. Strangely, the Syrians do not seem surprised. You'll be glad to know your fate is no longer in my hands." Turning, with obvious distaste, Ahmed spat into the urinal and departed.

For the first time Bill Kennedy dared to hope that he might see his wife and children again. Thank God, he thought, as pent up tears streamed down his face.

After what seemed like an eternity to Kennedy, but actually was nine hours later, Omar returned, again came into the latrine, and unlocked Kennedy's handcuffs, freeing him from the chain around the water pipe. Kennedy had a difficult time getting to his feet because of the loss of circulation in his legs, but managed to stand by grasping the sink and urinal for support. Omar gave him a brown paper bag containing his clothes, shoes, wallet, watch and diplomatic credentials. He also gave Kennedy a towel and a small bar of soap and suggested, in halting English and by gestures, that Kennedy might wash. Lastly, Omar brought some refreshment, a cup of goat's milk, a slab of unleavened bread and a crusty-looking piece of goat's cheese.

Although his spirits skyrocketed, Kennedy noted the irony that someone who had been arguing over whether to kill him could suggest, a short time later, that he might want to freshen up. One hour later, Omar came back into the latrine, announcing in Arabic, "Someone from Damascus is waiting in Ahmed's office for you."

As Kennedy was escorted into Ahmed's small, modern office he was relieved to recognize Brigadier General Affaz Briz. General Briz was one of Colonel Kennedy's closest contacts on the Syrian General Staff. Briz quickly got to his feet, shook Kennedy's hand and asked, "Bill, are you all right?"

Kennedy sternly replied, "I've been better, but I'm delighted to see you and anxious to leave this place."

Ahmed came around from behind his desk and walked over to Kennedy with a smile saying, "Colonel, sorry if we were too hard on you, but trespassing is a crime. Even in your country. But as two professionals, I hope there are no hard feelings," and extended his hand.

Kennedy squared his shoulders, looked Ahmed in the eyes and slowly said, "I cannot, by any stretch of the imagination, consider your cause—the senseless slaughter of innocent men, women and children—professional."

Ahmed withdrew his hand and quickly returned to the chair behind his desk. The hatred in his eyes was obvious.

During the ride back to the Syrian Foreign Ministry in Brigadier General Briz's staff car, the atmosphere was strained; not much conversation took place. Finally, Briz said, "Bill, I'm sure you are aware that this unfortunate incident has caused great embarrassment to my government. Based on your government's insistence, we will shut down the operation at the compound in Avon and ask the people there to leave Syria. We agreed to arrange your safe return and sincerely regret any mistreatment you may have suffered. I personally deplore these people and their actions, but you must understand the political realities of my country and the Middle East. My government does not take kindly to your role in this matter. You did not have the required permission of my office to be in Avon. From the Foreign Ministry's point of view you have exceeded your diplomatic privileges and embarrassed Syria in the eyes of the Arab world. My government insists that you be declared persona non grata and leave our country. You may be sure our government was aware of your plan to investigate the compound, Bill, although I will deny I told you this."

As they were pulling up in front of the Foreign Ministry, Kennedy was relieved to see the familiar faces of Ambassador Kizirian and Lieutenant Colonel Bob Taylor waiting at the entrance. Kennedy turned to his Syrian contact, "General Briz, I am grateful to you for coming to my rescue. I will always value our professional friendship and regret any differences our two governments may have. But you must know that Syria cannot be a true friend to the United States and continue to support international terrorism."

In Washington it was 2:10 p.m. and General Lowe was finishing up a phone conversation with Colonel Kennedy, who was back in his quarters with his family. "Bill, I know it's been a long day for you. Perhaps your longest day ever. You need to know that through your courage and determination, you have struck a significant blow against terrorism. We are very proud of you. You were one soldier all alone in an enemy camp, but one that the entire government of the United States quickly came on line for in a big way."

"Thank you sir; thank you for everything."

"Our DAS officers will assist you and Paula in your move back to the States. Let me know if you need my help. Good night and God bless," Lowe concluded. George Martin entered Bart's office and, as a man who had been awake and working a crisis for more than thirty hours straight said, in a bone-tired tone, "General, why don't we take the rest of the day off?"

"That's one hell of a good idea, George." Lowe stood up, stretched, realized how tired he also was, grabbed his hat and was quickly out of his office, into the elevator and on his way to the parking garage.

As General Lowe drove along the George Washington Parkway, en route to his quarters at Fort Myer, the Sunday afternoon traffic was light and the sun was warm. When he entered the gate at Fort Myer and returned the salute of the MP on duty, he was, as always, conscious of Arlington Cemetery on the left side of the road. Proceeding up the hill toward his quarters he vividly recalled the circumstances that, two years earlier, had brought him to this challenging job as Director of Attachés.

CHAPTER 2

THE GENERAL

Major General Barton Scott Lowe, USA, was an over-achiever. From the first day of his commissioning as a second lieutenant of infantry, he was recognized as a superior officer. He was promoted to major after only seven years of service. This exceptional achievement was followed by early promotions to lieutenant colonel and colonel. Many more senior officers he worked for, within the Army, and in joint service assignments, reported "this officer is destined to become a General." Their prophesy proved to be true. In 1982, at the age of 43, Lowe was promoted to Brigadier General.

Bart Lowe advanced to Major General in 1984 and was assigned to command the Army's most prestigious infantry division in Germany. For an infantry officer in the U.S. Army there is no greater satisfaction than serving at the head of a twenty-thousand strong fighting force. He relentlessly trained the young men and women of the 3rd Infantry Division on the terrain of West Germany where so many historic battles had taken place.

For Bart Lowe, Commanding General of the 3rd Infantry Division was the fulfillment of his boyhood dreams, an achievement beyond his fondest expectations. From the outset of his command he knew intuitively that anything after the division would be anti-climatic. As a result Lowe, then in his 20th month in command and in his 26th year of service, decided it was time for him to retire from the Army. He so advised the people in the General Officer Management Office, in Washington, and asked that they pass his intention along to the Chief of Staff of the Army, General Gordon Reiley.

General Reiley was disappointed to learn that one of his superstars was planning an early retirement. He decided he would not approve General Lowe's retirement until he met with Lowe to discuss the matter. Reiley planned to see Bart Lowe the following month during a visit to Army troops in Germany.

When General Reiley sat down with Bart in Regensberg, Germany, and heard Lowe's explanation for his early retirement, he reluctantly agreed to approve it. However in June of 1986, when Lowe had less than 30 days left in command and only a few weeks of Army service before retirement, the VII Corps Commander, Lowe's boss in Germany, surprised him with a late call on a Friday night. "Bart, I had a call from General Reiley this afternoon. He wanted to know if I could spare you for a few days; he wants to see you in Washington on Monday."

"Did you tell him that you or the division couldn't possibly do without me for a single day?"

"Hell no, Bart. My daddy didn't raise no fools. I told him of course the VII Corps and its hot-shot 3rd Infantry Division Commander would be delighted to support the request. And you make sure you get your ass on up to Frankfurt and get a flight back to the Pentagon pronto!

"What could the Chief want with me at this late date? I'm all but out the door."

"I didn't ask and the Chief didn't say. We both know the chief would never take a commander away from his troops if he didn't have a damn good reason."

"Yes sir." said Lowe.

"Then get on with it."

On Monday morning Lowe reported to the Chief of Staff of the Army's office at 0800 hours. He had been able to get a military flight from Rhein Main AFB to McGuire on Saturday night and a hop into Andrews AFB on Sunday morning. The Chief's Aide-de-Camp, Major Dick Dunkle, told Lowe, "the Chief will be able to see you at 0830 when he returns from morning briefings in the

Army Operations Center." Major Dunkle got General Lowe a cup of coffee and escorted him into the Chief's private waiting room.

As he sat in the small but comfortable anteroom, General Lowe was lost in the pleasant thoughts of the past and his earlier service in the Pentagon. He had lost track of time and was startled to hear someone say "Bart, Bart." He looked up from his reverie and saw General Reiley standing in the adjoining door of his offices.

"Come on in," the General invited. "Have you had enough coffee?"

"Yes sir," replied Bart.

"Then come on over and sit down." The chief motioned him to one of his office easy chairs and sat on the large couch opposite him. "Bart, as the saying goes," Reiley began, "you are probably wondering why I've asked you to come here. I want to make you an offer—an offer I hope you won't refuse."

"Two weeks ago the Chairman of The Joint Chiefs of Staff and his J2, Lieutenant General Lennie Murphy, came to see me with a problem. Maybe you know Murphy? He served in Germany last year at the U.S. Air Force Headquarters, Europe. He's the Director of the Defense Intelligence Agency. The crux of their problem," explained Reiley, "is that they need an officer to be the Director of the Defense Attaché Service, the DAS. Not just any officer. They need the right officer." Reiley went on. "The guy they currently have is ill and about to be medically retired. His replacement was supposed to come from the Navy, but the Navy says they don't have the right person available. The chairman could force their hand but he's worried that the officer they would send wouldn't be qualified. The bottom line is that while it's not the Army's turn, we've been asked to pick up the slack."

General Reiley continued. "The Chairman doesn't ask many favors. He spent a lot of time telling me how important the attachés we have are to the Defense Department, JCS, and the military services. General Murphy, the DIA boss, emphasized that because of the high visibility of the attaché service with Congress, the State Department, OSD, JCS, CIA, and the FBI, they require the kind of officer who can command the respect of those different interests ***and*** have the military savvy to be effective with the military leaders of foreign countries. I told the Chairman and Murphy that the Army would step up to the problem and nominate an officer.

At that point, Lowe started to protest, but before he could say anything Reiley stopped him with a wave of the hand. "Before you tell me all the reasons why I shouldn't nominate you for this job or about any plans you made for the future, I want you to go and see some people this week and talk to them about this job. Appointments have been made with their offices. When you have seen and talked to them, come back to see me on Friday afternoon and if you still think I shouldn't throw you into this briar patch then; well, we'll see. Now get the hell out of here and let me get on with running the Army." General Reiley stood up and returned to his desk. The meeting and any further discussion was obviously over.

Back in the small temporary office on the "C" ring of the Pentagon that the Army's Protocol Office provides for visiting general officers, Bart Lowe sat at his desk and reviewed the list of officials General Reiley had provided.

As Bart read the list he was impressed with the talent represented within the Washington power structure. Whatever the outcome, Lowe thought, it should be a very, very interesting week.

Lowe called his chief of staff at his infantry division in Europe to let him know he would be in Washington five more days. It occurred to him that it also might be useful to talk with two old friends who were presently serving in Washington. The first, a long standing acquaintance from Germany, Foreign Service Officer, B.J. Ross; the other a classmate from Lowe's year at the Naval War College, Rear Admiral Eugene Chomko, recently reassigned from his duties as the Defense and Naval Attaché in Moscow to the Naval Operations staff in the Pentagon.

Lowe located Chomko's phone number from the Pentagon directory and convinced Admiral Chomko's executive assistant that the general needed to talk to the admiral that morning. The two

friends agreed to meet for lunch in the Chief of Naval Operations' Mess.

Lowe was not as successful in reaching his other friend, Ambassador, B.J. Ross, Deputy of the Intelligence and Research Bureau for European Affairs. No amount of persuasion could convince her administrative assistant that Major General Lowe's call was more important than the series of meetings the ambassador was attending. The best Lowe could achieve was an agreement to pass his name and phone number to Ambassador Ross at the end of the day.

Bart was delighted to see his old friend Gene Chomko and almost before they could sit down at the two-person table in a corner of the Mess, Admiral Chomko asked, "I assume your schedule will allow for racquetball?"

"I thought you'd never ask," Bart replied.

"How about 6:30 a.m. tomorrow and Thursday? Or is that too early for a ground pounder?"

"No way. That's the middle of the afternoon for a good infantryman," Bart shot back.

The Navy steward served the two officers iced tea and they both ordered soup and salad.

Following twenty minutes or so of pleasantries and several servings of strong, black Navy coffee, Chomko asked, "So, what brings you to Washington?"

Bart related the proposition General Reiley had thrown him earlier in the morning, and also told Chomko of his tentative plans to accept an offer from a college classmate who was a land developer in Florida. "I don't know if you remember, but I served a two-year attaché tour as a major in Germany but that was 15 years ago and a lot has changed, I'm sure. I'd appreciate your views on the DAS, Gene, since you completed your assignment in Moscow a short time ago."

Admiral Chomko signaled the steward for a refill on his coffee, settled back in his chair and began. "My time in Moscow was the most meaningful in my career. A lot of that had to do with dealing with the Soviets and the changes and events that are taking place there now. I believe there are more to come. They're still our major adversary and, in my mind, our biggest threat. I came away with some satisfaction at what we were able to accomplish, also, with many frustrations—most with the Russians, but some with the State Department and many with the Washington bureaucracy."

Sipping his coffee, Chomko continued. "The Defense Attaché Service is a fine organization; it's brimming with talent from all the services, particularly the Army's Foreign Area Specialists. And career civilians give it excellent continuity. But the program is not without problems. Its budget lines and authorities are often not clear and its director is under the gun to be effective in the arenas where he must play. The current head of DAS, Tom Tibbets, has done a good job, but his health has failed, and lately I think he's overwhelmed with the responsibilities of having to deal with 135 countries, aging aircraft and vehicles, and international real estate accounts that would make ReMax green with envy. Add to that a constant running argument with each of the military services to make sure they provide the DAS with consistently top flight people, and the never-ending grind of interagency coordination in Washington to make sure you're not stepping too hard on the wrong toes. Not to mention the dealings with the Congressmen who believe they're really the ones in charge of every Defense program. Have I scared you off with all these negativcs?"

"Sounds challenging for the right person."

"I think so. Let me summarize by saying that the U.S. DAS is the best of its kind, ever, anywhere. Like any military organization DAS has its fair share of bad apples, discipline problems, and getting the right people in the right jobs at the right places, but a lot less than most military commands. If I hadn't already served my Moscow tour in the DAS, I would have fought

for Tibbets' job. I agree with your Chief. You're the right man for the job!"

"Well, it does sound like an interesting assignment. I'm not sure though it's the right time for me. Thanks, for your valuable insights."

Getting up, Chomko said, "I guess I'd better be getting back to that job of mine. It's great seeing you again. Don't forget—6:30 racquetball—tomorrow."

"I'll be there."

Back in the BOQ that evening Bart had just returned from a three mile run around the perimeter of Fort Myer. He pulled off his running shoes and his sweats, grabbed a bottle of mineral water from the mini-fridge and settled into the easy chair to watch the evening news on television. There's no place in the world, Bart thought, that can rival Washington's focus on the evening television news. After hearing the CNN headlines, he switched to CBS and was following a Dan Rather story on the environment when the phone rang.

"Bart Lowe."

"Is this the famous army general from Germany?"

"Is this the famous lady ambassador?" replied Bart, recognizing B.J. Ross' raspy voice.

"Bart, how are you? It's great to hear your voice again."

"I'm doing just fine, B.J., and the feeling is mutual."

"Well, tell me what you are doing here and how long you will be in town."

Bart told B.J. he was at Fort Myer, explained his offer from the Army's Chief of Staff, and told B.J. he'd appreciate hearing her views and experiences regarding the Defense Attaché Service.

"That explains why I saw your name on Bob Schoenfield's calendar for Wednesday," replied B.J. "Bob is a West Point graduate and, as I'm sure you know, was our Ambassador to Germany. You two will have a lot in common. Bart, I know it's

last minute, but if you're willing to take pot luck I can scare us up something from the kitchen."

Bart gladly accepted and B.J. said, "I'm at River House, just across from the Pentagon, not more than 10 minutes away. Slip into something casual and I'll pick you up in front of Wainwright Hall in 30 minutes."

"Yes ma'am! I'd be delighted to dine with the Ambassadress. I promise to clean the mud off my boots and bring my best table manners."

"In your ear, soldier!" B.J. fired back.

True to her word, she drove up in a sleek, black BMW to the front of Wainwright Hall precisely on time. It had been over three years since they had last seen each other. Bart was wearing a navy, double breasted blazer, tan casual trousers, a blue oxford button down shirt and black loafers. She noted his hair was a little grayer, but that, along with his piercing green eyes, added to the distinguished look about him that always attracted her.

Sliding into the front seat of the BMW Bart admired B.J.'s tailored, fit, strikingly attractive appearance. At age 45, she had no trace of gray in her thick, ash-blond hair. Dressed in conservative brown—long pants and matching pullover sweater and shirt, she was a model of mature beauty, health and confidence. As they exchanged friendly kisses on the cheek, Bart thought how fortunate he was to know this bright, exceptionally talented, and very, very attractive woman.

Following cocktails—Bart helped prepare a salad while B.J. concocted a delicious three bean soup, a long-standing family recipe she always kept in the freezer, she said, for unexpected guests. Their dinner by candlelight was a pleasant reminder of earlier times together. Amazing what a little wine, soft music and a beautiful woman will do for you, Bart thought.

During dinner, Bart and B.J. discussed his possible reassignment and B.J. provided a number of helpful insights based on her own experience with the DAS.

"The Military Attaché Service is, in my opinion, an indispensable capability the United States cannot do without," B.J.

said. "The individual attachés, in terms of linguistics and political-military insights are often among the most capable and visible Americans representing us abroad. Also," B.J. smiled, "for my money, the DAS couldn't pick a better leader than you, Bart Lowe."

On the following Friday morning Bart awoke at his usual time of 5:00 a.m. After 30 minutes of pushups, sit-ups, and stretching exercises, he shaved, showered, listened to the morning CNN updates and went down to the small mess in the basement of Wainwright Hall for breakfast. During the meal he read *The Washington Post, The New York Times* and scanned *The Wall Street Journal.* When he had finished, he was not yet certain on what he was going to tell General Reiley, that afternoon. He decided a run through nearby Arlington Cemetery would help him review the past week and lead him to the decision he must make.

In his earlier tours at the Pentagon, Bart always relished the opportunities to run through the Cemetery. The wind on his face helped to clear his head, and relieve the tensions of long, action-packed days. Now, as he jogged through the curving roads leading through row after row of white crosses and stars of David, he was once again humbled in the presence of so vivid a reminder of American military sacrifice and the country he loved. Lowe was proud to be an American soldier. As he ran, his thoughts turned to his family, his friends, and Florida. Bart's father had passed away when he was a lieutenant. His mother was living in the family home in Miami, but getting along in years and looking forward to having her only son nearby. The offer from his life-long friend, Dick Groveland, had been for more money than Lowe could imagine. Lowe had been looking forward to working with his old friend "Rags" Groveland.

The past week was both hectic and fascinating. His meetings with the officials General Reiley had arranged for him was like an instant graduate course in American civics and foreign policy. To a person, they characterized the attachés as unique sets of eyes and ears around the world, making an indispensable contribution to U.S. security, military assistance and foreign policy.

Lowe had been surprised to learn how much the State Department, CIA and FBI officials knew about the Defense Attaché Service and how important its efforts were to them in their own work. While Lowe had served a tour as an attaché and spoke three foreign languages, he realized he had thought of the DAS much along the lines of his own one-country experience and had never really appreciated or fully understood the big picture.

The only down side to what he had heard concerned the frequent interagency in-fighting that he was told took place regularly in Washington over roles and missions, manning, and funding. All the people he spoke with addressed the necessity of maintaining a high quality attaché capability for America in an ever-dangerous world.

Finally, Bart recalled his visit yesterday afternoon with the current head of the DAS, Brigadier General Tom Tibbets and the informal panel discussion Tibbets had arranged at the DAS Headquarters in Rosslyn, Virginia, with a dozen currently serving or former military attachés. The officers, representing all the military services, impressed Bart as proud, dedicated, and exceptionally competent. They addressed the internal workings of the Defense Attaché Service long term requirements for personnel, training, equipment and funding, and the strengths and weaknesses of the DAS. They stressed the importance of DAS's need for someone at the helm who could be counted on to fight the necessary bureaucratic battles, look after the attachés and their families, and provide cohesion and strong direction to the worldwide attaché offices. Clearly, the attachés had set high standards for themselves and high expectations for their leader.

Still running in Arlington Cemetery, but lost in his thoughts, Bart glanced down at his watch and realized he had been running for almost an hour. A light morning drizzle had become a steady rain and the rain was now coming down in earnest. Up ahead he noticed a freshly dug, but yet, unfilled grave, under a large, heavily branched tree. The tree offered some temporary shelter from the downpour and a place for him to rest. Okay, Lowe thought to himself, it's time to bite the bullet.

He had heard nothing during the week that would scare him away, but the job at the DAS, due to his inexperience, would certainly be a challenge for him. The lines of authority within the Army were clear cut, and the chain of command was a simple and effective one. Not so in the DAS, he was sure. The job could be fraught with frustration. But what about the positive side? There was a responsibility for keeping a U.S. military grip on the pulse of the world. Even the power of a modern infantry division paled when compared with DAS's area of operations. He needed to think of the DAS job as an opportunity; and Bart Lowe never met an opportunity he didn't like!

So, on a rainy summer morning in Arlington National Cemetery, in his 26th year of service to the Army, he decided, "What the hell. Who needs a lot of money? I'm ready for the DAS."

Ironically, a year earlier, another man who had devoted his life to serving his country also reached an important decision concerning his own future. His name was Harold Sema.

Sema had worked many years within a U.S. Government institution sworn to protect the country against all enemies foreign and domestic. With an exceptionally high IQ and an education from an Ivy League school, he began his government career with high expectation and optimism. The optimism faded and, although he was relatively successful over the years, advancing into the senior ranks of the institution, it was not enough. Never, Sema believed, had his true abilities or potential been recognized or rewarded. He resented that lesser people were given the best jobs and responsibilities, as he viewed his career.

Disappointment led to disgruntlement, then disillusion, then disaffection. But these feelings had been carefully concealed from colleagues.

So, on a rainy morning last year, Sema had walked the streets of Georgetown for several hours pondering his future. The thought of what to do with his unhappy life had been going on for some time and, like Bart, someone also had approached him with an offer that had to be either accepted or rejected. The more he thought about it, the more the offer appealed to him as a rare opportunity, a chance to make up for all his years of frustration.

That fateful morning, Harold Sema had decided to accept the offer. An offer to commit treason.

CHAPTER 3

THE ATTACHÉS

GENERAL ORDERS	HEADQUARTERS OF THE ARMY
No. 64	ADJUTANT GENERAL'S OFFICE
	WASHINGTON, August 25, 1880

Hereafter, officers of the Army traveling or stopping in foreign countries, whether on duty or leave of absence will be required to avail themselves of all opportunities, properly within their reach, for obtaining information of value to the military service of the United States, especially that pertaining to their own arm or branch of service. They will report fully in writing the result of their observation to the Adjutant General of the Army on their return to duty in the United States, if unable to do so at an earlier date.

By COMMAND OF GENERAL SHERMAN:

The U.S. Military Officers Manual, 6th Edition, revised in May 1917, in its instruction for military attachés, defined:

> "Requisites: Good address, intelligence, tact and industry; knowledge of the country where he is stationed, especially a speaking knowledge, and a sufficient income to live in a fitting manner and associate with his fellows of the Diplomatic Corps."
>
> "Duties: Consist in collecting whatever information would be useful, directly or indirectly to our government, concerning the country where he is stationed; organization, improvements in weapons, intentions, all new ideas and old ones not yet familiar to us.

Some of his reports are in answer to questions from his chief, but his most useful ones will be original."

"Guidance: A military attaché represents on every occasion his country and his military; he must not do or appear to do anything that can lower their prestige. He can afford to go only with the best company; frequent only the best places of amusement, hotels, etc. and present the appearance of a man of rank and dignity."

Through the WW I and WW II periods and into the 1960s each military service was responsible for its own attaché system. While this arrangement pleased the individual services, duplication existed at the attaché posts abroad and in information reporting, management and budget processes. Recognizing these shortcomings, in 1964, Robert McNamara, Secretary of Defense, made the decision to designate a senior defense attaché in each foreign country to support the U.S. Ambassador and to supervise the work of all U.S. attachés assigned to that country.

The Defense Attaché was charged with reporting to the Secretary of Defense through the Joint Chiefs of Staff. To further consolidate control over the military attachés, McNamara gave the newly established Defense Intelligence Agency, (DIA), operational, management and budget responsibilities for the new Defense Attaché Service. DAS was established in 1965 with approximately 2,000 personnel and attaché offices in nearly 100 countries.

The U.S. Military Services took umbrage at first to McNamara's actions, but acquiesced when promised that the services, the major U.S. military commanders around the world, and the JCS would be the principal customers of the DAS. The staffing of the DAS was from the combatant arms of each military service on rotating assignments, ensuring current professional thinking on land, sea and air warfare and technology. Many observers believed Robert McNamara created DIA and DAS to provide Defense an in-house information, intelligence and analysis capability as a counter-weight to CIA and State Department political/military reporters serving around the globe.

Most Defense Attaché Offices, (DAOs), were headed by colonels of the Army, Air Force and Marines, or Navy captains. Some of the larger countries, such as the USSR, China, France, Mexico, and Brazil had U.S. generals or admirals at the helm of the DAO. The senior commissioned officers were backed up by other officers and warrant officers and non-commissioned officers from all services to assist with the operational and administrative work. In the larger DAOs, Department of Defense civilians and host country foreign nationals augmented the military staffs.

The caliber of individuals who had served in the DAS was driven home to Lowe on the first day in his new job when his Executive Officer, Colonel George Martin, suggested Lowe visit the Attaché Hall of Fame. The Hall of Fame was fashioned in the form of historical attaché plaques, pictures and mementos similar to the many collections and displays in the Pentagon hallways honoring the nation's more well known military heroes.

"When I first came to the DAS, General Lowe, I had no idea how many of our best known military leaders had served as attachés, starting with General of the Armies, General John J. Pershing, who was our attaché to Japan in 1904."

"I didn't know that," Bart admitted.

"When you get to WW II," Martin said, pointing down the hall, "You'll find Generals Vinegar Joe Stilwell, and Max Tailor served earlier as attachés to China. Also, my own favorite, General Toey Spatz, who was the first Chief of our Air Force. Admiral Bull Halsey, served as an attaché in Denmark and Norway."

"George, is General Walters in the Hall of Fame?" Bart asked.

"Oh, yes sir. I think you can safely say that General Vernon Walters is an attachés 'attaché.' He is probably the most respected of those who have served as attachés based on linguistic and diplomatic skills and his service in Italy, Brazil, France, and at CIA and the UN."

"I am impressed, George, and I know I will find enough fascinating history here to keep me busy for a while. It was a good suggestion."

"Before I leave you, boss, let me point out that in that section at the end of the hall you'll find many other distinguished soldiers, sailors, airmen, and marines like Generals Brent Scowcroft, Samuel Wilson, William Odom, James Williams and Admiral Bobby Inman who served as attachés when they were junior officers and all rose to head important U.S. agencies such as the National Security Council, DIA, NSA and CIA. That's an important set of people for our young attachés in training because they are living proof that attaché duty is career enhancing. With that recruiting commercial, I'll leave you General to meander through the hallowed halls," George said, turning and walking away.

Forty-five minutes later, when he had finished his walk Lowe realized he was to follow in the footsteps of many great Americans.

☆ ☆ ☆

Two weeks had passed. It was Friday evening and at DAS headquarters in Rosslyn, Lowe watched a steady stream of headlights leaving the city.

While viewing the traffic from his 11th floor office window, Bart mentally reviewed the facilities and personnel that combined to provide him with an efficient headquarters.

DAS Headquarters was leased by the government and the owners had refurbished and remodeled the office spaces. Bart's predecessor had been in the new office for only a short time and it was in mint condition, tastefully decorated with pictures of tanks, ships, aircraft and missiles as well as military paintings from the past. Bart added his collection of small arms, fighting knives and swords, forwarded from Germany, that he had acquired during 26 years of Army service.

After his departure from Germany and thirty days leave in Florida with old friends, Bart returned to Washington, anxious to start his new job. General Reiley arranged for Bart's living quarters at Fort Myer. Although Bart was a bachelor, his attaché responsibilities made it necessary for him to have a home for formal entertaining to reciprocate for the social invitations that would come his way from embassies that reside in Washington. Bart enjoyed his Victorian-style, three story home at Fort Myer. He was doubly delighted when General Reiley told him he could also have his enlisted aide from his division, Master Sergeant Sam Wild, transferred to Washington from Germany to assist him at his quarters. Sergeant Wild had been in the enlisted aide program for many years and was an absolute master of military household matters. He could prepare a casual dinner for two or a formal one for 24. This was good news for Sergeant Wild whose family lived in the Washington area.

In the initial background briefings arranged for him, Bart learned the Defense Attaché Service had approximately 300 people in Washington to direct, support, assist, and manage 1500 attaché personnel serving around the world. DAS Headquarters was divided into eight divisions: an Operations Division, a Support Division, a Special Services Division and five geographical divisions—one for Eastern Europe and the USSR, one for Western Europe, one for the Middle East and Africa, one for South and Central America and one for the Pacific. The personnel, budget, logistics and real estate functions were handled in the Support Division. The Special Services Division dealt with sensitive activities, and worked closely with the CIA, FBI and the Military Service Intelligence and Security Organizations. The line divisions were headed up by colonels and/or Navy captains, who previously served in the field as attachés. A Senior Executive Service, (SES) civilian was in charge of the Support Division. The divisions were staffed with a mix of military and GS-13, GS-14 and GS-15 level civilians. Lowe was impressed with the knowledge, enthusiasm and professional caliber of the military and the civilians serving at attaché headquarters.

Lowe had two Deputies, Pete Kalitka, a Navy Captain, and Chuck Gregorios, the senior civilian. Chuck had entered the Department of Defense career service after a stint with the military. He was a rock solid manager with a firm grip on all activities at headquarters and Pete complemented him with his strong ties to Defense attachés in the field. Pete was a Navy SEAL with excellent special operations credentials.

General Lowe's personal staff consisted of his Executive Officer, Colonel George Martin, also a bachelor, the office secretary Joan Weber, an outgoing, older woman who made everyone feel their telephone call, visit, or subject was the most important one of the day, and a tireless, no nonsense, administrator, Navy Commander, Dolly West. From what Bart observed, their Herculean efforts allowed them to barely keep their heads above the heavy seas of messages and correspondence. After a few days of witnessing the fast pace of office activities, Bart Lowe was confident the DAS front office staff was exceptionally talented.

Still mesmerized by the fascinating Washington skyline, Bart ambled back to his desk and picked up a small black notebook, and moved over to one of the overstuffed, red leather chairs in the conversation group of sofa, chairs, tables, and lamps at the other end of his office. He settled back in one of the leather chairs, switched on the lamp on the adjoining table, removed his shoes, and put his feet up on the facing walnut coffee table. He turned to the notes that covered his meeting with Lieutenant General Lennie Murphy, the Director of the Defense Intelligence Agency.

He and Murphy had hit it off the first time they met. Murphy was a career Air Force officer, and an expert on the Soviet Union and strategic weapons systems with more than 30 years of service. By looking at his notes Bart was able to recall Murphy's words. "You've probably heard this before and will hear it again. The DAS is a unique resource for the United States. These highly trained attachés around the world provide us sets of eyes and ears that are indispensable to our national security. Our attachés are often in competition with their counterparts in the State Department and CIA, but when the chips are down and we need to know the bottom line on what countries or situations pose a security threat to the United States and its fighting forces, the attachés are the people we look to; they never let us down.

Our attachés do many important tasks across the spectrum of Defense needs such as information reporting, liaison with the host country's military, escorting Defense visits, administering military assistance programs, and assisting the U.S. Ambassador and his staff." Pointing his finger at Bart, Murphy continued, "You will run the Defense Attaché Service." Some people have the mistaken belief that, as Director of DIA, I'm in the day-to-day business of running the DAS. I do get a lot of calls, and communications on DAS matters, but I'll refer all those to you. I have more than I can possibly juggle trying to keep the Secretary and the Chairman and their staffs happy. DAS deserves and demands a full-time, completely dedicated leader and that's you. If you're clear on that," Murphy continued, banging his fist on his desk, "let's move on.

The Attaché Corps must have quality people. You shall insist that the military services provide only their best for attaché duty. The services, of course, have their own priority missions and they won't make this easy for you. Be tough! The Army's Foreign Area Officer program is by far the best foundation for attaché duty. See if you can persuade the other services to adopt similar programs. Again the emphasis must be on quality."

Slowing down a bit, Murphy concluded. "Finally, you need to look after the safety and security of our attachés and their families. Our folks are in harm's way everyday. Many are living in dangerous places and terrorist threats in many countries are present. The duties of our people take them off the beaten track of the diplomatic circles and their security is often at risk. Make sure you are doing all you can to look after their safety."

The last words still echoed in Bart's mind when he left Murphy's Pentagon office still echoed in Bart's mind.

As he sat in his easy chair with his feet propped up, thinking over his meeting with Lieutenant General Murphy details of a plan continued to formulate in Bart's mind—a plan on how to best take on his new responsibilities. He was anxious to get out to the field and meet the attachés where they were working but he knew this would be premature until he had a better understanding of how DAS headquarters operated and interfaced with other Washington organizations. Bart also wanted to know his headquarters people better, meet other department and agency heads and visit attaché training sites in the U.S. He estimated this probably would take at least 90 days. With those thoughts in mind Bart Lowe stood up, gathered his briefcase and hat and opened his office door.

George Martin, still at his desk, rose and said, "Had enough fun for today, boss?"

"You bet I have. I'll be in over the weekend to plow my way through the mounds of briefing and background papers you guys prepared for me. Also, you might alert the team in the Operations Center that I'll spend some time with them to learn how they monitor actions around the world. No need for you to be here, George. I'll be on the beeper or at my quarters if anyone should need me."

Going down the elevator, Bart's thoughts turned with pleasure to his 10:00 p.m. dinner with Ambassador B.J. Ross at Clyde's in Georgetown.

CHAPTER 4

HEAT SEEKER

Bart made the short drive from Rosslyn to his quarters at Fort Myer to change out of his uniform and shower before meeting B.J. in Georgetown. She had anticipated a late Friday at the State Department and told Bart she would meet him at the restaurant. Upon entering his quarters, Bart went directly to the kitchen, opened the fridge and took out a bottle of Heineken's and the frosted German beer glass that Master Sergeant Wild had left for him. After his first satisfying draught, Lowe moved out to the desk in the small alcove between the kitchen and dining room.

Bart looked first at the stack of telephone messages. They were mostly the flurry of social invitations that Bart had been receiving welcoming him to Washington and his new job. There was, however, one phone call that caught his eye; it was from an FBI official who had been Bart's classmate at a month's long Harvard international security forum in the early 1980's. Why hadn't his FBI friend called him at the office? Maybe it was social. Since it was late, Bart decided not to return the call until the next day. After scanning some letters he was anxious to read, he shuffled those to the top of the pile, prioritized the others, drained the last of his beer and headed up the stairs to shower and change clothes.

Sergeant Wild had laid out gray trousers, a blue shirt and a dark maroon sweater. It was uncanny the way Sam could anticipate the right clothes for the occasion and weather. Although the September days were still quite warm and the military in Washington would not go into winter uniforms until October, the evenings were cool. A sweater would feel good tonight on the streets of Georgetown. Georgetown had always been one of Lowe's favorite places in the world. Situated on the banks of the

Potomac River and home to many resident diplomats and two well known universities, Georgetown and American, the area was a fascinating locale. The variety of restaurants, entertainment, exclusive shops, art galleries, bookstores and late night watering holes served almost any interest, from preppie to sophisticated, from young to old, and from early to late evening. People-watching in Georgetown, in Bart's opinion, was among the best in the United States.

He was seated at a choice table in the rear corner of Clyde's. The restaurant, decorated like an American saloon, had long been a favorite of Bart and B.J.'s for a casual late night dinner. The maitre'd, a man who had been at Clyde's for years, either recognized Bart from earlier times or was clever enough to make Bart think so. He immediately honored Bart's request for a table with some degree of privacy. Along with his seating tip, Bart instructed the maitre'd to bring two Beefeater martinis, on the rocks, with olives, the instant a lady joined him at the table.

B.J. entered the front door of Clyde's at 10:10 p.m. Although always precise professionally, she had never been known for social punctuality. Even from a distance she was a striking woman, and Bart could see heads turning as she caught his signal and headed toward his table. She was dressed conservatively in a navy blue suit with white blouse, matching white hose and blue pumps. As she arrived, he stood to greet her. After they exchanged kisses on the cheek, she sat down with a noticeable sigh.

"What a day!" she said. "I need a martini."

Almost before the words were out of her mouth, an aproned waiter arrived with two chilled martinis. The drinks were served in oversized square cocktail glasses, frosting on the outside. Two large, pitted green olives on a toothpick crowned each inviting drink.

"Your wish is my command," Bart answered with a smile.

"I must say I'm impressed. What is it? Do they know you here? Do they know you're a general?"

"Of course not. They just recognize a man of distinction. When I told them I was dining with the future Secretary of State they couldn't do enough for me," he kidded.

"Bart, you really are too much some time," B.J. answered, not accustomed to much humor in her busy life. That was another reason she found Bart Lowe attractive.

They raised their glasses and Bart offered one of his favorite dinner toasts. "Here's to it and from it. If you ever get to it and don't do it, may you never get to it again!"

"You scoundrel." B.J. responded.

In her job at the State Department, Ambassador Ross was one of three ambassadors in the Intelligence and Research Bureau, or INR, who coordinated the interests and activities of other U.S. agencies. Her beat was East Germany, the Warsaw Pact countries and the Soviet Union. She took time, over her drink, to share some of the frustrations she and her colleagues had experienced during the week in dealing with some of the intractable, important problems of that region of the world. Lowe was a good listener and he sensed that it was helpful to B.J. to let off steam with a friend—one knowledgeable enough of the world to appreciate the difficulties and magnitude of the situations she was describing.

Their near perfect cocktail hour was briefly interrupted when two, slightly drunk men sat down at the next table and immediately lit cigars. "They probably didn't realize they were in the no-smoking section," Bart thought. Nevertheless, the smoke became bothersome and Bart asked the waiter to intervene. He did so promptly and persuaded the men, after a mild protest, to move to another table. Bart and B.J.'s solitude was returned.

After a brief glance at the extensive menu, B.J., said, "Bart why don't you order something for me. I'm tired of making decisions and I would like to feel like a kept woman tonight. Will you do the honors?"

"Gladly," he replied, suggesting Caesar salad, the blackened swordfish, mixed fresh vegetables and a bottle of Berringer California White Zinfandel.

The meal and the service did not disappoint them. In fact, the food was so light and tasty that Bart persuaded B.J. to try the raspberry parfait for dessert while he enjoyed a small caramel flan. Dessert was followed by hot, black cups of coffee.

"I did all the talking before dinner, Bart. Now it's your turn. How was your second week on the job?"

"It was a good week. I have a lot to learn and that will take some time. The acronyms, organizations and people are beginning to fall into place and I have some ideas on how I want to proceed. The worldwide scope of the operation is far greater than I thought. Or, for that matter, greater than I think most people realize, even well-informed ones. The activities of the attachés are markedly different from the Attaché Corps that I served in 10 years ago. What surprised me is the extent of attaché operations related to our national security in so many places. Many think attachés spend most of their time on the diplomatic cocktail circuit. Their operations are, as you know, carried out in coordination with the State Department, Defense and the CIA. Some really hot stuff is out there. You probably have a better feel for that than I do, B.J." Bart paused to refill their coffee cups from the silver serving pot that had been left at their table.

He continued, "I'm eager to visit some attachés on station, but to do that before I'm well grounded here in Washington would be a mistake. I probably won't head out before December. In the meantime, I've put some measures in place in the headquarters that I believe will allow me to get up to speed quickly and have a more complete understanding of what is going on. For example, I've directed my Operations Division to prepare and present a weekly briefing to me and the key staff on the significant operations taking place throughout the world; to include what successes or failures we are having, the number of terrorist or other security incidents, and what areas or countries of the world are facing increased threats. That kind of thing."

"Isn't that a lot of work for your people?" asked B.J.

"Yes, but I think when the briefing is in place, it will be useful not only to me but to all the attachés and staff personnel. I have the feeling that the people in the Pacific Division haven't the slightest idea what the people in the Western European Division are doing. If they are overworked, and they all are busting thcir humps from what I can tell, it may make them feel a little better to know that their buddies in another division are also overworked."

"Don't ask me if we have those kinds of problems at State. I'll take the fifth," B.J. said.

"I've also started a short end-of-day meeting with my six key senior people to share what has happened in each of their areas during the last 24 hours. It only lasts about 30 minutes and I have already learned a great deal about what is coming in and out of the DAS. I hope this will foster a feeling of team work and make my senior executives appreciate the importance of each other's jobs."

"That sounds like a good idea. I wish we could do something like that at State," B.J. said. "But we are just too large."

"You could never get that group of prima donnas at State to the same meeting each day at the same time," kidded Bart.

"Watch it, soldier. Don't press your luck."

"Two other things I have set in motion concern my communications with the attachés in the field and the value of regional attaché conferences. In the two weeks that I've been Director of Attachés I have received only five calls or messages from almost 100 senior defense attachés. My gut tells me that something is missing there. It may be that my predecessor preferred it that way or that the attachés feel they're working for so many people that they aren't sure who the boss really is. Just today I sent a cable to all the Defense Attachés to let them know I'm on board, how important I believe the attaché mission is, what I cxpect of them professionally, and my commitment to look after the attachés, their support staffs, and their families. I promised that I would send them an update cable from headquarters once a month and I'd expect the same from them. This will allow me and them to keep them informed on what's going on."

"I think," B.J. responded, "you'll find that useful, if you follow through and don't let yourself or your attachés forget the requirement or its purpose. We have a similar system at the State

Department with our ambassadors and it's one of our best management tools."

"The question of attaché conferences," Bart continued, "is a more difficult one, and the views at my headquarters are split as to the best mix of frequency, location, facilities and agendas. Not to mention the high cost of moving attachés around the world. The model I'm going to try, at least for my first year, is a quarterly regional conference at some central location in one of the regions where we will gather only Defense Attachés in that region and the minimum number of people from DAS Headquarters to make the conference worthwhile."

"Again, Bart, I think that's a logical way to proceed. In my experience the larger the conference, the less you accomplish. We have some excellent conference planners, and if you'd like, I can send a couple of our people over to see you and discuss some of our approaches."

"That would be great; please do. Now, I expect I've used you as a helpful sounding board more than enough for one night," Bart concluded, signaling for the check.

"My pleasure, General," B.J. drawled in her best southern accent. "Shall we go Dutch? Ambassadors make the big bucks, you know."

"Thank you, Scarlet O'Hara, but no. I still owe you one for the dinner at your place back in June."

"Well, thank you again, General, and I do hope you will come to Tara to see us again," B.J. carried on as they rose, linked arms and left the still crowded restaurant at midnight.

B.J. had found a parking place only a block away from Clyde's. As they neared her car, Bart turned to her and said, "How about a walk around the town?"

"No thank you. Even though walking in Georgetown is among my favorite pastimes, I'm a little tired tonight."

"Well, then, your earlier remark this evening about wanting to feel like a kept woman. Your place or mine?"

"No, again, although I must admit the thought has crossed my mind. As always, I'm tempted. If I can ask your forbearance,

I'd like to take a rain check. It's has been a long day, and unfortunately I have more of the same scheduled for tomorrow. Although I have been accused of being a Wonder Woman, some sleep is required. When that part of our friendship is renewed, I want it to be a special occasion."

Bart nodded his reluctant agreement. They shared a warm embrace and kiss and he helped B.J. into her car. As she pulled away from the curb, Bart smiled and waved good-bye and decided he would walk a while along the well-lighted and still crowded streets of Georgetown. "Need to update my people watching skills," he thought, and moved out at a brisk pace.

On Saturday morning Bart awoke at 7:00 a.m., dressed in a sweat suit, and, after a quick read of *The Washington Post* while catching the morning news on the radio, he headed out the back door for an easy thirty minute jog.

Although it was Saturday, Fort Myer was already a hubbub of cars and activity. The large number of military people—active and retired living in the Washington area—kept the exchanges and commissaries busy. The facilities at Fort Myer opened early on Saturday morning and at 8:30 a.m., judging from the full parking lots and heavy traffic, the stores were filled with military shoppers. Bart's run took him around the perimeter of Fort Myer.

Back at his quarters Bart returned the phone call he had received yesterday. The number John Kitchen had left was his office phone at FBI Headquarters in Washington. Bart hadn't seen John since their days at Harvard and he wasn't sure what John was doing now at the FBI.

The phone in Kitchen's office answered on the second ring. Bart thought he recognized the voice and said, "John, is that you? This is Bart Lowe."

"Yes, Bart. It's great to hear from you. Thanks for returning my call so promptly. I missed you in June when you came around to see Jack Gilbert. Congratulations on your new job. I'm delighted to see you in charge of the attachés."

After a few minutes of small talk Bart asked, "Well, what is it, John? Am I in some kind of trouble?"

John laughed and replied, "Of course not, Bart. I do have a matter that I'd like to discuss with you as soon as possible, not at your office or mine. Do you belong to the Pentagon Officers Athletic Club? And do you still play racquetball?"

"Aha," exclaimed Bart. "The real reason is out."

"Not really, but you know we don't have any racquetball facilities in the FBI Building, and we're always grateful when one of our defense colleagues invites us to use the Pentagon facilities."

"John, be my guest anytime."

"I know this is short notice, but I'll be finishing up here about 11:00 and could meet you at the Pentagon at 11:30. Can you squeeze that in?"

"Certainly, but when are you going to tell me what this is really all about?"

"Just as soon as I determine if you still have the old zip on the racquetball court. See you at 11:30."

Bart looked at his watch and saw the time was 9:35. It was too late to reserve a racquetball court, but Saturday was a slow day with most of the people out of the Pentagon. He shouldn't have any trouble in getting a court. He decided he would shave and just leave his sweats on until after the game. He had plenty of time to run by the building in Rosslyn, visit the Operations Center and get to the Pentagon by 11:30.

The security guards at the Defense Attaché Service Headquarters, and the team on duty in the Operations Center, were taken aback to see the new director at work on Saturday in his sweats. The Operations Center had been notified by Colonel Martin that the boss would probably be in, but they did not expect to see him in casual attire. The center was a small one as Operations Centers go, both in physical size and number of people on duty. The Operations Center Chief was Barbara Worthington. She gave Lowe the management overview. He learned that the center was staffed 24 hours a day by rotating teams consisting of a field grade officer in charge, and a mix of military and civilian desk officers and analysts from the regional divisions covering the world. The Operations Center was in regular contact with their counterparts at the National Military Command Center (NMCC) in the Pentagon and at the Operations Centers at DIA, CIA, NSA, FBI and the State Department, as well as the Operations and Intelligence Centers at the worldwide joint and specified military commands. The DAS Operations Center was in secure voice and message communication with each of the Defense Attaché Offices around the globe. The few, well trained people in the small, secure spaces of the Operations Center had a very sophisticated means to monitor the world's pulse for U.S. national security purposes and their supporting attaché role.

Bart left Rosslyn at 11:10 and was waiting for John Kitchen when John arrived at the POAC entrance at 11:25. The POAC was an old but well-equipped health facility located near the river entrance of the Pentagon. It consisted of racquet, squash, and basketball courts, an indoor swimming pool, and a wide array of exercise equipment and rooms. Lockers and changing rooms were provided for both men and women. He led John to the day lockers where he could leave his clothes, quickly got his own gear and went out on to the main floor of the POAC to locate a vacant racquetball court. He was soon joined by John and the two friends engaged in a best-of-three games match. Bart won the first one handily and suspected that his friend had not been playing regularly because his timing was off. Bart then made the mistake of easing off in the second game to make the competition closer. John got his second wind, recovered his timing and some of his better shots and beat Bart 15 to 13. Bart's military competitiveness roared back in the third game, and although it was close for most of the way, he was able to win 15-11.

After showering, Bart suggested that they have lunch in the POAC dining room. The dining room was fashioned somewhat like a Bavarian beer stube, with heavy wooden tables and chairs. Two meals a day—breakfast and lunch—were served cafeteria style. They both selected tossed salads and fresh lemonade, a POAC specialty.

After lunch, John said, "Bart, the matter I want to discuss with you is very sensitive. If my bearings are correct, I remember a track or road going from the rear entrance of the POAC into the North Parking Lot. Maybe we could get some fresh air and walk for a ways down that track. That would give us the privacy I need to talk to you."

As the two men distanced themselves from the rear entrance of the POAC, John Kitchen was satisfied the empty Pentagon parking lot provided a suitable location for the matter he wished to discuss.

"Bart, let me apologize for any undue anxiety I may have caused you. What I am about to tell you is, of necessity, one of America's most closely held secrets. Once I've shared it with you, you will agree never to discuss it with anyone else, other than a handful of people that I will indicate."

"I guess my first question, John, is why me?"

"That will become clear when I reveal the information."

"If you are absolutely sure I have a need to know, I agree."

"I am and you do." John then hesitated momentarily as a lone jogger went past them on his way toward the Memorial Bridge. When the runner was 50 or so feet beyond them he resumed. "Right now I'm heading up a small unit that conducts high level special investigations. Our most important project at this time concerns a leak somewhere in the government of highly classified and sensitive national security information. The information is being leaked to the Soviet Union with some disastrous results to our intelligence operations. Because of the quality and accuracy of the information being leaked we suspect that the leak is coming from a mole.

"The mole is someone completely trusted who has regular access to our most sensitive classified information. The mole has been recruited by a foreign intelligence service and has agreed to provide information very damaging to the United States. In this case we believe the leaked information is ending up at the KGB.

What we do not know is who the mole is and where he or she works. We have narrowed it down to the NSC, INR, DIA, CIA, the Attaché Service and my own agency, the FBI. We believe the mole to be in one of these places because in each of those organizations there are people who have access to the type of information being provided to the KGB."

By this time John and Bart had reached the end of the track, turned around and were heading back to the POAC.

"Why am I telling you all of this? Two of your people are aware of our investigation—Captain Pete Kalitka, your Deputy, and Colonel Bob Herrington, the Chief of your Special Services Division. Bob Herrington is a good man. I've worked with him for a number of years. Before taking the Attaché Service job he was formerly head of Army Counterintelligence."

"Yes. I remember him from some of the Army spy cases I was briefed on," Bart said.

"Your predecessor was not briefed. At the time we expanded our investigation to include the Defense Attaché Service, it was thought he would be retiring, and we are keeping our access list to the absolute minimum. We, of course, must have some knowledgeable points of contact at each agency in order to carry out our investigation. Before you ask, Bart, let me say that right now we do not have any suspects in the DAS. My purpose is to alert you to the investigation, and to solicit your cooperation for the future. By the way, our code name for the investigation is HEAT SEEKER. Results of the leaked information have impacted on some military operations. Bob Herrington will fill you in on the details."

The two men returned to the POAC, retrieved their work-out bags and shook hands. Kitchen thanked Bart and said, "I'm sorry to be the bearer of such bad tidings. I hope for all our sakes we can catch this bastard before he does much more damage. Thanks for your time, lunch, and the work out. I'll be in touch."

CHAPTER 5

EL SANTIAGO

On Monday morning Lowe arrived at his office at 7:00 a.m. His Executive Officer, Colonel Martin, had been there since 6:00 a.m., had read the cable traffic received over the weekend, screened out the most important messages and placed them in Lowe's action file along with his schedule of appointments and briefings for the day. George shared the outer office with the General's secretary and handled calmly the flood of telephone calls, visitors, staff problems, demands for the General's time and minor and major crises that would arise requiring solution, closure or compromise. The serene atmosphere of the DAS front office blended with the tasteful furnishings, Colonel Martin's southwestern watercolor paintings, Joan Weber's greenest of green plants and the hidden stereo that played a soft stream of light-classical music. George Martin's calm, impeccable appearance in his custom tailored, perfectly pressed, Air Force blue uniform belied the raging crisis management that took place regularly in other office spaces of the DAS Headquarters.

Mrs. Joan Weber, a well dressed and neatly coiffured woman in her late forties, who had served the previous three DAS Directors, arrived in the office shortly before 7:00 a.m. and served the General the first of many cups of coffee he would consume during the day. Joan Weber was typical of many women in the secretarial field in Washington: her abilities and service far exceeded the value of the salary she received. Like many of her contemporaries, her skills would have allowed her to move on years earlier to private industry for more money. But, because of a strong sense of loyalty to those she served and an appreciation for the importance of the missions her bosses were carrying out, she stayed on year after year in the same job, performing magnificently.

Lowe appreciated Joan's kindness in serving him coffee; the first time she did so, he assured her he was perfectly capable of getting his own coffee. She responded that she would be very disappointed if the General did not allow her to bring him coffee. She assured him that she took considerable pride in providing the coffee and tea service to him and the steady stream of people who visited his office. An important part of her job, she believed, was greeting, welcoming and providing refreshment to the foreign guests General Lowe received. Bart got the message and promised Joan Weber that she would not get any further flak from him on coffee service.

This morning he thanked her and asked, "Do you also make the coffee, Joan?"

"Oh, no," Joan replied. "The folks in Admin do that, but Colonel Martin and I always sample it after each pot is made to make sure it's just right."

After Joan left the office Bart returned to his action file. As he went through the fifty or so electronic messages he annotated some to give directions to the staff for follow-up action or, if he had questions or did not fully understand the issue, he made a note asking for clarifying information. When he had finished the file Colonel Martin would pick up any notes General Lowe had made and start the wheels in motion to get answers to any questions. By his third week Bart had pretty much decided on an office routine and schedule that worked for him. The first hour of the day was his quiet time for desk work and reading. Because of the complexity of both his job and the attaché missions he estimated he would be reading background and information papers for the first three months.

After his quiet hour he used the morning to continue his orientation tour at DAS Headquarters and receive the briefings necessary to understand the major operational and support functions of the DAS. He set aside the noon hour to have lunch with any attachés visiting headquarters from the field. He dined first with the attachés in from Prague and Tokyo and gained some revealing insights.

In most military organizations there is a view in the field about headquarters: "If we could just get those guys at headquarters to understand," and a view at headquarters about the field: "If we could just get those guys in the field to understand..." Bart quickly found that DAS was no exception. He knew that the challenge to the senior military commander is to get both the headquarters and field to appreciate the positions of each other and to work as a team, rather than working in a "we versus them mode." Lowe had found indications of this in the DAS and was beginning to make mental notes on ways to deal with it.

Bart set aside his afternoons for visitors to headquarters and time for him to continue his orientation with the other departments and agencies in Washington. George had scheduled these types of visits well into the next month. The official day concluded at DAS Headquarters with the end of day meeting in Bart's office at 5:00 p.m. He limited the meeting to thirty minutes and when that was over it gave Bart about another hour and a half for reading and more desk work; he was out the door by 7:00 p.m. Two days a week Bart played racquetball at the Pentagon at 6:30 a.m. and, on those days, he arrived later, in the office between 7:30 and 8:00 a.m.

The first item on his schedule this Monday after his quiet hour was an 8:00 a.m. briefing to be given by his Deputy, Navy Captain Pete Kalitka, on attaché training. Bart noted this when he first looked at the schedule but waited until 7:50 before pressing the button on his intercom to Pete's office.

"Captain Kalitka," the quiet voice answered.

"Pete, this is Bart Lowe, I see you are up first this morning to present your briefing on attaché training."

"Yes, sir."

"Will there be others sitting in on that briefing, Pete?"

"Yes, sir. Chuck Gregorios wanted to sit in as well as the training people from our Support Division, and Colonel Shelby from the Defense Intelligence College. Any problem?"

"No, I want to speak to you privately for a moment on a matter that came up over the weekend. Can you come over to my office a minute or two early?"

"Yes, sir, I'll be right there."

Captain Kalitka entered Bart's office and said "Good morning, sir."

Bart got up from his desk and moved to greet him. Rather than sitting down again, Bart moved to the window and motioned for Pete to accompany him. Pete was dressed in the Navy summer white uniform—white shirt, trousers and white shoes. Sharp! Pete had the look of a man who is habitually in exceptional physical condition. His black hair was closely cropped and the five rows of decorations on his short sleeved shirt were topped with the Navy Cross and Purple Heart. Kalitka was a man who not only had displayed extraordinary bravery in his career but had done so under hostile fire.

"Pete, I saw John Kitchen from the FBI this weekend and he briefed me on HEAT SEEKER. He told me that you and Colonel Herrington in the Special Services Division, were the only two in the DAS briefed on this operation. Any problems for us in the DAS that I need to be aware of?"

"I don't think so, sir. We don't believe HEAT SEEKER could be anyone in the DAS. Our greatest concern is for the risk to some of our operations and people. Bob Herrington has some theories based on his many years in Counterintelligence. You have a two-hour visit with the Special Services Division next week, and Bob is planning to bring you up to speed on all SSD knows. I recommend we wait until then to discuss this further. If you agree, I'll ask the others to join us now for the training brief."

Bart nodded and Captain Kalitka opened the door to the General's office and asked the others to come in and be seated. Bart knew everyone except Colonel Sean Shelby, the officer responsible for the attaché training at the Defense Intelligence College. Captain Kalitka introduced them, and Bart said, "Sean, I've been hearing good things about you and the training you are providing our attachés."

"Thank you, sir. I understand you are interested in going to Florida next week to observe our attaché field training exercise. I'd like to tell you about our training objectives, and, if you wish, accompany you to Florida."

"Sounds good," Bart replied. "Let's get my XO, George Martin, to work out the details. Now we need to hear from Pete."

Captain Kalitka walked over to a briefing chart that had been set up in the corner of the room, faced Bart Lowe and began the briefing. "General, the training of an American military attaché begins with the selection process of an individual by his or her military service. The DAS announces a vacancy at a particular Defense Attaché Office two to three years in advance and asks the appropriate military service to nominate a qualified individual to fill the projected attaché requirement. If the service nominates someone who has previously served in the DAS and/or is already proficient in the foreign language of the country where the attaché is needed, the training required may be relatively short."

"How short, Pete?" Bart asked.

"In that case training would consist of a few weeks of refresher training on attaché duties and a current information and policy update on the country where the attaché will serve. If the officer to be nominated has never served in the DAS and does not have the language we require, and this is often the case, then training will take from one to two years to complete. The service, after receiving our request for a nomination, will advertise the assignment and call for volunteers. Attaché service is a volunteer duty. The military service will screen the applicant's record and select the three best qualified individuals. These officers will then go before a board of senior officers who will pick the best qualified officer who, in turn, will be nominated to the DAS. Once we receive the nomination, our personnel people review the officer's record to see if we agree with his qualifications and motivation for attaché service. The nominated officer must have either the language for the country concerned or have already passed a language aptitude proficiency test. We are sticklers on this and weakness in this area often causes an officer's nomination to be rejected. When the officer has passed our administrative review, then the officer and spouse are interviewed by a board convened of former attachés. This ensures the volunteer really understands how demanding attaché training and duties will be. If our board recommends acceptance of the nominated officer, his complete attaché packet, consisting of his key service records, his scores on any aptitude tests and his picture are sent to you for approval or disapproval. As DAS Director, you may elect to interview the officer or act on the nomination on the basis of his or her file and the recommendation of our board."

"Pete, that sounds like an extensive process. Any undue duplication or bureaucratic red tape there?" asked General Lowe.

"No, sir. We want the services to do whatever is necessary to select their best people, and for the most part they do just that—particularly your own service, the Army. Whenever we get an Army Foreign Area Officer, or FAO, we know we are getting the best. However, due to a limited pool of personnel, all of the services at one time or another, will nominate an officer not suitable for attaché duty. The foreign language aptitude is usually the big discriminator. Unfortunately not everyone can master a foreign language to the skill level we require. An attaché in a foreign country who cannot speak the language will not be an effective performer."

"Did General Tibbets interview all of the attachés prior to his approval of their nomination?"

"No, sir. I believe that in the three years he was our boss he only interviewed two or three officers. He had great confidence in our own board reviews and recommendations. I believe you will also find that to be the case. The people who serve on our boards have all served in the field and know what it takes to be a successful attaché. They also recognize the officer who has volunteered for what he mistakenly thinks may be primarily an enjoyable social life. We can't use that type of officer in the DAS."

"Okay, I accept that. What happens after an officer's nomination has been approved?"

"At that point we scope the training time required, notify the service, and give them a date on which the officer must report to us to begin training. If an officer needs complete training, the training will consist of (1) language training, (2) attaché skills and techniques, (3) field training exercises, and, for some officers, (4) military security assistance or foreign military sales training. All of this, plus specialized orientation on the country in which the attaché will be serving. Whenever possible we try to begin with language training. This is done either at the Defense Language Institute, or DLI, in Monterey, California, the State Department's Foreign Service Institute here in Washington, or at selected universities throughout the United States."

"How much language training do we give them, Pete?"

"The objective is to reach a good speaking and understanding level of proficiency in the language. We use the Defense Language Test and the attachés must achieve a minimum of a 2/2 in speaking and reading on a five point scale. For the more difficult languages such as Russian, Chinese and Arabic one full year of study is normally required. For the romance languages like French and Spanish six months of study is the norm," explained Captain Kalitka. "The Army FAO officers we receive are already proficient in the language of the countries where they will serve as attachés. When language training is complete, the candidate attaché then begins four months of attaché professional training at the Defense Intelligence College at Bolling AFB in Washington. This is usually the first time you or I will meet the new crop of perspective attachés. Either you or I or Chuck Gregorios will go to Bolling to welcome them to their first day of class and then we—that is, most of the staff in the Headquarters—will join the faculty at the College that evening for a welcome aboard reception for the new attaché class. General, there is a class in session now at the College that will be starting their Field Training Exercise, or FTX, next week in Florida. I'm sure you will want to go down there and see that training."

"Concur, Pete. George Martin told me you would be briefing me on training and he has blocked the calendar for the FTX in Florida so that I would be free to go."

"While at the College," Kalitha continued, "they will learn about diplomatic protocol, diplomatic immunity, the roles and missions of other U.S. agencies serving abroad, defense information reporting requirements, techniques of observation, foreign Army, Navy and Air Force cultures, foreign weapons systems, foreign customs, how other societies view Americans, and the threat of terrorism to U.S. diplomats. In addition to the classroom instructions, the attaché trainees have many hours of practical exercises to develop the skills and techniques used by attachés serving in foreign countries.

"To test them on all they have learned, we then take them to a major field training exercise in Florida we call an FTX and see how they perform under simulated but very realistic conditions. I won't spoil the Florida exercise briefing Colonel Sean Shelby will give you. Many of our prospective attachés are surprised at the realism and how much we throw at them during the short duration of the FTX."

After a few questions and some comments by the others, Lowe thanked Captain Kalitka for the briefing and adjourned the meeting.

The following week Colonel Martin arranged for the U.S. Air Force's Military Airlift Command to provide a C-20 small executive jet aircraft for General Lowe and Colonel Sean Shelby for the trip to Florida. Lowe, in the pre-brief, learned that the FTX was conducted at and around Homestead Air Force Base in the Miami, Florida, area.

During the Tuesday afternoon flight to Florida, Colonel Shelby covered the details of the FTX for Bart. He indicated that the prime objective of the Florida FTX was to expose the attachés to a "worst-case" set of circumstances that could possibly happen to them while serving in a foreign country. In this week's training scenario, Shelby explained, the attachés would assume that they had just been assigned as new Army, Navy, Air Force, Marine and

Coast Guard Attachés to a fictional country, El Santiago. For most of its history, El Santiago had been a small, relatively poor, agrarian country without much interest shown by the rest of the world. Seven years ago extensive oil reserves were discovered in the swampy interior of the country. Since that time El Santiago had changed dramatically. The former impoverished country had become rich overnight, and the small government had been overthrown by an ambitious military officer, a former head of the country's army. The country's new dictator, El Presidente, had opened the country to the highest bidders. And they came from every corner of the globe, much to the chagrin of El Santiago's former chief ally, the United States and neighboring democratic countries.

Miami, the fictional capitol of El Santiago became a mecca not only for Middle East extremists, but for South American drug cartels. Gambling casinos, world class resorts and tourist attractions quickly sprang up and Miami became an international capitol where all things were possible: high finance, legal and illegal drugs, prostitution, gun running, espionage, duty free trade, counterfeiting, and a safe haven for terrorists.

El Presidente, while lining his own pockets, had not neglected the military services of his country, and although they had no particular enemies, he traded oil to provide his military with the best equipment and technology available. The United States had been able to maintain a small embassy and staff in the country, albeit with tense diplomatic relations. The U.S. military attachés in El Santiago had been able to continue a dialogue with their counterparts largely because the president and so many members of his government had come from the El Santiago Military. While military rapport with their U.S. military attaché counterparts was cordial they were clearly attempting to hide the extent of their activities with the communists, the Libyans, Iraqis, Iranians, PLO and North Koreans.

Then, much to the alarm of Washington, the CIA came up with some information that indicated that El Santiago had made overtures to some of their new friends to acquire weapons of mass destruction. The mission then, for the U.S. attachés serving in El Santiago, is to report any information on weapons of mass destruction entering or already present in El Santiago.

"Once on the ground at Homestead," Shelby said, "the attachés are told that a building we use at Homestead Air Force Base and for the FTX will be the U.S. Embassy. The rest of the base belongs to El Santiago. Whenever they leave the U.S. Embassy they are in El Santiago's sovereign territory and subject to the laws and rules of that country. Where they sleep, eat, and where they go may be monitored. The attachés are then briefed on the internal security forces of El Santiago—and these forces are extensive. El Santiago, while not communist, is essentially a police state. Human rights violations are considered business as usual. The attachés are given targets to cover consistent with their own service roles. For example, the Naval Attachés will be assigned to look for certain foreign ships at Port Everglades and at the port in Biscayne Bay; the Air Force Attachés will cover the Homestead Air Force Base and the military airport at Opalocka; and the Marine and Coast Guard Attachés will be responsible for coverage of the Coast Guard District located at Dinner Key and the coastal areas of Miami. The Army Attachés will be assigned to cover the International Airports and the numerous Army National Guard Units situated throughout the Miami area. All attachés will have their El Santiago contacts at the Foreign Office and respective service headquarters, manned by our role players. For the FTX we assume that all attachés are fluent in Spanish, the primary language of El Santiago. Spanish is a widespread secondary language in Miami and the attachés who speak Spanish will have an edge. Do you speak Spanish?" Colonel Shelby asked.

"I'm not a linguist, Sean, but being from Miami, I understand it. I also studied both German and Russian. What will the attaché's assignment be?" Lowe asked.

"The training requirement for the student attachés is to observe and report information concerning weapons of mass destruction in El Santiago without attracting attention from the El Santiago security forces. They may use any source of information available to them: their own observations, the local press and media, contacts within the host military or government, information from dissident groups or casual sources they encounter by living and being in El Santiago. The attachés will have some resources normally available to them in any embassy and country. For example, their own Defense Attaché Office, consisting of an office, and files, and communications with DAS Headquarters, contact at the Embassy with other helpful U.S. agencies, such as the State Department, CIA and FBI, transportation to move about the country, a camera, and binoculars. The trainee attachés are told that the FTX is supported by a number of role players designed to facilitate the exercise and aid the attachés in satisfying their requirements, provided the attachés recognize which role players can actually help and which role players may mislead or present obstacles to the attaché's mission. The attachés will also be given leads on where and how to obtain pertinent information. Some of these leads are basic, and others are more subtle, requiring follow-up by the attachés to get at the information they are seeking; and, finally, the attachés will encounter a number of events and activities that are not related to, but may hinder, their mission requirement. These are the kind of things our attachés regularly run into in foreign countries, such as the friendly individual seeking assistance from the United States, the potential defector who wants political asylum in the United States, the mentally unstable person or government plant who tries to get the U.S. attaché in a compromising position, and the individual who offers to provide the attaché sensitive information about his country in exchange for money or favors."

Bart Lowe listened intently as Colonel Shelby described the intricate FTX. He was impressed with the sophistication and forethought that had gone into planning the exercise.

"Sean, are there any hidden agendas?"

"The hidden agenda will be the number, extent and involvement of the El Santiago security forces. The attachés go into this FTX with the idea that it will pretty much be a friendly force exercise without any real enemy. What they don't know, and are always surprised to find out, is that we are able to create the realistic environment of around-the-clock surveillance, technical monitoring of activities, suspicious law enforcement and counterintelligence officials, and agent provocation. We are able to do this with the volunteer support and involvement of the FBI, DEA, Customs, the Army, Navy, Air Force and Coast Guard Security Services, and the Florida and Miami law enforcement agencies. It is a remarkable coordinated effort. I think you will be amazed to see the amount of support we receive from our colleagues in the other agencies and how well it works in providing realistic training to our future attachés."

"Sean, we've learned time and time again the lesson of the importance of training in my military career. I'm anxious to see this 'remarkable' exercise you've described. As long as I'm the Director of the Attaché Service, you can count on my commitment to the best possible training for our attachés."

The flight steward walked back to Lowe's seat and said, "General, we are on our final approach for landing at Homestead Air Force Base and we should be on the ground in ten minutes."

After thanking the C-20 pilots and the flight steward Lowe and Shelby disembarked and moved to a waiting sedan where the Homestead Base Commander welcomed them. After exchanging salutes and offering Lowe any support he required, the base commander took his leave and turned Bart and Sean over to a second waiting officer, Marine Colonel Donovan.

Colonel Frank Donovan was the epitome of a Marine Corps officer. He was tall and tanned with a rangy, muscled fullness and impressive in his distinctive, short sleeve khaki uniform. His decorations spoke volumes about the many places where he had served his country. Donovan was the senior attaché training instructor and Director of the FTX. According to Colonel Shelby, Donovan had served as the Naval Attaché in Moscow and was famous in attaché circles for some of his exploits in the Soviet Union. He had once been held incommunicado by the Russians for 24 hours in Leningrad when they thought he had ventured too close to one of their nuclear attack submarines. He had narrowly avoided being declared persona non grata several times during his tour, and his Russian counterparts, who rather liked Donovan personally, told him in private that the KGB devoted more surveillance agents to him than to any other foreign military attaché. Donovan was the ideal trainer to run the FTX because he knew from personal experience the many measures the security services in an unfriendly foreign country can use to make a military attaché and his family miserable.

After getting Lowe and Shelby settled in their accommodations at Homestead Air Force Base, Donovan invited them to an eight o'clock dinner with the other attaché training cadre at a nearby seafood restaurant. Bart enjoyed both the excellent dinner and the opportunity to get to know Donovan and the other attaché instructors.

When he awoke at 6:00 the next morning he took a leisurely thirty minute jog around the air base to reacquaint himself with the facilities. He had last been at Homestead in 1960 as a new Army lieutenant involved in working the Cuban problem. After his graduation from the University of Florida and his commissioning, he had gone to Fort Benning, Georgia, for his infantry officer basic training. He was scheduled to join an infantry division in Europe after Benning for his first assignment. Then, during his last week of training at Fort Benning, he was approached by two men in suits and snap-brim hats who made it clear that they had an offer he couldn't refuse. The bottom line was that a screen of Army records had shown his residence and family in Miami, and his basic knowledge of Spanish and Russian studied in high school and college. He was needed, the men told him, for a joint CIA/FBI Army project dealing with Castro and Cuba. Nothing that Bart said could dissuade them he was not the right man for their job, and he was packed off back to Miami when he finished his training at Fort Benning.

As it turned out, the assignment proved to be an exciting adventure for a young man. Bart learned a lot from his FBI and CIA colleagues, the time had passed quickly, and when the Berlin

Wall crisis came along the following year, he was transferred to Europe and returned to the infantry.

Donovan and Shelby met him with a sedan at 7:55 and together they made the short drive from the BOQ to the building that served as the U.S. Embassy in El Santiago for the FTX. Once inside the building Donovan led the way to a small, "cadre-only" briefing room that was off limits to the student attachés. Lowe was offered a comfortable chair at the head of a small conference table and a cup of steaming hot Colombian coffee.

Seated at the table with Lowe and Shelby were a Navy commander and an Air Force major—two of Colonel Donovan's assistant instructors whom Lowe had met the previous night at the seafood restaurant. Colonel Donovan stood in front of the table beside a small slide carousel and projector pointed at a built-in screen in the facing wall. For the next 45 minutes Donovan used 35 mm color slides taken during previous FTX's to highlight the action events and the specific missions and tasks to be carried out by the attaché trainees.

"General Lowe, as you know, we are a little over half way through the exercise. At the beginning of the FTX, we assign each attaché a specific set of tasks to accomplish. We don't tell them how much time to spend on each aspect of the task, and when they first receive and review their tasks, they think it will be a piece of cake. They find out that's not the case. They learn that information is not always easy to obtain and they have not counted on the obstacles we throw at them. By the time the critique begins at 2:00 o'clock on Friday afternoon we have a bunch of tired puppies, General. Most of them will have worked for about 14 to 16 hours a day this week. Our purpose is to determine if the four months of intensive training we have given them has prepared them sufficiently to perform effectively under the adverse circumstances and harassment that we simulate in the staged situations I have shown you. During the next two days we intend to present four different situations where you will see Army, Navy, Air Force and Coast Guard officers actually performing their portion of the week's mission. I can tell you now that we expect this attaché class of 42 officers to be one of our most outstanding classes. They are doing exceptionally well so far, and we believe, will continue to do so, for the rest of the exercise. Three attachés we have selected for you to see in action, are as good as any I've seen go through the attaché school. I predict all three will become superstars when they get on station. The first officer is Army Colonel Noel Coyne. He is an Army FAO who is scheduled to be the Army Attaché in Prague, Czechoslovakia. He served an earlier tour there as a major, took a Czech language refresher course before beginning the attaché professional training and has been an outstanding student. His FTX mission is to develop a contact in the El Santiago Army who has knowledge of their weapons of mass destruction activities. His counterpart in the El Santiago Army introduced Coyne to a colonel who is responsible for the Customs Police in El Santiago. This customs officer has provided Coyne some helpful information and told Coyne that he is dissatisfied with the corruption in the military and the government. He has hinted that he may be willing to tell all if granted asylum in the United States. Colonel Coyne has reported this to the ambassador and the CIA station chief, and has received tentative approval to offer our friend asylum. Coyne is scheduled to have a 'chance' meeting with the colonel tomorrow night at a local restaurant and hopes to obtain the information. He must be careful not to be bilked with false information or to be obvious to the El Santiago Security Service who may be tailing him or the customs officer."

"Very interesting, Frank. But how will I be able to observe this kind of activity?"

"We've determined that Colonel Coyne has never met you and would probably not recognize you in a crowded restaurant. You'll be having dinner and seated at a table that we have selected for our El Santiago Security Service role players. This will also give you an idea of what our role players are looking for in their surveillance and how discreet Coyne will be in carrying out his important but theoretically risky task."

"Okay, sounds good!" acknowledged General Lowe. "I look forward to it."

"The second scenario," continued Colonel Donovan, "involves Air Force Lieutenant Colonel Elizabeth Hemmingway. Beth Hemmingway is one of the U.S. Air Force's first female transport pilots. Although she has had no previous attaché service she volunteered for an assignment in the Middle East. Beth came out with flying colors in the Arabic language course and is one of our best students. She is very popular in the class and has a great sense of humor. She will certainly need it. Most of the countries outside of the United States do not treat women in the military on equal terms. Most foreign military services are still very macho, and this is a major challenge for our female attachés. Beth's FTX mission is to monitor military flights and cargo coming into El Santiago for any indications of weapons of mass destruction. She has fared well with her El Santiago Air Force counterparts and our macho-acting role players, in overcoming the male superiority factor. Her good rapport and professional demeanor have allowed her to obtain some very valuable information. In a development that will take place later today Lieutenant Colonel Hemmingway will learn from a female NCO in the El Santiago Air Force that a 'special' shipment will arrive by air transport just after midnight. According to the NCO the shipment will be unloaded immediately and moved to a secret location. The problem Beth Hemmingway will face is that the area where the transport aircraft will be unloaded is in a restricted area of the El Santiago base, one that is off limits to foreign attaché personnel. The highest priority of Hemmingway's mission is to, if at all possible, obtain photographic evidence of any suspected weapons of mass destruction in El Santiago. Her dilemma will be whether or not to risk being caught in an officially restricted area. She is a gutsy officer and we think she will take the risk. If she does, she will be apprehended by our security service role players and held in confinement overnight. Tomorrow morning she will be subjected to a hostile interrogation by the El Santiago Security Service. Of course Lieutenant Colonel Hemmingway will not be harmed in any way, but the techniques will be real and similar to those our attachés have encountered in the field. As you may know General, I have had some first hand experience in this regard and I can tell you that our exercise play is realistic. We will be using real world Air Force security facilities for the interrogation and their two-way mirror interview room will allow you to see the interrogation as it takes place."

"What if Lieutenant Colonel Hemmingway doesn't take the bait and get caught in the restricted area?" asked General Lowe.

"We have a similar scenario planned for several other attachés and if that becomes the case we will switch you to one of those. However, General, if you are a betting man, I would be willing to bet a beer that Lieutenant Colonel Hemmingway will not only get caught in that restricted area but will have some plausible reason for being there."

"I occasionally bet," replied Bart, "but I think I'll wait for an opportunity when the odds are better."

Donovan smiled, clearly confident in his prediction. "The third situation is what we call the 'needle in the haystack' problem. In this class there are ten Naval and Marine officers training to be Naval Attachés. The senior officer is Navy Captain Lance Hargrove. He is being assigned to Singapore as the Defense Attaché. For the FTX, because of the large number of ports in Miami, Captain Hargrove has the responsibility of coordinating all of the Naval Attachés' activities. We've given them the description of a suspect ship that we believe is carrying chemicals that can be used for biological weapons. No name, no registration, no port destination and they are not sure whether the ship, an actual one, is already in port or just on its way. Information is available from their El Santiago counterparts, and shipping schedules from various sources in Miami. But the numbers are overwhelming. Some 3,000 ships with many registrations are in ports in and around Miami at any given time. What we know, and the attachés do not, is that the actual ship we have in mind will not dock until Friday morning. Key to the Naval Attaché effort being successful is how they organize themselves, sift the information they are gathering and avoid the wild goose chases we will try to send them on. To a great extent they will be at the beck and call of their El

Santiago foreign liaison overseers with meetings, requests for information, social dates that must be adhered to, etc. They are actually doing pretty well in their collection of information efforts and may even be a little ahead of schedule. They don't realize that, and they are getting increasingly worried that they will not locate the suspect ship before exercise time runs out. Captain Hargrove has two meetings a day to coordinate their activities. The morning one is at 0730 and there's an evening meeting at 1800 to go over the results of the day. We have arranged for you to monitor these meetings on closed circuit television . The attachés have all been informed that they are subject to electronic monitoring for exercise purposes, but they have no idea that you are here and will be watching and listening to them. We think that this will give you a good look at how they perform as individuals and as a military team. Both skills are required to successfully accomplish the exercise mission."

Bart Lowe again indicated his agreement.

"Finally, the last item we want you to be aware of is not the kind of subject we like to deal with but it is important to find out in the training environment if any of our student attachés have character flaws that could prove embarrassing to themselves and the United States while serving in a foreign country. There is an officer in this class who appears to be in that category. He is Commander Lawton Harris of the U.S. Coast Guard."

Colonel Donovan then explained that at the beginning of the class the attachés were told that there are three things that can get attachés in trouble. 'Booze, broads, and bucks.'

"We explain that abuse of alcohol, or involvement in a compromising situation with a member of the opposite sex could result in blackmail or a security compromise. We have noted during this exercise, General, that Commander Harris is regularly consuming alcohol well beyond any social context and, more importantly, when under the influence he appears to be very free in describing to others his duties as an attaché. Unlike the other trainees, he has managed to squeeze out a couple of hours each evening of the exercise to visit a local bar. Fortunately the bar is one in which we have positioned some of our role players for the purpose of safeguarding the security of our FTX. Harris also has been hitting on one of our female role players and has described in considerable detail what he is doing here in Miami, all of which is a clear violation of our real-world security guidelines. We are now keeping him under close surveillance to avoid any compromises."

"Has this happened often in the past?" General Lowe wanted to know.

"No, sir. This is a rare exception." responded Colonel Donovan.

"General Lowe," added Colonel Shelby, "this is a disappointment for us, but knowing that bad news never improves with age, we wanted you to know right away. Also, we think this case demonstrates the effectiveness of the FTX in identifying susceptible individuals before they go out on station."

"Well, let's do what we have to do," the General directed.

"Yes, sir, we'll be back to you on this one. That about covers my pitch." Colonel Donovan then walked back to the table, opened a manila folder, removed a typed schedule of the next three days and passed copies across to General Lowe and Colonel Shelby.

"We have taken the liberty, General, to schedule some of your time for visits to other agencies in Miami that are supporting the FTX. They are anxious to meet you and your visit here will let them know how much we appreciate their assistance. I've also allowed some time for you to meet our role players and, if we haven't completely tired you out, Bob Shelby and I would like to challenge you to a game of cut throat racquetball. The courts are pretty good here and I understand you like to play."

Bart Lowe accepted the recommendation and the challenge. "Colonel Donovan, you're on. Thanks for a very informative rundown of the FTX. I'm most anxious to see our future attachés in action."

CHAPTER 6

BEHIND THE GREEN DOOR

After the attaché FTX concluded on Friday, Bart decided to remain in Miami for the weekend. George Martin had given Bart an update on the secure telephone and told him there were no urgent matters requiring his attention in Washington before Monday. He took advantage of the break to visit his mother at the family home in Hialeah.

On Sunday morning Bart had gone scuba diving with his developer friend of many years, Dick Groveland, and his wife Mary. The Grovelands owned a 52-foot Chris Craft Cruiser and were delightful hosts. Dick had been disappointed when Bart decided not to accept his offer to return to Miami and work with him, but he respected Bart's decision.

He returned to Washington rested, refreshed, and upbeat for the prospects of the weeks ahead. The more he saw and learned about the Defense Attaché Service, the more he liked. Times and training methods had certainly changed since his own days as an attaché.

The attaché FTX had been informative. Colonel Coyne had handled the potential El Santiago defector as smooth as any professional. His actions did not cause any undue attention to himself or the man he was meeting, and he obtained the information that was needed. Lieutenant Colonel Beth Hemmingway did indeed get caught in the El Santiago restricted area but was not intimidated by the hostile interrogation or her interrogators. She stuck by her status and privilege as a U.S. diplomat and was subsequently released by the El Santiago Security Service. She also managed to conceal the film that revealed the El Santiago Military was receiving either weapons or material for weapons of mass destruction. At 11:00 a.m. on Friday,

Captain Hargrove and the his contingent of Naval attachés finally located the suspect ship at Port Everglades that was supposedly transporting illegal chemicals. A close call.

Bart agreed with Colonels Donovan and Shelby on the outstanding caliber of the class. He also was impressed by the way the various role players and supporting agencies combined efforts to conduct a realistic exercise. This realism was obvious during the FTX critique on Friday afternoon to judge by the surprised expressions on the faces of the attachés when the extent of the monitoring and coverage of their activities, and the identity of the key role players, were revealed. The only unfortunate aspect of the exercise was the Coast Guard officer whose adverse conduct had necessitated his "return to service." Bart had approved the relief for cause and phoned the senior U.S. Coast Guard personnel officer to advise him of Commander Harris' return. It had not been a pleasant business, but a necessary one.

Monday—Bart's first day back at the office—was spent catching up on paperwork and returning phone calls. Bart was amazed at how many official papers arrived at his desk for his signature, approval, coordination or review. The volume was staggering in spite of the efforts of his two very active deputies, Chuck Gregorios and Pete Kalitka, who took everything they could handle at their level and only sent Bart the "must sees" that by law or regulation could only be approved by him.

Seeing how much could pile up in three days, Bart asked his XO, "George, what the hell happens to all of this paper when I'm on a long trip out of the country for two or three weeks? Does it just sit here?"

"Au contraire, mon General," replied George. "It will follow you like the wind. No matter where in the world you are you will either be at one of our DAOs or close by. We simply forward all the cables and messages to you. Ditto for some of the other correspondence. After all, we have moved into the era of the fax. Timely and secure. If it's big and bulky we simply send it via the diplomatic courier system the State Department operates for all the embassies around the world. You are doomed to be followed by this paper for all the days you dwell in the house of the attachés."

"We'll see about that," a slightly frustrated Bart Lowe murmured.

"But not to worry, boss. I make most of the trips with you, and I'll help you keep the old paperwork flowing."

"No hill for a climber, huh, George?" Noting George's ever present smile and positive attitude Bart went back to his pile of paper with renewed determination.

Bart did not leave the office that evening until almost nine o'clock. In looking at the week's calendar, most of the items looked routine except Tuesday's three hours in the Special Services Division (SSD), and on Friday a scheduled appearance before the Senate Select Committee on Intelligence. The SSCI, as it was called, was responsible for the defense appropriations that supported the attachés. His appearance would be an opportunity to let the committee know what the attaché financial requirements were for the upcoming budget year and also to seek their support. Bart made a mental note to make sure he allowed sufficient time before Friday to prepare his testimony.

He was also anxious to better understand the mission and responsibilities of the SSD, and the HEAT SEEKER problem that SSD was aware existed.

On Tuesday morning Bart was escorted to the seventh floor of the DAS Headquarters building, into the "inner sanctum" of the SSD. SSD was an "eavesdropping proof" secure room within a physically secure area. The people who worked in SSD all wore a second special security badge that had to be shown to the armed guard at the SSD entrance. The other people working at the DAS Headquarters "thought" they knew what the people in SSD were doing, but they were really never sure because of SSD's cloak of security. Until that day, even Major General Bart Lowe, who was responsible for everything the SSD did or did not do, wasn't aware of all of their activities. Once inside SSD, he was given a schedule that broke his three hour visit into specific times and subjects.

Back in his office, with no one scheduled for lunch, he was sitting at his work table eating a tuna salad sandwich that Joan Weber had picked up for him in the basement deli that catered to the DAS Headquarters. As he finished the sandwich, he took a long drink from his glass of iced tea and began to mull over all he had heard and seen in Special Services Division. He had been reassured by the knowledge and professional acumen of Colonel Bob Herrington and the other military and civilian men and women working for Bob in SSD, doubly so when he learned they were involved in sensitive national security operations. Most of these operations he had only read about in the newspapers in the last few years without any first-hand knowledge. He was sobered by learning the extent of sensitive U.S military operations around the world. And Bart had been surprised to learn how much authority had been delegated to his subordinates for approving these sensitive Defense Department operations. It wasn't that Bart didn't trust his subordinates, but in his career he had seen cases where senior officers and government officials had delegated almost everything to their subordinates; when something went wrong, they claimed they didn't know anything about it.

The SSD, was organized into desks responsible for geographical regions of the world, e.g., the Soviet Union and Eastern Europe, North Korea, Cuba, China, etc. The difference between the desks in the DAS and those in the SSD was that the DAS desk officers monitored and directed the myriad of normal operations that military attachés around the world were involved with: protocol, military-to-military agreements, security assistance, foreign sales, defense related information and advice and assistance to U.S. ambassadors and the host country's military representatives. The SSD, additionally and in contrast, monitored, coordinated and approved for the Department of Defense, only the involvement of the U.S. Military in sensitive activities, special operations and foreign counterintelligence.

"These kinds of operations," Bob Herrington told Bart, "are only undertaken by the military to satisfy the combat information and intelligence requirements of war fighting military commanders when the required information cannot be obtained by other agencies or means. For example," Herrington had explained, "when the Commander-in-Chief of Central Command based in Tampa, Florida, requires military information on potential adversaries he goes to the national security community and asks that they satisfy his requirements. In practice," Herrington added, "the national community of DIA, CIA, NSA, FBI, State and the military services are able through all source intelligence to satisfy 90% of the CINC's information needs. The military attachés and the DAS play a major role in this mission. But almost always," Herrington pointed out, "there's about 10% of the CINC's requirements, more in certain countries, that do not get answered. The CINC then looks to the military intelligence units in his assigned service component commands to satisfy these requirements.

When a service component intelligence unit proposes an operation in a foreign country to satisfy a CINC requirement," Herrington continued, "our guys in SSD review it for operational soundness and coordinate it with our colleagues at DIA, CIA and State. And if we, and by this we mean you, General Lowe, believe the risk of possible embarrassment is acceptable if the operation is compromised, versus the gain of satisfying the CINC requirement, then we approve the operation in the name of the Secretary of Defense. There are high stakes for all of us in these operations because failure to satisfy the CINC's requirements could result in the loss of American military lives when the fighting begins."

Colonel Herrington also explained that on some occasions all attempts to satisfy some CINC or JCS requirements are unsuccessful; then the resident military attaché becomes the last resort and only hope to satisfy a critical requirement. "This happened," he said, "a number of times in the Soviet Union."

In his overview of the SSD mission Herrington also outlined SSD's role in working with the FBI and the U.S. Military Service Counterintelligence authorities against the worldwide hostile intelligence threat to the U.S. military services. The espionage directed against U.S. military technology, readiness and war plans by more than a dozen hostile intelligence services was massive, persistent and too often successful. The national security agencies and military services feared technical and human penetration and, as Herrington had indicated, rightly so, citing a number of espionage cases where spies had been caught red-handed, though not before considerable damage had been done to U.S. national security.

After Colonel Herrington had completed his overview of the SSD mission, he was followed by his civilian deputy and two of the SSD branch chiefs who went into specific ongoing operations and results achieved around the world. Bart Lowe had been the recipient of information and intelligence on America's real and potential adversaries for many years, but he had had little exposure to details and the mechanics of how "difficult-to-obtain" information was garnered by human and technical means.

"Frankly speaking," he had told his subordinates in SSD, "as a battlefield warrior for the past twenty-odd years, I concentrated on the skills of my profession...how to fight and how to win. I appreciated the importance of tactical intelligence and combat information and the U.S. Army had the best; but, for the answers to strategic questions, and as to who and how they were answered, I expected someone would automatically send them down to me. You have given me a new appreciation of what it must take in the way of people-talent and operational know-how to answer the strategic mail."

Before the walk-through of SSD, Colonel Herrington had cleared the room of everyone except Captain Pete Kalitka, Bart's deputy and General Lowe. Herrington then went over the details of HEAT SEEKER much the same as John Kitchen. The chief difference was that Bob Herrington put a military spin on it and shared his thoughts with Lowe on where the mole was located. Herrington explained that John Kitchen had first alerted SSD earlier in late 1985 on the possibility of HEAT SEEKER based on operational compromises. Then, in early 1986, it had been reported to SSD from military and defense sources that three long-term operations in Europe had been compromised abruptly. Later, two

CIA agents focused against Eastern Europe were apprehended. In both cases supporting nets had been rolled up with nine suspected deaths and a complete shutdown of the very valuable information the operations had been providing. At this point Herrington provided Lowe a written summary of the known losses. A security leak was suspected and counterintelligence investigations were immediately undertaken. SSD had been kept in the loop concerning these investigations. The investigations had tentatively concluded that the leak or leaks had not come from within Department of Defense activities. Herrington agreed. He told Bart that he believed that HEAT SEEKER would probably be found in one of three places: (1) the CIA (2) the FBI (3) or, a small staff cell of the National Security Council. At each of these locations a small number of people had access to foreign agent operations information. The FBI's access was normally limited to counterintelligence-type agent information or investigations where compromise was taking place such as "HEAT SEEKER". SSD technically had access only to Defense operations, but in working closely with the CIA, some agent operations were mutually supportive and gave the SSD people access to some CIA operations. The National Security Council staff could call for access to any and all agent operations. And, according to them, had done so in the past to determine source reliability concerning grave national security matters and judgments.

Only the CIA had complete information concerning all agent operations of the U.S. Government and was number one on Colonel Herrington's suspect list. He explained that within CIA there were three distinct groups: the analysts, the operators and the counterintelligence people. "Part of the problem," he said, "was that the CIA was pretty much its own watchdog and resented attempts by the FBI to move into CIA turf. "Also," he added, "CIA had recently transferred some operators to outlying regions from headquarters as an internal security measure they wouldn't discuss."

"It's fair to say, General, that the FBI does not trust the CIA and vice versa," Herrington had told Lowe. Herrington was loath to believe that any member of the SSD staff could be the HEAT SEEKER mole, but he assured General Lowe that he was working with the FBI, CIA and the service counter intelligence chiefs to root out the mole. Lastly, Herrington told Lowe that some attachés in the Bloc countries and the Soviet Union had reported their best sources of information had disappeared. Herrington and Kalitka were both concerned over a HEAT SEEKER connection.

Bart became more and more uncomfortable about HEAT SEEKER as the briefing progressed.

"Bob, recognizing that my job as head of the DAS will keep me busy with many things both here and abroad, what percentage of my time do you think I need to devote to playing an active role in your areas of responsibility?'

Herrington replied, "General, I've never seen a more busy or demanding job than the one you now have. If you could devote ten percent of your time staying abreast of all we are doing here, it would be great."

"Fair enough," Bart replied. "But until I learn more about what you are doing, I plan to double my involvement, and I'll find the necessary time. Look for new ways to keep me informed on what's going on and let's start with me personally exercising approval authority for all Defense Department intelligence and sensitive operations SecDef has delegated to me." Recognizing the panic on Herrington's face as Herrington thought about what he would do about an urgent, time sensitive operation when he couldn't reach the General, Lowe added, "when I go back to the office I'll have my XO get together with you to work out a system for you and your people to get to me for operational approvals on a regular basis."

After the meeting, Bart Lowe then instructed Colonel Martin that he did not want to go any longer than 24 hours without Colonel Herrington's people being able to reach him for important business.

At the conclusion of the end-of-the-day meeting in his office, Bart, speaking to his deputy, Pete Kalitka, said, "during my visit to SSD today I decided to make some policy changes regarding the delegation of approval authority for sensitive operations. I told Colonel Herrington what I wanted and instructed George Martin to set up a system with Herrington and SSD to allow them to get to me on a timely basis." Then, turning to Chuck Gregorios, Lowe said, "Chuck, Pete was with me for the SSD visit but I would like to kick the matter around with both of you for a few minutes if you two can stay behind."

Both men nodded and Chuck Gregorios suggested, "You may want George to sit in with us and he can write a memo on the policy changes you wish to be made."

"Good idea, Chuck. Call George back in, please."

When the three men were all seated again Bart asked, "Any problem with the SSD changes I've made?"

Pete Kalitka was the first to speak. "No problem from my perspective. My only concern is that Bob Herrington may think you are doing this because of some lack of confidence in his abilities."

"I would throw in my two cents of agreement to that," added Chuck." Pete and I speculated that it was probably only a matter of time before you would want to become more involved in SSD. Your predecessor didn't like that side of the business and was comfortable with letting Bob Herrington run it. Recognizing the potential problems inherent in the activities of SSD, and to protect General Tibbets, Pete and I kept a close eye on SSD. But, to tell you the truth Bob Herrington knows that side of the business cold. He's never been a cowboy and won't tolerate one working in SSD. Bob has always gone out of his way to keep Pete and me informed."

"That's all very reassuring," Bart said. "Now you need to help me convince Bob that my only reason for taking back the SSD operational approval authority is to return it to its intended level. I see nothing different in Bob's and SSD's responsibilities other than when it comes time to sign a 'go-or-no-go' on the dotted line, the signature will be mine. I'll need all the help I can get from Bob

Herrington and his SSD people, and for that matter, from you three, as I continue to break into this new business. I also would welcome any thoughts you have on how I might establish a closer working rapport with my opposite numbers in the community, particularly at the agency and bureau."

CHAPTER 7

CROSSING THE POTOMAC

It was 9:30 Friday morning. Bart Lowe was sitting alone in his office going over his congressional testimony for the fifth time, testimony to be delivered later that morning to the Senate Select Committee on Intelligence (SSCI) at the Rayburn Congressional Office Building, "on the hill." Bart planned to leave the DAS Headquarters at 10:10, allowing 30 minutes for the drive from Rosslyn into Washington and 15 to 20 minutes to get into the hearing room and set up a slide presentation for his testimony. Bart knew that Senators and Congressmen often kept others waiting, yet insisted that scheduled hearings begin promptly. The chairman or vice chairman of a committee who had called a hearing would always be present at the hearing and on time. Individual members of a committee, on the other hand, could afford to miss a scheduled hearing. They were covered by their professional staffers who were assigned regular places on the committee room's back bench where they could take notes on the proceedings. Bart was cautioned not to be disappointed if only the chairman and one or two other senators and two dozen staffers were present for his hearing. He was told this was usually par for the course. Full member attendance normally occurred when hearings were open to the media and/or were being televised. Bart's DAS hearing was a closed hearing where classified Defense Department information would be discussed.

Bart completed his final review of the testimony. The typed, double-spaced pages were a summary of the actual testimony that would be submitted for the record to the SSCI. A less formal draft would be used by Bart as a talking paper to make key points.

In preparing the testimony, Chuck Gregorios suggested the condensed, summary format to Bart and recommended that he work with a person from the Operations Division, one from the Budget Branch and a third person from the DAS Congressional Liaison Office. Bart met with the three individuals several times. Bill Barnes, the man from Operations, was a seasoned middle-aged civilian who knew operations and the needs of the DAS and the service military intelligence organizations. The budget officer, Air Force Lieutenant Colonel Bernie Cox, covered funding and resource programs and future requirements for the DAS. The congressional liaison officer, Robin Fitch, provided Lowe insights on how the congressional hearing process really worked, particularly the "behind-the-scenes-play."

Ms. Fitch spoke with an authoritative view gained from five years of service as a staff member on the hill, she kept an extensive book on the SSCI members and their staffers, their voting track records on DAS programs, and issues of concern to members. She highlighted the important role played by the professional staffer for the habitually busy Senator or Congressman. Robin recommended that General Lowe use his first appearance before the SSCI as a foundation for an active program to cultivate the congressional staffers. She suggested that he keep them informed on all the DAS was doing and seek their help and assistance on matters of import to the DAS. When Bart appeared uncomfortable with this approach, Fitch quickly clarified that she was not suggesting favoritism or anything unethical. She was, she said, "simply pointing out one of the realities of Washington and the U.S. Congress. Those who do not understand the role of the professional staffer and bypass them are usually doomed to failure in gaining support for their programs in Congress. The reality of the congressional staff," she said, "is that it is a power base only the most naive players ignore and the smartest Washington players include in their approach in dealing with Congress."

Fitch recommended he meet the Congressional staffers head-on, pay them their just dues and respect and be forthright and candid with them in all matters. "They are," she said, "quick to recognize something that makes good sense for the country and their members and will lend their support to making it happen. That is why," she said, "the DAS has always enjoyed an excellent reputation with the Congress."

Fitch also made it equally clear that some staffers and members on the SSCI and on the House Permanent Select Committee on Intelligence (HPSCI) were not as supportive on military service involvement in sensitive and special operations as they were for pure attaché matters. This was partly because they understood the more routine attaché activities better, and because, in the minds of many, sensitive operations that could prove embarrassing to the United States should only be conducted by the CIA. The problem was further complicated because the CIA had never been willing to assume full responsibility for providing war fighting commanders with all the information necessary for commanders to fight a war. Nor would the military commanders be willing to be dependent solely on CIA for their wartime information and intelligence support.

The task then that fell to Lowe was to convince the Congress—members and staffers—that the military intelligence organizations, missions and roles he was responsible for were an essential and critical part of the overall U.S. Defense preparedness efforts in peace, crisis and war. General Lowe also needed to reassure the Congress that all operations were carried out in coordination with other appropriate U.S. agencies, such as State, CIA, and the FBI, and complied with the spirit and letter of U.S. legal and ethical guidelines.

Bart Lowe's staff did their homework in gathering pre-hearing information on how the DAS might fare this year with the SSCI. The consensus was that if General Lowe was not a complete flop in front of the SSCI, he would probably come away with Congressional support for most of the attaché program budget items, including new vehicles, communications and office machine modernization, secure fax capabilities, increased aircraft maintenance and safety equipment costs, escalating foreign housing costs, and training dollars for advanced foreign language training at field locations. Most Senators and staffers had heard about these needs from their visits to foreign locations and their contact with the attachés on station.

Lowe's toughest sell, his staff estimated, would be his endorsement of the military service initiatives, and particularly SSD's involvement in what was identified as human intelligence. This area was contentious with the Congress because many legislators were not in favor of the military services being involved in this sensitive program. This was a CIA role, Congress maintained. The funding for such human intelligence (HUMINT) operations was contained in the individual service programs, but the DAS support for the program and the DAS evaluation of the need for and success of the programs were keys to any Congressional support. Accordingly, the DAS written testimony and Bart Lowe's verbal pitch left the service items to last, somewhat to the Special Services Division's chagrin.

During the week Bart had spoken with each of the service intelligence chiefs and the service intelligence and security commanders. The Army's programs, Bart's own service, would be the most difficult to gain support for because of their size, number and cost. The Army's programs were larger than all the other services put together. There was a congressional concern, Bart was told, that if not checked, the Army programs would rival the CIA, NSA and DIA programs. Bart's people suspected the CIA fanned some of those concerns.

At 10:05 George Martin came into Bart's office and announced, "Time to mount up, General; go forth and educate the great Congress of the U.S.A."

Bart stood up from his work table, stretched and said. "Okay George, I'm as ready as I'll ever be." He pushed the material he had been reviewing across the table to Colonel Martin, and said, "Please put this into the large travel briefcase and pass it to Bill Barnes. He's going to accompany me to the Hill. I'm going to change my shirt."

Because the building in Rosslyn was a leased facility, not subject to the normal federal building specifications and restrictions, some of the executive offices had private rest rooms. Bart's office area had a toilet, wash basin, shower and a full length mirror. There was also room for a wall locker where he could keep a change of uniforms, civilian clothes and his athletic gear. As he changed from short sleeve, open collar shirt to the more formal long sleeve green shirt with black tie, military French cuffs and regimental cuff links, he thought that of all the trappings that sometimes went with senior military rank such as aides, and drivers and stately old military quarters, the one he ranked as most desirable was the private latrine in his office.

After washing his hands, he slipped on his green blouse with stars and full military decorations. He would have preferred the informality of the short sleeve shirt but the Class A uniform was appropriate for the occasion. Uniform complete, Major General Bart Lowe left his office and crossed the Potomac River into Washington, to report to the U.S. Congress.

Brian Cobry, the Staff Director for the SSCI met General Lowe and his two assistants at the entrance of the Rayburn Building and escorted them to a small hearing room on the second floor. After they had shown their identification cards to the guard at the hearing room door and gained admission, Cobry briefed General Lowe on the proceedings. "General Lowe, my boss, Senator Charles Corbett, the Chairman of the SSCI, will be chairing the hearing today. He is not here yet and probably won't arrive until just a minute or so before 11:00. He asked me to tell you that he probably won't get a chance to chat with you informally today but he invites you to come see him at your leisure. If you do not already know this, Senator Corbett is a true friend of the military. During the relatively short time he has been Chairman of the SSCI he has also been a friend to the DAS. He, of course, is a tremendously busy man, but if at any time you feel strongly about something and need his help, I think you can count on him being there for you."

Cobry acknowledged that the DAS formal testimony submissions, both the unclassified and classified versions, had been received and distributed to all concerned. He also explained the set-up of the hearing room. In the front of the room there were two large witness tables complete with sound systems. Lowe could have his choice. Behind the witness tables were rows of chairs to be used by people accompanying the witnesses or other congressional spectators, provided they had the necessary security clearances to be admitted. In front of the witness table was a horseshoe shaped dais with seats for all the committee members. The Chairman would sit in the middle and the other members to his left and right according to their seniority. Behind the members was a semi-circle of chairs known as the "back bench." There was a second entrance at the rear of the room to permit the members and staffers to come and go during the hearing without interrupting the proceedings.

"General Lowe, I'm informed that the Vice Chairman, Senator Thomas of New Hampshire will also be here today. That is unusual. I suspect that he's coming because you are new and he wants to have a look at you," Cobry opined.

Bart remembered that Ms. Fitch had indicated that Senator Thomas and his staffers were the leading opponents on the committee concerning military sensitive operations.

"My information is that in addition to the Chairman and Vice Chairman, five other Senators have indicated their intention to attend, including the Senator from your home state of Florida, Senator Bob Jones."

Bart nodded and said, "I noted that Senator Jones was on the SSCI. He and I both graduated from the University of Florida, but he's not someone I know personally. I'm looking forward to meeting him."

"On the timing, General, and I'm sure Robin Fitch has briefed you, the hearing is scheduled for 90 minutes. It will never go that long. I would be surprised if the Chairman could stay for more than one hour. I would strongly suggest that you try to get in the important points during the first 30 minutes. By that time the members will be ready to put their questions to you. Thirty more minutes should suffice. The remaining 30 minutes of the allotted 90 minute hearing time, if you are willing to remain after the Senators have departed, could be used for staffers' questions. It would be a good opportunity for them to get to know you, and vice-versa."

Bart indicated his willingness to stay behind with the staffers, thanked Mr. Cobry for the informative overview and with only five minutes remaining before the hearing, huddled briefly with Bill Barnes and Robin Fitch, who assured him his notes were in place and all was ready to proceed. The Chairman, Senator Charles Corbett, entered the hearing room with about fifteen seconds to spare. He was preceded by the six other Senators and about twenty staffers. After briefly greeting the other Senators, he took his seat and banged his gavel to signal that the "SSCI Hearing on Attaché Affairs" was officially open.

"General Lowe, speaking for myself, and I'm sure the other members of the Senate Select Committee on Intelligence, I want to extend a warm welcome to you and say how happy we are to have you appear before us today. We have all, I believe, read your biography and are pleased to have such a distinguished soldier in our midst. To a man, and lady, I might hastily add," referring to Senator Barbara Haskins, "this committee has the greatest respect for the Defense Attaché Service. All of us have had many opportunities to observe our splendid Army, Navy, Air Force, Marine, and Coast Guard attachés serving around the world. We have never been disappointed in their representation of the United States and roundly applaud their dedication and service to country."

Bart Lowe was sitting ram-rod straight at the witness table listening carefully to Senator Corbett's opening remarks. He could not help but be somewhat taken aback by the florid compliments.

Less than one minute ago there was only one individual behind the dais, Brian Cobry; now there were almost 30 people. Senator Corbett was talking slowly as if he had been waiting for his audience. Other Senators and staffers appeared almost instantly as Senator Corbett started speaking, as if they were students who had just heard the last bell for class. Robin Fitch had warned Bart that while Senator Corbett was an ally and supporter, he was foremost a politician through and through and Bart could expect some grandstanding for the record. Bart smiled to himself as Ms. Fitch's estimate proved to be right on the mark.

"General," the senior Senator from Arizona continued, "as you may know, time for most of us here is of the essence. We received your written testimony and we and our staffs will be going over that in detail. For today I would ask that you keep your remarks as brief as possible and allow sufficient time for the Senators' questions." Turning business-like now, Senator Corbett asked, "Do you have any questions before we begin?"

"No, Senator," replied Bart.

"Very well, then let's begin."

"Senator Corbett, Senator Thomas and other distinguished members of the Senate Select Committee on Intelligence, I am honored to have the opportunity to appear before you today to discuss the present and future posture of the Defense Attaché Service. As you are aware I have been the Director of the Defense Attaché Service, or as we call it, the DAS for only a short period of time. However, I was privileged to serve as an Army attaché earlier in my military career. It is my firm conviction that the requirement for a DAS has never been greater in the history of our country than at the present time. I can also report to you that this conviction is shared by my superiors in the Defense Department. Before I elaborate I would first like to highlight for you some brief examples of DAS accomplishments during the last year. First slide please...," and so Bart Lowe began his testimony.

Even though it was his first appearance before a Congressional committee, Bart had wanted to try something unique. Instead of just telling the Senators what the attachés had accomplished, he wanted to show them. Bart had picked the idea up some years ago as a young officer serving on the staff of the Commander-in-Chief, Pacific, in Hawaii. Bart's boss at that time, Admiral John McCain was a very popular warrior with the

Congress and, during the Vietnam War years, made many appearances before Congress. Bart had assisted the Admiral in his presentations and the Admiral always used graphic aides in closed hearings. This was done, according to the Admiral, to make his points to the Congressmen dramatically clear and, as far as Bart could tell, it always worked.

Bart selected twelve examples of outstanding attaché work and had his staff convert these examples into color graphics, reduced to 35mm slides. The items he selected dealt with information or evidence the attachés had reported concerning matters of high national interest such as nuclear weapons proliferation, biological warfare, terrorist incidents, new weapons developments in Russia, China and North Korea, drug trafficking in South America, the Iran-Iraq War, and various other conflicts in Nicaragua, El Salvador, Angola and Chad. Bart's advisors were not too keen on the idea of using slides and were concerned that they might turn the Senators off. The medium the Senators were most comfortable with, they argued, was words; they were not certain how the slides would be received.

Bill Barnes, at Bart's direction, had positioned the slide projector at a right angle from the dais and positioned the large screen on the other side of the room facing the Senators. The effect was that the Senators hardly noticed the screen until Bart had the first slide projected. He watched their expressions closely as he began to show and explain the actions represented on the slides. For the first one or two slides, he saw some movement and surprised expressions on the face of the Senators and a lot of movement on the part of the back bench staffers as they whispered to each other. By the time he was on the fourth slide, he detected rapt interest on the part of the Senators and most of the staffers.

At the end of the twelve attaché examples he showed three additional slides, showing impressive results obtained from human intelligence operations, (HUMINT ops), conducted by the Army, Navy and Air Force Military Intelligence Units. Concerning these last three, he thought he detected some consternation and conversation going on among the staffers and noted Senator

Thomas making notes. The slide portion of his pitch took 15 minutes—right on schedule—and Bart quickly returned to his seat and began his prepared remarks. His delivery took another 15 minutes and he could detect no fidgeting on the part of the Senators. All appeared attentive and interested. Just as the clock on the hearing room wall reached 11:30, Bart said. "And that concludes my prepared remarks, Mr. Chairman. I'm now ready for your questions."

"Thank you, General. A most interesting presentation. Particularly your little slide show," began the Chairman. "Was it your thought that if you regaled us with those bright colors and pretty pictures that it might keep some of us more senior Senators awake? Well, if that was your intention, General, I think you can conclude it worked. We know you fellows over in the Pentagon are big on high tech and slide presentations. But we fellows on the Hill are big on words. We like to hold people responsible for what they say or what they commit to writing. I'm not so sure we can hold you responsible for what you show us in a picture show." Corbett smiled and winked at Senator Thomas. "Now, let me ask the first question. I'm interested in the study of foreign languages. If we approve the money you have asked for over the next five years, is that just for the purpose of being nice to your attachés and their families or can we expect to see some improved proficiency in the language skills of the people?"

"By all means, Senator. All of our advanced language programs, at the stations where we can afford them, begin with a diagnostic test. The test is designed to identify weaknesses in the language; we then design a tailored course of study to correct the deficiencies and enhance proficiency in the language. At the end of the language training, the individual is again tested to measure improvement. We've been keeping stats on this for some time and believe the money spent is worth the improvement in proficiency. We can provide your staff with our analysis if you would like, Senator," Bart responded.

"Please do so, General, and keep your people's nose to the grindstone in learning those foreign languages. Now I'll yield to other Senators for their questions."

Each of the other Senators had a question or two. For the most part, the questions were friendly and straight forward, reflecting the Senators' long service on the SSCI and familiarity with the DAS. Bart had been able to respond satisfactorily and promised follow up information when a question called for a more detailed answer. Time was almost running out, and Senator Thomas had not yet asked a question. Then, just as Senator Corbett was getting ready to close the hearing, the Senator from New Hampshire turned to Senator Corbett to signal he needed a little more time and then turned toward Bart.

"General, I have two questions for you. One, this human intelligence business involves agent-operations—really sensitive operations conducted by the military. Shouldn't all of that be CIA's responsibility?"

Before Bart could attempt an answer Senator Thomas raised a hand and said, "You don't have to answer that today. I know you are new in your job and will require some time to sort out your views on that subject, but I want you to give me an answer as soon as you feel comfortable in doing so. Now my second question is do you know that both the Army and Air Force recently had serious compromises of some of their agent operations?"

Bart was surprised at the question. It was the only one involving classified matters he had received. SSD had told him that they didn't think anyone on the Hill was aware of the compromises. "Was Senator Thomas or his staffers aware of HEAT SEEKER?" Bart wondered. Not that anyone was hiding anything from the Hill; it was just premature. His staff had told him not to inform the Congressional Committees until more was learned about the cause of the compromises.

Bart did not show any surprise outwardly and responded to Senator Thomas by replying. "Yes, Senator, I'm aware of those compromises and my staff has briefed me. The Army and Air Force are both conducting investigations into the causes of the compromises. As soon as we know more, we will be happy to provide you any information you desire."

"Good, General; I'll look forward to hearing from you." Then Senator Thomas turned to Senator Corbett and said, "No more questions, Mr. Chairman."

With that Senator Corbett's gavel sounded and the formal hearing was over.

Senator Corbett immediately left the hearing room. The other Senators came down off the dais and each, in turn, shook hands with Bart, thanked him for his testimony and complimented the DAS. Senator Bob Jones, the junior Senator from Florida, purposely hung back to be last.

"General, thank you for a very informative run down on the DAS. I think you made your case very clear, and I would not be surprised to see this committee fully supporting the programs you have requested."

"Senator, please call me Bart, and thank you for your kind remarks."

"All right Bart, I'll do that, and you call me Bob. I understand we are classmates and us Gators need to stick together. There are a lot of Seminoles in the Washington woods."

Bart Lowe had known of Senator Bob Jones for a long time. Jones had been two years ahead of Bart at the University of Florida. He had been a young man of independent wealth; his family had made a fortune in Florida in diary farms. Jones had always been what the fraternity men at Florida had called a "politico," and a successful one. He had been president of the student body. After his undergraduate days, he had gone on to law school, and after graduation he joined a law firm in Miami. It was only a matter of time before Jones became involved in state politics and subsequently ran for governor of the state. He had two successful terms as governor and was a shoe-in when he ran for U.S. Senator.

"Bart, my staffers tell me that you play racquetball, and I was thinking that if you wanted to get together for a game, we might add lunch and I could give you a little run down, from one

Floridian to the other, on how things work over here and how we see the world."

"I'd very much like to do that."

"Okay!. I'll have my staff assistant, Teri McCannon, contact your folks to arrange a time. By the way, feel free to contact Ms. McCannon if she can assist you. She is one sharp lady. Now I must get back to the Senate floor."

Bart had heard that Senator Jones, with all his wealth and success, had never let that go to his head. He seemed like a regular guy, and Bart had heard he was probably one of Congress' true statesman. Bart looked forward to knowing the Senator better.

After Senator Jones departed, Brian Cobry brought Bart Lowe and his two assistants some coffee. "General Lowe, may I suggest that you move up to the dais and make yourself comfortable, and we can give the staffers a crack at you."

Bart agreed, removed his uniform blouse and hung it on the back of a chair. As he moved up to the dais and settled into one of the executive chairs the remaining staffers gathered around, introduced themselves to Bart and began their informal questions. This differed from the formal hearing in that none of the questions or answers now would end up in the Congressional Record. The staffers were a lively and interested group. Most were well dressed, relatively young people, generally, in their mid-thirties. One notable exception was a man named Merle Kiley, probably in his late fifties who, according to Ms. Fitch, had been a professional staffer for years. Four of the staffers were women, one of whom was Senator Jones' staffer, Teri McCannon. Ms. McCannon was an attractive woman, confident and articulate in her manner and questions.

None of the questions or comments made by the staffers were frivolous. All of the questions demonstrated solid understanding of the DAS. If there was a pattern to the questions that Bart could discern, it was one of getting to know him as they tried to pick his brain on his approach to his job. Did he bring any prejudices to this assignment? Was he going to introduce any radical changes? Had he been given any new charges from his superiors at the Defense Department?

The only exception to the friendly, "getting to know you" type questions were the ones put to Bart from Senator Thomas' staffer, Milt Cohen, an aggressive young man who said he had worked at DIA before becoming a staffer. His questions dealt solely with the role of the military service intelligence units and their missions. Bart fielded Cohen's questions by indicating that since overseeing the military services' missions was only a small part of his overall responsibilities he was getting into this area slowly and carefully, still formulating his own views. In the meantime he was satisfied that operations were being carried out in compliance with all legal and congressional guidelines. There was more than a hint of concern on Cohen's part. Bart made a mental note to follow up on the subjects raised by Mr. Cohen.

The remaining 30 minutes went by quickly, and promptly at 12:00, Brian Cobry, still acting as host announced: "Well, ladies and gentlemen, I'm sure General Lowe is on a tight schedule and needs to get underway. General, again on behalf of Senator Corbett and all of the staffers present, we thank you for sharing your time with us today and wish you every success in your new and important responsibilities."

Riding back in the sedan to Rosslyn, Bart and his two assistants went over the details of the hearing. Bill Barnes had taken notes and would, with Robin Fitch's help, prepare a "memorandum for the record" highlighting follow-up actions to be taken. Bill believed that the proceedings had gone well with the slide show serving as a catalyst for the Senators' understanding and appreciation of the attachés' work.

Robin Fitch said, "the preliminary feedback from the staffers at the break was all positive. General Lowe, I think it's safe to say that in your first skirmish you have taken the Hill."

"Taken the Hill, Robin? Probably not. I think I'll settle for establishing a beachhead."

Bart appreciated the enthusiasm and optimism of his two able assistants, but the underlying issues behind Senator Thomas' questions and the questions and comments of his staffer, Milt Cohen, would need to be followed up. Maybe Senator Bob Jones could help with that.

At the same time Bart Lowe was getting into his sedan to return to Rosslyn, Harold Sema was leaving his office to meet his foreign contacts in Georgetown for lunch. The responsibilities of his job actually called for him to meet with his foreign colleagues as often as he deemed appropriate. Summer was ending in Washington and the drive on a sunny day in his new Lexus 400 was relaxing to Sema.

During the first couple of months after he had agreed to work for the Russians he had some misgivings and almost gave it up, particularly when they told him what they wanted. They gave him a wish list and asked him to review it and let them know what items he could obtain.

Sema had a photographic memory. If the information they wanted was under his control he would review it carefully before he went home, and then that night, in the privacy of his study, he would replicate the information on his home computer. For information he didn't control, he would first locate where it was and then use some research excuse to review the information and then follow the same technique.

Sema's responsibilities at his work permitted him wide latitude for requesting the kinds of information his Russian friends were interested in without arousing suspicion. And the money! He couldn't believe what they were willing to pay. Beyond his wildest expectations.

If only his friends, he thought, could see him now. The reality, of course, was that he did not have any real friends. There was another down side. The Russians failed to keep their promise of not letting it be known that they had his information. They had blown it shortly after he provided them with some real hot stuff. Names of people, places and dates, including the kinds of information the US was getting about the Russians. Contrary to what they had told him, they overreacted to shut down their losses and some people were hurt. Well, what the hell," he thought. "It's a dangerous business."

The problem was the Russians were so damn heavy-handed. Not cautious at all. He told them in no uncertain terms that if they didn't clean up their act they could kiss him good-bye. They sure as hell didn't want that to happen. They assured him they would be more careful and eased his feelings with more money. It helped.

As he pulled his car into the underground parking garage next to the Georgetown Mall, he had to admit that he was looking forward to meeting with Katyu and Boris, a husband and wife team. It took two of them to stay up with him. Nevertheless, they were far better than that idiot colonel they had thrown at him in the beginning. As he left the parking garage he lit his first cigar of the day.

CHAPTER 8

THE WASHINGTON PLAYING FIELD

Following his trip to the Hill, Bart settled into the day-to-day running of the DAS. The weekly operational briefings he initiated with the Operations Division and Geographical Divisions allowed him to get up to speed and become involved with the high volume of operational activities around the world. He included the Support Division in the weekly updates to stay abreast of the logistical, finance and resource problems.

After the first two months he made the decision to have Colonel Herrington and the Special Services Division provide him, his two deputies, and the Operations and Geographical Division Chiefs, with a weekly snapshot of sensitive operations at the end of the weekly update. Herrington grumbled about this at first on security compartment grounds but quickly saw the value of including the opinions of other key DAS personnel in gauging the risk of sensitive operations.

The increased pace was not without casualties. Bart decided to replace the Chief of the Operations Division, an officer who had not responded well to change, and the DAS Chief of Communications, a good technical person, but one who had difficulty in designing a communications architecture for future DAS requirements. He intended to keep the joint service mix of officers at headquarters, but until he got to know the other service personnel officers better, he used his contacts in the Army to jump-start some key positions. The Army agreed to assign a Colonel Nick Tortellie, a very successful brigade commander with extensive national security experience to the DAS, to be Bart's Operations Chief, and to loan him, for one year, one of the Army's brightest Signal Corps officers, a Lieutenant Colonel Jerry Kirsh. Kirsh had commanded a signal battalion for Lowe in Germany. He was a futuristic thinker, a technical expert, and the ideal man to design the future information and communications needs of the DAS.

The DAS management team was falling into place. The feedback coming in regularly from the Defense Attaché Offices allowed Lowe to assess the relative effectiveness, strengths, and weaknesses of the various attaché staffs around the world. He used this information to prepare for his future visits to the DAOs.

Bart Lowe also had made progress with his counterparts at the other national security agencies in Washington. He devised a scheme to have coffee, breakfast, or lunch once a month with Judge Lamont, the Director of the FBI; Art Cheek, the Deputy Director for Operations, DDO, at CIA; Vice Admiral Bud Weaver, the Director of NSA; and Lieutenant General Lenny Murphy, the Director of DIA. He also met routinely and informally with the commanders of the Military Service's Intelligence Commands. Bart scheduled each of the meetings separately. All turned out to be productive for the informal exchange of mutual-interest information. It would have been more practical to get all of the group together for one function, but coordinating their individual schedules would have been a nightmare, and the exchange of information would have been far less candid. As the new kid on the block, Bart had the most to gain and he was more than willing to make the extra effort. The "one-on-ones" also facilitated the discussion of HEAT SEEKER.

In the early days of his new job, through these informal meetings and exchanges of information, Lowe was able to gain insights into the national agencies, their real agendas, the players, and the roles and missions they carried out in the United States and around the world. He knew the knowledge he gained would serve him well in the years ahead.

The Director of the CIA, was largely a figurehead leader of the agency. He spent most of his time mending fences with the oversight committees of Congress, or responding to National Security Council and White House staff requests. The two workhorses at the CIA were the Deputy Director for Intelligence,

DDI, and the Deputy Director for Operations, DDO. The former was responsible for the myriad of national intelligence estimates required by the government, and the latter was almost solely responsible for the direction of CIA's worldwide intelligence operations. The main DAS interface with CIA was with the DDO organization in Washington, and through its attachés, to the CIA station chiefs (COS) at U.S. embassies around the world.

Bart Lowe enjoyed his association with his CIA contacts, all very talented and capable professionals, but he discerned a subtle, and sometimes not so subtle, attitude that announced, "We are in charge. Our mission is the most important one and we will help you with your mission if we think it's a good idea. But this assistance will be on our time schedule, not yours, and, by the way, while we want to know everything you are doing in your operations, even the smallest details, don't ask about anything we are doing, because you don't have a need to know." There were many exceptions to this harsh generalization, but it didn't take Lowe long to detect a sense of frustration throughout the DAS and in the military services' operations in their dealings with CIA.

Fortunately, the greatest information reporting successes of the Defense Attachés came from their unique abilities to gather strategic political, military, and tactical information on an overt basis, a procedure not requiring approval by the CIA.

The FBI was a kindred spirit to the uniformed men and women of the Armed Forces and Defense Attaché Corps. There was a commonality of missions. The U.S. military services and the FBI were both protecting the United States. FBI agents were men and women of their word. There were never any hidden agendas in DAS's mutual operations with the FBI. The Bureau could be counted upon to fulfill any commitments it made. The FBI's coordination process was straightforward and their cooperation genuine. The very real terrorist threat at home and abroad and the terrorist related missions that fell to the FBI, the DAS and the military counter terrorist and counterintelligence forces made them logical team players, willing to support each other's mission requirements.

The National Security Agency, the nation's czar for codes and communications security and signals intelligence, was the most closed and secret agency of the federal government. It was a joint military/civilian effort staffed by the military services' cryptologic experts and resident civilian work force at Fort Meade, Maryland. The NSA, since its inception had been headed up by a three-star officer from either the Army, Navy or Air Force on a rotating basis. The real continuity and strength of NSA came from a large cadre of super grade senior civilians that staffed the upper management echelons of the agency. It was this group of highly skilled men and women who strived tirelessly and successfully to keep NSA the best signals intelligence service in the world.

Concerns over NSA support came in from U.S. military combat commanders who were not convinced that NSA would be able or willing to support them in times of hostilities because of the security restrictions on NSA's acquired information. The senior military commanders viewed NSA like the CIA whose focus of support and priorities were toward the centers of government rather than to the military in the field. As a result, military commanders felt strongly that they needed their own supporting intelligence forces rather than relying on CIA and NSA.

The solution, Bart recognized, was achieving a balance between the spectrum of U.S. civilian and military information gathering agencies to meet the disparate strategic needs of the national command authority in Washington, the operational requirements of the Unified and Specified Commands around the globe and the tactical information and intelligence required by land, sea, and air forces. Having served at the bottom end of the information and intelligence flow for so long, Bart Lowe rapidly became an articulate voice for balanced strategic, operational and tactical support from the DAS seat at the table.

The Defense Intelligence Agency, Lowe thought, had the most difficult and thankless job of any agency in the superstructure of U.S. information and intelligence organizations. DIA's charter was to provide information and intelligence support to the Secretary of Defense, the Chairman of the Joint Chiefs of Staff and the chiefs' large and demanding staffs, the Unified and Specified Command CINCs and the military services. Even though their customers and requirements were clearly the most demanding in terms of numbers and urgency, DIA was the smallest of the national agencies and worked from the leanest budget. DIA often found itself at odds or in competition with the CIA on key judgments concerning strategic matters of utmost concern to the United States. The CIA sometimes was not above basing some of its judgments on information it held and had not shared with DIA for fear that the source of CIA information might be compromised.

All national security agencies had access to the technical information and intelligence gathered around the world by America's superior technology and sophisticated hardware, but none of that fully answered the question about the plans and intentions of foreign powers, rogue rulers, terrorists, and a wide variety of assorted crazies that posed a threat to the United States. Thus the human source of information and intelligence the HUMINT aspect, took on a critical degree of importance in arriving at key national security judgments. It was this human element in the national security process that made Bart Lowe's DAS and the attachés stationed in 130 countries unique to the Defense Department and so critical to DIA information and intelligence analysts in arriving at estimates of what others might do that would impact on the security of the United States. Bart Lowe concluded that the global Attaché Information Reports steadily arriving around the clock at DIA and throughout the Defense Department, formed the bedrock of reliable defense and military information on foreign countries. It did not take Bart Lowe long to recognize the value of having one or two DAS people on the ground to answer the question of what was really going on in country X—particularly if the CIA and State Department's reports were at odds; unfortunately, as Bart was learning, being at odds was not an unusual occurrence.

One other relatively small player in the national security scene, but one significant to the DAS was the State Department's Intelligence and Research Bureau, or INR. This modest office, headquartered at the State Department in Washington, was headed by a career Foreign Service Officer with ambassadorial rank and the status of Assistant Secretary of State. INR was responsible for disseminating intelligence and threat information to embassies world wide.

The INR was a place at the State Department where requests from the DAS for help or assistance were favorably received. The DAS requests were often in terms of numbers of attaché positions needed at a given embassy to respond to some new crisis or mission in that country. Professionals in INR recognized the importance of the military information flow from the DAS. INR was a friend in court to the DAS, and often the only higher court of appeal in a case of a difference of opinion between the DAS and a particular ambassador.

Bart Lowe was very comfortable in dealing with the military service chiefs, field operators and intelligence officers and commanders. Their requirements and military, strategic, operational, and tactical information needs were clear; these translated well into specific missions for the DAS and the attachés operating in foreign countries. In the monthly breakfasts Bart had begun with the military service intelligence commanders it became apparent to him that there would be no hidden agendas, and the service commanders would look to him as their advocate and a conduit to gain support for their requirements and operations from high Defense Department and National Security officials.

As promised, Bart was invited back to the Hill for lunch with Senator Bob Jones. The Senator had been a gracious host. He had taken Bart to the Senate Dining Room in the Capitol Building for lunch and treated him to a true Florida Everglades luncheon of gator tail appetizer, stone crab soup and fresh Florida lobster. Following lunch, Senator Jones had personally given Bart the VIP tour of the Capitol Building and taken him back to his office for coffee and a private discussion. Bob Jones had been especially helpful and candid in his description of the way things worked in the U.S. Senate and Congress. He told Bart the names of those Senators and staffers on the SCCI whom Bart and the DAS could count on for support. He warned Bart that Senator Thomas of New Hampshire was not a friend of the DAS and the military service intelligence organizations, and that Bart would do well to watch his flanks when dealing with Senator Thomas and his staffers.

"Remember, Bart," Senator Jones concluded, "things in Washington are as they are, not as they should be. Never, never, underestimate the importance of politics in this town."

Bart had taken Senator Jones' advice as gospel and proceeded carefully with all the DAS's dealings with Congress.

In Bart's view the DAS fared better than most with congressional support. For that he was thankful and he never missed an opportunity to express his appreciation to the appropriate committees. He watched over and reviewed carefully, his staff's response to congressional queries. There were many—the vast majority from congressional staffers. Most were routine, some in search of an issue that their members could use for criticism of the Administration, or as leverage for increased congressional control of Defense/DAS-related matters. The best response, he quickly learned, was a complete, forthright, rapid answer with nothing held back.

During the first three months in his new position Bart threw himself into every aspect of the job. He worked from early morning to well into the evening of each weekday and a part of every Saturday and Sunday. Lowe accepted every official social invitation and soon was recognized on the embassy and government official and social circuits. He made overnight trips to the DAOs in Canada and Mexico for his first DAS excursions outside the United States, and used these visits to the closest DAOs to formulate his thoughts and ideas for future visits and attaché conferences. Finally, acting on the assumption that all work and no play would make Lowe a dull general, Bart availed himself of the many cultural attractions and athletic events in the Washington area. He squeezed in a play here, a visit to a museum there, a band concert on the Mall and, when he was lucky enough to get tickets, an afternoon at RFK Stadium watching the Redskins. Bart preferred, and was usually successful, in obtaining female companionship for these excursions. His first choice was B.J. Ross, but her schedule at the Department of State was as demanding as his own, and she was often not available. Bart Lowe had no trouble in finding women whose company he enjoyed. However, no relationships beyond the casual came from these dates.

Bart Lowe was well known for his perseverance, and persevere he did with B.J. Ross until wonder-of-wonders, they found that they would both be free for Thanksgiving and agreed to spend the time together.

Bart was successful in renting the Lodge at Fort A.P. Hill for three days. Fort A.P. Hill is a small Army Post located in the heavily forested terrain of central Virginia. The post is used to train Virginia National Guard and Army Reserve units. In a remote corner of the post, a game preserve and wildlife recreation area has been set aside for the use of military personnel and their families and guests. In addition to many fishing and hunting locations in the preserve, the area contains a small number of widely dispersed cabins that may be used for overnight accommodations. The flagship of these cabins is an old hunting lodge originally built in 1919 before the government acquired the land. It is nestled in the woods sitting high upon a hill overlooking a fresh water lake. The Lodge can accommodate a large hunting party or family and is also a popular location for seminars, meetings, and weekend events. Bart had first learned of the Lodge several years earlier when he had attended an off-site conference there. The Lodge was so popular that reservations usually needed to be made six months in advance. Bart Lowe was fortunate when he called to check its availability and found that A.P. Hill just received a last minute cancellation. The Lodge contained all the amenities for a comfortable sojourn in the woods including a stocked fishing lake and fireplaces with stacks of seasoned firewood. Bart Lowe had always been lucky, and he was about to get luckier.

Bart met Ambassador Ross at her River House condo at 7:00 p.m. on Wednesday evening. He had told her to pack lightly because of limited space in the Corvette. She, like Bart, was a seasoned traveler and had no difficulty in getting three days of warm casual clothing in her Samsonite overnight bag. Her suitcase slipped in nicely on the luggage shelf behind the Corvette passenger seat, along with Bart's black leather overnighter, and the picnic hamper of food and a small cooler that Sergeant Wild had prepared for their three-day stay. B.J. was dressed in jeans, blue sweater with a matching hair scarf and three-quarter-length hiking boots. She carried a dark green down winter jacket. Bart was also wearing jeans, with black leather Reebok walking shoes and a red long-sleeve wool lumberjack shirt. He had a winter jacket behind his seat and suggested to B.J. that she also stow her jacket for the trip to A.P. Hill, telling her that it would be comfortably warm in the Corvette. As Bart helped B.J. into the car, he thought how elegant she looked, even in jeans. From the River House they headed south on Interstate 395 finding the traffic very heavy.

As they slid into bumper-to-bumper commuter traffic, B.J. turned to Bart, placed her hand on his arm and said, "Bart, this is going to be great! I can't remember when I last had three days to call my own. No meetings, no telephone calls, no international crisis. I have about had it up to here," she said, gesturing to nose level, "with crisis management."

"Feel strongly about it, do you?" Bart replied, covering her hand with his.

"For the last couple of weeks, it's just been non-stop. If it's not the Administration deciding to modify its foreign policy, then it's Congress pinging on us about enforcing some policy, or the Israeli or Arab lobbies complaining we are partial to one side over the other. I'll tell you, soldier, it's damn hard for a professional diplomat to be diplomatic in this town. Sometimes I feel like telling the lot of them—screw you—strong letter follows!"

"Whoa, Madam Ambassador. It sounds to me like you really need these few days of rest and recuperation prescribed by Doctor Lowe. I'd better step on the gas and get you to our wooded retreat and begin treatment pronto."

Slipping down into the contoured brown leather seat of the Corvette and stretching her arms and long legs into a more comfortable position, B.J. relaxed, smiled at Bart and said, "Now that I've answered the question how I am doing, tell me, how is the attaché business?"

"Well, I can honestly report that I am getting the hang of running the Attaché Service, even some international crisis management, but certainly nothing near the scale you're encountering, Madam Ambassador," joked Bart.

"Screw you, soldier, and the horse you rode in on," B.J. shot back, eyes flashing.

"Seriously," continued Bart, "since we talked last, my days and nights have been filled with a steady stream of problems and puzzles to be taken on, solved or resolved. Never a dull day would be an understatement."

"What kinds of specific things have you been doing?"

"Let's see, I've been summoned now twice by the SecDef and three times by the Chairman for special taskings for our attachés in Russia, South Korea, Norway, Indonesia, Great Britain and Panama. I have been chastised by your Assistant Secretary of State for Western Europe on the political/military reporting of our attachés in Paris, for not being consistent with the embassy's reports on France. Incidently, we believe the attachés' reporting has been accurate although not flattering to the French. I have briefed, in rough numbers, twenty new U.S. ambassadors en route to their new stations, spoken with another twenty-five regarding various complaints, requests, or kudos for the attachés and met and dispatched thirty odd new attachés. I now know all my counterparts in the National Security agencies, including your INR Chief, Jeff Lavin. I argued my first defense of the attaché budget for 1987-92 with Defense officials, had my first encounter with Senator Thomas and two of his staffers on the merits of military service intelligence organizations and operations—he's against them—we're for them. I've launched two studies on DAS communications and aircraft requirements for the future years, made a one-day visit to the DAO, Ottawa and an overnight visit to DAO, Mexico City. Finally, I think I can say that I've met most of the senior foreign attachés serving in Washington, either in calls at my office or at the many, many embassy social functions I have dutifully attended."

"Thank God I don't have too many of those to do," interjected B.J.

"And I've missed your company, but fortunately some other interesting women turn up from time to time."

"I'll bet," B.J. commented.

"And I have made firm plans for a first Regional Attaché Conference and my first major overseas trip. The conference will be held in Garmisch, Germany, next month for our Russian and Communist Bloc country attachés. Following that conference, I plan to visit Vienna, Prague, Warsaw, Budapest, Bucharest and Moscow. By the way, B.J., the people you sent over to work with my folks on the development of a conference model were very helpful. I sent the State Department a letter expressing our appreciation for their assistance."

"Yes, I saw that. Lisa Brown and Brett Wells are two of our brightest young foreign service officers. You have been busy. Any regrets so far?"

"No, none. As you know, Washington is at the center of the diplomatic world and the opportunity for me to be a player in United States involvement around the globe is fascinating and exciting, not to mention demanding as hell. In spite of all that takes place in Washington to keep the adrenaline flowing and the gray matter engaged, I am anxious to get to the field. I want to get to know the attachés on the front lines better and experience first hand what they are up against in accomplishing their missions. I'm looking forward to my first field conference and the follow-on road trip."

"Spoken like a true military man, Bart. Get the hell out of the headquarters and leave the bureaucratic work to the headquarters pukes, right?" B.J. taunted him.

"There is one perplexing matter that I am not sure how to handle."

"What's that Bart?" B.J. asked, turning toward him as she sensed the concern in his voice.

"I'm not even sure if we should talk about it, but, I checked with John Kitchen and I know you're cleared for HEAT SEEKER."

"Oh, yes. That."

"I guess my problem is what to do about it and if we collectively, mainly the FBI, are doing enough?"

B.J. hesitated for a moment and then offered, "I don't know if I can help you Bart, but let me try. I have been briefed on HEAT SEEKER. Often in our busy lives, with the heavy demands of our jobs that we face each day, we have a tendency to think that a HEAT SEEKER is a CIA or FBI problem and that we have enough on our own plates to worry about. When I first joined the Department, and even before that—when I was studying Russian at Harvard, I was fascinated by the spy cases of World War II, and the post world war years when the cold war began. The Rosenbergs, Alger Hiss, Philby, et. al., and the motives that caused those people to betray their countries, has always fascinated me. If I learned one thing from my review of those cases it is how extensive the damage is."

"I can believe that. I read the suspected HEAT SEEKER Defense Department losses include long-standing agents, their nets, the cut off of information, and loss of human life. And, as I understand it, there are also losses to CIA and the FBI."

"You're right, Bart."

"What can we do about it, B.J.? With John Kitchen at the lead at FBI, I would guess that all that can be done is being done. The FBI, for my money is tops, and I think John is their best. The CIA on the other hand probably has the most to be concerned about, but they are a difficult breed to read and always seem to hold their cards close to the chest."

"What do you do, general? You do what the military always does best; you shore up the perimeter, tighten security, put out your reconnaissance, and keep your ears to the ground. You watch for a break and then attack. That's what you do!" B.J. advised.

Then B.J. leaned over close to Bart and whispered in his ear, "And you, mister hot shot general, better keep a close eye on me. Remember, I speak fluent Russian. I deal with the Russian Embassy all the time and I have access to everything going on in Eastern Europe and the USSR. Who knows, maybe I am HEAT SEEKER."

If B.J.'s intention was to startle Bart, she succeeded. He jerked his head and the Corvettes' steering wheel to the right and looked into her eyes.

For about 15 seconds B.J. sternly returned Bart's surprised look. She then turned in her seat, slapped her leg, threw her head back, and said, "Gotcha!"

Because of the holiday eve traffic and the beginning snow flurries—the area's first snowfall of the year—the drive to A.P. Hill took more than two and one-half hours.

B.J. and Bart enjoyed being together and the time passed quickly. The keys to the Lodge had been left for General Lowe with the sentry at the front gate along with directions to the Lodge. During the fifteen minute drive through the game preserve to the Lodge it became apparent that the snowfall was much heavier in the wooded area; about two inches covered the hill leading up to the lodge. The Corvette negotiated the hill without problem. A night light had been left on in the Lodge, and as they pulled to the front door it seemed as though Bart and B.J. had arrived at the scene of a picture perfect winter wonderland.

B.J., obviously surprised and pleased, said, "Bart, how beautiful. This must be one of the best kept secrets in Washington."

After they were inside and Bart had unloaded their things from the Corvette they each selected one of the two master bedroom suites that adjoined the great room and sun porch of the lodge. Bart then turned to getting a fire started in one of the two walk-in size fireplaces that dominated the great room.

When B.J. came out of her bedroom, Bart said, "B.J. I put the picnic hamper and cooler in the kitchen. Sam Wild put some coffee and snacks in there for tonight. You want to see what there is and maybe brew us a hot cup of coffee?"

"At your service, general. Coming right up. Too bad you couldn't have brought Sam along," B.J. commented, moving toward the kitchen.

"It was either him or you, and he lost," Bart quipped.

Within 10 minutes a fire was roaring in the fireplace and they had pulled easy chairs and a coffee table up close. B.J. brought out a platter of cold cuts, vegetables, horseradish, pickles and dark breads prepared by Sergeant Wild. They quickly wolfed the tasty snacks and settled back into their chairs with shoes off and feet up, their hands wrapped around steaming mugs of coffee, totally relaxed, sipping their coffees and warmed by the fire, making only small talk until almost midnight. Then B.J. stood up, stretched and leaned over into Bart's face. She gave him a warm and gentle kiss and whispered in his ear, "I think what I need most tonight is a good night's rest. Any problem with that?"

Bart hesitated and then replied, "No..oo. I guess if you can restrain yourself so can I. After all, I am an officer and a gentleman. But before you head off to bed walk with me to the sun porch and let's have a look at the lake."

Bart turned the lights off in the great room and once their eyes had adjusted to the dark, they could see down the surrounding hill, white with snow, to the lake below. It was a picture of winter serenity. Bart held B.J. close while they shared the intoxication of the still falling snow.

"Okay." Bart said to B.J. "Off you go. Sweet dreams and I'll see you in the morning for breakfast. Reveille comes pretty early around here."

Bart was the first one up the next morning. He awoke shortly after six and showered and shaved by the time the sun began to appear. The snow had stopped sometime during the night but not before depositing about six inches of white, wet remembrance. Bart noted from the sun porch that a plow had already cleared the snow from the road along the lake leading to the Lodge. He put a pot of coffee on to brew, started a fire in the fireplace and, still not hearing any movement from B.J.'s bedroom, decided to drive into Bowling Green, the small town outside the front gate of A.P. Hill, to pick up morning papers. He left B.J. a note on the kitchen table.

The round trip took just 35 minutes, and when he returned he found B.J. sitting in front of the fireplace with a mug of hot coffee. B.J. was dressed in a white turtleneck shirt, a blue and green sweat suit and athletic socks without shoes. She looked rested and refreshed.

"Good morning, Madam Ambassador. I trust you slept well?"

"Absolutely. I was just waking up when I heard you driving off. My God, I thought, he's been called back to the office and when I go out into the Lodge I'll find a note saying I'll be back as soon as possible'. I was relieved to find your note."

Bart passed *The Washington Post* and the *Richmond Times* to B.J. and said, "Why don't you look these over and I'll cook breakfast."

He enjoyed preparing things in the kitchen but rarely had time to pursue anything complex. Bart considered breakfast one of his best meals and relished the opportunity to prepare something for B.J. At his request Sam Wild had included the ingredients for a mushroom omelet, several strips of center cut bacon and English muffins. The kitchen at the Lodge contained an old-fashioned grill that made cooking the breakfast both easy and fun. Plenty of room to turn and fold the omelet and lots of space for the bacon strips.

B.J. was delighted by Bart's delicious menu and impressed by his culinary skills. Breakfast was a huge success. After the morning meal they took fresh mugs of coffee to the sun porch and read the newspapers. This was followed by their first walk along the road around the lake, a distance of approximately three miles.

The plow had done a good job in clearing the road of the snow and their footing was solid. Bart and B.J. walked briskly along, hand-in-hand, touching only on the lightest of subjects and memories of earlier Thanksgiving days with their families. They decided to eat their Thanksgiving meal early in the afternoon and allow themselves more time to enjoy the snow. Shortly after they returned from their walk around the lake to the Lodge, they prepared their Thanksgiving dinner. Resourceful Sam Wild had thought of everything, packing the small picnic hamper efficiently with all the ingredients for a sumptuous Thanksgiving feast.

The meal consisted of a turkey breast, large enough for the meal and for follow-up cold sandwiches, chestnut dressing, candied sweet potatoes, a thermos of giblet gravy, sweet English peas, cranberry slices, fresh carrots and celery, and ample wedges of mince and pumpkin pies. This was accompanied by a bottle of Robert Mondavi cabernet sauvignon—they both preferred red wine. Sergeant Wild had even included the appropriate heating and cooking times and serving instructions.

B.J. and Bart savored the bountiful meal and each other, lighting candles with romantic ceremony. The only hint of formality was the china, crystal glassware and candelabra provided by the Lodge and the traditional blessing voiced by both as they held hands and gave thanks for their good fortune.

Following the meal and some drowsy time spent with desert and coffee by the fireplace, they ventured out again into the snow. This time Bart discovered a wooden sled behind the Lodge and determined that the hill leading down from the back of the Lodge offered an excellent sled run. They tried this, individually and together, more times than they could count. If seen from a distance they would have been mistaken for teenagers. This frivolity finally ended in a snowball fight with combatants getting soaked from the wet snow. The setting sun slipped behind the horizon of green and white forest reminding them that it was time to seek the warmth of the Lodge and the inviting fireplace. Once inside and still laughing, Bart removed his green parka and gloves and helped B.J. out of her very wet jacket. As he removed the jacket from her shoulders, she turned with a sparkle in her eyes said. "Bart, I think what I need now is a hot shower. Would you care to join me?"

Bart was momentarily surprised by this unexpected invitation, but quickly recovered. "I thought you would never ask."

"Yeah, right, "she said.

In less than a minute they both had stripped, dropping their wet clothes where they stood and were quickly toe-to-toe in the large glass enclosed shower in B.J.'s room with streams of steaming hot water flowing over their reddening bodies. The natural foreplay brought about by the hot water and their naked bodies aroused them as they kissed and touched each other, taking turns soaping and washing each other's backs.

Their passion gradually but steadily built to the point where they knew it was time to shut off the shower and move to B.J.'s nearby bed. Bart grabbed towels from the bathroom rack and hastily threw them around their wet bodies. They moved into the bedroom, hurriedly threw back the covers and slipped under the sheets. Cooled in the move from the shower into the bedroom they moved quickly together, each seeking the warmth of the other's body.

It had been six years since Bart Lowe and B.J. Ross had been intimate during their earlier service together in Europe, but there was no awkwardness in their love making. He was a caring and considerate lover and she met his every caress with one of her own.

By 9:30 that night they had made love three times.

Bart placed B.J.'s head between his hands, saying, "Your cheeks are flushed and you're radiating a look of contentment."

"And you're smiling a lot!" B.J. responded.

They both considered themselves "caught up" and at 10:00 p.m. decided they were ravenous and eagerly consumed cold turkey sandwiches. That Thanksgiving Bart Lowe and B.J. Ross agreed they had a lot to be thankful for.

General Barton Lowe and Ambassador B.J. Ross spent three glorious, snow-filled, fun-filled days and nights together.

They walked, they talked, they napped, they loved, they built morning fires, afternoon fires and evening fires. They renewed a warm intimate relationship that was better than ever. And, briefly, they thought about what it might be like to spend their lives together. When they returned to Washington their morale was high, their outlook optimistic and, like most dedicated workaholics, they were anxious to get back to their professions.

CHAPTER 9

ON THE ROAD

The snow was beginning to fall as they reached the end of the Autobahn from Munich to Garmisch, Germany. Garmisch was still twenty kilometers south but the drive along the two-lane road was pleasant and scenic. The mountains surrounding Garmisch were now visible through a curtain of light snowfall.

General Lowe's party had departed Washington's Dulles International Airport at 6:30 on Saturday evening on Pan American's nonstop flight to Munich, Germany. Bart was accompanied by his Executive Officer, George Martin, and his Eastern and Western Europe Division Chiefs, Army Colonel Kurt Kavenaugh and Navy Captain Michael Niceman. The DAS's new Operations Division Chief, Colonel Nick Tortellie and his assistant Barbara Barnsworth had preceded the General to Garmisch to set up the Regional Attaché Conference.

At 7:30 a.m. on Sunday morning Lowe and his party were met at the Munich-Reim Airport by Colonel James Bartlett, the Defense Attaché in Bonn, Germany. Bartlett was in his mid-forties and of medium build; he was dressed in sports coat, flannel trousers, shirt and tie and carried a London Fog raincoat. Because the Attaché Conference was being held in Germany, Colonel Bartlett was acting as host. Working with Nick Tortellie he had made the necessary arrangements for the conference with the U.S. Armed Forces Recreation Area authorities in Garmisch for the billeting and conference facilities, and for transportation from Munich to Garmisch for arriving attachés. Jim Bartlett's impeccable German and obvious rapport with the German customs officials allowed General Lowe and the others with him to move quickly through the security and passport checks.

Their processing was accomplished in less than fifteen minutes while the Lowe party waited in a VIP transient lounge. Once the luggage was available and placed in the two Mercedes sedans, they left for Garmisch. Bartlett, Lowe, and Martin were in the lead sedan. As they had pulled away from the airport, Bartlett introduced the German driver, Herr Stadler, as one of Bonn's Defense Attaché Office's regular drivers. He told Lowe Herr Stadler would act as the General's driver during his visit to Germany.

"General Lowe, it's good to see you again," Colonel Bartlett said when they met. They had met previously when Lowe was commander of the 3rd Infantry Division. "I trust your flight over was satisfactory?"

"Yes, indeed, Jim. It was quite comfortable. George was able to convince Pan Am that our frequent traveler miles were enough for an upgrade, and the first-class treatment provided by the Pan Am flight attendants couldn't have been better. The only down-side was the six hours we lost between Washington and Europe."

"Well, General, the conference doesn't start until Monday and you'll have plenty of time to recover from any jet lag. Our drive to Garmisch should take a little over one hour, and the weather here in Munich is clear as a bell; however, Garmisch is now getting fresh snow.

Garmisch-Parten-Kirchen had been the site of the 1936 Winter Olympics and was renowned for its excellent winter sports and skiing facilities.

When the two Mercedes reached the city limits of Garmisch they proceeded to the General Patton Hotel. Colonel Bartlett informed Lowe he had arranged for all of the attachés and conference attendees to stay at the Patton; it was one of the five remaining hotels in Garmisch that still belonged to the U.S. Army from the original 144 hotels and inns taken over by the U.S. Army at the end of World War II. The others had gradually been returned to the Federal Republic of Germany as its economy had improved and its tourist industry rekindled. Bart Lowe had first visited

Garmisch in the 1960s as a captain and returned often as a visitor during his later tours in Germany. He had skied the slopes in and around Garmisch and nearby Austria many times. The small picturesque Bavarian town was one of his favorite places.

Colonel Bartlett had pre-registered General Lowe and his party and, as they moved into the hotel lobby, he passed out individual room keys and escorted Lowe and Martin to their respective rooms. Bart Lowe's accommodation was a small but warmly furnished and comfortable three-room suite with a breathtaking view of the Zugspitze, the highest mountain in Germany, and the surrounding Bavarian Alps. The morning's light snow had stopped as quickly as it had started and the sun was shining on the nearby snow covered peaks. Breathtaking.

"General Lowe, your baggage will be right up, along with some fresh coffee and German pastry. George Martin's room is right across the hall if you need him. Your secure telephone is on the desk in the small study room in your suite. You can talk with DAS Headquarters or any other U.S. facility in the world. Most of the attachés and their spouses and the other conference people arrived last night. Your folks have been hard at work here since Thursday and I believe we are going to have a super conference. I recommend you take a couple of hours rest until we meet again at 12:30 for a working lunch. Nick Tortellie and Barbara Barnsworth are prepared to brief you then if that meets with your approval."

"Sounds like a plan to me...I concur."

"I should mention that we also intend to get the group together tonight for a buffet dinner and mixer. Casual civilian dress for tonight and today's lunch, if that's okay, sir?"

"Roger that," acknowledged Bart, as Bartlett left, leaving Bart alone with a spectacular view of the Zugspitze, a hot cup of coffee and a fresh brotchen. As he enjoyed the refreshment and the scenery, he couldn't help but wonder, "Does it get any better than this?"

Bart took a two hour nap, showered, shaved and put on brown corduroy trousers, an open collar shirt and an olive-green pullover sweater and brown suede walking shoes. Feeling rested and refreshed, he entered the Bavarian stube at the rear of the hotel where George Martin was waiting to lead him to a small private room with a table set for seven for lunch. Two waitresses dressed in the traditional Bavarian dirndl stood by to take their orders. Seated at the table were Colonels Bartlett, Kavenaugh, Tortellie, Captain Niceman and Ms. Barnsworth. After they ordered lunch, Nick Tortellie began the review of the conference. Tortellie was a great hulk of a man whose receding hair and hint of a paunch did not conceal the powerful physique of the tight end he had been at Notre Dame. Already known at the DAS Headquarters for his tireless work ethics and savvy, the good humored officer passed a copy of the conference schedule to Lowe.

"Boss, please take a minute to review the schedule for the next four days. I know you've seen and approved the earlier draft we provided you in Rosslyn, but because of some last minute travel problems with conference guests we've had to make changes. I've highlighted those in yellow."

Tortellie waited until Lowe had read the schedule and looked up and then continued, "Day one will cover the conference objectives and the various presentations from the National and European Theater people. We are all set with CIA, DIA, NSA, European Command and U.S. Embassy people in Bonn to give their current estimates on prospects for the Soviet Union and the Bloc countries. Time has been built in for questions and discussions by our attachés. Day two will be devoted to presentations by our Defense Attachés on their local situations, on how they see developments in their respective countries and where they see the region going. Time also has been allotted for us to ask our attachés any questions or raise subjects we wish to discuss."

Bart nodded as a signal that he understood and for Tortellie to press on.

The lunch arrived and after everyone was served, Tortellie suggested, "I'll continue and let Barbara get started on her lunch. When I've finished she will pick up her portion of the brief."

Bart again nodded his agreement and cut into his first bite of a German wurst and sweet mustard.

"Day three," continued Tortellie, "will be our DAS nuts and bolts day. In the morning we'll provide the attachés some report card feedback on how well they are accomplishing their missions and covering their objectives. We expect to hear from them on how well they think we are supporting their operations. The afternoon will be spent with our Support Division guys on budget, equipment, and the status of our various programs. This will give the attachés an opportunity to influence input or changes for the upcoming DAS mid-year budget review. Finally, boss, the morning of the fourth day will be for wrap-up of the conference. The afternoon will be available for any private time the attachés want with you or free time with their spouses. Friday, we'll break camp."

General Lowe finished a bite of German potato salad, and said, "Nick, that all sounds good. I just want to make damn sure our attachés don't feel as though we are giving them a fire hose treatment with only limited opportunities for them to participate."

"Boss, I'm confident that won't be the case. While there are a considerable number of presentations, the time allotted for the formal pitches will be tightly controlled to permit the maximum question and discussion time," replied Tortellie.

"If I may, General Lowe," spoke up Jim Bartlett, "I've had the opportunity to go over the schedule with Nick and Barbara and I believe it's right on the mark. It is oriented toward our needs in the field, and I think it will be well received by the other attachés. Also, I can assure you that none of the attachés attending this first conference are bashful. They are all seasoned, experienced attachés who won't hesitate to speak up if they don't like the way something is going."

"Thanks, Jim." Bart answered. "Your comments are helpful. I am anxious to see how effective this first conference will be in meeting both field and DAS Headquarters requirements. It's obviously expensive to pull everyone together like this and it will be very important to get the most bang for our bucks."

"I read you loud and clear, sir," said Bartlett, "I also want to let you know that your idea of including the spouses for the conference has already been well received. The wives and husbands are such a key part of the attaché profession that it's important to include them whenever and wherever possible. I've also reviewed the spouse schedule and believe that, too, will be effective. My wife, Andrea, has worked closely with Barbara on the agenda and she thinks we have a winner."

"Good." said Bart. "That probably is the right introduction for Ms. Barnsworth's portion of this brief.

Barbara Barnsworth passed a single sheet of paper to Lowe. "Now, General," she instructed respectfully, "let's review the schedule for the spouses."

An attractive blond in her late 30's, Barbara started her career in the DAS right out of college as a civilian in the London DAO. A natural for foreign service and the attaché business, the quick-witted woman rapidly advanced to the grade of GS-14, the equivalent of lieutenant colonel. Widely respected by her colleagues for her intelligence and no-nonsense approach, she was clearly on her way up and everyone knew it. When Barbara spoke, her male colleagues listened. A bachelorette, in whose wake one could find many disappointed men, Barbara understood the traps of office romance. Her social life was active but discreet. Lowe noted that, as usual, Barbara was fashionably attired in blue ski pants, blue turtleneck and white sweater.

"We have included the spouses in all of the unclassified presentations that attachés will receive. The blue highlighted items on the schedule indicate the joint sessions. In addition, we have arranged for State Department, Defense and European Command representatives to provide status reports and future plans to the spouses on embassy commissaries, school programs and medical support. These were items that were suggested by the spouses when we asked for candidate items from the field. Nick also scheduled to discuss their support to attaché operations and highlight some of their successes. Note, General Lowe, that you're scheduled to give the unclassified version of your congressional pitch to the spouses on Monday following your welcome to them.

George Martin tells me he brought the slides with him and he will run through them this afternoon and check the projector set-up."

"Thanks, Barbara," Bart acknowledged. "Do we have some time scheduled for the spouses to provide their own assessments of what's going on in the countries where they are serving?"

"Yes, we do; that takes place on day three, Wednesday. We did it that way so you will be able to sit in on that session," replied Barbara.

Looking again at the schedule Bart said, "Oh! Yes, I see it now. How about refreshing my memory on who will be here."

"Just about to get to that, sir," replied Barbara with a slight grin. She remembered that the General had a tendency to get ahead of briefers. "From our Air Force Defense Attachés in the Eastern European Division we have Brigadier General Alton from the Soviet Union, and Colonels Simon, Davis, and Gregory from Czechoslovakia, Hungary and Yugoslavia. The Army Defense Attachés are Colonel Warcheck from Poland, Colonel Roskowski from Romania, Lieutenant Colonel Weaver from Bulgaria and, of course, Colonel Bartlett from Bonn, Germany. Colonel Ruth Davis' spouse Alan Davis, is a State Department employee at the embassy in Budapest and will participate in our program," explained Barbara.

"General Roberts, the SHAPE Commander, will fly in for an hour tomorrow afternoon. He will give a thirty minute overview of theater operations and then allow time for discussion with the attachés. Colonel Bartlett was successful in persuading Ambassador Reader to be our last presenter for tomorrow and he will be arriving from Bonn by train. He will be staying for dinner with us Monday night and fly back to Bonn on Tuesday morning."

Barbara then passed a list of names of the other presenters to General Lowe. "I don't believe you know all of these people from the national agencies and the military organizations in the European Theater, but they are all well known to us and are the best analysts and experts in their fields. They will be participating with us on days one and two, and then they'll be gone. I hope you have a chance to meet and chat with them, if only briefly. I think you will find them very interesting. Finally, General Lowe," Barbara said as she passed over another list: "The social events. The hotel has reserved a private dining room for us tonight and, beginning tomorrow, we will take three meals a day together there. We have a set menu for all meals to keep down the confusion, but a good variety of European cuisine and some American specialties. No dinner at the hotel Thursday night and Friday. Each night we'll have a thirty minute social hour beginning at 6:30 with dinner at 7:00. Open seating, but we plan to put you at a different table each night." Barbara made eye contact at this point to make sure there was no objection on the seating arrangements.

"We have a Christmas caroling session planned for Monday night here at the hotel to get us all in the mood for Christmas, a bus trip Tuesday evening to a local beer stube for a Bavarian shoe platz dance show, and on Wednesday an evening of night skiing at the nearby Hausberg ski slope. The Armed Forces Recreation Area will provide the ski equipment and even some ski instructors and lessons if anyone needs them. Thursday will be an open night to allow for visits to local restaurants or time with family and friends. That covers my pitch, General. Unless you have questions I'll turn it back to Nick," Barbara concluded.

"No more at this time, but I'm sure I'll think of some as we begin the conference. Very impressive, Barbara. Thanks. Nick? Anyone else, questions or comments?"

"Okay boss, with your approval of the schedule we'll put these into the conference books we've prepared and distribute them this evening. Please note that everything we have discussed here and everything contained in the Attaché Conference Book is unclassified. Of course, some of the presentations will be classified and the main conference room for the attachés is in a secure area. The conference rooms, one for the attachés, and one for spouses, are both in the nearby Sheridan Military Kaserne where the Headquarters of the U.S. Armed Forces Recreation Area is located. The Kaserne is just a few blocks up the street from the hotel. We have a bus that will run between the hotel and Sheridan Kaserne three times a day. Some may want to walk back and forth depending on the weather. The uniform for the conference will be open collar with winter sweaters and wind breakers except for General Rodger's presentation and the conference photograph. We will put on our ties and blouses with decorations for those two occasions. Start time is 0800 each morning, break for lunch at 1130 hours, resume at 1300 and finish each day at 1630 hours or when discussions are completed."

Looking through his notes, Colonel Tortellie said, "Oh! One other item. The Rec Area people have also provided us sufficient space for our admin headquarters and communications center, an area where the attachés can receive messages and stay in touch with their DAOs, and office space for you and Colonel Martin. George has already checked it out and has some info for you. George...."

"Yes, sir," replied George Martin. "I think you will find the office comfortable and suitable for our needs. I recommend you arrive at the conference location at 0700 each morning. By then I will have screened the cable traffic that headquarters has forwarded to us, prepared a read file for you, and served up the world wide opns/intell briefing from our operations center to you. I'll then assist with any outgoing cable traffic you wish to send and ensure that you have plenty of excellent German coffee from a source I have already identified." George said this with the confident smile and a twinkle in his eye that Bart had come to recognize as George's trademark.

"Given the time difference of six hours we can use the afternoon or the evening for any calls that you need to make or to consult with your people in Rosslyn."

"Sounds like you are on top of everything, George," commented Bart. It was obvious that while Bart had been resting, George had been doing his homework.

"General, I'm sure you know this, but let me make sure." These words came from Navy Captain Mike Niceman. "Ordinarily Jim Bartlett in Bonn and I would not be at this Eastern Europe countries' conference since they are the responsibility of Colonel Kavenaugh. But because of the close association of all the Bloc country attachés and DAO Bonn and Germany, Nick, Pete and Chuck all thought it would be a good idea for Jim to host and for me to sit in as a primer for when we hold the Western Europe Regional Attaché Conference later."

"I'm aware of that, Mike, and agreed that it would be a good idea to have both you and Jim involved in this conference," acknowledged Bart.

"Since none of our present Defense Attachés in the Bloc countries are naval officers, I may also be able to help Kurt out with any Soviet or other naval matters during the conference. Also, I am prepared to help prep you for your visit to Vienna when you depart Garmisch at the conclusion of the conference here."

"Thanks, Mike. George has all the background papers for the visit and after I have gone over those, it will be helpful to compare notes with you."

The DAS Eastern Europe/Soviet Union Regional Attaché Conference went off without a hitch. The facilities, accommodations and service provided by the Armed Forces Recreation Area were first class. No one had any complaints. Maybe it was the Christmas season that put everyone in such good spirits. Maybe it was the magic of the little Bavarian town of Garmisch.

General Roberts had given a spell-binding overview of SHAPE Command, the most demanding military job in the free world. He was pessimistic in his estimate for any positive changes in Soviet plans and policies and believed that the importance of NATO had never been greater.

Ambassador Reader from Bonn gave the attachés an insightful view of the German political and governmental apparatus and its continuing concern for the size of its armed forces.

The analysts and area experts from Washington gave sterling presentations on the political, economic, and military situations in the region, clearly impressing the attachés on how much they knew about the countries where the attachés were serving. This group also was lavish in its praise for the work of the attachés and commented on how the analysts valued highly their information and reports.

The spouses were pleased to be participating in the main stream of attaché business and appreciated being recognized as important members of the team. Bart Lowe was surprised to learn he was held in high esteem by the spouses, and told by more than one that he was the first DAS Director to pay anymore than lip service to their role. It would, he thought, remain to be seen if he could maintain that exalted status with the spouses. That would depend on his success with some of the housing, support, medical, and educational program costs that he was obliged to arm wrestle over with the Congress, Defense, State Department, and the Theater and Service Commanders.

Lastly, the social part of the conference allowed the attendees to get to know each other better and to think of themselves as part of a world wide team—a military team—and also a family that cared for one another and had a lot in common. Many faced the same type of problems or challenges whether they happened to be in Washington or Bulgaria, Germany or the Soviet Union. The conference, Bart knew, would serve as a springboard for him with the attachés and their families when he visited them at their stations. He would be a known entity. He had enjoyed talking to them, listening to them, and in fact every minute of the conference. He even managed to get in time on the racquetball court at the end of the conference days with two or three of the attachés and a couple of ringers from Stuttgart. The attaché from Sofia, Lieutenant Colonel Weaver had almost, but just almost, taken Bart. Weaver was hungry.

In his closing remarks to the attachés on the last day of the conference, Bart shared with them his recent charge from the Chairman of the Joint Chiefs of Staff. "The Chairman," Bart said, "has related to me that in spite of the President's continued advocacy for a strong defense posture, some Congressional wolves and others are beginning to come out of the woodwork looking for Defense related issues. The smart money does not envision any diminution of the Soviet strategic threat to the United States. Most of the national intelligence agencies, according to the Chairman, are forecasting continued Soviet strategic weapons research and development and heavy USSR spending—in effect a continuation of the cold war at a sustained or even accelerated pace. In fact," Bart continued, "most of what you heard at this conference supports that view."

Bart also told the attachés about the growing concern among senior U.S. leadership that the Soviet threat was being oversold. "The Chairman, the Sec Def, and the President do not want to be accused of padding the threat or learn from some second guessers that we may be losing our best threat." Bart emphasized that challenges to the National Intelligence Estimates concerning the Soviet Union were appearing in increasing numbers in the U.S. press, and a number of the Washington based think-tanks were beginning to question the validity of the USSR threat and the high cost of U.S. weapons modernization to counter that threat. The Strategic Defense Initiative (SDI) was coming under increasing criticism for its high cost and specious requirements. "The bottom line," Bart summed up, "is that we have spent forty years tracking the strengths of the Soviet Union and have done a remarkable job in discovering each advancement in military technology and weapons development they have made. This is due primarily to the magnificent efforts of people like you and those who served before you. You must continue to do this. But now you must also ensure that you give equal priority and attention to discovering their weaknesses and how these may impact the future. I want each of you to consider the proposition, unthinkable to this point in history, that the 'Evil Empire' has reached its zenith and will disintegrate. Your task is to aggressively seek out any and all information that will confirm or deny this proposition."

Bart mentioned to George Martin that he had been impressed with many of the germane observations on the subject of the Russians made by Brigadier General Erv Alton the Defense

Attaché in Moscow. He added that he was anxious to visit the USSR and spend more time with Erv and the other attachés there, and anticipated the visit to the Soviet Union would be the high point of his follow-on road trip.

The attachés elected to have some private time with General Lowe on Thursday afternoon. Most of this time was used by the attachés to identify issues peculiar to their own stations. These one-on-one meetings would serve as the foundation for further discussions during Bart's upcoming visits. Bart made notes and turned them over to George Martin to link them up with trip briefs and issue papers prepared by the staff in Rosslyn and sent along for Bart's review prior to visiting the individual attaché stations. No surprises surfaced, but questions concerning adequate housing for the attachés and their families, aging vehicles, and inadequate DAO budgets were recurring themes. Bart questioned each of the attachés on losses of sources of particularly valuable information during the past year. Each DAO had at least one unexplained loss; Moscow had three. Two cases he wanted to know more about in Prague and Moscow, Bart decided could be HEAT SEEKER-related.

By Friday morning most of the attachés had departed, Bart's staff was wrapping up the conference administration, and Bart spent most of the day in his temporary office in Sheridan Kaserne with George Martin catching up on DAS Headquarters business. His Executive Officer had been absolutely right. Paper followed him everywhere he went. To his credit, George had an uncanny sense of those things that were really important and essential. As Bart's XO, he used every available minute prudently to keep Bart fully informed and productive in the role of running the world-wide DAS. Also helpful to Bart had been his daily phone conversations with his deputies Chuck and Pete in Rosslyn, keeping him abreast of significant actions and events happening in Washington and elsewhere in the world.

On Friday afternoon General Lowe and Colonel Kavenaugh spent two hours with the staff at the U.S. Army Russian Institute getting their perspective on the USSR. They all had served previously in Moscow or in Potsdam, East Germany, and the current attachés in Moscow were graduates of the Institute.

The last item on the Friday agenda was thirty minutes with Captain Niceman. Mike Niceman went over the DAO Vienna, Austria, visit brief with Bart, and then he and Nick Tortellie, Barbara Barnsworth, and Kurt Kavenaugh left for Washington. George left later that night by train to spend Christmas in Wiesbaden, Germany.

Bart was picked up at 8:00 p.m. in a horse-driven sleigh by a long time German friend, General Major Fritz Steiner. Steiner had recently retired from command of the 10th Mountain Division of the German Bundeswehr and now resided at his family farm outside Garmisch. Bart had contacted his old friend when he first arrived in Garmisch and Fritz had persuaded him to spend a Bavarian Christmas, or Weihnachten as the Germans call it, with him and his wife, Anke. Following Christmas with the Steiners, Bart was scheduled to return to Garmisch on Tuesday where a helicopter would fly him to Bonn for a visit to the U.S. Embassy and the DAO.

For the rest of the week, Bart would first be accompanied by the Defense Attaché, Colonel Bartlett, on visits to the German Armed Forces Headquarters, then on to Wiesbaden, where he would be joined by George Martin. They would also visit Stuttgart and Munich, the locations of the U.S. European Command, and the U.S. Military Intelligence and Security Organizations based in Germany. Munich was the headquarters of the German Intelligence Service, the Bundesnachrichtendienst, or BND. Bart and George would then leave for Austria by train Friday night from Munich, spending the New Years' holiday with the U.S. Defense Attaché in Vienna, Colonel Preston Bernhardt.

CHAPTER 10

LA BOHEME

The Schnellzug pulled out of the Munich Hauptbahnhof precisely at 8:00 on Friday evening. The "fast" German train would take just a shade over three hours to reach its final destination—Vienna, Austria. Bart Lowe and George Martin with their winter coats, hats and gloves removed, were settled comfortably in a private, first-class compartment. Rail travel in Europe was still one of the most affordable luxuries. George had ordered coffee and cognacs for each of them from the porter who appeared soon after a push on the service call button.

"Well, boss, was that a whirlwind four days or what?" said Colonel Martin feigning a deep breath.

"It was that, George," replied Bart.

By the time the train passed through the Munich suburbs, and running fast through the snow-covered Bavarian countryside, the coffee and cognac had been served; Bart had removed his suit jacket, tie and shoes, reclined his seat and broken out a mystery novel. George had earlier asked General Lowe for any notes that he had made during the day to add to George's own running account of notes that eventually would become an official trip report when they returned to Washington. He would be certain nothing of import escaped recording.

As Bart was enjoying his light reading material, a novel about a private investigator in West Palm Beach, Florida, one Archie McNally, and taking an occasional pull on his Remy Martin cognac, he reflected on the Weihnacten spent with the Steiners. He and Fritz had enjoyed cross country skiing each day, and his old friend delighted in giving Bart a complete tour of the farm and introducing him to his Bavarian neighbors. The evenings were spent around the Steiners wood stove in their informal living room following delicious meals of German cold cuts, homemade salads and liters of local Garmischerbrau beer. The Steiners' two sons and their wives were home for the holiday, and much to Bart's surprise and delight a former classmate of Anke's from her days at Heidelberg University, Herta Baldry, an attractive red-headed woman and well known German artist was also their house guest. And Herta was very good company... The combination of people and Anke and Fritz's uncommonly warm hospitality made for one of the most memorable holidays Bart could remember. He even had enjoyed the traditional Weihnacten Day goose. Well, almost.

The return to Bonn and visit to the Defense Attaché Office was nostalgic for Bart; he had served there as an attaché in the 1960's. The DAO was a large one, given the amount of Defense Department business with Germany and the 400,000 American military forces stationed there. Colonel Jim Bartlett and the other military attachés were favorites of the ambassador and had virtually no problems in working relationships at the Embassy. The same rapport Bart had seen demonstrated by Jim Bartlett in Munich was evident on Tuesday afternoon when General Lowe was welcomed at the headquarters of the German Armed Forces.

Bart Lowe's last appointment of the day in Bonn had been with the CIA's Chief of Station, (COS), Walter Sutton. After giving Bart and Jim Bartlett an overview of CIA operations in Germany with emphasis on East Germany and the Communist Bloc countries, he asked that Colonel Bartlett allow him some private time with General Lowe to discuss a sensitive matter. After Bartlett departed, Mr. Sutton told Bart that his headquarters at Langley had given him permission to discuss HEAT SEEKER. Sutton went on to say that when he first learned of the compromise of some of the U.S. Army and Air Force intelligence operations in Russia and the Warsaw Pact countries, he thought it was due to some security compromise by military operators. However, when he learned that CIA operations were also involved, it was apparent that a leak of sensitive information was taking place somewhere within the entire United States system. Sutton had no idea where the compromise might be taking place. Sutton was one of those

CIA officials who, like Senator Thomas, was not convinced that the U.S. military services needed to be involved in sensitive operations. He also gave Lowe the impression that he viewed military service operations in competition with CIA. Lowe made a mental note to discuss Mr. Sutton's "attitude" with the CIA's Deputy Director of Operations at Langley when he returned to Washington.

Bart concluded his visit to Bonn with an evening out with the DAO Bonn staff and their families at a festive waterfront restaurant on the banks of the Rhine River. Because of the season, they enjoyed the house specialty of the seasonably available Jager (Hunter) Schnitzels complemented with pitchers of fine house wine—Rhine, of course.

Wednesday was spent with the European Detachment of the U.S. Air Force Special Activities Command, or AFSAC, in Wiesbaden. This Detachment was responsible for the Air Forces' Human Intelligence operations supporting the U.S. Air Force, Europe and the U.S. European Command. Their major targets were the Soviet and Bloc country Air Forces. The Detachment Commander, Colonel William Bell, and his people were delighted that General Lowe was paying them a visit. They understood how important his support with the JCS and the Congress was to the future of their service sensitive operations. The briefings he received were well thought out, carefully prepared and presented with the utmost care to emphasize the security and professionalism with which their operations were conducted. When asked about their working relationship with CIA in Bonn they did not badmouth CIA's Chief of Station, Mr. Sutton and his staff, but made it clear that obtaining COS Bonn coordination for their operations was difficult. On the other hand, the Detachment was very complimentary of the supporting roles played by Colonel Herrington and the Special Services Division staff at Rosslyn.

After Colonel Bell and his staff had run the gamut of their operations and operational successes, Bell cleared the room of everyone else except himself, his deputy, Bart, and two Special Agents from the Counterintelligence Wing of the Air Force Office of Special Investigations, OSI, who had assisted in the investigation of the compromise of two AFSAC operations. With painstaking deliberation, the two youthful special agents, dressed in dark business suits, outlined those ill-fated operations from start to finish. The foreign agents, one an East German airfield radar repair man and the second a Russian MIG pilot, had been providing information to AFSAC for many years and had provided consistently accurate, confirmed data on Soviet airfields in East Germany, including tactics and armaments of Soviet aircraft. The AFSAC officers who worked with the agents were among the most experienced AFSAC personnel.

The agents had been arrested by the East German Security Service and had not been seen or heard from again following their arrest. It was possible, the OSI Special Agents pointed out, that the compromises were due to some mistake made by the agents themselves, or compromise within Air Force channels. Both possibilities had been thoroughly investigated, and the OSI had not been able to discover any evidence supporting either premise.

"These operations were our best ones and just too good to be burnt in this way, General Lowe. I would stake my life on the professionalism of our two officers. I have to believe that somewhere, someone on our side blew the whistle on these two guys," opined Colonel Bell. "The loss of information has cost us dearly."

Lowe conveyed his sympathy to Colonel Bell, but knowing that the Colonel was not aware of the HEAT SEEKER investigation, he did not risk further discussion. He thanked the two OSI Special Agents, and assured Colonel Bell of his personal support for the AFSAC mission.

When Bart Lowe and Colonel Martin left Wiesbaden Wednesday afternoon, they flew south to Stuttgart. The schedule called for an overnight stay in Stuttgart, with dinner at a local restaurant with the staff officers of the European Command (EUCOM). Thursday would bring briefings throughout the day at

EUCOM Headquarters and a call at 1600 hours on the Deputy Commander-in-Chief (DCINC), EUCOM, Air Force General, Ned Tailor. General Roberts, the SHAPE Commander was dual hatted as the CINC of all the U.S. Forces in Europe, but his allied duties in Mons, Belgium, kept him so busy it was necessary to have a four-star deputy for the day-to-day running of EUCOM. General Tailor had been doing that for two years.

Lowe's briefings at EUCOM gave him an excellent overview of that command's extensive responsibilities reaching across Europe to Russia, running the width of the Balkans, into the Middle East and extending southward to the tip of Africa. Any trouble in that area alerted EUCOM and triggered an instant response. These briefings also confirmed for Bart the importance of the attaché information reports and the military services' human intelligence program to EUCOM.

In his afternoon call with General Tailor, Bart had been pleased to find out that Tailor was familiar with the work of the DAS and the attachés who were serving in the EUCOM area of operations. He told Bart he had been to each of the EUCOM countries. On those visits he always spent some time with the attachés, had seen them in action and asked for feedback from the host country's military staff officers on what they liked or disliked about the U.S. attachés. Tailor said their opinions were almost always favorable and EUCOM considered the attachés their eyes and ears. Tailor regularly read the attachés' political-military reports and relied heavily on their estimates. He added, "That the attachés in the Middle East and African countries are equally important to EUCOM. This is true," General Tailor said, "because those areas are far more volatile and remote than the traditional Bloc countries. The attachés in those areas are the only game in town; the only ones to warn of impending disaster or conflict that will cause the deployment of U.S. Forces from Europe." General Tailor's concern had been a heads up for Bart. He made an entry in his notes to reconsider his travel plans for the next few months following his return to the United States.

Lowe and Martin departed Stuttgart by Military C-12 Aircraft for the short flight to Munich. They were met by a U.S. military escort at a small German Military Field, Neubeberg, near Perlach, a suburb of Munich.

Lowe and Martin were billeted at a comfortable U.S. guest house in McGraw Kaserne near Perlacher Forest and hosted to a boisterous evening at the world famous beer hall, the Hofbrau House in downtown Munich, by the Commander of the 66th MI Brigade, Colonel Ben Kelsey and the officers and NCOs of the command.

The briefings at the 66th the next morning covered the Brigade's multi-discipline intelligence support program to the large contingent of ground troops in Europe. Bart was impressed with the scope and quality of the 66th's operations and their working relationships with their European counterparts. The 66th, like its Air Force sister unit, AFSAC, conducted human intelligence missions, including debriefing refugees, document exploitation, and foreign intelligence operations targeted on the USSR and Warsaw Pact nations. The 66th also had recently experienced unexplained compromises of some of their operations. The Intelligence and Security Command, INSCOM, the 66th's parent headquarters in Washington, had conducted counterintelligence investigations of the compromised operations and had been unable to pinpoint any Army leak. The 66th officers told General Lowe that many of their long standing sources of information had simply disappeared. They feared the worst for their sources. The 66th operators had compared notes with AFSAC on the compromised operations, and like AFSAC, felt that there was a leak somewhere on the United States side.

Following the morning's briefing at the 66th, Bart played a spirited game of racquetball at the McGraw Kaserne Gym with Colonel Kelsey and Captain Harold Schneider, the U.S. Navy Commander of Task Force 78, a HUMINT activity. After the workout Captain Schneider took Lowe to the Navy facility located in the nearby suburb of Gruenwald. T.F. 78's activities included the debriefing of selected refugees from the USSR who had knowledge of Soviet Naval operations, research and development and capabilities. The unit worked in a cooperative effort with the U.S. Army and Air Force and in coordination with the Germans. Captain Schneider and his shipmates solicited General Lowe's support for continued funding of the task force.

Bart's last stop in Munich was the visit to the German BND, located in Perlach on the site of a sprawling former German military kaserne. Like many of the traditional German kasernes it consisted of one large building that served as headquarters, and several other buildings that housed the working departments. While it was a civilian-chartered and civilian-run federal agency—like the CIA—the BND compound still had a decidedly military look about it, clean, neat and orderly. That was due, Bart imagined, to the influence of its roots.

Bart remembered from his days in Bonn that the BND had grown out of the Gehlen Organization. Lieutenant General Gehlen had headed the intelligence effort for the German Wehrmacht at the end of World War II. In the last year of the war Gehlen moved his headquarters and all its files to the still relatively safe Bavarian capital of Munich. When the war ended, the Gehlen compound, its files and many of its experts, particularly on the Soviet Union, were intact and ready to go to work for the occupying U.S. Army. General Gehlen and his intelligence files proved to be very valuable to the Americans, especially during the early days of the cold war with Russia. When the U.S. occupation ended and Germany became a federal republic, Gehlen still had the infrastructure in place needed to provide the fledgling democracy with its own intelligence service. In its evolution since World War II, the BND had tried to avoid any political taint and concentrated exclusively on East Germany, the USSR and the Warsaw Pact as its targets.

All of this flashed through Bart Lowe's mind when he, Ben Kelsey, George Martin, and the 66th BND Liaison officer, Edward Beck, arrived at the BND compound. His German hosts treated him to a full afternoon of BND history, an overview of the BND organization, their working relationships with the CIA and the various cooperative arrangements with other U.S. agencies and the U.S. military that had grown out of their years association since World War II. The BND was familiar with the role exercised by General Lowe and the human intelligence activities of the U.S. military in Germany. The BND was also conversant with the DAS's worldwide attaché stations and knew many of the individual attachés in the Bloc countries and the Soviet Union. Lowe was told that it was the BND's objective to work closely with their U.S. allies, including the attachés, wherever possible, and share in what the U.S. and U.S. military services knew about real or potential adversaries.

At the end of the day, Colonel Kelsey, Bart and George, and Mr. Beck, were escorted to the BND Foreign Liaison Building for cocktails and dinner hosted by the BND Deputy Director, Klaus Werner.

The Liaison Building had been designed to provide a place where foreign visitors could be hosted in comfortable surroundings, without risk or public disclosure, and where private or sensitive discussion could take place without fear of compromise. From the anteway Lowe's party had been taken by their escort to an open room with easy chairs arranged around a small fireplace. A fire had been lit some time ago, and was projecting considerable heat. Once Herr Werner introduced himself, he introduced Bart to the other five gentlemen already there. Herr Werner then offered Bart the chair to his right and summoned a nearby waiter.

"Herr General, will you try a mug of our Bavarian beer?" Herr Werner asked.

"By all means," Bart replied. "I've long admired German beer, particularly the ones brewed in Bavaria."

Once the beer was served, Herr Werner pointed to the game birds and animal heads mounted on the walls of the room.

"General, these fine birds and animals are all from our nearby Perlacher Forest. Perlacher is one of Bavaria's finest forests and for hundreds of years was one of Europe's best hunting locales. Now, civilization has encroached on the forest and the hunting season has grown shorter and shorter. There was a time when you could have entered the forest and selected anything you see on this wall for your table."

Bart was impressed with the display and related some of his own hunting experiences in the Everglades as a youngster growing up in Florida.

Herr Werner was a stocky man in his late fifties with a full head of salt and pepper hair; he was dressed as the other BND officials, in a dark business suit. He appeared to be naturally gregarious and very comfortable in his role as host. According to the information Edward Beck had provided to Bart, Herr Werner was a career officer with the BND who had risen through the ranks to his present position. Beck pointed out that Werner had served as the BND representative in Washington for three years.

When the beer mugs had been twice drained, Herr Werner invited Lowe and the others to follow him into the adjoining dining room. A splendid meal of wild fowl and rice was flawlessly served and topped off with one of the very best known German specialties—Schwarzwalderkerschtorte—Black Forest cake for dessert. The dinner was served by two waiters at an unhurried pace, permitting maximum time for conversation. The conversation had been a general one on the world situation, with emphasis on Europe. Herr Werner had not tabled any issues during dinner and Bart wondered if the gracious BND hospitality was extended simply to get to know him. This was clarified at the end of the evening when goodnights were being exchanged and Herr Werner drew Bart and Edward Beck aside.

"General Lowe, I have two brief items for your ears only," began Herr Werner. "First I want to express my personal and official appreciation for the work over the last 10 years of Herr Beck, who is a superb liaison officer. His linguistic abilities and his understanding of our history and culture are remarkable. His untiring efforts and professionalism have been a model for our own BND officers and the rapport that he long ago established has allowed us and the U.S. military to maintain splendid cooperation. Your country could not be better served."

Edward Beck, every bit the outstanding civil servant and skilled operative, was surprised and somewhat embarrassed by the unexpected praise. Concerned that General Lowe might think he had put Herr Werner up to this endorsement, he quickly interjected, "Herr Werner, the hour is growing late and the general has a train to catch."

"Yes, of course, Herr Beck," Werner acknowledged. "Unfortunately, General, the next matter is not so pleasant. In fact, it is rather delicate. I am sure you are familiar with the many compromises my government has had over the years vis a vis the German Democratic Republic. Well, we have had our problems and will probably have more. It now appears that your side may be having a problem."

Bart was surprised by this comment, and not knowing what Herr Werner meant, merely said. "Oh, how's that?"

"General, in our business, like yours, we have many sources of information. And our sources tell us that the Russians recently obtained information concerning American operations, and as a result some important operations have been compromised."

Bart was not at liberty to discuss any of the details of military operations compromises with the BND. But he immediately thought of HEAT SEEKER.

"Herr Werner. I appreciate your candor. If true, that certainly is a disturbing situation. Can you give me any additional details?"

"No. I'm afraid not. My aim in telling you this is that we have reason to believe the leak is American and we want your side to do everything you can to stop it. These things have a way of snowballing, and eventually affecting us all."

"Thank you. I'll certainly look into it," replied Bart.

And, with that, Bart and George departed for the Bahnhof.

The day in Munich had been another interesting and instructive visit for Bart. As George had put it, the short week had been a "whirlwind four days." And more HEAT SEEKER insinuations to worry about.

The night train ride through the Bavarian and Austrian countryside was quiet, relaxing, and uneventful, with two brief stops at Salzburg and Linz. When the train slowed for its approach into Vienna, or Wien as the Austrians correctly called it, bright lights were everywhere in spite of the late hour. As the train backed into the Hauptbahnhof it seemed more like a huge medieval castle than a train station. As soon as the train stopped, and as Bart and George prepared to get off, General Lowe's friend, Colonel Preston Bernhardt appeared. Colonel Bernhardt was a tall man dressed in a gray suit and topcoat, dark green hat and gloves.

"Pres, you old son-of-a-gun," exclaimed Bart, grasping Colonel Bernhardt's right hand and putting his other hand on Bernhardt's shoulder. "How the hell did you get here so fast? We just this instant stopped."

"Good information from the Austrians on where the train would be arriving and even better information from George Martin on your car and compartment number; he phoned me before you left Munich. The rest is elementary, my dear Watson," laughed Bernhardt. "Or, as I probably should say, my dear General, or sir, or all of the above."

"We've known each other too long for that, Pres."

"Right you are, Bart, but I could at least say boss," And with that, he grabbed one of Bart's suitcases and said, "Follow me. We need to get you out of this train station and into more comfortable surroundings. You must be tired. I know I would be just by looking at your schedule for the last few days."

Colonel Bernhardt led them through the train station and out to a waiting black Opel sedan. The driver jumped from the car the minute he saw them coming and quickly arranged the luggage in the trunk of the car. Once under way, Colonel Bernhardt introduced his driver, Wolfgang Tanner, to General Lowe and Colonel Martin. He then explained that the trip to his quarters would only take about 30 minutes.

Bart Lowe and Preston Bernhardt had served together as majors and briefing officers at the Pacific Command Headquarters in Hawaii in the early 1970s, sharing the rigors of jobs that started at 4:00 a.m. during the last years of the Vietnam War. Preston Bernhardt had always been the picture of a dashing, confident Army officer. He had graduated from West Point and married the homecoming queen from his hometown college. He was an armored cavalry officer and looked like a stately colonel from a John Wayne movie. Bart had not seen Preston for more than 10 years.

"Is Anna as beautiful as ever?" asked Bart.

"I think even more so, but then I'll let you be the judge when you see her," acknowledged Preston.

"I hope you haven't kept her up waiting for us at this late hour."

"You don't think for a minute that Anna would miss a chance to welcome her favorite bachelor in the world, do you, Bart? Seriously, she has been beside herself since we first learned you would be visiting us. We are delighted you are going to be with us for the New Year's Holiday."

The drive through Vienna went quickly. The streets they traveled were wide boulevards, well lit, clear of all snow, with six and seven story, sturdy gray buildings shadowed behind the lights. It seemed to Bart that hardly any time had gone by before the sedan pulled into the circular driveway of a magnificent old three-story mansion in the hill country on the outskirts of Vienna overlooking the Danube River. The house had been confiscated by the U.S. Army at the end of WWII and made into a residence for the general in charge of the U.S. forces in the American sector of Vienna. When the U.S. and Russian occupation ended in 1955, the house was given to the U.S. Army Attaché, and then passed on when the DAS was formed.

No sooner had the sedan pulled into the driveway, under a large portico adjoining the house entrance, than the double door opened and out came Anna Bernhardt. With many hugs and kisses, Bart and George were officially welcomed to Vienna and into the home of two old and dear friends. Anna had prepared a welcome snack of Austrian pastries and hot chocolate and no excuses were going to dissuade her that these goodies were not just the ticket her guests needed before retiring. Anna also insisted on a brief tour of the downstairs and entertaining areas of the home. Preston suspected that George Martin was more than ready for a good night's sleep and considerately offered to whisk George away to his bedroom. But, Bart was not that tired because of the restful time spent on the train, and he enjoyed catching up on the lives of his friends until the wee hours of the morning. When he finally retired, he reflected that Anna was just as beautiful as ever.

On Saturday morning, Preston took Bart for a jog along the Blue Danube River and George went into the DAO in the embassy to review the incoming cable traffic. If there was anything Bart needed to act on immediately, George would make a determination whether it was necessary for General Lowe to come into the embassy, or if it could be handled telephonically from the Bernhardt quarters.

When Preston and Bart returned from their morning run, the Bernhardt's cook prepared a scrumptious breakfast and served it on the glassed-in terrace overlooking a very large and well manicured garden. Although it was winter, it was obvious that the garden was an extraordinary one, crisscrossed with crushed rock paths and sprinkled with statues and white gazeboes. Anna explained that the garden was part of the grounds of the estate on which the attaché quarters sat. It was a full time job for a professional gardener to maintain. The natural beauty of the garden was well known in Vienna and used extensively throughout the warm months for attaché and other embassy functions. Both Anna and Preston came from ethnic European/American families, spoke fluent German and had a keen sense of appreciation for nature's beauty.

"Bart, I know that the expense of maintaining this house and garden are contentious and that you will have to make a decision whether the DAS can afford to keep them. Preston and I have been here for more than two years and I believe the good will toward the United States resulting from the old world setting of this grand old estate more than justifies its expense. I've said my piece and you have my word I won't mention it again," Anna said, with obvious feeling.

Both Bart and Preston laughed, and Bart said, "Anna, I read you loud and clear," thinking to himself that this would not be the last time he would hear an impassioned plea from an attachés' distaff side.

Following breakfast and a walk in the "famous" garden, Preston took Bart into the roomy study that he used for his office to go over the schedule he had planned for him. Preston explained that the reception Anna would give that evening was to be a mess dress, black tie affair. The holiday season would insure a good turn out of guests, and afford Bart the opportunity of seeing his Vienna-based attachés in action in a "live" situation. It would also allow Bart to gauge the performance of the other countries' attachés as they tried subtly, and not so subtly, to learn as much about General Lowe as possible. Bart should be aware, Preston informed him, that he would be the target of opportunity that evening and should not be surprised if some of the most sophisticated and penetrating questions came from the attachés' wives.

"I know you are going on to the Bloc countries and the USSR after Vienna but you need to know that those countries all accredit attachés to Austria and they have all accepted our invitation. Duty in Vienna is a real plum for the Soviets and the Bloc guys and you will be seeing some of their smoothest operators tonight."

"I've had some limited exposure to the bad guys in Washington on embassy circuit parties; I'm looking forward to a little friendly West vs. East arm wrestling," Bart replied.

Preston then told Bart that the rest of the schedule would follow the guidance he had received from DAS Headquarters. He highlighted the specifics of a Sunday tour of Vienna, Monday at the Austrian Ministry of Defense, and Tuesday, the first day after the New Year's holiday, at the U.S. Embassy, with calls on the embassy principals and the rest of the day with the DAO.

While Bart was looking over the written agenda, Preston moved behind his desk and pressed two switches on a panel mounted on the side of the desk. The sounds of classical music streamed from speakers in the four corners of the room. Bernhardt explained that the first switch initiated a electronic jamming technique against all electronic power and wiring entering and leaving the room—lights, telephones, etc. The second switch activated the sound system as a barrier to any acoustic listening device that might be present in the room. This system permitted the discussion of sensitive information.

Preston then gave Bart an overview of the Vienna DAO and the U.S. Embassy. The Defense Attaché Office was typical of a small DAO—one Defense Attaché, Colonel Bernhardt, dual hatted as the Army Attaché; one Air Force Attaché, Colonel Smith; and two Assistant Army and Air Force Attachés, Lieutenant Colonel Boyd and Major Burns. Additionally, one Army Chief Warrant Officer, Chief Stevens, and three NCOs from the U.S. Army, Navy and Air Force handled the administration and communications. DAO Vienna was weighted with more army people because the Austrian Army was by far the largest service and required the most army attaché support. In addition to the U.S. staff, the DAO employed three Austrian Nationals who served as drivers.

The Vienna embassy was also relatively small, with its largest sections devoted to commerce, cultural affairs, and economic interests. The political-military activities of the embassy were low key, but important because of the neutral country status Austria provided to both East and West. Vienna in particular was the classic middle ground where opposing ideologies and nations could take on each other with immunity in many areas—business, technology, trade and espionage—provided they were discreet in carrying out their many affairs.

The U.S. Ambassador was a young man, a political appointee who was very active and successful in representing the United States in ceremonial and social events. He left the day-today running of the embassy, and the interaction with the Austrian government, to his Deputy Chief of Mission, Felix Hoffman and the State Department's professional Foreign Service Officers. The CIA had a large station at the embassy for all of the aforementioned reasons and CIA's Chief of Station was one of the best. The incumbent COS and Preston Bernhardt had arrived in Vienna at about the same time and worked well together.

In the strictest of confidence Preston told Bart that he had some concern with DCM Hoffman that he had not been able to convey to DAS Headquarters. He explained that Hoffman, a career Foreign Service Officer of ethnic Austrian parents, ran the embassy with an authoritarian hand." "This in itself," Preston explained, "was not too unusual, many DCMs are that way, and DCM Hoffman was considered an exceptionally competent officer and superb linguist, well respected by the Austrians.

"The rub came," Preston continued, "when the DCM took an extraordinary interest in the business of the DAO and was interested in knowing everything that the DAO was doing. For example, the DCM was reading all of the DAO outgoing cable traffic. When called on this, Hoffman claimed he was merely exercising his authority for embassy coordination on any activities conducted by embassy personnel that had the potential for embarrassment to the United States. In carrying out that role, the DCM always asked an inordinate amount of questions about DAO operations."

Concerned with this, Preston queried the CIA's Chief of Station and learned that he shared the same concerns about the DCM; Hoffman had tried on many occasions to learn more about the details of CIA operations than the COS believed he was entitled to or had a need to know. As a result, both Preston and the COS were cautious about sharing certain sensitive Defense Department and CIA information with the DCM. Germane to all of this, Preston added, was the DAO operation code named GREENFIELDS.

GREENFIELDS was a 77-year-old Austrian woman who had been providing valuable military information on the USSR for many years. A member of the pre-war Austrian royal family, Countess Eva Laressa had been captured in the last days of the war by advancing Russian troops and interned by them in the occupied Russian sector of Austria. When she was later released she returned to her home in the American sector and volunteered her services to the U.S. Army Counter Intelligence Corps. Using well connected friends and family, she organized a spy network leading from Austria into the Soviet Union. When the occupation ended and the U.S. Army left Austria, control of the operation was turned over to the Army Attaché because the Countess refused to leave Austria for meetings, and categorically refused to have anything to do with the CIA. Because of the great value of the operation, CIA tried many times to gain control of GREENFIELDS but had been unsuccessful.

To CIA's credit, they were helpful in monitoring the security of the operation and always provided whatever assistance was required to ensure that the personal meetings between the attaché and the Countess were in a secure place and free from surveillance. A number of Army and Defense Attachés had worked with Countess Laressa over the years, carefully transferring her control from one to the other. Countess Laressa had faithfully passed along volumes of highly classified Soviet defense information, information that CIA and DIA believed was coming from multiple Russian sources the Countess' network recruited. The countess had never asked for anything in return for the information she provided and rebuffed all suggestions for remuneration. Her continuing hatred for the Russians was apparent and her admiration for the Americans and the U.S. Army steadfast.

Abruptly, thirty days ago, the Countess announced to Colonel Bernhardt that she would not be turning over any further information. She declined to give any reason, but said she would be willing to discuss it further with Colonel Bernhardt's Commanding General, if that person could come from Washington and meet her in Vienna. She assured the perplexed Bernhardt that it had nothing to do with him; in fact, she told him, he was one of her all-time favorites.

"You know the rest. I have compared notes with the Chief of Stations, John Ormond, and he has no idea what her problem is. Based on your earlier approval, I have arranged for you to meet Countess Laressa at the Vienna Opera House tomorrow night." Preston explained that on the third level of the Opera House there was a private "Patrons of the Opera" box which Countess Laressa and other prominent Austrians used when attending the opera. It was not unusual to make a seat available in that box to visiting dignitaries particularly on slow nights. A seat had been arranged for General Lowe. The rest of the seats in the Patrons' box that night would be filled by other members of the Countess' family. The plan was that during the intermission of *La Boheme*, Sunday night, the other family members would leave the box and go to the lobby for refreshments. The Countess and General Lowe would remain in the box and have approximately twenty minutes together privately for whatever she wished to tell him.

The New Year's Eve party Saturday night was a regal event attended by more than 100 people. The Vienna Attaché Corps—East and West—turned out in great numbers as Preston had predicted, as well as the U.S. Ambassador and senior officers from the Austrian Defense Ministry. After one glass of excellent Austrian sekt, Bart switched to the standard drink of the U.S. Attaché Corps—a tall glass of soda water with lime.

The foreign attachés were impressive in their dress uniforms. Bart found he was the object of their deliberate attention and questions. He gave most high marks for their diplomatic skills and discretion. Some were obvious: the Russian Attaché, accompanied by a younger woman who was there because her memory was better than that of her boss, and the Chinese Attaché, who confessed he was having difficulty determining how many nuclear weapons the U.S. had in Europe, and would appreciate any help he could get. He even suggested providing information on his own Army in return. The Hungarian and the Romanian attachés pointedly told Bart that he could expect a warm welcome by his counterparts in their countries and hinted that they would have important matters to discuss.

The tour of Vienna on Sunday was a wonderful experience for both Bart and George. Preston and Anna Bernhardt were knowledgeable tour guidcs and their articulate descriptions of the many castles, museums and magnificent buildings and architecture made for a memorable day.

The meeting at the Vienna Opera House with Countess Laressa was filled with intrigue and mystery. *La Boheme* was an artistic feast, the sounds of which brought tears to most listeners eyes. The Countess was a most charming grand dame and her four accompanying family members were pleasant company. They spoke fluent English, but were comfortable with Bart's German. The son, his wife and two teenage grandchildren all departed promptly at intermission leaving Bart and the Countess alone. At first they made small talk about the General's visit to Vienna and asked how he was enjoying the opera. Then she asked Bart if he had read the story of *La Boheme* in the Opera Program as she opened her program to the page containing an English version of the *La Boheme* story. Bart immediately saw the short handwritten note inserted by the Countess. The note read:

> My contacts in the Soviet Union and elsewhere have told me that our efforts to assist you may be at risk. They tell me that the KGB has received new information concerning several successful espionage operations against them. It is not certain but the KGB may have information that indicates that Vienna is one of the locations from which information concerning the Russians is being passed. I have no reason to suspect Colonel B but I do not trust the CIA or the Ambassador's assistant, Mr. Hoffman. If you want to continue to receive information from me we need to work out some other arrangement for passing the information. Can you help?

Bart continued to look at the Opera program but took his pen from his inside coat pocket and wrote a short reply on the Countess' note:

> YES. I CERTAINLY WANT THE INFORMATION TO CONTINUE. IT WILL TAKE ME ABOUT 30 DAYS TO REVIEW THE SITUATION AND WORK OUT A NEW ARRANGEMENT. I WILL GET WORD BACK TO YOU THROUGH COLONEL B. IS THAT AGREEABLE?

He then passed the program back and said aloud. "Countess Laressa, I had not read the story of *La Boheme*. It is a very romantic and sad story. Thank you."

The Countess read Bart's note and nodded her agreement. Her family returned at the end of the intermission, and *La Boheme* continued to its sad conclusion. After the applause ended and the curtain calls had been taken, Bart thanked Countess Laressa and her family for sharing an evening at the opera and made his way to the Opera House entrance and hailed a taxi for his return to the Bernhardt residence. As the white Mercedes taxi sped quietly through the streets of Vienna, Bart pondered whether or not this new problem with GREENFIELDS was somehow connected with HEAT SEEKER. It was not a subject he could discuss with Preston Bernhardt; he would have to wait until he returned to Washington. He would, however, call SSD on the secure phone and get Bob Herrington started on it.

On Monday, the Austrians at the Ministry of Defense welcomed General Lowe and provided him with a comprehensive overview of their armed forces. As their international status was officially neutral and their capabilities limited, it was painfully obvious they would look to their friends in the West for assistance if any Bloc threat materialized. The Austrians, as they had on Saturday night, complimented the efforts of Colonel Bernhardt and the U.S. attachés.

High marks for Preston and the DAO also were noted during Bart's visit to the U.S. Embassy, particularly by the

Ambassador and Mr. Hoffman, the DCM. At the end of the day, Bart sat down with Preston Bernhardt and CIA's John Ormond in Bernhardt's office to discuss the GREENFIELDS problem. As Chief of Station, Ormond shared the concerns he had about the overzealous involvement of the DCM, Felix Hoffman, into DAO and CIA operations. He told Bart he also passed along his concerns to CIA Headquarters. He said he had no reason to believe Mr. Hoffman was aware of GREENFIELDS' true identify because that was closely held. Ormond offered the use of his COS secure communications with CIA in Washington as a way in which Preston could relay communications to General Lowe, if necessary for the security of GREENFIELDS or other sensitive operations. This would prevent the DCM's access.

Bart thanked the COS for his offer but declined until such time as Bart's Special Services Division staff had a chance to review the operation. Bart had already talked to Colonel Herrington on the secure phone and had tasked him to take on the GREENFIELDS' problem and provide him with some recommendations. Bart also indicated to Preston and John Ormond that he intended to discuss GREENFIELDS with CIA's DDO when he had the results of the SSD review.

CHAPTER 11

THE WARSAW PACT

During the cold war the western military alliance viewed the Eastern Bloc countries—principally East Germany, Poland, Czechoslovakia, Hungary, Romania, Bulgaria and Yugoslavia—as the forward area of the USSR, an area inextricably tied to the "Evil Empire" of the Soviet Union. The fact that the Russian presence and influence had been imposed on these countries by brutal military and political force was sometimes lost when the United States and its NATO allies estimated who the opposing forces would be in any conflict on the European continent. It was therefore taken for granted that the Bloc countries, tied by the Warsaw Pact, would reinforce the USSR and do their bidding in any conflict with the West.

In the early days of the cold war the Iron Curtain dividing east from west limited western knowledge about the quality of the opposing military forces in the forward area. The USSR and the Bloc countries were known in the National Security community as the "denied area." NATO nations depended heavily on overhead reconnaissance, technical intelligence, defectors, a limited number of legal travelers and the handful of diplomats and military attachés serving behind the Iron Curtain for estimates on these potential enemies' strength, equipment, training and will to fight. The professional military service commanders in the United States accepted these estimates as accurate; there was really no other choice. Yet, there was always a burning curiosity that asked: "Are these guys really that good? Are they really 10 feet tall? Do they have the best war fighting weapons, training and doctrine in the world?"

With that concern swirling around in his mind, Major General Bart Lowe, accompanied by Colonel George Martin, disembarked from the morning Russian Aeroflot flight in Warsaw, Poland, and were met at the foot of the aircraft ramp by a Polish naval officer and two armed security guards. The officer introduced himself as Lieutenant Commander Milsudski, a foreign liaison officer of the Ministry of Defense. He escorted General Lowe and Colonel Martin across the tarmac to a waiting bus. They proceeded to the main terminal building and to a small lounge where a uniformed Polish customs official was waiting to take their passports. Bart's first impression of the International Air Terminal could best be described as "early drab." There was a dreary, dirty grayness to the buildings that was present with few exceptions throughout the Eastern Bloc.

Commander Milsudski explained that the Polish bureaucracy was painfully slow and suggested that the general and his assistant make themselves comfortable in the lounge. The lounge where Lowe and Martin waited was a room approximately 20 x 15 feet in size with no windows. It contained two vintage couches, two easy chairs, a single battered coffee table, and a large picture of the Polish ruler, General Wojclech Jaruzelski. The lounge's single luxury was a small adjoining lavatory with essential, no-frills toilet and wash bowl facilities. Bart took advantage of this amenity; as he returned a young woman in military uniform was bringing in a tray containing a pot of coffee and three porcelain mugs. Bart found the coffee to be tolerable although bitterly strong.

Commander Milsudski, a blond, ruddy-faced individual of medium height offered cigarettes, lit one himself and seemed genuinely surprised that neither the general nor colonel smoked. He was anxious to demonstrate his proficiency in English and proved to be friendly and talkative. After Bart asked him a number of questions about his naval experiences, none of which were answered coherently, Milsudski admitted he was not really a naval officer. He explained, somewhat embarrassingly, that his superior, General Raslav, had been criticized for not having a naval officer on the Foreign Liaison staff. Raslav instructed Milsudski to get some naval uniforms and satisfy the naval requirement until such time as a qualified naval officer could be found. Commander Milsudski was then in his second week of being a naval officer.

After an interminable time, the passports were returned, the baggage claimed, and Lowe officially welcomed to Warsaw by Colonel Dennis Warcheck. They passed through the near empty terminal and exited the building. Commander Milsudski insisted that Bart ride in a black official car with him and an armed security guard with two motorcycle police serving as escorts. The two colonels followed in the attaché sedan with the luggage. The immediate impression he had as a first time traveler behind the Iron Curtain was that he was in a time warp. The buildings, the streets, the people on the streets, the traffic, the cars, all looked like something out of the 1930s, as if time, somehow had been arrested. Later, as he continued his trip throughout the Eastern Bloc and the USSR, Bart found this impression would return time and time again. The old buildings of magnificent architecture and form seemed to be in an advanced state of deterioration with no evident maintenance. The newer, multiple dwelling buildings built from Soviet design in the post WWII period looked worse than the old buildings, with broken, boarded up windows starkly visible everywhere. The smoke from wood burning and coal fires whipped up by the cold January winds hung over the city like a gray threadbare blanket.

The Foreign Ministry was located on Wiejska Street among a cluster of government buildings in the center of Warsaw. The Foreign Military Liaison Office was located on the fourth floor. The elevators were out of order. After climbing the ancient stairs, Bart and the two colonels were ushered into General Raslav's large, sparsely furnished office. The General, a short, stocky man with dark brown hair was dressed in the greenish-khaki uniform of his country's army. He came around the side of his desk to welcome them. He spoke acceptable English with a heavy accent. Counting Bart and his party and the Polish escort officer, there were a total of 10 officers in the room. General Raslav offered Bart a choice between a Polish Zubrowka, a Russian vodka, and the famous Hungarian pepper drink, Slivovitz. Bart considered declining, but realized his refusal would offend his host, who was obviously looking forward to having a drink. Bart accepted a small glass of Slivovitz in what looked like good Polish crystal, and General Raslav poured himself a stiff portion of Zubrowka. Then the Colonel who had brought the tray poured drinks for the others.

Raslav was anxious to learn if Lowe had an agenda, or any complaints requiring his attention during this visit. When Bart assured him that the visit was purely routine to check on his attachés, Raslav seemed relieved and became more animated and talkative. He complimented Colonel Warcheck on his fluency in Polish and then, in a condescending way, said, "Colonel Warcheck and his attachés are pretty good boys. Most of the time they behave themselves and only occasionally get in trouble. Then, of course, I must scold them. We have restricted areas where we must safeguard our military and state secrets. Sometimes we find your attachés in these areas. The restricted areas are always clearly marked and we give them and the other western attachés maps designating these restricted areas, but still they show up there and claim they are lost."

Bart acknowledged Raslav's complaint and replied that he would certainly take the matter up with Colonel Warcheck and the other attachés during his visit. Colonel Warcheck entered the conversation at this point and tactfully made light of the General's remarks. Denny Warcheck was an old Polish hand, having served two tours in Warsaw. His genial rapport with General Raslav and his colleagues was obvious, and he seemed to know just how far to go in needling Raslav, then skillfully backing off when he had pushed far enough.

"Even so, General Lowe," Raslav continued. "I think relations between our two countries are improving. We have many people of Polish extraction in the United States, and we like Americans. I am sure that Colonel Warcheck has told you we permitted him and the other western attachés to observe our major war game exercise last month. This was the first time any western observers attended a Warsaw Pact exercise."

Bart recalled reading Denny Warcheck's report of the exercise at the time, and the event had been precedent setting. The State Department and Defense analysts were still looking for the quid the Poles would request.

The meeting terminated after about 45 minutes, much to Bart's relief; the smoke filled room, without ventilation, had been a strong test of his diplomatic skill.

Enroute back to the U.S. Embassy, Denny told Bart that he thought the meeting had gone well. He explained that the Poles would often use the visit of any senior U.S. official, no matter what his field, to unload some policy grievance or Communist Party complaint. These outbursts usually came without any advance warning. Warcheck then pointed out the civilian sedan following their attaché car. Warcheck told General Lowe he could count on being followed by the SB—Polish State Security—during the entire time he was in Poland.

"Nothing personal," Denny said. "It's just the standard treatment all western attachés receive. We all have Polish SB guards at our homes, put there ostensibly for our protection, but really to keep an eye on us and report our comings and goings. Sometimes they relax their vehicular surveillance within the city of Warsaw, but the minute we get on the roads leading out of the capital SB police are on our tails. It's a challenge to elude them. Sometimes we are successful, but they are good at what they do. And, with the exception of the secure phone lines in the DAO in the Embassy, you can count on any phone you use to be monitored. Other than that, General Lowe, welcome to Warsaw."

The first two days of the visit proceeded as planned. On the second evening of the visit Bart and George were scheduled to have a quiet dinner with Denny and Mary Warcheck at the Defense Attaché's house. They walked from the embassy back to Colonel Warcheck's quarters. After they had been there about an hour Denny was called away to answer the phone. When he returned, he was ashen-faced and had obviously received some bad news.

"General Lowe, that was the embassy. We have apparently had an incident involving the assistant Air Attaché, Lieutenant

Colonel Charles James. I'm told that the incident will be aired at eight o'clock on Polish National Television and it may involve you."

"Say again!" Bart Lowe exclaimed.

After repeating the shocking news, Warcheck suggested they go into the front room and turn on the television.

It was the lead story on the Polish National news broadcast. The film footage panned General Lowe's and Colonel Martin's arrival at the airport. There were shots of them entering and exiting the Foreign Ministry Building before arriving at the U.S. Embassy. Then there was footage of two individuals being arrested at a table in a local restaurant. A final section of film showed Lieutenant Colonel James in his U.S. Air Force uniform in front of a large number of Polish journalists with a microphone in his face. He was saying, "I am from the U.S. Embassy and I'm here in response to a call from the SB Headquarters asking the embassy to send someone to pick up an American who has been detained."

Bart did not understand Polish, but as soon as the broadcast item concluded, Colonel Warcheck, with a grim face, explained.

"According to the broadcast, a Polish national was arrested this afternoon on suspicion of espionage. The individual, a man identified as Pavlov Strauss, a local journalist, was meeting with a second individual, also arrested, and identified as Victor Huber, a commercial official from the U.S. Embassy. The story went on to say that Mr. Huber is a member of the American CIA. When informed, the U.S. Embassy sent an attaché, Lieutenant Colonel James, to pick up the CIA agent. It is implied that U.S. military attachés are working with CIA. And finally, Polish officials suggest that the visit to Warsaw by a high ranking U.S. military official was for the purpose of supervising such espionage operations. It's fair to say," Denny concluded, "that they mean you and the shit has hit the fan."

No sooner had Denny Warcheck finished this explanation than the phone rang. This time it was the DCM calling on behalf of the ambassador to announce a meeting at the embassy in 30 minutes and requesting that Colonel Warcheck, General Lowe and Lieutenant Colonel James be present.

When Lowe, Martin and Warcheck arrived at the DAO, Lieutenant Colonel James was already there. He explained that his involvement in the incident was because he happened to be the embassy duty officer for that day and had responded to a routine after-duty-hours-call from the Polish SB saying they had detained an American. No further specifics were given, other than they wanted someone from the U.S. Embassy to pick the person up at SB Headquarters.

Lieutenant Colonel James assumed he would be making a routine pick up of an American visitor who had been involved in some minor altercation. When he arrived at the SB Headquarters and announced his purpose for being there he was directed to a room on the main floor of the Headquarters building. As soon as he went through the closed door and saw the large number of television cameras and microphones, he realized that it was a set-up, a timed event designed to embarrass the United States.

Armed with this background, Lowe, Warcheck, and James left the DAO and went up the elevator to the fifth floor and the ambassador's office. George Martin stayed in the DAO to alert the DAS headquarters in Washington. As they entered the room the Ambassador, Walter Lockhart, came from around his desk and shook hands with Bart.

"General, I didn't expect to see you so soon. I hope you had a chance for dinner before all this. The SB has staged this incident to embarrass us. They will try to get as much propaganda value out of it as possible. We have spoken to our contacts at the Foreign Ministry, and I understand your people have contacted the Polish Foreign Military Liaison. Bill Taber, our Chief of Station, has touched base with his contacts in the government, and they all deny any involvement with this nasty business. It's our preliminary conclusion that the whole affair was orchestrated by the SB. They are a bad bunch."

"I am sure you are wondering what our Mr. Huber was up to today," said Bill Taber. "Vic has known Strauss, a Polish journalist, for more than two years. We have used him as a casual source, and he has been helpful to us, but he is not a clandestine source and that was not a clandestine meeting today. It was all open and above board. It is not unusual for the SB to look for an opportunity such as your visit, general, to tie in a trumped-up charge to put us in a bad light—in this case both the DAS and the CIA. If I had to guess, I think this incident probably was conducted in retaliation for something the FBI did to their SB people in Washington."

"General," the Ambassador continued, "the main thing we have to do now is make sure we have all the pertinent facts in order to respond to the landslide of state-side queries that we are about to receive. Greta Reinhold, our public affairs officer, has learned that the broadcast we heard here was also released to the major wire services in Europe and the United States. The time differences will ensure that an avalanche of questions will be forthcoming here throughout the night. I have our political-military people working on a cable to send to State, and I have already called our Assistant Secretary for Eastern Europe, Reuben Workman. Greta is drafting a press release for the Polish press and the U.S. wire services. I'd appreciate it if you and Denny would look over our cable and news release and make sure we haven't overlooked anything important."

"I'd be happy to, Ambassador Lockhart," Bart replied. "The main question I have now is will the Poles take any other action against our people here or try to further involve me?"

"I don't think so," said the ambassador. "The usual course is to make the most of the bad press, but they may attempt to use it as leverage against us in the future for anything we do that they don't like. The important thing for us to do now is get a categorical denial on the street as soon as possible and stonewall their propaganda efforts. The other thing you may see, general, is that other Warsaw Pact countries may pick this up and attempt to hassle you about it. Have the visas for your visits to the other Eastern European countries and the Soviet Union been approved?"

"Yes, we have them in hand."

"I will be surprised if we don't see some movement by the others, particularly the Russians," volunteered Colonel Warcheck.

The Ambassador nodded agreement and the meeting broke up. As they were leaving the Ambassador's office, Bart realized that he might have his first major flap on his hands. When they returned to the DAO they found that half of the DAO staff had returned to the office to assist with the anticipated crisis. The phones were ringing, one after another, and the communication center had already advised the DAO of multiple incoming cables. George Martin had already alerted the DAS headquarters. While they were waiting for the State Department messages, Bart sat down and drafted a message for the Secretary of Defense and other Washington officials. Bart also conferred with Captain Pete Kalitka and Chuck Gregorios and asked them to pass on the necessary facts to the key Washington people. He asked Chuck to contact John Kitchen at the FBI to see if there were any recent FBI actions against the Poles in Washington that might have served as the basis for the events in Warsaw.

Bart then called Lieutenant General Lennie Murphy on the secure line. The Director of Defense Intelligence Agency was the one official in the Defense Department who would get the most questions concerning anything military that happened behind the Iron Curtain. General Murphy thanked Bart for the heads-up and ended his phone call with, "Again, Bart, welcome to the wonderful world of attachés."

By midnight, Bart and DAO Warsaw had stemmed the tide of curiosity surrounding the alleged spy incident in Poland and headed back to quarters for a little well earned and much needed sack time. Bart's last thought before slipping away to sleep was: What is this? Just another day of normal attaché business or some sinister plot by the other side to discredit DAS and attaché operations? Bart could not help but wonder, "Is HEAT SEEKER behind all of this?"

Bart's third and last day was spent visiting the DAO family quarters and touring Warsaw, a sadly beautiful, and now dilapidated city. In the afternoon he and Colonel Warcheck returned to the embassy and linked up with George Martin and the other attachés who had been monitoring the follow-up actions to last night's incident.

The Polish SB, through the Polish Foreign Ministry, requested the departure of the CIA officer, Vic Huber, within 72 hours on a persona non grata basis, but there was no mention of the attaché, Lieutenant Colonel James. Word had been relayed from DAS Headquarters that Bulgaria had canceled General Lowe's and Colonel Martin's visas and that the USSR had suspended the Lowe and Martin visas until such time as they could review the facts in the Warsaw incident.

"What does that mean? Suspended our visas?" Bart asked Denny Warcheck.

"It means they are going to let you sweat it while they take their sweet time in deciding. I'll bet they let you wait until the last possible minute," Denny said.

"And what about the Bulgarians?"

"I don't think those guys ever change their minds. I would bet you can consider that a closed deal."

George Martin looked at the remaining portion of the trip. "Boss, we were going from here to Prague, Budapest, Bucharest, Sofia and then Moscow. If Sofia falls out, we can have Lieutenant Colonel Weaver from Sofia come up to Bucharest and join us there, and if we don't get the go ahead from the Soviets we can always go back to the States from Belgrade."

Bart agreed and directed George to put the necessary travel contingencies in place. Bart was disappointed the visit to the Soviet Union might be at risk. It was going to be the highlight of the long trip and an opportunity Bart had thought about most of his life.

Next on the agenda was Prague. The Czechoslovakian capital was the best cared-for city that Bart would see on his tour of the Warsaw Pact countries. Air Force Colonel Nick Simon, the Defense Attaché, and his wife, Samantha, met Bart and George

Martin at the airport. The entry procedures for diplomats at the International Airport in Prague were not as stringent as in Warsaw. Bart and George were both billeted at Colonel Simon's house. In the interest of security, General Lowe was staying with the attachés in the Warsaw Pact countries whenever possible. The Simons lived in a comfortable old house in the diplomatic residential section of Prague, assisted by a cook, housemaid, and a gardener who doubled as butler, handyman, waiter and major domo.

On General Lowe's first night in Prague the Simons hosted a dinner party, attended by the U.S. Ambassador, his wife and the British and French attachés and their wives. Bart was seated between Ambassador Strobe and Mrs. Strobe and found them to be a delightful couple. Bart told the Ambassador that George Martin had recently read an article in an American magazine that contained a story about the U.S. Ambassador's residence in Prague. The story, illustrated with a number of pictures, described the residence as a small castle filled with priceless antiques, several grand pianos and a swimming pool in the basement that had cost more than a million dollars to build. The Ambassador confirmed that the residence was all that the story suggested and more, and compared it to living in a museum. The house had been ceded to the U.S. at the end of WWII.

"Unfortunately," the Ambassador said to Bart, "my wife and I are leaving on the midnight train for Paris to attend a conference and will not be here during the rest of your visit." He reached into his pocket, pulled out a key and said, "This is an extra key to the residence. Please go there and see it whenever you like. All of the rooms are open except our private sleeping quarters; the domestic staff will be there to show you around.

The next day Bart, George, and the Simons were joined by the Army Attaché, Colonel Noel Coyne and his spouse Carol. Colonel Coyne was the attaché General Lowe had first met in training in Florida. The Coynes had been in Prague just a short time, but based on their previous tour, according to Nick Simon, they had hit the ground running and were fully settled and productive.

A cold but sunny day was ideal for a tour of Old Prague, Wenceslas Square and the major historic and cultural sites of the city to include ride-bys of the many military installations in and around Prague. Sunday afternoon and evening were spent at the ambassador's spectacular quarters where Bart and the rest of the group found out that George Martin could not only "talk the talk" when it came to pianos, but he could also "walk the walk" with an impressive repertoire of classical, and popular piano music.

The next two days at the DAO and embassy in Prague were informative and the DAO staff continued to add to Bart Lowe's database on DAOs and how they are run. He began to realize that the DAOs, like their parent U.S. Embassies, had things in common. At the same time, each had its individuality and no two DAOs, or embassies were exactly alike. Each DAO took on the look and personality akin to the military service of the senior Defense Attaché—Army, Navy, Air Force, or Marine Corps. And the demeanor of the Defense Attaché seemed to set the tone. This was certainly the case with Colonel Simon in Prague. The DAO had an exceptionally fine track record in the DAS and produced a high volume of information, with a superlative record of identifying advanced technology weapons in Czechoslovakia.

During Bart's visit Colonel Simon described the Czech military as a professional service with excellent war fighting capabilities but little enthusiasm for any real conflict. He said, "The majority of the military has little love for the Soviets, but the Communist Party and a small number of communist hard liners in the military keep the army in check. We've been able to maintain a good give-and-take relationship with the senior officers at the Military Headquarters of the Czech Armed Forces. However, the DAO is still recovering from the shock two years ago when an attaché and his spouse were brutally handled and detained for several hours by a group of paramilitary border guards when returning from a road trip to Germany. The couple were finally returned safely, but the incident left a scar with us."

Colonel Simon then turned Bart over to Colonel Coyne. Coyne had quickly moved into the right circles among the Czech military giving him regular access to a cooperating senior Czech officer who had worked with Coyne's predecessor. But, recently, to Coyne's chagrin, one of the things the Czech officer passed on to Noel was that he had learned from a friend he was suspected by Statni Tasna Bezpecnost, the State Secret Security Service, of providing information to the Americans and the officer thought that he and his family were now in danger.

"The cutoff of this Czech officer's information would represent a loss of one of the DAS's and Defense's most prolific sources of information on the Warsaw Pact," Coyne said.

Lowe was developing a premonition that each DAO in the Warsaw Pact would have some new sinister development that somehow would be linked to HEAT SEEKER. He could not discuss this subject with anyone at the embassy in Prague, so he just filed it away as another item to be taken up upon his return to Washington. He then instructed Nick Simon and Noel Coyne to low key their contact with the Czech officer so as not to put their source into any further danger, and to keep the Special Services Division and DAS Headquarters in Washington informed of any developments.

When Bart and George departed Prague for Budapest, Hungary, again on an Aeroflot plane, there still had been no movement on the USSR visas. Bart asked Chuck Gregorios to start pinging the Soviet Embassy in Washington. He also asked Chuck to have a cable sent to BG Alton in Moscow to see if he could do anything to break the visa loose.

Colonel Ruth Davis, the Defense Attaché to Hungary, had persuaded the Hungarian Airport Security and Customs officials to let her accompany them when they met General Lowe and Colonel Martin plane-side on his arrival in Budapest. Ruth Davis was a strong-willed, no-nonsense individual, who prevailed upon her Hungarian counterparts by confident determination and excellent linguistic skills. She was accompanied by a Hungarian Army major from the Foreign Office who was genuinely helpful. The airport in Budapest gave yet another different impression than those of Poland and Czechoslovakia. There was far more activity. Commercial advertising signs hawking international hotels, restaurants, gasoline and scenic locations throughout the country were conspicuously evident. The Hungarian people also lacked the grim, depressed looks of the Poles and Czechs. They seemed more open and prone to occasional smiles.

Based on a conversation that Bart had with Colonel Davis in Garmisch, she had made a special effort to arrange a meeting between General Lowe and his Hungarian counterpart, a Major General Czarny. During the trip into Budapest from the airport, Colonel Davis reported that she had been successful in arranging the meeting with Czarny and that it would take place the next day at noon. She explained that she would accompany General Lowe for the first part of the meeting, which would take place at the Hungarian Army Headquarters. After the meeting, General Lowe would be asked to stay and share a private lunch with General Czarny in his office. This type of meeting was virtually unprecedented, according to Colonel Davis. In this case, the U.S. Ambassador wholeheartedly supported the meeting, she added.

Ambassador Martin Sorrenson was one of those farsighted individuals who, unlike many of his contemporaries, thought the Iron Curtain had rusted sufficiently during the years of the Cold War. Colonel Ruth Davis told General Lowe that Ambassador Sorrenson was most anxious to see him and go over some of his initiatives with the Hungarians, and that Sorrenson was one of the few U.S. Ambassadors who supported increased U.S. military to Bloc military contacts as one possible way to uproot the strong hold of communist rule.

The ambassador had charged Colonel Davis to look for ways in which to increase her contact with the Hungarian Military. As a female, she was been rebuffed by her male Hungarian counterparts, but through perseverance she was having limited success. Most recently her suggestion of holding seminars at the Hungarian War College on the differences between western and eastern war fighting doctrine, and allowing the NATO attachés in Budapest to take part in the seminars, had been accepted by the Hungarians.

At the DAO Budapest briefings the next morning, Colonel Davis told Bart she was very pleased with her DAO staff. In addition to the normal complement of service staff, she was supporting two U.S. Army officers in their final stage of in-country training as Hungarian Foreign Area Officers. These two individuals had been particularly helpful to Davis in her military-to-military initiatives with the Hungarians. "The Ambassador could not be more supportive," she said, "although his political-military people were not enthusiastic over her military-to-military contacts. Colonel Davis also spent time to make strong and convincing arguments to Bart for an increase in her annual budget and replacement of her high-mileaged vehicles.

In Bart's meeting with Ambassador Sorrenson, the ambassador indicated that he thought the meeting with General Czarny was being arranged by the Hungarians so Czarny could pass on some message intended to be for a government-to-government level. He believed Czarny did not have the authority to suggest such a meeting without the approval of his superiors and their superiors. The Ambassador's personal assessment was that the key senior officials in the Hungarian government were ready for a change in the hard core communist doctrine and were searching for some way to start the ball rolling in bringing about change without losing face with their own people or provoking the Russians to take some oppressive action.

For his visit to the Hungarian Army Headquarters, Bart wore his green uniform, and black all-weather coat. He and Colonel Davis, tall and slim in her Air Force blue uniform and blue raincoat, attracted all eyes as they entered the old sandstone colored building and went on into a large alcove filled with the flags of the Hungarian Army Units. An escort was waiting to take them to the fourth floor, and Major General Czarny's office. After the introductions they went into a small, sparsely furnished conference room with a single large table and pictures of

Hungary's current military leaders on three walls and a projection screen on the fourth. They were offered worn chairs and joined by four other officers, apparently from Czarny's staff. Two enlisted soldiers served hot black syrupy-looking coffee in standard Hungarian Army issue coffee mugs. On the table were several packs of Hungarian cigarettes and everyone except General Lowe and Colonel Davis lit up. Bart hoped that this part of the meeting wouldn't last long.

General Czarny was eight or nine years older than Lowe and, according to the biography provided to Bart, Czarny was the head of Hungarian Military Intelligence, responsible for Hungary's attachés in other countries and for monitoring foreign attachés accredited to Budapest. He was a career infantry officer and had been in his present job for two years. He had graying, sandy hair, stooped shoulders and a pot belly was visible inside his khaki green tunic. He frequently frowned, but was cordial and his Hungarian, which Colonel Davis translated, was friendly in tone. A staff officer, identified as Colonel Babor ran a color video tape of the Hungarian Army in action. It was a typical propaganda film, set to background music, with the narrator speaking perfect English. The film ran approximately 20 minutes and was long on distant shots of major military forces in battle formations with tanks, guns and aircraft supporting them. There were very few close ups or weapons specifics.

When the film was over, Bart asked a few questions about Hungarian conscription, and lengths of military training for the various combat skills which were answered with reasonable candor. His hosts, in turn, asked essentially the same questions, which Bart answered directly. Nothing sensitive—just soldier-to-soldier talk. At that point General Czarny indicated in Hungarian that the Hungarian Army was pleased with Colonel Davis and had no complaints to register with General Lowe. General Czarny then stood up indicating that portion of the meeting was over.

General Czarny asked Bart in English to join him in his office. Bart followed General Czarny out of the conference room and down the corridor to his office. General Czarny led Bart through his outer office where three uniformed soldiers sat behind desks and into his inner office. Czarny's inner office was comfortably large, but by no means plush. It contained a desk and chair, a sofa, a large coffee table, one easy chair and four straight back chairs. Behind Czarny's desk a small work table held several phones. Bart wondered where those lines connected. Who could pull Czarny's chain and whose chain could Czarny pull? Aside from the furniture, there were two flags in the corner of the room and a handful of pictures and plaques on the walls. Not a lot different, Bart thought, from an American military officer's office. The most noticeable feature of General Czarny's office was the heavy odor of cigarette smoke. Czarny was close to being a chain smoker, and lit up a fresh cigarette the moment they entered the office. Czarny invited Bart to sit on the couch, and he took the easy chair.

"General Lowe, would you care for an aperitif?" Czarny offered and when Bart declined, he said, "Then if you have no objection I will go ahead and order our lunch. We have a kitchen and eating facility in the basement of the building for the Army Headquarters people. Because of my duties with the foreign attachés, I have meals served in my office for guests. Actually the quality of the food is better because we wouldn't want our guests to think we had anything but the best," he laughed.

They made only small talk until the lunch was served from a restaurant-like serving cart that kept the food and the plates warm. The meal was a Hungarian specialty of three types of meat with a spicy sauce, noodles and green vegetables with brown bread on the side, accompanied by a sweet tasting white Hungarian wine. It was served by a soldier in a dining steward's uniform and supervised by the general's aide. They ate at the coffee table, and when the luncheon dishes were cleared away, a pot of very hot, very strong and very syrupy coffee was placed on the table. General Czarny then began to tell Bart about his career in the Hungarian Army. He made it clear that he had no particular affinity for the Russians, but that their presence in his country was a political reality. He revealed his current job was his first assignment in intelligence. He went on to say that he was involved only in military intelligence work and had nothing to do with the Hungarian civilian security services.

"Those people," he said, "are heavily involved with and controlled by the KGB." Which was not the case, he explained, with the Hungarian Army. He had no real problems with the NATO attachés but spent a lot of time responding to complaints from the Soviets about the attachés. Czarny's monologue echoed the case often made by the Warsaw Pact countries: "We are okay and want to be your friends. The Russians are the real bad guys." Or, put another way, "The Devil made me do it."

Then, suddenly, Czarny launched into an area that Bart recognized as new ground. "General Lowe, each year, the Soviets have what you call troop rotation whereby the USSR takes the soldiers who have been in the Warsaw Pact countries, including Hungary, for one year and returns them to the Soviet Union, replacing them with fresh troops. Your country and NATO watch this closely to make sure that the Russians do not send more troops forward than they take out. The Soviets are considering reducing their military presence in Hungary. They now have 65,000. This talk of reductions has come about as a result of our urging them to do so. Although the numbers we proposed are small, I think you will find that in the future their presence in Hungary will dramatically decrease. Candidly, our countrymen want to get rid of the Russians altogether and improve our country economically."

After lighting another cigarette, and refilling both coffee cups, Czarny continued. "As you can see we are still a backward country. We realize that in spite of our ability to wage and perhaps win a war with sophisticated weapons, the rest of our economy is a disaster. We have made some progress in opening our country to the West and want to do much more for the future. Now, General Lowe, if the things I have suggested hypothetically take place, would your country be willing to assist us in our areas of greatest need? The number one priority for my army in this hypothetical situation would be to learn and do more about our environment. To learn from you what long range actions would be necessary to clean up our environment and make our country more attractive to the West. We know, for example, that your army has a Corps of Engineers heavily involved in maintaining and improving the environment in the United States. My army is very interested in this approach and mission for the future."

Bart Lowe wasn't shocked, but he was surprised. At the end of their meeting, he told General Czarny he would be sure that the hypothetical situation Czarny described would be passed to the right people in Washington, and that Czarny and Lowe would then have to wait and see what developments took place. Bart told General Czarny that Colonel Davis would keep him informed.

Bart wasn't entirely sure of the result of his meeting with General Czarny, but Ambassador Sorrenson thought it was a clear signal for an upcoming major change in United States-Hungarian relationships and portended new possibilities vis a vis the Soviet Union.

The next two days in Budapest were spent in answering follow-on questions concerning the Lowe-Czarny meeting and in getting to know the rest of the DAO staff members and their families. As in the other Warsaw Pact capitals, a tour of the city and the cultural/historic landmarks was arranged. Bart was impressed by the old historic houses and buildings of the "VAR" area overlooking the Danube River. Bart had the opportunity to sample the famous Hungarian goulash soup, a tasty treat never prepared quite the same at any two places.

The flight to Bucharest, Saturday morning, was short. There were few travelers on the Aeroflot plane, mostly grim-faced Romanian and Russian businessmen. Leaving Hungary and arriving in Romania was like going from one world to another vastly different world. Both countries were a part of the Warsaw Pact but that was where the similarity ended.

After disembarking—they were the last people off the aircraft because the foreigner section on the Aeroflot aircraft was always secluded at the rear of the plane—Bart and George got into a slow moving line through the Romanian Customs and Passport gates. Bart and George were traveling on black U.S. passports reserved for diplomats and honored by most of the civilized countries of the world, yet there had been no indication any preferential treatment would be given until they reached the customs point and presented their passports and bags for inspection. After a glaring look at the passports and a cursory look at the outside of their suitcases, the customs officials waved them through and pointed to a door across the terminal marked "private." Once through that door, Colonel Roskowski appeared with a Romanian official.

Frank Roskowski, a short, stocky infantry officer in his late 40s, with a dark brown crew cut was wearing a gray sports coat and red tie and navy blue trousers. He had lost the argument with a Romanian official on being permitted to meet his boss at the arrival gate. Frank, still red-faced, indicated that he had not taken the rebuff lightly, and he apologized for not being able to extend the courtesy of personally meeting Bart.

After getting settled into the attaché sedan for the fifty minute ride into Bucharest, Colonel Roskowski assured General Lowe that he was basically an easy going gentleman who rarely, if ever, lost his cool. But dealing with the Romanians over the last two years had caused his frustration level to climb. He was confident all arrangements had been made for the General's arrival and just to be sure had shown up an hour early. But to his chagrin the official he had made the arrangements with wasn't there and his replacement knew nothing and would not budge. After about 10 minutes into the ride along a fairly deserted two-lane highway Colonel Roskowski said, "I should know by now to never be surprised. In fact, I'm usually surprised if I'm not surprised by the Romanians."

Colonel Roskowski declared, that "Romania is a disaster and getting worse. Its leader, Mr. Ceausescu, is the worse possible despot, and his son is bleeding the country's treasury dry." As they passed a grim-looking 10 or 11 story building Roskowski pointed out that it was the kind of place where most Romanians lived. He recounted a standing joke that he said was a painfully accurate reflection on the sad state of affairs of most people: "Mr. Electricity and Mr. Water met at the front entrance of an apartment building and when they both could not pass through at the same time Mr. Water said, 'Please, after you. I am only going to the third floor and I cannot stay long.' 'Thank you,' replied Mr. Electricity. 'After you. Although I hope to get to the sixth floor, I can only stay for two hours.'"

Colonel "Bronko" Roskowski further described the regime in Romania as ultra-oppressive. In his reporting to the DAS, as well as in his briefing to General Lowe, he emphasized that the country was divided into essentially four groups. One, the people, poor, living in shameful conditions. Two, the Communist Party holding the government together with blind dogmatism. Three, the military infrastructure, the most stable institution, also very unhappy, but kept in check by the Communist Party. And the fourth group, the country's leader, Ceausescu, backed by the party and a small number of ruthless and very powerful men. There was, according to Bronko, great frustration among the professional military leaders over the sorry state of affairs in their country. But so far none had been willing to come forward and take on Ceausescu.

By the time Bronko completed his summation, they arrived at the Defense Attaché villa on the outskirts of Bucharest. An electronic steel gate opened into spacious, completely walled grounds of the large residence. Bronko's wife, Montie, met them at the front door with the same good humor displayed by her husband.

"General Lowe, Colonel Martin," she said with outstretched arms. "Welcome to Transylvania and Castle Dracula."

One of the great strengths of Americans, Bart thought, is their inherent ability to make the best of almost any situation, no matter how grim. And from what Bart had been able to tell so far, Romania looked pretty damn grim.

Colonel Roskowski had arranged for both General Lowe and George Martin to stay at his quarters. They had converted one of the two wings of the one-hundred year old house into two small but comfortable apartments that Montie had made into a refuge for visitors to the DAO.

Bronko explained that none of the official calls that he had proposed for General Lowe with the senior Romanian Military had been approved and as a result they would spend the entire day in the embassy on Monday. The good news was that a number of the Romanian military officers were coming to the attaché cocktail party to be hosted that evening by Bronko and Montie. The cocktail party, Bronko said, would allow General Lowe to talk with the head of the Romanian attachés, a Romanian Navy admiral and the Deputy Chief of Staff of the Romanian Army, as well as a number of other luminaries, including some Communist Party officials. The communists, Bronko joked, were always willing to eat and drink American refreshments under the guise of keeping an eye on the Romanian Military.

After they were settled into their accommodations, Bronko suggested that he, General Lowe, and Colonel Martin go for a jog in the nearby woods. George begged off, pleading fatigue, knowing that Lowe would want some time alone with Bronko. Bronko reported that there was no snow and that a number of clear paths were available for running and walking, and the area was safe. The Romanian surveillance detail—not so discreet—according to Bronko, would keep an eye on them, but they would stay a reasonable distance away.

Outside the air was crisp and clear and Bart welcomed the exercise. Bronko, like Bart, had spent most of his military career as an infantry officer and was more comfortable out on the terrain than on the cocktail circuit, but he had proven to be a good observer of the Romanian military. As they jogged slowly, Bronko talked about his views on Romania. "I think the time is ripe for better relations between the United States and Romania. The Ambassador agrees and has been searching for a palatable idea. Ceausescu is such a tyrant that the Ambassador doesn't see much possibility there. He and I both think that the military offer the best potential for a breakthrough. Our idea is for the military here to invite a senior U.S. military officer, at least a four-bagger, to visit the country, and following that, propose a reciprocal visit to the United States."

"Have you any support for this idea?" Bart asked.

"Yes, sir. I believe quite a bit. We have been planting that seed for quite a while and I will be surprised and disappointed tonight if General Bodin, the Deputy Chief of Staff, doesn't mention it to you. If you have no problem with it, I'll make sure the two of you get together tonight for at least a few minutes of private conversation."

That night, Bart's first impression was that the Romanian military was stand-offish and only intended to make small talk. As the evening wore on and the alcohol flowed, the Communist Party watchers spent more time around the food table and the open bar, and less time watching the Romanian military. Bart then found the Romanian officers more receptive to substantive conversations. He gleaned three consistent themes. One, no love for the Russians. Two, no love for their civilian leader, Ceausescu. And, three, an interest in better rapport with America and its military. True to Bronko's prediction, General Bodin, a chain smoker and heavy drinker, minced no words when they were alone in a corner: "We would like to invite your Chairman, JCS, or the Chief of Staff of your Army to visit our country. Do you think such an invitation would be well received? And would you be willing to invite our Chief, General Lazarus, to your country?"

Bart explained the politics of such a request and pointed out that he could not commit his country but thought that such a plan would be a good start toward improving relations with the United States. Bart then asked General Bodin if he believed the military could gain Ceausescu's support for the invitation. Bodin said that he was convinced that Ceausescu could be persuaded on the basis that such an action could possibly produce much needed assistance for Romania from the United States. Bart told Bodin that he would relay the question to the U.S. military and an answer would be passed to Bodin by Colonel Roskowski.

Bart was genuinely surprised when the Chief of the Romanian attachés, Admiral Zorn, after several unsuccessful attempts at privacy, put the question to him, "Would your country be willing to help Romania learn how to establish a tourist industry?"

Bart first thought Admiral Zorn was just asking a rhetorical question, but the Admiral made it clear that he was posing an official question from his government. While Zorn was not at liberty to say where the request was coming from, it was equally clear that he was thinking of the economic potential for his country, including a role for the military. Bart initially thought the two requests incongruous, even bizarre, but then considered that perhaps what he was hearing were the cries of desperation of a government and a military near chaos. He gave essentially the same answer to Zorn he had to Bodin.

Unlike the attaché receptions in Washington where most of the guests have departed by the end of the time shown on the invitation for the affair, at 8:30, the scheduled concluding time of the DAO Bucharest party, it was still going strong and none of the guests, especially the Romanians, showed the slightest interest in leaving. The longer they stayed, the more comfortable they seemed in their manner and speech, even the Communist Party officials.

When Bart and Bronko, who had been acting as Bart's interpreter, joined a group of five Romanian officers, it was apparent they had arrived at the end of a joke told by one of the officers that had produced boisterous laughter. When Bronko asked about the joke, the officer repeated it in Romanian and suggested that Bronko translate it into English for the General.

Bronko then turned to Bart and said, "This is how it goes. It seems that Mr. Ceausescu made a trip to the Soviet Union and spent some time with Chairman Gorbachev. When Mr. Ceausescu returned from Moscow he told his Chief of Staff that he wanted to see Romania's finest plastic surgeon as quickly as possible. The doctor was summoned and sent in to Mr. Ceausescu. Ceausescu dismissed the others there and said to the doctor, 'Can you take some skin from somewhere on my body, graft it here (pointing to the left side of his forehead) and make a birthmark?'

'Of course, Comrade Ceausescu, but why would you want to do that?' the doctor asked.

'Ceausescu replied 'I have my reasons but I don't wish to reveal them.'

'But Comrade Ceausescu,' the doctor insisted, 'I could never undertake such a delicate operation without knowing what you hope to achieve.'

'Very well then,' Ceausescu conceded, 'but you must promise never to tell anyone what I am about to tell you. When I was in Moscow with Chairman Gorbachev I asked his advice on how to deal with the many problems we are having in Romania. Chairman Gorbachev turned away from me for a few moments deep in thought and finally turned to me and said, 'The trouble with you, Comrade Ceausescu, is that you have nothing up here,' pointing to his forehead."

Again laughter broke out as Bronko reached the punch line. Even in English, the Romanians found the cruel joke about their leader humorous.

The last of the Romanians left the party about ten o'clock, and Bart then spent some time with the American attachés before turning in for the night. Bart, Bronko and George Martin compared notes on what had taken place. Bart wasn't sure if the two messages he had been asked to relay were sincere or some form of entrapment designed to embarrass the DAS and the United States. Bronko was convinced that the messages were genuine and he was confident that Ambassador David Slayman would agree when they saw him on Monday.

On Sunday, lunch at the McElroys was pleasant and the subsequent riding tour of Bucharest was interesting, but even Ceausescu's Palace was bleak. The Ambassador shared Bronko's views on the Romanians and pledged to try to get the State

Department on board for the reciprocal military visits proposal. Bart had sent no messages to the Secretary of Defense and Chairman of the JCS in his 26 years of military service before coming to the DAS. He had now sent them three messages in the last three days. He suspected they were thinking, "Who the hell is this guy Bart Lowe?"

On Monday afternoon Bronko informed him that there was still no word on the Soviet visa approval, but that the Romanians had approved Bronko's request to drive General Lowe and Colonel Martin to Belgrade, Yugoslavia, the next day. It was an easy day's drive and would permit Lowe to see some of the places the DAO Bucharest attachés traveled on their driving tours, which would include some of the Romanian military installations. Bronko was proud of himself because he had requested permission for two driving tours. He had specified the tour to the north toward Transylvania as his first choice, when in reality he wanted the tour to the south as his first priority. The Romanians approved the second choice and both sides were happy with the diplomatic compromise.

The drive from Bucharest to Belgrade was a good change of pace from the hassle of the Aeroflot flights. The weather and the roads remained clear and cold. The day-long drive, although somewhat circuitous because of the restricted areas that the NATO attachés were forbidden to enter, passed quickly. The countryside of Romania, like the cities, cried out in its stagnation and poverty. The series of Romanian Police checkpoints along the routes that Colonel Roskowski had filed with the Romanians for his tour allowed the Romanian Police to track the progress of their trip. The Air Attaché, Colonel Biff Rosedale, accompanied Bronko, which allowed both attachés to use their ever-present touring cameras and binoculars as they passed in the vicinity of the Romanian Army and Air Force installations. Both attachés were experienced senior officers, adept at their assignments. They did nothing to put

General Lowe at risk or to arouse the suspicions of the Romanian Security Forces. Nevertheless, the very fact that the American officers were driving alone under surveillance well behind the Iron Curtain was sufficient, Bart found out, to increase the adrenaline flow.

The trip and the border crossing into Yugoslavia passed without incident. In Belgrade Colonel Bronko Roskowski turned General Lowe and Colonel Martin over to his colleague, Air Force Colonel Gene Gregory, the U.S. Defense Attaché for Yugoslavia. Gregory informed Bart that there was no new information concerning the visas for General Lowe's visit to the Soviet Union. Following that disappointing note, Colonel Gregory pointed out that there was considerable DAS message traffic and phone calls waiting for the General at DAO, Belgrade.

The most sobering information Bart took away from the Belgrade visit was how fractious the country was. Yugoslavia, the country team pointed out time and time again, was many countries and peoples loosely lashed together. The Croats, Slovenians, Serbs, Bosnians, people from Herzogovenia, Montenegro and Macedonia; the list was almost endless and the differences between the peoples seemed intractable. Colonel Gregory, whose ancestors came from Serbia, was confident that Yugoslavia posed no threat to anyone outside its borders.

"The threat, if there is one," he said, "is internal." He described Yugoslavia as a powder keg with a slow burning fuse. "The fuse," he said, "is already lit and while no one knows exactly when the powder keg is going to blow, one day it will."

Bart found the DAO to be in good shape, working well within the embassy. There were some minor personnel problems with the in-country FAO students concerning their housing and mail, and Bart realized that DAO Belgrade hadn't fared well with the attaché budget. Its fleet of vehicles was old and mostly unrepairable. He intended to correct those shortcomings.

On Friday night, the Gregorys treated Bart to an excellent mixed grill platter at a local restaurant. When they returned to the residence, he had a nightcap with Gene, discussed a wrap-up of the visit and then went upstairs about 10:00 to finish packing.

At 11:15 as Bart was reading the second mystery novel he had brought along on the trip, he heard the phone ringing downstairs. Shortly thereafter there was a knock on his door.

"Yes."

"General Lowe? Sorry to bother you, but Brigadier General Alton in Moscow is on the phone for you."

"Okay, Gene. Give me a minute." Bart pulled on the sweatsuit he planned to wear on the plane the next day and hurried down the stairs to where Colonel Gregory was holding the phone. "Erv, what's up?"

"General, you are not going to believe this, but the Soviets have released the hold on yours and Colonel Martin's visas. The green light is on if you can still make it."

"Well, I'll be damned, Erv. Any explanation for the delay or the turnaround?"

"None at all. It's just their way. They may tell us why sometime; then again, we may never know."

"Well, if we can make the necessary travel arrangements, we will be on our way as soon as possible. I wouldn't want to miss Moscow. Many thanks, my friend, and we'll be in touch."

"Roger that and out here," Erv Alton signed off.

Lowe then turned to Gene and said, "Can we reach George Martin?"

"Yes, sir," replied Colonel Gregory, retrieving the telephone and dialing the number of the air attaché quarters where George was staying. George came on the line in less than thirty seconds and Gregory returned the phone to a pacing Bart Lowe.

"George?'

"Yes, sir."

"The Sovs have just released the visas; if it's not too late I want to cancel the trip to the United States and get the trip back on track to Moscow. Can we do it?"

"Not a problem, boss. I didn't give up all our contingencies, and I believe that I can get us on an Aeroflot flight to Moscow tomorrow afternoon. When you wake up in the morning, I'll have all the details for you," George said in his most confident and optimistic voice.

"Great! See you in the morning. Evil Empire, here we come."

CHAPTER 12

THE KREMLIN

George worked his magic and was able to re-book their original reservations for the Saturday afternoon Aeroflot flight from Belgrade to Moscow. The flight was almost forty-five minutes late and Bart and George were among the last to board. They were escorted by an Aeroflot representative to their seats in the rear compartment, reserved for non-USSR passport holders and diplomats. The rear compartment windows of the Aeroflot triple engine jet were covered to preclude any unwanted photography or observation. Fortunately, there were only three other individuals in the rear compartment, so Bart and George had plenty of space for the four-hour flight. The Russian flight attendants actually were quite helpful. They spoke some English and seemed puzzled when Bart turned down their offer of complimentary vodka.

Bart used the flight time to review again the briefing papers he had brought along describing the history, background and economy of the USSR. Not knowing what to expect, he and George were careful not to include anything classified.

The Aeroflot flight did not make up the time lost in its late departure and arrived at Moscow's Sheremetyevo Airport shortly after dark, one hour behind schedule. There was no sign of Erv Alton, but an Aeroflot representative arrived to escort the rear compartment passengers to the area for processing foreign visitors and diplomats. After a short walk through a series of vacant corridors, they arrived at a large, controlled hallway with approximately six lines of people. Two lines were for diplomats. Bart and George were left by the Aeroflot representative in the shorter of the two lines. Twenty minutes later, they were in front of two uniformed passport control officers who methodically examined their black diplomatic passports and the Russian customs cards they had filled out on the aircraft. When they noted that Bart and George were U.S. military, they also demanded to see their military I.D. cards.

There was a certain disdain on the part of the two Russian officials toward Lowe and Martin, but it was difficult to tell if it was because they were American, or because Bart and George were just two more in an endless line to be processed through the cumbersome Russian bureaucracy.

When they left the passport control desk they were directed through two large doors to the baggage waiting area. This large public area was not unlike other international airports of the world except for the large number of uniformed people in the room. Bart immediately spotted Brigadier General Erv Alton's 6'4" frame; he was with Colonel Gordon Sojak, the Army Attaché, waiting at the exit from the passport room.

"Welcome to Moscow," both men chimed.

"I hope you received word on our delay and haven't been waiting too long," Bart said.

"Gordon came out early because we are never certain whether arriving flights will be early or late. He called me as soon as you were in-bound and I've just been here a few minutes," Erv replied.

"Sir, we are going to suggest that we depart into Moscow now and not wait for your baggage," Colonel Sojak said. "The Russians take their time on the baggage, and it's not unusual for them to take up to six hours before they will release it. One of the Russian nationals we employ will pick it up for you as long as he has the Aeroflot claim tickets."

The four men left the airport in a large carry-all driven by one of the DAO Moscow NCOs. "General Lowe, the drive into the embassy will take about 40 minutes. Right from the get-go I want to point out something that my predecessor, Admiral Chomko, pointed out to me," Erv Alton announced. "Please take note of the road. It is about 20 miles of the very best road in the entire country."

By this time, they had left the airport service road and were on what Bart assumed was the main road to Moscow. Because it was dark, he couldn't tell much about it, although it was heavily traveled, judging from the number of vehicles that were coming and going. It was a four-lane highway and seemed to be well paved based on the fairly smooth ride of their van.

"The Russians spend a lot of time on this road, repaving, filling pot holes, etc.," Alton added. They know this road will be the first thing visitors coming to Russia will notice and they want it to make a good impression. Generally it does; except, you can feel the van going up and down and rolling slightly."

"Feels like a road with many little hills, doesn't it?" Erv asked. "This is what it's like the whole stretch to Moscow. The road's not level. When they built the road they did not do, as we do in the States, go to the extra expense of reinforcement in order to achieve a level road. And it wasn't because they didn't understand the technology or have the capability. They made a conscious decision not to incur the extra expense of proper leveling. Now think about that. The world's second leading super power; a country with the world's largest and most lethal armed forces; and, a country with the technological know-how to build nuclear weapons, intercontinental ballistic missiles, backfire bombers, nuclear submarines, satellites, and laser guided-weapons. But no level roads. And this is the best road in the entire country. When you leave Moscow, it's like going back into an 18th-century agricultural countryside. When a country like the Soviet Union plows almost every available ruble back into military technology something, somehow, sometime has got to give. That's my main thesis for the cracks in the Kremlin wall," Erv Alton explained, with more than a little emotion. "There are other things I plan to point out to you during this visit."

"Music to my ears, Erv," Bart assured him.

"Well, so much for now. Tomorrow we will give you the Cooks' Tour of Moscow. We'll start with the Kremlin, Lenin's Tomb, and the changing of the guard at the Grave of the Russian Unknown Soldier. We'll give you a riding tour of the city. There's an afternoon bus tour that Intourist runs and, believe me, it's the best way to see everything of interest in Moscow. I know you speak some Russian, but the guides speak excellent English. They give you the major highlights of Russian history and every building and monument of interest in the city. You'll have to put up with the liberties they take with history and a good amount of pure propaganda.

We will spend Monday at the embassy, meet all our people, and call on the Ambassador, DCM, COS and a few others. Tuesday, we'll go to the Foreign Military Liaison Office for a visit with the attaché czar, Admiral Krutznov, then tour the Kremlin Armory and the Russian War Museum at the Red Army Frunze Academy.

"Tonight Ashlyn and I are planning a light dinner at our quarters to give you a chance to meet some attachés and their wives. Gordon and his wife Sonja will be joining us. The rest of the week depends on what we can get the Russians to agree to."

"Why is that, Erv?"

"You asked us to arrange visits to two other Russian cities. Our original request to the Russians was for Leningrad and Kiev. When they released your visas last night, they gave the okay for Leningrad, provided your visit is an Intourist escorted tour. They said nothing about Kiev; it may be only an oversight but we expect they left it off on purpose. It is their way of exercising control. They wouldn't want to be too accommodating."

"I see," said Bart.

"We have already gone back for clarification," Erv continued, " but right now we are just planning on Leningrad. The way it will work is for you to go up on the train at midnight on Tuesday. They won't book anything on the day trains—afraid you might see—too much. There's really not much to see, but if you are willing to stay up and it's a clear night, you'll get a good feel for the Russian countryside and the people. The train makes many stops. We'll send Lieutenant Colonel Boyle with you. He's a Marine, one of our Assistant Naval Attachés. Leningrad is his beat."

"I have taken the train through East Germany to Berlin. This sounds similar," Bart commented.

"I think that's true," Erv agreed. "There's a regular contingent of the Soviet Baltic Fleet in Leningrad and Boyle spends considerable time up there at our consulate. The Russians would prefer that you begin the tour in Moscow and have Intourist fly you up, but we think our option is better. We are telling them that you wish to spend the day at the consulate. There isn't really much going on at the consulate, but we have an apartment in the consulate that Colonel Boyle uses, so if you don't get any sleep on the train, you can grab a couple of hours there. Boyle can take you around the city. Then we'll tell the Russians that your business at the consulate will be finished at 1700 hours, and they can pick you up there."

"Sounds good to me," Bart said.

"They will insist that you stay at one of their Intourist Hotels, and they will stay by your side the rest of the visit. It will be heavily weighted on the cultural side and their economic successes. One of the places they will take you is the Hermitage Museum. It is one of the finest in the world and they are very proud of it. The art collection there rivals the Louvre."

"I've heard about the Hermitage for years, Erv, and wondered if it is really as good as they say?"

"I am sure you won't be disappointed," Erv replied. "Your Intourist guide may be a woman. They tend to do that with Americans. Male or female the guide will certainly be KGB. And they may attempt to get you into a compromising situation. The ambassador is a little worried about that. I assured the ambassador that you were capable of looking after yourself."

"Let's hope you are right Erv," Bart said.

"If they try to pull any fast stuff, and I don't think they will, all you need to do is call a halt to the tour and demand that they return you to the U.S. Consulate. Lieutenant Colonel Boyle will be standing by in the event that you need any assistance. You will have his phone number and the consulate's number. I don't think you will have any problems. From what I can tell most of the incidents embarrassing to Americans happened because the individuals themselves didn't use good judgment and allowed themselves to get into compromising situations. As we now have it scheduled, you will spend Wednesday, Thursday, and Friday in Leningrad, then take the train back Friday night."

Lowe nodded his understanding; then Colonel Sojak picked up the brief. "General Lowe, we found the Aeroflot flights to Frankfurt and New York on Saturday and Sunday are booked. There is, however, a Saturday afternoon flight to Berlin, and we have made reservations. Although it gets into Berlin after all the flights to the States have departed, you can remain overnight there and get a good night's sleep and catch the Pan American Sunday morning flight to New York. It makes for a better day. If that sounds okay to you, we'll press on and work out all the details with George Martin. By the way, the Sovs did not approve the Leningrad portion for George. That is not too unusual. They probably figure they will have a better shot at you alone."

"But don't worry about Colonel Martin; I am sure we can find something to keep him busy at the embassy," added Alton. "By the way, George, you will be staying with Jack Ryder, the Air Attaché. He and the Naval Attaché, Captain Teswillenger, and their wives, will also be there to meet us at my quarters for dinner."

When they arrived at the U.S. Embassy, an old Russian pre-revolution building in downtown Moscow, they entered a side gate to the large U.S. compound and went directly to Brigadier General Alton's quarters. The Altons lived in a comfortable modern townhouse, one of 75 quarters inside the compound. The Alton's townhouse had just been completed the year before and was a welcome relief, according to Ashlyn Alton, from the old, cold and dreary apartment provided by the Russians miles away from the embassy. The family housing constructed under U.S. specifications at the embassy compound was only about half completed with another 75 units still to be built. The very desirable units had gone to the largest families and the senior State and Defense Department people first. Eventually all embassy personnel would be living at the embassy compound. The morale of those living inside the compound had improved greatly when they were relieved of the burden of uncomfortable living conditions in old apartments and the cumbersome commute across Moscow each day. Even though it was dark as they entered the compound, it was impossible to miss the large multiple-story red brick skyscraper-like building that was to be the "new" U.S. Embassy standing behind the old four-story U.S. Embassy.

Bart's first night in the capital of the "Evil Empire" was a restful one. He slept until 6:00 a.m.; he and Erv Alton then went for a 30-minute run, taking several laps around the inside of the embassy compound. When they returned to the quarters, the Altons' Russian nanny, Olga, had cups of hot tea laced with honey, and freshly baked Russian bagels waiting for them. The bagels were served with sour cream and homemade currant jam, compliments of Olga. Olga had been passed on from the Alton's predecessor, and she served the Alton family well. She was a traditional grey "Babushka" in her mid-fifties who wore the full skirt, blouse, and long great coat of her working class. Olga was never without a shawl over her head when going to and from the embassy compound. She had an outgoing personality and was quick to tell stories about Americans she had served in the 20-odd years she had been working for the U.S. Embassy.

Erv Alton revealed there was no doubt Olga was one of "theirs" as compared to one of "ours." "It is," he said, "one of those things you must take for granted in the Soviet Union. Olga is a prime example of a whole host of people who have learned to survive during the Cold War by working both sides of the street."

On the Sunday Intourist bus tour Bart and George were seated by three new Assistant Attachés and their spouses, all in their first month of service in Moscow. None were old Russian hands and Bart recognized them from the attaché training classes. The English speaking tour was completely booked; the two Intourist guides spoke perfect "King's English."

The January day was bitter cold and all the bus riders wore coats, hats and gloves. The bus was well heated (only the Intourist ones were), and the sky was crystal clear and deep blue. The guides' emphasis was on Russian history and the achievements of the past, and the tour covered every major monument, building, memorial park and cathedral in the Russian capital. To Bart's mind the tour and the dialogue from the two Intourist guides were subtle attempts to get the visitor to think of Russia in positive terms of the glorious past, the time of the Czars, The Napoleonic Wars, Peter the Great, Marshall Zhukov, and all the other great Russians, rather than the Communist government of the present.

One of the new assistant attachés, an Army Major, Tom Jethro, and his wife spoke excellent Russian and each time they asked a question in Russian about present-day conditions in Moscow or the Soviet Union, the guides always answered in English, skillfully avoided any confrontation.

But, the two highlights of the day were the visit to Red Square and the famous Russian Bolshoi Theater. Red Square was all he had ever seen in films or May Day parades: the gigantic Kremlin walls, the onion-shaped towers, thousands of people in the square standing in line to file past Lenin, the goose-stepping guards at the Tomb and the ever-present Soviet soldiers with their weapons and armored vehicles in the not-so-subtle background. All of these images moved against a backdrop of hundreds of red flags.

Near the end of the tour the guides took the group into the massive Bolshoi Theater, home of the Russian Ballet. That day, fortunately, the Red Army Band was rehearsing for a concert to be given that evening. The tour group was seated half-way down the orchestra section, and after they had heard the history of the Bolshoi they were treated to a Russian overture that had been written after the Russian victory in WWII, played by the Red Army Band. The music was spectacular and stirring. While the seats were somewhat smaller and a lot less comfortable than those in American theaters, the acoustics were impressive. The Red Army Band was on a par with the best of the military service bands in Washington.

Dinner that night was in an Intourist restaurant in downtown Moscow. When their tour arrived, the restaurant was full, apparently with other Intourist tours. Bart's group was taken to the second floor of the restaurant to a room that was somewhat like a terrace with many windows and a good view of the center of the city. Waiters immediately took drink orders and offered several of the best known European brands of liquor and beers. Bart asked for a Russian vodka and ice water. After the beverages, English menus were passed out and Bart was surprised to see that the menu contained most entrees a visitor would find in any country in Europe. The waiters pointed out that, unfortunately, only the chicken or fish entrees were available. Some excuses were made half-heartedly by the guides, but Major Jethro told Bart this was typical of the Intourist restaurants—a flashy menu to impress, but only a very limited offering in reality. Other restaurants in Moscow, he said, were often closed for days at a time because there was no food supply, and most of what they did serve, when they could, came from the black market.

The dinner was palatable, nothing to write home about, and the service was less than enthusiastic. But, the Russian vodka was numbingly good, as Bart had always heard. At the end of the evening he tried his rusty Russian to express his appreciation to the Intourist guides. He despaired at how obviously intelligent and well educated people could live a life of such obvious subterfuge and duplicity. When he crawled into bed that night he was pleased with his tour, but was anxious to see what the official side of the USSR looked like.

The next morning began at 7:30 in the embassy chancellery in Erv Alton's office. Erv had blocked an hour and a half for his update briefing to General Lowe.

"It's hard to believe that almost five months have gone by since I first met you in your office in Rosslyn," Erv said to Bart. "You told me that you had hardly been in your job long enough to know what yours' was, much less mine. You did say, as I recall, that I was about to take charge of the largest DAO in the world, the most active and aggressive. Your charge to me was to take care of our people, keep those reports coming, hold down the PNGs and rapidly inform all those who needed to know."

"That's it in a nutshell, Erv, and let me say you and your team have done a superlative job.

"Thank you, sir," Erv said, with a big grin. "We aim to please."

Erv Alton was not your run-of-the-mill career military officer. He had attended the Air Force Academy excelling in academics and athletics, and his basketball skills had netted several offers from the pros. He elected to accept a Rhodes Scholarship instead, but was severely disappointed when he learned in his senior year that he had a latent vision problem disqualifying him from ever flying high performance aircraft. Erv subsequently separated from the active Air Force, became a reserve officer and completed his studies for a doctorate in Russian and Slavic history. He spent many years at a midwestern college teaching history. In his mid-forties the Air Force Academy asked him to be the Dean of Academics with the tenure of a Brigadier General. After three years at Colorado Springs, Erv Alton was amazed, he said, when the Air Force told him they were going to recall him to active duty as a Brigadier General and nominate him to be the Defense Attaché to Moscow.

He and Ashlyn had been surprised by this development but decided it was probably going to be the adventure of a lifetime and they both eagerly said yes. Erv, who earlier had studied the Russian language in his academic days, went into a six month total emersion refresher course and finished the course as an excellent linguist.

"General Lowe, I don't have any other embassy experience to compare this with, so let me just describe what we see going on here, and you can be the judge of how it tracks with other places. The U.S. Ambassador here is definitely the outside man. He is a political appointee, well qualified to dialogue with the Russians, but the points of contention are so great that he spends most of his time either at the Kremlin, the Foreign Ministry or recalled to the States for consultation. The poor guy hardly has any life of his own. The DCM runs the embassy and takes on all of the support problems which, to use your words, 'are monumental.' Some problems you know about—the new embassy building problems, and the question of resupplying foodstuffs for the embassy commissary. No matter what they are paying the DCM here, it's not enough."

"And the rest of the embassy, Erv?"

"The rest of the Embassy, our DAO, the POL/MIL Section, the other U.S. agencies, the COS, all pretty much go their own way. The pace of life is so fast, and the demand from many places so heavy, that you don't pay much attention to what the other guy is doing. You just press on with your own mission." After a short pause to refill their coffee cups, Erv continued. "All our attaché activities are conducted openly. For years, the DAO has had several official sources who provided us information regularly. We get our information in essentially two ways. One, through our intensive contact with military officials here in Moscow, or two, by touring the countryside, observing the Soviet Military forces and weapons, weapons testing, and where the weapons and forces are deployed. The Soviets know this and take every action they can to prevent us from touring."

"Judging from the number of reports the DAO generates, the Soviets haven't been able to hold you back," Lowe commented.

"When you asked me to hold down the number of persona non grata cases, I took that as a first order of business when I arrived. I found then that the attachés often were taking one person tours. That increased their vulnerability. I changed that to make it mandatory for two or more people on a tour. That way, if a chance to collect information presents itself, one attaché can do the collecting while the other watches his back. So far so good. No PNGs. Of course I can't control what may happen in Washington if the FBI busts any Soviet military attachés. Then the Sovs here will reciprocate. And they will select someone without cause, usually someone who has just arrived, knowing that we do not have anyone in the pipeline to replace him, and we will be shorthanded for some time. The old timers who have been here before say that this reciprocity thing is very big with the Russians. They say something may happen to them in Washington, caused by Americans, or even someplace else in the world, and the Sovs will use that to take away something from us here."

"Tell me about how much our people are watched by the Soviets," Bart asked.

"The Soviet surveillance of our attachés is around the clock and intense. Their guys are good at it. But they do so much of it, including watching all the other country attachés, that sometimes they get careless, and that is when we make a hit. Even though we may lose surveillance, often someone at the target we are trying to cover still may see us and report it. When that happens, Admiral Krutznov will haul me in on the carpet, rant and rave and threaten to have the attachés PNG'ed. We, of course, deny any wrongdoing and blame the poor Soviet road markings and lack of reliable maps. And believe me, you can get lost almost anywhere in this country. By the way Krutznov is a piece of work. He is like something out of a James Bond movie. He really plays the role. But I don't know if his heart is really in it. Sometimes I have the feeling he is going through the motions because that's his job."

"Erv, what about the case of those three Russian officers that you mentioned to me in Garmisch?" Bart asked, looking for any HEAT SEEKER connection without tipping his hand.

"That remains a mystery. The officers were literally here in Moscow one day and gone the next, along with their families. 'Transferred' was the official explanation."

Erv complimented the DAS targeting and feedback system Bart had initiated. He said it greatly simplified the ever-present question in the attachés' mind of what priorities would yield the most important results.

Bart had a number of questions regarding the operational techniques of the attachés, and wanted specifics about the equipment and logistic support of the DAS.

Erv made a plea for a new fleet of European built vehicles. His present ones were old and difficult to maintain. He also asked for two additional civilian admin personnel to help with the increasing volume of information reports prepared by the DAO.

"Now Erv, in the remaining 10 minutes or so before I move on to see the DAO and the rest of this huge embassy, tell me more about the JCS Chairman's sixty-four thousand dollar question on cracks in the Kremlin wall," Bart asked.

"I guess my bottom line is that it's too soon for me to know. I haven't been here long enough to form any hard judgments. I would tell you though that my first impressions tell me the chairman is probably right. The underlying current is that dramatic change is waiting in the wings. What will trigger that change—or if it has already been triggered, what caused it—is not clear. Many think Gorbachev's days are numbered and that the old time hard-liners will rise up, dispense with Gorbachev and get things back on the hard line track. I just don't know yet. The DCM and the Pol/Mil crowd here want to review anything we are putting out except pure military equipment reporting. They are, of course, being asked the same questions and don't want to be second guessed or surprised. One new significant area is that some of our long standing requests for our attachés to call on Soviet senior military officers, even their retired ones, which have always been stonewalled, now are being reconsidered. I hope you read my cable on that subject. The chairman called me and said he was very interested, and told me to let him know when there are any developments." At that point Alton looked at the clock on his wall and said, "Since we have run out of time and we want to keep you on this killer schedule, let me suggest we take up that discussion tonight at dinner at a place in Moscow we want to show you."

Bart looked at his watch, then at Erv Alton and nodded his head in agreement.

Bart spent the remainder of the morning in the Defense Attaché Office, meeting the rest of the staff, and receiving briefings from each of the service attachés on their special areas of interest within the Soviet Military. After visiting the embassy motor pool to see the wear and tear on the DAO vehicles, Lowe and Alton paid a hurried call on the ambassador, then had a working lunch with the Deputy Chief of Mission.

The rest of the day was spent on short calls on the other principal offices in the embassy and with George Martin for a quick review of other DAS business from headquarters. The last appointment of the day was at five o'clock with CIA's Chief of Station. Erv dropped Bart off at the COS office and said he would meet Bart back at the DAO.

George Kamamyer, the COS, was a slight, thin man, bespectacled and with receding hair. He was conservatively dressed and looked as though he could blend into any crowd. Bart's first impression was that Kamamyer had the perfect nondescript appearance to be a professional spy. After offering Lowe a cup of coffee, which Bart accepted, he introduced his deputy and then made the usual small talk of "How's the trip going? What have you seen so far?"

Then, out of the blue, he said, "Look, unless you have some specific questions, I'll just tell you that Erv and I arrived about the same time here, hit it off right away, and there aren't any problems between us. He and his people are always helpful, and I try to be helpful to them whenever I can. We pretty much go our separate ways."

This last comment was made in such a way that Bart thought the meeting was over. He started to get up out of his chair when Kamamyer continued. "General Lowe, I do have a matter I would like to discuss with you. But, I would rather discuss it in the bubble down the hall."

Lowe followed Kamamyer out of the COS offices, down the corridor to a separate door guarded by a Marine sentry. Once the sentry verified their access badges, they passed into a clear, totally self-contained plastic bubble containing a small conference table and several chairs. Bart knew U.S. Embassies around the world had sterile security facilities to permit the discussion of sensitive information without fear of clandestine listening devices or other technical intrusion devices.

After sitting down, George Kamamyer said, "General, I understand you are cleared for HEAT SEEKER, and I have received permission from my headquarters to discuss it with you." With that, he reached into his coat pocket and took out a cable, which he handed to Lowe from the CIA headquarters at Langley. It verified Lowe's access to HEAT SEEKER and gave permission for Kamamyer to talk with General Lowe, provided no other person was present. Bart read the cable, acknowledged its contents and looked at Kamamyer.

Then the quiet, up-to-now conservative appearing gentleman across the table from Bart, suddenly jumped up, removed his coat, threw it into the next chair, and with considerable agitation said, "I don't know how much you really know about this fucking disaster, but it's driving me and my people up the wall."

Bart was completely surprised by Kamamyer's outburst, and braced himself for some kind of salvo that was going to blame him or the DAS for whatever Kamamyer was so exercised about.

But as quickly as his outburst had taken place, it quickly passed, and then Kamamyer said, "General, please forgive me. It is just that this thing has been so frustrating and yet so closely held in the Moscow station that it is difficult sometimes to control my feelings. Part of the frustration is that we are not at liberty to discuss HEAT SEEKER with anyone at the embassy. Even the ambassador and the DCM have only the briefest data and none of your people or the State Department people have access. I thought it might be helpful to go over some of the details with you to see if you can throw additional light on the subject from your vantage point."

Bart told Kamamyer he was willing to do so, but held little hope that he could be helpful.

"General, I believe HEAT SEEKER first began in the fall of 1985. I was serving as the Assistant COS in Bonn at that time and was working with a young KGB major who was posted to Bonn as a TASS correspondent. He was among the best KGB agents we had ever recruited. He was particularly helpful to us in determining what the KGB and Glavnoye Razvedyvatelnoye Upravleniye (GRU) military intelligence targets were in Europe. This information allowed the U.S. and NATO military to plan against Soviet efforts. One night he didn't show up for a meeting, and we never heard from him again. We later learned he was returned to Moscow and executed. This was also the same time frame that some of the agents in the military service operations began to disappear. Frankly, at the time, I never connected the two. Then by the summer of 1986, when I returned to Washington and learned that I was coming here, I was shocked to find out that more than 20 Russian CIA agents had been compromised, given long prison terms or had been executed. This number did not include the military service agents.

At first CIA thought it could place the blame on the CIA defector Edward Howard who showed up in Moscow in 1986. When we looked at Howard's access list we found he was familiar with some of the agents, but by no means all. And since he defected the compromises and arrests have continued. As you know, we had to investigate the possibility that we had been penetrated. Langley and the FBI formed task forces to work the problem, and HEAT SEEKER was born. The problem is I haven't seen any progress in Washington in getting to the bottom of this. My people—hell, me and my people are running scared for our own operations and for the poor guys who came over to work for us. The word is out on the street, and this thing has damn near shut us down. What is even worse, I'm not convinced that CIA headquarters really gives a damn." Kamamyer paused and let out a deep breath.

"After Howard defected all Chiefs of Station and attachés had to purge their files, break contact with their sources and figure out new ways to contact them without putting their safety at risk. And still the spate of compromises and arrests continue. What happened here, in Bonn and elsewhere has been put into the HEAT SEEKER investigation but has still not answered the questions. Assuming the Soviets are still getting information on our sources and agents here, that still would not be enough to account for the

CIA and military service agents rolled up in other places. But if the Sovs are able to penetrate our communications and draw information from Langley, as we do, then that could explain HEAT SEEKER. And just suppose there is still someone in this or some other embassy in, say, the DAO or State Department or my station, who assists the KGB? Someone who has been doing it for years, someone at my headquarters, or your headquarters?" Kamamyer stopped his burst of information momentarily.

"General, you are probably wondering what's my bottom line? Well, my bottom line is this: We are sitting astride a catastrophic problem that is costing us dearly in lost information. HEAT SEEKER has already taken a number of lives and will certainly take more if we don't solve this puzzle. If there is anything you can do in Washington to light a fire under HEAT SEEKER to give it more of a sense of urgency, please do so."

Bart told Mr. Kamamyer that the information he had shared would be helpful as he continued to investigate the impact of HEAT SEEKER on the DAS and U.S. military. Bart now believed events in Moscow were linked to the DAO in Vienna and the military operations in Germany. Too many questions, so few answers, he thought.

When Bart returned to the DAO, Erv Alton was curious why Bart had spent so much time with George Kamamyer. Bart told him that it concerned a matter in the United States involving the DAS and CIA headquarters. Erv accepted that, not pushing any further for information, and reiterated that he and the COS got along great. Bart made a mental note to request that Erv be added to thc HEAT SEEKER access list when he returned to Washington.

Bart awakened the next morning to the kind of weather he had always imagined in Moscow in January. The skies were grey, and wet snow was falling steadily. And like any major city in the world confronting snow, the early morning traffic was snarled, moving at a snail's pace. After a breakfast of yogurt, poached eggs, and black bread toast, Bart and Erv left for the DAO to review what Lowe might encounter in his ten o'clock appointment with Admiral Krutznov. Upon arriving at the DAO, General Lowe and Brigadier General Alton spent the first 30 minutes reviewing the previous night's cable traffic. With coffee mugs in hand Bart and Erv settled into the two easy chairs in the corner of his office.

"Up until now you have seen what I would call the more pleasant side of Russia. You are now about to see the other side of the Russians. I call it the Soviet side," Erv declared. "When we go to see old Krutznov we never know what to expect, but I can't think of a single time in my dealings with him that he has even been close to civil. Don't be too surprised if he comes up with some grievance or some favor he expects you to perform for the Russian Attaché Corps in Washington. Although he speaks perfect English—he served as the Soviet Naval Attaché to Great Britain when he was a Captain—he will only speak to you in Russian. They will provide a translator for you and I will allow him or her to translate for you unless they miss the meaning. Sometimes when something is particularly offensive, the translator will try to soften the offensive word or thought."

"Does the meeting take place in his office?" Bart asked.

"No, and that's another point I want to explain. The meeting will not be held in the Kremlin. They have a Foreign Military Liaison Office several blocks from the Kremlin in a building used exclusively for the purpose of meetings with foreign attachés. The meeting will be in a large conference room with all the trappings of a Spanish inquisition. We will be the first to arrive and be seated at one end of a long table. He will probably keep us waiting. They will put on the table a tray containing bottled water and three or four Russian soft drinks to give the impression of hospitality but no one ever offers you anything. It is like so many things here—strictly for show. I always insist on having something, usually the bottled water, just to make them go through the motions. One time I asked for soft drinks, and it must have taken them ten minutes to find an opener." With that Erv looked at his watch and said, "With the new snow we need to get underway. It will take a while to get there and if we were to be late, they would probably cancel the meeting."

The trip across Moscow in the 4-wheel drive DAO vehicle was slow, but they arrived at five minutes to the hour. The building was an old one with a brick security wall around it. The vehicle passed through the guarded gate after the U.S. Embassy diplomatic cards were shown to the Ministry of Internal Affairs (MVD) Security Guard.

Bart and Erv, in Army green and Air Force blue uniforms, were let out at the front entrance and were met by a short, youngish-looking major in the green uniform of the Red Army.

"This is Major Tutlov," Brigadier General Alton said, and introduced the major to General Lowe.

"Major Tutlov is from the Foreign Military Liaison Protocol Office. He is one of the good Russians, and is almost helpful sometimes. Right, Major Tutlov?" Erv inquired.

"I don't know what you mean by that, General Alton, but please let's make haste," he said, leading the way inside the building and up a set of stairs toward the second floor. "We don't want to be late for the Admiral."

"Not likely," remarked Brigadier General Alton.

On their way to the meeting room, they passed eight armed, grey uniformed MVD security guards including one in front of the meeting room door. Bart wondered what they could possibly be guarding. It seemed like an unnecessary show of force. Once inside the meeting room, it did indeed seem like something from a James Bond movie. There was a small anteroom with a single chair and a coat rack. The men hung their coats and hats there and went into the large adjacent meeting room. The ceilings were 16 feet high. The two side walls were covered with heavy red velvet drapes, the back wall with long red hammer-and-sickle flags, and the windows overlooking the courtyard were heavily draped, allowing hardly any light into the room. There were a half dozen straight-back chairs around the walls, and in the center of the room was an old, long, heavy wooden conference table. Four chairs had been placed at the table; two near the end of the table and one at the opposite far end, presumably for Krutznov. One chair had been set up half way down the table, probably for the translator, although Erv had said the translators often stood during the meetings. Small lamps high up on the walls scarcely lighted the room.

Just as Erv had predicted, a small tray containing four glasses and several small bottles that were set just out of reach of the two chairs Major Tutlov had designated for the American officers.

At five past the hour, Erv said to Major Tutlov, "Major, I assume you have advised Admiral Krutznov that General Lowe is here and waiting?"

"Of course, sir. I am sure that the Admiral will be here any minute. I am also sure the General knows that Admiral Krutznov is a very busy man," the Major replied, politely, but as if he had made this statement many times.

When five minutes more had passed, Erv said to Bart, "Sir, I suggest that we help ourselves to some of this delicious Russian water." Erv then rose, selected two bottles, opened them, and handed one to Bart.

Bart poured a glass of the water and tasted it; there was nothing special there. Bland water at room temperature.

At 10:15 and still no Krutznov, Erv said to Bart, "This is a game with them, and sometimes we have to play hard ball or they will just run over us. I'm going to tell Tutlov that if he can't produce Krutznov pronto, we are out of here. Okay, boss?"

"Erv, it's your turf and I'll back your judgment," Bart told him.

With that, Erv walked up very close to Major Tutlov, looked down at him with the appropriate amount of disdain and said, "Major, my patience has about run out. We have other appointments to keep, and we can't be sitting around here waiting all morning for your Admiral." Erv looked at his watch, turned again to the major and said, "Let me suggest that you inform the Admiral that if he is not here in three minutes we will be out of here and lodge an official complaint."

Major Tutlov and exited the door at the opposite end of the room. About two and one-half minutes later, Admiral Krutznov burst through the door. Both Erv and Bart rose from their chairs, thinking that Krutznov would come to the other end of the table to greet them and make some lame excuse for being late but, he merely sat down at his end of the table and immediately began a diatribe, so vitriolic that it even surprised General Alton. This tirade went non-stop for almost five minutes with Krutznov talking so fast that twice Major Tutlov told him he could not keep up the pace of the translation. The essence of the diatribe was:

"Esteemed General Lowe, welcome to Moscow and the glorious Union of Soviet Socialist Republics. I am glad you are finally here. Maybe now you can control your attachés. It is obvious that General Alton cannot. Your attachés conduct themselves like a bunch of bandits and hooligans. They are all over my country like horseflies. I can't keep track of them. They are everywhere, and always in places they shouldn't be."

Krutznov then read off a list of six U.S. attachés he said were suspected (he had said "guilty," but Major Tutlov changed it to "suspected") of many violations of Soviet rules governing foreign military attachés.

"It is becoming clear," the Admiral said, "that unless General Lowe can do something about the criminal conduct of his attachés that I will have no choice but to PNG the whole lot of them."

Erv Alton did not take kindly to this outrageous display of Russian theatrics by his chief tormentor, particularly in front of his boss. His face reddened and he began to respond to the Admiral's broadsides in crisp clear Russian.

Major Tutlov concluded his translations were no longer needed, and he sat silently while the Admiral and General Alton shouted at each other. Bart watched the whole procedure, understanding most of which was said.

Then, almost as abruptly as the "meeting" had begun, Admiral Krutznov stood and said, "General Lowe, I regret if I detained you unnecessarily this morning, but I am very busy with many important affairs of state and I must now go." With that, he turned and exited. Major Tutlov handled the final translation.

When they departed the Foreign Liaison compound Lowe said to General Alton, "Erv, I see what you mean about the Soviet side of Russia. What the hell was that all about?"

"To tell you the truth, I'm not sure I know. Even for Krutznov, who is a hard-liner, that display of temper and frustration is unusual. Krutznov might be under pressure from somewhere in his hierarchy. The alleged incidents he mentioned were all routine trumped-up charges that they regularly throw at us on any tour, no matter how innocuous. There is a routine procedure. They send a letter to the embassy saying it has been reported that on such and such a date an American military attaché was seen at such and such location. If this is true then it is a violation of such and such. All of these reports have been answered saying 'not so.' Maybe they heard of something that's going to happen to their people in Washington and they believe they must be ready to respond here."

"If something were about to happen in Washington, we should have been alerted by now. When we get back to the embassy I'll get to a secure line and call Chuck Gregorios and ask him to check it out," Bart told Erv.

The snowfall had increased and the return trip to the embassy took even longer than the morning trip. At noon, when Lowe and Alton walked back into the DAO, Colonel Martin and Captain Herb Teswillenger, the Naval Attaché, were waiting at Alton's office with concerned looks.

Martin spoke first. "Boss, this cable came in for you about an hour after you left the embassy this morning." He handed the message to Bart. "If we could have sent it to you before your meeting, we would have."

Bart read the message:

EYES ONLY FOR MAJOR GENERAL BARTON LOWE, DIRECTOR, DAS, CURRENTLY TDY TO US EMBASSY

MOSCOW FROM MR. CHARLES GREGORIOS, DEP DIR, DAS, WASH, D.C.
SUBJECT: SOVIET ATTACHÉS ARRESTED FOR ESPIONAGE

1. FYI, at 2345, 21 Jan 87, DAS OPNS CTN received notification that two Soviet Military Attachés had been arrested by the FBI in Arlington, VA for espionage. FBI has notified the Soviet Embassy here and will request PNG action by US State Department later today. A press release is scheduled for 0730 hours local. Follow up information, names and particulars of the Soviet Attachés will be passed to DAO, Moscow by the Eastern European Division as soon as received.

2. Based on past track record believe Soviets will quickly initiate reciprocal action against U.S. Military Attachés, Moscow. Regret to be bearer of bad news. Very Respectfully, Chuck - Deliver immediately upon receipt.

Bart quickly passed the message to Erv and after he read it, he said, "No point in jumping to any conclusions yet. I guess the ball is in Krutznov's court and we will have to wait until he makes his move."

General Lowe's afternoon visits were escorted by the Army Attaché Colonel, Gordon Sojak. Colonel Sojak was the "old Russian hand" on the DAO Moscow team and was confident in his dealings with the Russian Army General staff. As a result, he had been able to arrange a limited tour of the Russian War Museum and one of the Russian War colleges, the Frunze Academy. The Russian War Museum was fascinating to Bart, and although its major exhibits and themes were of WWII, it was impossible to leave there without appreciating the massive destruction and loss of life the Russian people and their military had suffered at the hands of the Germans during WWII.

Although the Russian officers who briefed Lowe at the Frunze Academy declined to answer all of Bart's questions on their current military tactics and training, it was clear to Bart that the lessons learned from the successful combinations of armor, artillery and infantry forces used in WWII formed the basis of current Russian military doctrine.

For Lowe's last night in Moscow, Colonel Sojak had planned an evening at an indoor ice rink near Gorky Park. The rink restaurant had only a few items of Russian fare for food, but it was spacious and could easily accommodate a large group. Most of the assistant attachés, and the staff of the DAO and their spouses attended in spite of the freshly falling snow in Moscow. Gordon had an extra pair of ice skates that fit Bart and although it had been years since Bart had ice skated, he managed to take several successful turns around the rink. After a few more turns around the ice, a hot bowl of potato soup, a chunk of black bread and a Russian beer tasted good. Bart shifted his conversation from table to table as the DAO people moved to and from the ice. It was a fun evening.

Gordon Sojak and George Martin accompanied Bart to the train station after he said his last good nights. Bart had packed a bag earlier and stowed it in Gordon's four-wheel drive DAO vehicle. George had worked out an emergency communication scheme with Lieutenant Colonel Dan Boyle and the U.S. Consulate in Leningrad in the event some message came along for General Lowe that absolutely could not wait.

Lieutenant Colonel Boyle, dressed in casual clothes, met them at the entrance of the train station and told them that everything was "A-O.K." The train was on time, the compartments were secured and Boyle had boarded the train and inspected the compartments. His baggage was on the train, and all they had to do was get the general aboard.

Bart and Dan Boyle had two adjoining compartments separated by only a door. Lieutenant Colonel Boyle joined Bart at his request for the first 30 minutes and gave Bart an idea of what they might see along the Russian countryside. Dan explained how to convert their bench seats into rough and narrow, but adequate beds. Each bed paralleled a window and Bart could easily see out to the passing countryside.

After Lieutenant Colonel Boyle departed, Bart stretched out on the bench seat as Boyle had suggested. The night passed quickly with smidgens of sleep, miles of rolling countryside, old houses and barns, blurs of MVD guards passing by, and many, mostly deserted, train stations. Sometime, well before dawn, as the train moved to the northwest of Leningrad and approached the coastal water and winds of the Gulf of Finland, the snow cover ended. When the train pulled into the old St. Petersburg station, close to its scheduled arrival time of 8:30, the sun was already moving upward in a cold, clear blue sky. With travel bags in hand, Bart Lowe and Dan Boyle walked out to the station entrance and found the DAO vehicle and driver waiting. As they pulled away from the curb and entered the early morning traffic pattern, Boyle called Bart's attention to the black Russian Lada sedan, the third car behind them.

"There's our tail. Whenever this vehicle or our other one leaves the compound, the tail begins and lasts as long as the vehicle is away from the consulate," Boyle explained.

"What if you leave the vehicle?" Bart asked.

"Depends on where you are. Sometimes they will dismount and follow you on foot; other times they will call for back up. If you just go downtown, they usually stay with the vehicle and record where you have been. We have some evasive techniques I can tell you about, but while you are here we will do nothing that could arouse suspicion. What I suggest we do, General, is go directly to the consulate—it's only 10 minutes away—and when we get there, I recommend you grab a couple of hours sleep. You're probably going to need them. We'll have lunch with the Consul General and then this afternoon I'll give you a tour of the harbor followed by a walk in downtown Leningrad. There's something there your Intourist guide may not show you."

Dan Boyle had been right. Bart needed the rest. After two hours sleep and a cold shower, he felt fresh and ready to enjoy lunch with the Consul General (CG). The CG was a middle-aged Foreign Service Officer who really knew Russia and particularly Leningrad.

For the next two hours after lunch Lieutenant Colonel Boyle showed Bart around Leningrad Harbor, including most of the ship works and the quay in the distance where the Soviet Navy's Baltic Sea ships and subs moved in and out of port. Boyle pointed out that while you could not see the ship's identifying numbers with a naked eye, binoculars brought that vital information into range easily. Dan Boyle impressed Bart with his knowledge of the Baltic Fleet's order of battle and the extensive information he could recite about each ship or submarine's characteristics. He told Bart an amazing story about the Soviet Naval Museum on the edge of the Leningrad Harbor. They drove by it, but did not go in. Boyle recommended that Bart tell the Intourist people that the Museum was one of the places he wanted to visit, and Boyle was sure they would accommodate him. The Museum contained, in model form, a replica of each of the Soviet Navy's ships and submarines. The scale models were almost exact and the details of each ship's, boat's or submarine's armament, electronic gear or any other characteristic that was visible on the outer shell of the crafts was configured exactly on the model.

When the Soviets launched a new ship or sub and U.S. surveillance had not yet visually picked it up, an attaché could visit the Naval Museum, discreetly photograph the model and send it home to U.S. Navy analysts who could begin to ascertain the new characteristics, sometimes before the ship or sub berthed in its new port. The driving force behind the timely delivery of the new ship's model to the Naval Museum was the Communist Government's strong desire that the Russian public, particularly school children, take pride in the sophisticated armaments of the nation.

The last highlight Boyle showed General Lowe was in downtown Leningrad where a "foot zone" had been created. This was akin to the malls and shopping zones in Europe and the United States where all vehicular traffic is prohibited, permitting shoppers to shop at their leisure and criss-cross from one side of the mall-like area to the other without having to worry about being hit by a vehicle. As he and Bart strolled along the "foot zone" Bart pointed out a large number of people with stands or carts in the zone selling items not found in the stores.

"General Alton calls this 'creeping capitalism.' And the government is letting it happen," Boyle explained. "Look at the people who are walking up and down here. Some Russians, but a significant number of tourists. The Russians are letting more and more tourists in for the hard currency it produces. This is the by-product they might not be able to curtail or turn it off. And one other thing General, see that young Russian over there?" Dan Boyle pointed out a neatly dressed short-haired man talking to a blond couple, probably Scandinavian, dressed in blue jeans and leather jackets.

"He has just offered them a huge amount of rubles for those jeans. He knows that they have paid an outrageous exchange rate in their own currency for rubles, and he is offering them black market rubles in the amount of three or four times what it will cost them to replace the jeans when they go back home. If they agree to the sale, the jeans will end up on one of these stalls. The remarkable thing is that the government is aware of this black market activity, and officials are just turning their heads, or as some believe, participating in it. I guess we might consider this one of those cracks in the Kremlin wall you are looking for, General."

"Yes indeed, Dan, yes indeed!"

Back at the U.S. Consulate at exactly 5:00, a black, official-looking Russian sedan pulled into the circular drive. A second sedan containing two men that appeared to be following the first car parked just outside the consulate drive entrance.

Bart had changed into a blue pin-striped suit and tie after he and Dan Boyle had returned to the consulate and proceeded to the lobby of the consulate with his travel bag to await his Intourist guide. He had watched the two cars pull up as he looked through the consulate lobby windows. From the first sedan a woman wearing a navy blue winter coat and a Russian fur hat, gloves and boots got out of the passenger side of the sedan and walked into the lobby of the consulate. At first she headed toward the Marine sentry in the glass guard booth, but then spotted Bart, the only person in the lobby, and walked up to him saying, "General Barton Lowe?"

"Yes," Bart replied.

"I am Tatayana Romanov from Intourist. I am here to take you to your hotel."

Bart offered his hand, which she quickly took and returned a firm, steady-handed shake. Before he could say anything else, she said, "Please don't ask if I am any relation to the former Russian Czar. It is my married name, and my husband is not related to that Romanov family."

"All right," Bart said, surprised by her directness.

Before he could say or do anything else, she picked his bag up, turned toward the door and said, "Please follow me."

The driver of the sedan, a slight man in a black suit, got out of the car, took the bag from Mrs. Romanov and placed it in the trunk. Mrs. Romanov asked Bart to get into the right rear passenger side. She went around the car and got into the seat beside him. Once they were underway, she reached into a small, imitation leather-like folder and removed a sheet of paper which she passed to him. It was an itinerary for his visit, typed in English on both sides of the page.

"This is a schedule for the time you will spend with us in Leningrad. I suggest you review it this evening at your hotel and if you have any questions, I will answer those for you in the morning. Should there be something missing from the schedule that you wanted to do in Leningrad then you can let me know and I will see if it is possible to arrange. You know, of course, that I cannot arrange for visits to any military installations or activities that are a part of state security." She looked purposefully at Lowe to make sure he understood before continuing.

"You will be staying at the Intourist Hotel Europa, a new hotel overlooking the harbor. It is the finest hotel in Leningrad. You must pay for your hotel room and any refreshments and food you have. Tickets to state sponsored cultural sites on your tour, such as the Hermitage Museum, will be complimentary for you, as our guest, but if you want me to act as your guide and accompany you, then you must pay for my tickets." Then she added, "I am sorry but it is the Intourist way."

Bart immediately sensed that she was a very proud woman who found discussing the financial arrangements awkward. When they arrived at the hotel, the driver turned Bart's travel bag over to a bellman. Mrs. Romanov accompanied him to the front desk. When she asked for his reservation, a discussion in Russian between her and the clerk ensued. Bart could tell that something was amiss.

After a few almost heated exchanges she turned to Bart and said, "There has been an error. When the reservation was made for you from Moscow, it said for one person—a single. The rooms have two beds, and in your room there is already one man. It means that you will have to share the room. Is that agreeable to you?"

Bart, obviously surprised, quickly replied. "No! That would be unacceptable. In my country we respect the privacy of the individual, and I expect you to honor that for me as your guest."

"I did not think so, but I was obliged to ask," Mrs. Romanov replied. Turning back to the clerk, she demanded to see the hotel manager.

From what Bart was able to understand from the discussion between the hotel manager and his Intourist guide, definitely heated, the manager was not about to take the blame for some Moscow bureaucrat's mistake and he wasn't sure he had the authority to change the reservation and give the American a private room. Mrs. Romanov, clearly the more determined of the two, finally convinced him that he did have the authority and that her boss would square it with Moscow.

A key was produced, and the bellman, Bart and Mrs. Romanov finally went up the elevator to a room on the eighth floor with a view overlooking the harbor—the civilian commercial side—not the Soviet Naval docks. After the bellman departed, Mrs. Romanov apologized profusely for the confusion at the front desk. As quickly as her anger surged, it subsided, and she returned to her role as Intourist guide.

"General Lowe, I think you will be comfortable in this room. Just call the desk if you require anything. This room is equipped with English explanations of the hotel facilities. The literature will tell you there is a hard currency bar with live music and a hard currency restaurant. That is where you should go for cocktails and dinner, but you must pay in dollars, no rubles."

Bart knew about the hard currency rule, a technique used by the Soviets to increase the flow of western money much needed into the country.

"If you have no further questions, I can meet you after breakfast, and we can begin our tour," Mrs. Romanov said. With a final, firm handshake, she left.

The next 48 hours were some of the most interesting of Bart Lowe's life. The good weather held and he was fascinated by the slices of Russian history that Tatayana Romanov ably and articulately described to him. The Hermitage tour was as good or better than Bart expected. The number of old Masters' paintings was astounding. But Tatayana's exceptional knowledge of art made that portion of the museum particularly memorable. Tatayana was able to juggle the Friday schedule to permit Bart's visit to the Soviet Naval Museum and the ship models were as Lieutenant Colonel Boyle had described them. Bart was also able to persuade Tatayana to show him where she lived. She could not, she said, risk taking him into her apartment, but she could take him to a future Five-Year City Plan display for Leningrad that sat in front of the Government housing building where she lived.

In every free moment, between explanations of what they were seeing and doing, Bart bombarded Tatayana with questions. At first she thought out each question and answer carefully, in order to decide if he had any hidden agenda. Once she was satisfied he did not, she answered candidly, quickly following with a question of her own. They both had insatiable appetites to learn as much as possible about the other's lives and country. By the afternoon of the third day, Tatayana was providing Bart with a basic course in Russian civics, the composition of the government, and how it worked in reality at the town and village level. Bart, in turn, was explaining the American democratic two-party system at national, state, and local levels.

The final evening of Bart's visit included attending a performance of Russian folk dancing, in kind of a dinner show building, and the ballet, where a rendition of Swan Lake, at the Kirlov Theater, proved exceptional in its artistry and simplicity. In looking at Tatayana and other Russians as they watched the ballet he could tell that the Soviet people held music and art in its many forms in the highest esteem.

In the final sad scene of Swan Lake, as the stage darkened, Tatayana discreetly reached for Bart's hand and squeezed it tightly, wanting, he suspected, to share the emotional moment. As the curtain fell, she quickly retrieved her hand and returned to her role as an efficient, articulate, and very professional Intourist guide.

Bart had checked out of the Hotel Europa before going to the ballet. Tatayana and the ever present KGB security escort accompanied Bart directly to the consulate from the Kirlov Theater. Lieutenant Colonel Boyle was waiting there in the DAO vehicle, ready to depart for Bart's train ride to Moscow.

After retrieving his bag from the Intourist driver and placing it in the DAO vehicle, Bart turned to Tatayana for one last firm handshake and said, "Mrs. Romanov, dasvedanya. You've made my visit to Leningrad one I will not forget. My sincere thanks to you and to Intourist. It is my hope that you and your family will someday have the opportunity to visit the United States. If you do, I hope you will come and see me."

"General Lowe, dasvedanya to you. Although I doubt it will be possible, I, too, hope to see you again."

And Bart Lowe saw a warmth in Tatayana's eyes that forever in time has transcended differences between people, politics, and countries.

Riding back that night on the train to Moscow, Bart reflected on what he had heard and learned from Tatayana. He pictured Tatayana along with a great number of other Russians born after WWII who grew up and were educated to love their country, and believe in the Communist Revolution for Russia and the world. They were raised to believe that Socialism offered the greatest good for the greatest number of people and they were taught to sacrifice whatever was necessary in their personal lives for the good of the State. They were proud of their sacrifices to protect the homeland against many enemies. There was always the promise of a better tomorrow. But as their youth passed, they became increasingly disappointed in the government and its lethargic performance in improving living conditions for the people. And as information about the alleged enemies and how the rest of the world lived began invariably to filter into Russia, the people's doubts began to turn to suspicion and then to disgruntlement with the government. People wanted better treatment for themselves.

The bottom line, Bart believed, was that the status quo was at grave risk in the Soviet Union. The set of people, like Tatayana, who had formed the backbone strength of Russia, were on the brink of demanding the changes they had long awaited, and if they didn't get them, they would probably trample the Kremlin wall down. Before falling asleep, he made some notes that he could use when he returned to the United States to make a memo for the Chairman and SecDef.

When the train pulled into Moscow, Saturday morning, the sun was out and the snow was cleared from the streets. He and Lieutenant Colonel Boyle were met by Captain Herb Teswillenger and Bart's XO, Colonel Martin. They left quickly by DAO vehicle for the embassy compound.

On the way there, George said, "Well boss, I hope you had a great visit to old St. Petersburg. Now you will just have time for one more of Olga's breakfasts at the Alton's quarters and a shower before you get into your travel togs for the afternoon flight to Berlin and drop by the embassy for a final wrap-up with General Alton. I'm afraid General Alton has some bad news; Captain Teswillenger is here to break it to you."

"Oh, sorry to hear that, Herb," Bart replied, "but first, let me tell you that the Leningrad trip was a real eye opener, and Dan Boyle here did a superb job in setting everything up for me. Now, what's your news?"

"I am afraid that part of the news concerns Dan, and that's why I'm here. We didn't want him to hear it on TV or radio, or read it in the paper first," Captain Teswillenger began.

Dan Boyle's normally easy-going face tightened in a frown.

"As you know, General, the FBI asked the State Department in Washington to expel two Soviet attachés. The Soviets reciprocated this morning by announcing Lieutenant Colonel Boyle and Major Jethro will be PNG'ed, and they have 48 hours to leave the country. Although we expected it, we'll certainly hate to lose you, Dan, and Major Jethro."

Bart was saddened at the news and turned to Colonel Boyle, put his hand on his shoulder, and said, "Dan, that's tough and you certainly don't deserve it."

"It's okay, sir. I'm actually not surprised. We've had two years here and Ginny, and the kids, will be glad to be going home."

Later in Erv Alton's office, after discussing the trip and the PNGs, Erv said, "Boss, it looks like we have two more casualties of the Cold War. I wonder if it will ever end?"

"I certainly hope so, Erv. I pray we will see it end in our lifetime and never have to fight these guys on a battlefield. If the impressions I have garnered here and in the Warsaw Pact countries prove to be correct, I believe we are beginning to see glimpses of light at the end of the tunnel. But are we?" And then, smiling broadly as he prepared to leave, Bart said, "That question is for me to think about and for you and all our people here, to find out about. You certainly have your work ahead."

"Yes, sir," Erv noted, saluting in respect and farewell.

Bart's first trip to the "Evil Empire" officially ended at 1:05 p.m. when their Aeroflot flight bound for Berlin lifted from the runway at Sheremetyevo Airport, crossed the Moskva River and turned toward the West.

CHAPTER 13

NO REGRETS

While General Bart Lowe was in Europe amid the cold winter snows of Bavaria and Russia worrying about HEAT SEEKER, Navy Captain Chester Baldwin, and his family were enjoying the sun and mild climate of Athens, Greece. Chet Baldwin, a Naval Surface Warfare Officer, had been the U.S. Defense and Naval Attaché in Athens since July 1984. Chet was scheduled to go home in the summer of 1987, and during the first week in January had talked with his Navy detailer about possible future assignments. Whatever this next assignment, it would be Chet's last because he would complete 30 years of service and face mandatory retirement. That was okay. The Navy had been good to Chet and he had no regrets.

Chet enjoyed being the DATT in Athens, even though the embassy was considered by the State Department to be one of the most threatened in the world because of terrorist activity in Greece. State Department personnel even received hazardous duty pay for serving in Greece. But Chet Baldwin just didn't believe the threat against Americans was as high as the State Department security profile and the CIA painted it.

On the Monday morning General Lowe visited the DAO, Moscow, Captain Baldwin rose, as usual, at 5:30 a.m., pulled on some sweats, and went downstairs to a small room in the basement he used as a workout room. He did twenty minutes of calisthenics, went upstairs to the kitchen, put on the coffee and had juice and cereal for breakfast. By 6:25 he had showered, shaved and dressed in a business suit, white shirt and tie. Uniforms were worn only one day a week at the DAO, and on special occasions as appropriate. By leaving at 6:30 each morning, Chet could be at his desk in the

DAO by 7:00 with his second cup of coffee of the day and the cables and news from Washington.

At 6:29 Chet entered the garage from the inside of the house, turned off the garage security alarm, climbed into the front seat of the car and started the engine of the small Toyota that he used to commute to and from the embassy. He then pressed the remote control to raise the garage door in front of him, headed down the left side of the circular driveway to the security gate, and opened the gate, also with his remote control. After pulling out far enough to re-close the gate, he checked the residential street for any traffic. Seeing none, he turned left and drove slowly down the hill toward the intersection approximately one-half mile away that would cross the main access road into Athens.

Chet Baldwin had been very conscientious in all security matters. He would leave his house at a different time each day and come home at randomly different times. He would vary the routes, and by turning off a few blocks from his villa, he could arrive back at the villa from the other direction. In his second year, he became less concerned because he knew his neighborhood was a safe and secure region of Athens, one of the best. By the third year, because of the traffic pattern, Chet had settled into a regular routine that worked well for him. The early morning departure avoided the traffic, and he was always in the DAO early. He also found that by leaving no later than 5:00 in the evenings from the embassy he could avoid the heaviest rush hour traffic leaving Athens.

Today, however, as Captain Baldwin's Toyota disappeared down the hill in front of his villa, two sets of eyes from the house across the street watched it disappear in the distance.

From the second floor bedroom in the house a female voice speaking in Greek said, "He was alone in the car and departed at precisely 0630. The car is a late model black Japanese Toyota, diplomatic license plate number X956461."

A male voice behind her, also speaking in Greek said, "Good. I have recorded it in the log."

"Did you record the time the first light came on in the house, the time the garage door opened, and that the garage door and the security gate are apparently remotely controlled?" the woman purposefully asked.

"Yes it's all here in the log." the man replied.

"And did you also make a note that there are apparently no security guards at the house?"

"Yes, that too," he again replied.

"Good. Then I am going to get some sleep. You have the watch." As she said this, she passed the man a pair of small, powerful binoculars. "Make sure that you record anything that you see. If I don't wake up sooner, call me at noon and I will relieve you."

The woman moved into the adjoining bedroom, reached into a small black knapsack and pulled out a rolled-up sleeping bag, shook it out and laid it on the bare floor. She removed her shoes and sweater, left her jeans and swcatshirt on and crawled into the sleeping bag. It had been a long night.

The house across the street from the Baldwins' villa was owned by a Greek family named Matakios. They had recently sold their import-export business in Athens and moved to Thessaloniki in the north. They had not decided whether to sell the home, and as a result, they had taken all their furniture and belongings from the house and closed and locked all the windows and door shutters. The house had been standing vacant for about two months. But the gardener had been retained by the family to keep the grass cut and to look after any needed repairs. After a few weeks the vacant house seemed just a normal part of the neighborhood.

The man and woman who now occupied its second floor bedrooms had broken into the house the night before, shortly after midnight. The break-in was quiet and professional. Both were members of the Greek terrorist organization known as 17 November. The woman, Felicia Athlas, was 29 years old, unmarried and had been a member of 17 November since she was 19. The man, Christopher Kalis, was 26 years old and had only been a member of 17 November for four years. But he was already highly regarded for his dedication to the cause and his willingness to carry out the organization's bidding, no matter what the risk or danger. Felicia was the senior of the two and gave the orders. 17 November was anti-government, anti-military and anti-American. The organization had sufficient line soldiers like Felicia and Christopher who were committed to carrying out terrorist actions. Felicia and Christopher were part of a target assessment team who investigated people and places as potential targets.

The name of Captain Chester Baldwin, USN, U.S. Defense and Naval Attaché to Greece, along with his official and residential address, had been given to the target assessment team by an unknown source, at least unknown to them. Felicia and Christopher were selected for this specific mission by their team leader in Athens. Other members of the team would do vehicle surveillance and monitor Chet's movements to and from the U.S. Embassy and around Athens.

Felicia had conducted many target assessments and had been doing them with Christopher for more than a year. Often, when they thought the assessment suggested a perfect target, the target would not be selected by the target selection team leader. It was not their position to worry about such things; they just did their jobs. The Sunday night they came to the vacant house they were driven to a point, thick with trees, approximately two blocks away from the house and proceeded from there on foot to the rear of the house. Once they were satisfied they had not been followed, they entered through a basement door and made their way to the second floor with the assistance of shielded pen lights. They carried only small black knapsacks, containing their sleeping bags, one change of clothes, enough tinned food for 24 hours, a water bottle and a thermos of black, extra strong Greek coffee. Their water, coffee and food would be replenished every 24 hours by a courier who would pick up their log entries and trash. Neither had a gun, only a small all-purpose Swiss army knife. After cutting small peep holes in the shutters to give them a view of the villa and the street, they checked the rest of the house. The first night they both stayed up all night so they could watch the villa carefully and, at the same time, be alert to any movement that might take place in the neighborhood. At 2:00 a.m., Felicia sent Christopher to the basement to turn the water source on so that they could use the toilet facilities. After the first night, they planned to alternate in shifts.

On Monday morning at 7:45, a school bus arrived at the front gate to pick up one child; the bus returned her at 3:30 in the afternoon. On Monday evening Captain Baldwin returned to the villa at 5:58, apparently opening the security gate with a remote control device from inside his car, and drove inside the fence. The gate closed and the captain drove up to the top of the driveway, pulled over to the left and when the garage door opened, he backed the Toyota into the garage. No other events were recorded in the terrorist log that day.

When Chet Baldwin had gone into the Defense Attaché Office that Monday he received a call on the secure phone line from his old friend, Captain Mike Niceman, the Western Europe Division Chief at DAS Headquarters in Rosslyn.

Mike said, "Good-day to you, Chet. I hope all's well with you and the attaché gang. While you are basking in the warm sun of Athens, we are freezing our buns off here in Washington."

"Things are great, Mike. I just came back from lunch with a colleague, we had Greek salads at one of those little sidewalk cafes along the coast, and the sun was so hot we had to get the waiter to move an umbrella over to our table to give us some relief from the heat."

"You sure know how to hurt a guy, Chet. Actually, I'm calling you for two reasons. The first is that I wanted to give you some feedback on that series of information reports you and your guys have done on the reaction in the Greek military to the recent political scandals and the upcoming elections. We've received kudos from just about everybody in town on the insights provided by those reports. And we continue to get high marks from the CIA on your personal reporting on Russian activities in Greece. Please pass on my well done to all concerned. I know that the boss will want to send a flag note to you when he returns."

"That's great, Mike, thanks for passing on the word. Our Greek FAO attachés and all the operations people really worked hard on those reports and will appreciate the feedback. By the way, when will the general be back in Washington?" Chet asked.

"Glad you asked. That's my second subject. General Lowe is beginning the last week of his trip today in Moscow. He is scheduled to depart Moscow on Saturday but Chuck Gregorios talked to George Martin in Moscow, who said they can't make the regular Moscow-to-Frankfurt-to-Washington flight, and they are looking for alternate routes. George said if the route they come up with takes them through any country that has a DAO the general has not visited, the general would want to stop, however briefly, and see the DATT. I don't think it likely, but I'm notifying the Western European DATTs of the possibility."

"Okay Mike, thanks for the heads up. If the boss shows up in sunny Athens you can count on us to be ready."

"That's it, Chet. All the best to the DAO guys and Meriam."

Chet did not think that a visit from General Lowe was very likely, but he put out the word to the DAO staff and alerted the Operations Coordinator to begin to spruce up the brief in the event they needed it. Before leaving the office on Monday Chet reviewed the rest of the week's schedule. It was a busy one.

The same week moved slowly for Felicia Athlas and Christopher Kalis. The log on Tuesday recorded the same routine as Monday, the same times of comings and goings for the captain except that he and a blond woman, evidently his wife, left the villa at 7:00 in the evening and returned at 10:00. In the morning, a female, believed to be a domestic, showed up at 9:00 in a car that was left outside the fence. She was admitted to the house using an intercom on the security gate. When she was recognized, the gate was electronically opened. She stayed until 10:15 Tuesday night, departing after the captain and his wife returned. The same woman came again on Wednesday, Thursday and Friday. On those days that the captain or his wife did not leave the villa in the evening the woman departed at 7:00 p.m. A man in a truck came on Thursday at 10:00 a.m. and was admitted inside the security fence with his truck after being identified at the intercom. He was the gardener and departed at 3:00 in the afternoon after cutting the grass and the shrubs surrounding the house.

A second villa car was seen on Wednesday morning at 11:00 coming from the garage, driven by the captain's wife. The car was a white Ford station wagon, diplomatic license number AX93346; it exited the same gate as used by the Toyota and went down the hill towards Athens. The station wagon returned at 4:00 in the afternoon. The captain and his wife departed the villa in the Toyota at 6:30 in the evening and returned at 9:45. On Thursday, the captain's wife made two trips in and out of the villa in the morning and afternoon. On Friday, the captain and his wife left the villa in the station wagon at 7:30 that night and did not return until 12:30 in the morning. The captain was wearing a white uniform. The domestic woman departed at 12:45 a.m.

On Saturday morning, because of the late night at General Cozinities' party, neither Chet nor Meriam woke before 8:00 a.m. Their daughter, Valerie, always an early riser, was up at 7:00.

At breakfast later that morning Chet said, "How would my girl like to go for a sail today?"

"Oh Daddy," Valerie replied, "I would love to go sailing, but I have a birthday party today at Sally Benjamin's house at noon."

"We have to drop Valerie off and then pick her up at 4:00. Will that give us enough time to go sailing?" asked Meriam.

"Sure, a couple of hours on the blue seas is all we need, and the Benjamin's apartment is not too far from the marina."

By 12:30 Chet and Meriam had dropped Valerie off at the birthday party, proceeded to the marina, and working together, had launched their 27" Bristol Sailor. The day was another beautiful one, not a cloud in the deep blue sky. A good wind made for excellent sailing. They headed for a small island a short distance off the Greek mainland. It made for a good fast run with the prevailing winds and when they reached the island, it offered a small, wind-protected, cove where they anchored and had their lunch.

Meriam laid out the offerings on the galley table: slices of cold white chicken, goat cheese, celery and carrot sticks, Greek hard rolls, and a bottle of Chardonney already chilled in the boat's ice locker.

After lunch they went up on deck again with steaming mugs of coffee and stretched out enjoying the natural beauty of the water, sky and the day. The rest of the afternoon passed quickly; they returned to the marina, stowed their sails, secured the boat and picked up Valerie from the birthday party. They were back at the villa by 5:00.

On Saturday afternoon at 5:00 when the Baldwins returned to the villa, Felicia dutifully noted the time and details of their return. It was just the second log entry of the day, the other when the station wagon departed that morning. Neither Felicia nor Christopher had any way of knowing, at that time, that the 5:00 p.m. log entry would be the last one. They both were thinking the mission was almost over, and it would be good to get back to their own places, clean up and have a decent meal.

The rest of the day passed without event. That night at 1:00 a.m., when the courier was scheduled to drop their last resupply and pick up the log entries, Felicia, who was listening for the courier, was surprised when she opened the door slightly and saw that the courier was her team leader, Georg Mandakas.

He motioned for Felicia to let him in and once inside said, "Where is Christopher?"

"He has the watch. He is upstairs."

"Good, let's go up. I want to talk to you both."

When they reached the second floor, Christopher was also surprised to see Mandakas and said, "Georg, what brings you here?"

"Christopher, you can continue to watch the house, but listen carefully to what I want to tell you and Felicia. But first, anything unusual in the log entry for today?"

"No," Felicia replied. "The captain and his wife and daughter were out at 10:15 this morning and returned at 5:00 this evening. That was the only activity for the day."

"Good, then you two need to know that the target selection team met earlier tonight and your target has been selected for an action. The action is to take place Monday morning. Before I explain the action, let me see the house, the driveway and the security gate the captain uses."

Georg then joined Christopher at the window, and he pointed out the items that Georg had asked to see.

"All right. I have it." Georg said, and stepped back. "Here is how it will go down." He told them that at 1:30 a.m. Monday, Petra Metka would bring a car near to the front of the house and park it. Petra would then join Felicia and Christopher inside and wait until the captain left the villa for the U.S. Embassy. When he finished, Georg asked if there were any questions.

"What if the captain should leave on Sunday and not return?" Felicia asked.

"Then the action is off and you will leave the house tomorrow night, when Petra arrives."

"What if the Captain's family are in the car with him on Monday morning?"

"If anyone else is in the car riding with him on Monday morning then the action is also off," answered Georg. "If, after Petra arrives on Sunday night, anyone discovers the car or disturbs the car, you three should leave the house immediately and wait at the rendezvous point for pick-up."

Sunday seemed the longest day Felicia and Christopher spent waiting in the house. There was no movement in or out of the villa. They were surprised the captain had been selected as a target—not that the terrorists were concerned about him personally. They were well beyond that, but it was a question of the value of the action. A single person in a lone car in a residential area? Felicia thought the impact would be greater if the action were carried out near the U.S. Embassy. And Christopher thought the action would have been better done on a crowded street during the height of traffic.

As day turned into night and late night into morning, with still no movement in or out of the villa, Felicia and Christopher became resolved that the action was going to be a go. They both started watching the front street very closely after 1:00 a.m. At 1:27 a.m., a car was seen approaching from above the villa with just its parking lights lit. As it approached the house they could not hear a sound. Perhaps Petra was coasting. At any rate, the car stopped precisely at the location Georg had indicated, and the lights went out. They could make out a figure in dark clothes exiting the car with a small bag in his hand. Felicia left the window and went to the basement to await Petra's soft knock. It came as soon as she arrived, and after opening the door only a crack at first to make sure it was Petra, she opened the door wide and let him pass.

Felicia led the way upstairs where Petra removed a small remote control device from his bag checking the line of sight from the window to the car. He then told Felicia he was going to get some sleep, and asked to be called at 5:00 a.m., or sooner if there were any developments. Petra was known in 17 November jargon as a "shooter." He was one of only a very few members of 17 November who pulled the trigger in the actions they carried out. While Petra slept, Felicia and Christopher took turns standing two-hour watches. They had long since readied their knapsacks for a fast departure.

At 5:00 a.m. Felicia woke Petra who poured himself some black coffee from a thermos. Jarred alert by the caffeine, he satisfied himself that the car was still in place. Then he retrieved his remote control device, checking it thoroughly. He positioned himself at the window providing the best vantage point of the security gate. At 5:30 a.m., all three terrorists saw the kitchen light go on, and felt a rush of adrenalin.

In the villa in his exercise room Chet Baldwin was whistling as he did his calisthenics. He couldn't remember a more relaxed weekend. While he was showering, he thought about the work to be done during the week and he was anxious to get to the DAO and begin. After he was dressed, and before he went back downstairs, he went over to the bed and kissed Meriam lightly on the head.

"Mmm," she moaned, and sleepily asked, "Is the coffee on?"

"Of course. Just awaiting 'My Lady's' presence," Chet replied.

"Well, have a good day," she said and rolled over and went back to sleep.

When Chet entered the garage to turn off the security alarm he glanced at his wrist watch. It read 6:29. " Good," he thought. "Right on time."

When the garage door opened, three sets of eyes looking on from the house across the street became even more intensely alert. As the car began its roll down the hill, the three terrorists had different thoughts.

Felicia thought," I will be glad to get out of here and have a long bath and wash my hair."

Christopher thought, " I wonder if I really want to do this kind of thing my whole life?"

And Petra thought, "One more time," feeling his thumb over the remote control button tingle.

Chet drove through the security gate and pushed his remote control button again to close the gate when he first noticed the car parked in front of the house across the street. "I don't think I've seen that car there before," he thought.

As he turned his car to the left and pulled out fully onto the street, coming alongside the parked car, Petra, standing in the upstairs bedroom, pushed the remote control button triggering the huge amount of high explosives that had been packed into the parked car.

Chet Baldwin's last thought in the split second that he sensed the blinding light and intense heat was "What the..."

CHAPTER 14

A HERO RETURNS

When General Lowe and Colonel Martin departed Moscow on the Aeroflot flight to Berlin, Bart did not realize at first the flight would be going into East Berlin, rather than West Berlin. His XO, George Martin learned earlier that this would be the case and had contacted the Commander of the U.S. Military Liaison Mission (USMLM) to the Soviet Forces in Germany headquartered in Potsdam, requesting that a USMLM officer meet their party and transport them to West Berlin.

When the Aeroflot plane landed and taxied in, Bart and George, the only passengers in the closed rear compartment, were detained, while the passengers from the main cabin disembarked. After the last of the other passengers had departed, the Aeroflot representative showed up to escort Bart and George to the passport control office. When Bart started down the landing steps and looked up, the first building he saw was an old run-down terminal that hadn't been painted in years, the only signs of color coming from the huge flags of the DDR and the USSR which hung oppressively above it.

Colonel Tom Kilkane from the USMLM met them in the passport control office with a Russian Army officer and between the two of them, they had Bart and George processed in and out of the DDR terminal in less than 20 minutes—probably a new record for the DDR, Bart thought. Once they were safely in the USMLM black Chrysler Sedan with its American flag and special license tag, Colonel Kilkane waved farewell to the Soviet Officer and said, "Yuri, I owe you one."

Bart Lowe remembered Colonel Kilkane from the U.S. Army Europe Commanders Conference he had attended. When

Kilkane climbed in beside Lowe, Bart asked, “A Russian being helpful, how did you pull that off, Tom?”

“Yuri is an officer I have known for years. I first met him when I was serving as an attaché in Moscow. Yuri was the protocol officer at the Foreign Liaison Office. Then later when I was serving at V Corps in Frankfurt, Yuri was a tour officer in the Soviet Liaison Mission, our counterpart in Frankfurt. Yuri is now stationed in the Group Soviet Forces, Germany Headquarters. The only way you can get anything done on this side of the wall is to know someone with enough clout to make it happen.

“General, I have taken the liberty of reserving the Berlin Commander’s Guest House for you and Colonel Martin for the night. We’ll go directly there, drop you off, and then pick you up tomorrow morning at 10:30. That will allow plenty of time to get you to Tegel airport and checked in for your noon flight to Washington. I have already confirmed your reservations with Pan Am.”

“Tom, that suits me fine.”

The U.S. Berlin Commander’s Guest House was a pre-World War II mansion that sat on the west bank of the Wannsee Lake that separated West and East Berlin. The house was one of the few left standing at the end of the war, and it was selected as the official residence for General Lucius Clay, the first American Commander of Berlin. As the city rebuilt in the post-war years the house was too far from the center of the American sector and the U.S. Commander shifted his residence to a nearer location. The Clay house was put into service as a guest house for visiting U.S. dignitaries.

When they arrived, Hans, the “Hausmeister,” came out to greet them. “General Lowe, welcome to Berlin.”

The guest house kept a full staff: a cook, gardener, maids and the major domo, Hans. They could look after one person or a dozen. Hans, a native Berliner, had first joined the staff of the guest house more than thirty years ago as a boy and had worked his way up to “Meister.” Hans was a master at his profession. He never forgot the eating and drinking preferences of a guest.

After Bart was settled in his suite on the second floor, with a splendid view of the Wannsee, Hans inquired, "General Lowe, will you be having a Manhattan and would you prefer Cordon Bleu or the Chateau Briand for dinner?"

"A Manhattan to be sure, and I think the Cordon Bleu. I can still remember how delicious the last one was that I had here."

As Bart and George sat down to an excellent dinner, George told Bart that he had checked in with the Operations Center at the DAS to provide them the phone number where they could be reached in Berlin. Barbara Worthington was on duty and said that Captain Kalitka had left a box of personal messages in the operations center containing the most urgent DAS actions ongoing in the event that the General wanted to come into the office when they got back in on Sunday.

"What time will we get in George?" asked Bart.

"In the early afternoon, Washington time. The flight will take about eight hours, and because of the difference in time we'll get there almost the same time we leave here."

Bart retired early on Saturday and was up early Sunday morning, as soon as the light came through his bedroom window. There was still too much snow and ice on the ground for jogging, but the sidewalks around the guest house had been cleared and salted, so Bart went out for a 30-minute walk before breakfast. When Lowe returned from his invigorating walk, he enjoyed Hans' delicious breakfast of eggs, sausage, ham, cheese, fresh brotchen and jams.

Colonel Kilkane arrived in time to have a final cup of coffee with Bart while George Martin readied the suitcases and briefcases. When the Chrysler was loaded, the good-byes said and the sedan was rolling down the drive leading them away from the guest house, Bart turned to look at the grand old relic that had seen much of history and wondered, "Will I ever see this old beauty again or will this be the last time?"

During the Pan Am flight back to Washington, Martin reviewed the outline of the memo he was putting together for Bart's signature, to be passed to the DAS staff. George had sent to Rosslyn information of real significance on time-sensitive matters by informal message or secure telephone. The trip report memo would be for wider distribution to the DAS staff and for tasking individual members of the staff for follow-up actions. Bart gave George several specifics he wanted added, and then went to work on the memo he intended to send to the JCS Chairman, the Secretary of Defense and a number of others on changes he speculated were taking place in the USSR and the Warsaw Pact countries. Bart knew that the memo would be contentious in Washington. He wanted to choose his words and conclusions carefully. He suspected, as he began his first draft, that it would take more than one draft before he got it right. He finished a first draft just before the flight attendant came around to begin preparation for the evening meal.

The flight arrived fifteen minutes early at Dulles due to light head winds. The sky was clear, there was no snow on the ground, and the ground temperature in Washington was a brisk 37 degrees. Lewis Ridges, the limo driver DAS utilized for its airport trips had anticipated the early arrival, and met Lowe and Martin at the exit of the U.S. Customs Gate.

"Welcome home, General," Lewis drawled in his heavy Virginia accent, taking two suitcases from Bart and George.

The bags were quickly placed in the trunk of the Lincoln limo, and the limo was on its way to northern Virginia via the Dulles Access Road. Lewis dropped General Lowe first, at Fort Myer, and then Colonel Martin at his high-rise condominium in Arlington.

Master Sergeant Sam Wild was waiting for Bart when he reached his quarters at Fort Myer. A broad grin announced that Sam was glad to see General Lowe. The only duty Sergeant Wild could not tolerate was not having enough to do. Bart imagined that even though he had forced Sam to take ten days' leave with his family while Bart was gone, the silver in the quarters had been polished and re-polished to perfection.

"By the way Sam, it's Sunday and I appreciate you being here, but why don't you take off now and get a fresh start tomorrow."

"You know me better than that, General," Sam said as he started picking up the general's suitcases from the front room, "I want to get started putting your trip things away, sorting out the laundry and dry cleaning, and making sure you get your first home cooked meal."

Bart threw up his hands in surrender as Sam headed up the stairs. "Okay, you win, Sam, but nothing to eat before tomorrow morning. Bart went into the kitchen, fixed himself a tall glass of ice water and then moved back into the dining room to begin to sort the phone messages and mail. The mail was the normal assortment of personal correspondence, bills, junk mail, magazines and, as always, several social invitations. Sam had taken or transcribed phone calls from Bart's answering machine, placing them in clear, well-written order. Most were routine: Bart's mother in Miami, some other relatives, old friends passing through Washington, and a number of foreign attachés' calls. Four of the yellow phone messages caught his eye: one from B.J. Ross, saying that she was leaving town and would see him next weekend, one from John Kitchen at the FBI, also on Friday, asking that Bart get in touch as soon as he returned, and two calls recorded just yesterday from Colonel Preston Bernhardt in Vienna. The last message was from General Reiley, asking that Bart call him at his quarters at Fort Myer. "What could that mean?" Bart thought.

Bart went to his desk and pulled the world-wide attaché roster from it and looked up Preston Bernhardt's home phone number in Vienna. It was 3:20 p.m. in Washington, and although it was 11:20 at night in Vienna, Bart thought that Preston would still be awake. He obtained dialing instructions from the Fort Myer operator, and in just seconds Preston was on the line.

"Preston, this is Bart. I just got in a short while ago and found your message. Since you called my quarters rather than the office, I thought it must be important."

"Yes, sir. Sorry to disturb you so soon, but something happened that I thought you should know about right away. You remember the person you had a special meeting with here?"

"Yes," Bart answered, not completely sure if Preston meant Countess Laressa or the CIA Station Chief, John Ormond.

"Well, that person contacted me and asked if I had an address for you where something could be sent to you by mail. The request was not for an official address but a personal one and the person ruled out having me send whatever it is to you. Bottom line, I took the liberty of providing the person your quarter's address at Fort Myer. I hope that was okay?"

"Not a problem, Preston, but you have no idea what it may be?"

"No, but the person indicated it was a matter of the utmost urgency. The request came on Thursday, so I would think you should receive something this upcoming week."

"Okay, Preston, I've got it. I'll be on the lookout for whatever it is. Look, I have a thousand things to do here, so I'll be in touch with you if and when anything arrives."

"Roger that, boss. Out, here."

Next, Bart called General Reiley's quarters, but his enlisted aide answered and said that General Reiley was out for the day and would not return until 2100 hours that evening. Bart asked the aide to give General Reiley the message that he had called and would be at his quarters all evening.

Bart worked the mail until 4:30, at which time Sam Wild departed for the day, telling Bart he had left a cold turkey sandwich in the fridge just in case the general got hungry. Bart, feeling a little drowsy, decided a few minutes later he would go for a run around his usual path at Fort Myer.

The run in the cold air cleared his head, and after a shower he was feeling great. He called the Operations Center Duty Officer and told him he would be coming in. He dressed in casual trousers, loafers, a button-down shirt and a heavy pull-over sweater, and went out to the garage and got into the Corvette. It was, as always, an exhilarating fecling to be behind the wheel of the Corvette and feel the response of power to the slightest touch to the accelerator. When he came out of the rear gate at Fort Myer, he turned right and drove down to the Pentagon, then on to I-395, and then back onto the George Washington Parkway to Rosslyn, and into the underground parking garage at the DAS Headquarters.

When he got off the elevator on the 11th floor, he headed directly to the Operations Center. As he entered, he was surprised to see the Operations Center Chief, Barbara Worthington. She came over immediately and extended her hand and said, "Welcome home, General Lowe."

"Thank you Barbara, it's good to be back; it was a fantastic trip." Bart answered. Then he took time to shake hands with the Duty Officer and the Operations Center team members.

"I am surprised to see you, Barbara. What brings you here on a Sunday night?" Bart asked.

"Well, after I talked to Colonel Martin, I thought you might come in, and then Major Baylor, the Duty Officer called me and said you were definitely coming, so I thought I would be here to explain the pile of things Captain Kalitka left for you and see if you required any assistance."

"That's very kind, Barbara, but not necessary. Please show me what you have and then you can be on your way."

Barbara had set up a table in a quiet corner of the Operations Center with a thermal pitcher of coffee, a cup, and a leather-backed desk chair. She explained that she had arranged the material to be reviewed in three stacks. "Sir, the first stack contains any ongoing crises or events around the world affecting attachés. For example, the PNGs in Moscow, an attaché beating in Singapore, a shooting incident at an attachés' residence in Panama, and a DAS C-12 plane crash in Africa. No casualties. The second stack, by far the largest, is a summary of significant DAS events and activities during your absence. The third stack is a summary of major DAS activities in Washington in the next 30 days, with those that you must personally be involved in highlighted."

"Whoa, Barbara, that sounds like thirty days of work just to review these stacks."

Barbara laughed and said, "I am sure, General Lowe, that you will whip through all of this with your usual speed."

"I wish. Now go on, Barbara. I'm just going to sit here for about an hour, hour and a half tops; and, if I need any assistance, I am sure Major Baylor can help me. I appreciate what you have already done and I'll see you tomorrow."

With that, Bart read continuously for about an hour and a half while drinking two cups of coffee, but finally had to give into that drowsy feeling again. He had been awake almost 21 hours. Bart asked Major Baylor to drop the remaining material off at his office tomorrow morning and then departed. Back at his quarters he turned on CNN to catch the news updates. He realized that he had not watched any television in almost a month. Not wanting Sam Wild to be disappointed, Bart ate the cold turkey sandwich. He called his mother in Miami to let her know he had returned, and at 9:30, after looking through some of the magazines that had piled up while he had been away, was about ready for bed. Just then the phone rang.

"General Lowe," Bart answered as he picked up the phone.

"Bart, this is Gordon Reiley. I understand you have been in the Soviet Union. Are the Russians really ten feet tall?"

"Yes, sir. I have been to the USSR, and no sir, I don't think the Russians are ten feet tall. I did at one time, but I no longer think that is the case. There are changes taking place there now that are dramatic, and ones I believe are going to work to our advantage. I am going to prepare a memo for the Chairman that will cover my observations during my trip, and I think it may surprise some people. I'll send you a copy of the memo if you would like."

"Damn right I would like, and don't make it long after you have given it to the Chairman. I am sure he will want to discuss it with the Chiefs."

"Yes, sir, I'll take care of it."

"Bart, what I called you about concerns a matter that was brought to my attention by my Chiefs of Intelligence and Legislative Liaison. Senator Thomas of New Hampshire and his staffers have been after Chuck Ikelaby's guys to cut out Army Human Intelligence operations. It seems the Senator feels strongly that HUMINT should only be performed by the CIA. My guys say not so, and they insist the take from the HUMINT operations is very important to our Unified and Combat Commanders. They claim we don't always get what we need from the CIA. Chuck Ikelaby says that you are the guy that answers that mail for Defense. Lennie Murphy at DIA also says you're the guy who needs to carry that water for us. Can you get this senator off our back?"

"General Reiley, it's my job and I'll work it. Senator Thomas raised the subject with me at the congressional hearings last fall and I asked him for time to review the situation, not just for the Army, but for the other services as well. I thought he had agreed, but evidently, he's end running me. I can't promise I can get him off your back, but I'll work with the Senator and keep you informed of any progress."

"Okay, Bart, I appreciate anything you can do for us," he said as he hung up.

At 10:05, Bart slid into his king-sized bed and switched off his night light on the table beside his bed. He was too tired to read from one of the half dozen books he kept at his bedside. His thoughts were filled with Moscow PNGs, HEAT SEEKER, good friends, and Senator Thomas. Always the optimist, his last thought before sleep was, "These problems are no hill for a climber. We'll work through them, do what is right and things will undoubtedly get better before they get worse." He was wrong.

At 12:31 a.m. Washington time, the high explosives that took the life of Captain Chet Baldwin exploded... The tremendous blast shattered a number of windows on the front of the DATT

villa in Athens, waking Meriam Baldwin and her daughter with a frightening suddenness.

Valerie ran into her Mother's room crying, "Mother, mother, what is wrong?"

Meriam, quickly gathering her thoughts and running to Valerie said, "I don't know, but I am going to find out. You go back to your room and stay there until I tell you that it is safe to come out."

When Meriam ran down the stairs and looked out a front window she could see the broken glass and a fire in the street near their gate with black smoke hovering above it. Her first thought was that there must have been a terrible accident. She did not think of Chet because, in her sudden waking, she imagined that Chet had departed long ago. Meriam knew that she should probably call the police, but she wasn't sure what she would tell them. She decided she needed to go outside and down the driveway to see what had happened.

Meriam started down the drive and as she got nearer to the street she could only see scattered piles of burning debris spread across the street and into the yard of the vacant house across the street. "Strange," she thought. She didn't see any people. Then she noticed something that looked like the rear end of a car resting against the fence. In this hunk of metal was a license tag, a diplomatic tag. "My God," she thought, " that's Chet's tag." Meriam almost fainted but somehow had the presence of mind to realize that she and Valerie might also be in danger. As she turned back to the house, out of the corner of her eye she could see other people coming out of their houses and running toward the fire in the street. She ran as fast as she could and, once inside, locked the door.

Valerie, upstairs, hearing the slamming door cried, "Mommy, Mommy, what has happened?"

Hearing Valerie's frantic call seemed to snap Meriam out of the shock that had taken hold of her, and she knew she had to regain control, calm Valerie, and somehow get help. After reassuring Valerie, she went to the phone in her bedroom and called Lieutenant Colonel Charles Papalardo, the Assistant Army Attaché. The Papalardos lived only a few minutes from the Baldwins and Meriam knew that Charles did not go into the DAO as early as Chet. Charles answered after two rings and Meriam, trying not to be hysterical, but unable to hold back the sobs, described as best she could what had happened and, what she feared, and asked him to come quickly. Lieutenant Colonel Papalardo told Meriam to stay in a safe place in the house and not to open the door until he arrived at the villa. Papalardo immediately departed for the Baldwins taking his cellular phone with him.

Papalardo was a Greek Foreign Area Officer and the DAO's best Greek linguist. After Meriam's call, he phoned the Greek Counter-Terrorist Police, knowing they would respond the fastest and were the most professional. He then called the Embassy Security Office and asked them to dispatch a team to the scene. Finally he called the DAO and alerted them to the possibility of what may have happened, asking that the next senior officer, Colonel Lawrence, the Air Force Attaché be informed. Papalardo cautioned the duty officer taking his call not to make any reports to the DAS headquarters until such time as more information was known.

Lieutenant Colonel Papalardo reached the Baldwin villa 20 minutes after Meriam called. The Greek Counter-Terrorist police were already at the scene, had moved the gathering crowd back and were cordoning off the area. After presenting his diplomatic identification, Papalardo was taken to the officer-in-charge of the scene and told what they had been able to determine thus far. The debris was from two automobiles, and the remains of one body had been found in several pieces. The officer asked Papalardo to look at them and see if an identification was possible. After doing so, regrettably, there was no doubt in Papalardo's mind that Captain Baldwin was the victim. The officer also told Papalardo that his unit had called for other units and his men would secure the area and begin to search for anyone who might have been involved. Papalardo told the officer that people from the U.S. Embassy would be coming to the scene soon and asked for both his cooperation and security for Mrs. Baldwin. Then Lieutenant Colonel Papalardo went to the villa intercom and began the heartbreaking task of informing Meriam Baldwin of the horrible tragedy that had taken place.

By the time the Greek and American investigators searched the area for any follow-on bombs, and declared the area safe, gathered up the remains, completed the victim's identification and notified the American embassy and their own government superiors, it was 2:30 a.m., Washington local time. At 3:05 a.m. the U.S. Ambassador to Greece had released a spot report to the State Department in Washington, and the Athens DAO had sent an immediate cable to the Operations Center at the DAS. At 3:20 a.m., Bart Lowe thought he heard a phone ringing, but it sounded far off. It just kept ringing and ringing. Finally, from the deepest of sleeps, Bart realized it was his phone. He turned over, picking up the receiver and said, "Bart Lowe here."

"Boss, welcome home." The voice was speaking slowly and sounded familiar to Bart. "This is Pete Kalitka, and I hate to wake you from a night's sleep."

"Pete," Bart said, now becoming more awake, "That's all right. What is it?" He glanced over at the luminous digital clock.

"I am afraid I have the worst kind of news. The Operations Center has received a cable from DAO Athens saying that the DATT, Captain Chet Baldwin, was blown away by a terrorist bomb early this morning in front of his house."

"Oh my God, Pete." Bart muttered. "Are we sure that he is dead and not just injured?"

"There is no doubt, general. Evidently his body or what was left of it was identified," Pete said, explaining what additional information was known.

"Pete, should I go back out there?" Bart asked.

"I don't think so, boss. There is really little you could do. The State Department will have responsibility for the investigation and will be working with the Greeks to try and catch the terrorists. We will want to move the family and Chet's remains home as soon as possible because there will be nothing there for them now. It will be a good idea, though, to have someone from here go out to assist the family and make the trip back home with them. The Navy will, of course, appoint a Survivors Assistance Officer (SAO) to work with the family. Probably someone from the European Theater. We should have someone there the family knows. I think Mike Niceman is a friend of the Baldwins; if you agree, I'll get Mike on his way to Athens ASAP."

"Good idea, Pete, go with it. Pete, what about me calling Captain Baldwin's widow? You know, I don't even know her first name."

"Her name is Meriam, and from all reports she has been one of our best attaché spouses. The Baldwins have an eleven year old daughter, Valerie. I think you should call her, General Lowe, but you might wait until the initial shock is over. We'll tell our folks there that you are anxious to speak to her and ask them to let us know when she is ready. Probably tonight sometime, depending on how she holds up."

"Okay, Pete, but ask the Operations Center to put together a draft message of condolence for me to Mrs. Baldwin and the family. And when I get in the office, I can personalize it and send it on its way, okay?"

"Can do, boss. I don't know of anything else you can do at the office right away, so why don't you try and get a few more hours' sleep?"

"Thanks for the thought Pete, but I don't think I can sleep after that kind of news. My heart aches for Captain Baldwin's family."

"I hear you, boss. It is indeed a black day," Pete said and rang off.

Bart, now fully awake, got out of bed, went downstairs to the kitchen and put on some coffee. He then went back up to take a cold shower.

Bart arrived at the office at 0445 hours and was not surprised to learn that George Martin and Pete Kalitka were already there. Also, Commander Dolly West and the DAS Admin Shop were in full swing, as was the Greek Desk in the Western Europe Division. Bart found the draft condolence message already on his desk. He made a few changes to the text and passed it to George Martin for immediate dispatch.

At 0500, Bart called the Chief of Naval Operations duty desk in the Pentagon to obtain a residence phone number for the CNO to inform him of Captain Baldwin's death and learned that the CNO was out of town. He was given the phone number of the Vice CNO, Admiral Ledney. Bart called and expressed his regrets to Admiral Ledney on the death of Captain Baldwin. He also told Ledney that the DAS had learned that the story of the assassination would air at 0600 Washington time or CNN and all the major networks. Prior to 0600 Bart, Pete and George had collaborated on a list of Defense Department officials to be notified before the public announcement aired on the T.V. and radio networks.

When Chuck Gregorios and Joan Weber came in at their usual time of 0700, the sad news immediately dampened what would have been a happy day of welcoming back their boss from a long trip. The death in Athens was a sad, sobering shock wave that ran throughout the entire DAS staff. Fortunately, Joan had scheduled no appointments for General Lowe's first day back, and he was able to deal with the somber blanket that had fallen over him and the DAS by doggedly plowing his way through the stack of paper that had grown high during his four-week absence.

Lowe talked with Meriam Baldwin in the afternoon and assured her that her DAS family was there to assist her and her daughter in every way possible. Bart's first impression of Meriam was that she was a remarkably strong woman who was immensely proud of her husband and his service to his country. He said he hoped that in time she would be able to sustain herself and her daughter emotionally through the overwhelming grief and anger she was now feeling. Lowe also returned calls to those senior naval officers who wanted to know if the DAS had any information beyond that in the media. The only additional news concerning the assassination was the announcement that the 17 November organization had claimed responsibility for the terrorist action.

Petroangelo went on, "Without blinking an eye, Shashkin told me that if I wished, he could help me out with the necessary money to cover my house payments and maybe with a loan to pay off the house. At first I thought Shashkin was kidding and I asked him if he was serious. When Shashkin answered that he was indeed serious, I said I would think it over and let him know next week.

Colonel Blaseman and the CIA Chief of Station as well as the security staffs at DAS and CIA headquarters agreed that they did not yet have enough information to be certain I had received a pitch to commit espionage in exchange for money from the USSR, or if the Russian attaché was just blowing smoke. It was decided to send me back to meet again, feigning interest and putting several questions to Shashkin that would definitely clear the air. I met with him today."

Lowe halted, whistling softly. "This is very interesting Mike, keep going."

"When I met Lieutenant Colonel Shashkin at lunch today, Shashkin floored me by telling me that he was a member of the GRU, that he had been for quite a while, and it was his job to try and recruit an American military officer in Jakarta.

"Shashkin then told me, when he reported his last week's conversation to his boss, a GRU colonel, the colonel authorized him to offer me $250,000, the price of my house in Washington, for future cooperation with the GRU.

"Shashkin told me he had been thinking about the matter all week, and he didn't think it would be a good idea for me to accept. Shashkin said he was worried about the changes taking place in his country and wasn't sure what would happen to him, the GRU, the KGB or for that matter the Soviet Government. He might want to ask for political asylum sometime in the future and to demonstrate his good faith, he wanted to pass something on to me that he thought the Americans would find very valuable."

Shashkin then related an incredible story to Petroangelo. "The essence of the story, general, was that when Shashkin served in the United States as a military attaché in 1984-86 he had a comrade, Georgi Kapustin, at the Soviet Embassy who was a KGB

At the end-of-the-day meeting, Pete Kalitka reported that a SAO had been appointed by the Navy to assist Meriam and was now in Athens, as was Captain Niceman. The return of the remains and family would be by an Air Force Special Mission Aircraft leaving Athens Wednesday morning and arriving at Dover Air Force Base, Delaware, at 1100 Wednesday. Mike Niceman and the SAO would be on the flight, with Meriam and her daughter. The family would then stay overnight at Dover while the Defense Mortuary Division at Dover prepared the remains for burial. "An Honor Guard will welcome the returning remains at Dover," Pete explained. "I recommend that you go up to Dover Wednesday morning and be there for the arrival and ceremony. The rest of the Baldwin family, his father and mother and two sisters will be there, as well as Meriam's family. The Vice CNO plans to be there, representing the Navy."

"I definitely want to do that. Make it happen, George." Bart said.

"After the arrival and short ceremony, the family will be moved to a reception room. I recommend you talk to Mike Niceman first to bring you up to speed, then you can talk with Meriam, her daughter and the Baldwin family members there," Pete continued. "The family will remain overnight at Dover and then on Thursday, the Air Force will fly the remains and family to Andrews Air Force Base and, from there, to the Main Chapel at Fort Myer for the military funeral at 2:00, Thursday afternoon. Meriam has made the decision that there will be no civilian funeral in Rhode Island, and Captain Baldwin will be buried in Arlington National Cemetery."

"What about the Chaplain and the eulogy, Pete, are we handling all of that?" Bart asked.

"No sir, it's strictly a Navy show. While an officer is assigned to the DAS as an attaché, he is in a joint assignment and belongs to us. But when the officer becomes a casualty, he or she is immediately returned to the parent service's control," Pete explained. "Meriam plans to remain in Washington for three days, and we have made arrangements for her to stay in guest quarters at the Washington Navy Yard. Mike Niceman will be with her until she leaves Washington, and the SAO will accompany her to the Baldwin's home in Rhode Island," Pete concluded.

On Tuesday, Joan managed to postpone most of Bart's appointments, and he spent most of the day on the second draft of his memo to the JCS Chairman on his visit to the USSR. He only returned one phone call, and that was to John Kitchen at the FBI. As he suspected, the subject was HEAT SEEKER. There had been some developments, and John wanted to get together for an update. Bart agreed to a meeting the following week.

The trip up to Dover Air Force Base and back was a sad and heartfelt one. Admiral Ledney, the Vice CNO, offered Bart a ride on his plane, and Bart was happy to accept. Ledney was newly appointed to his position and had a number of questions about the Navy's participation in the Defense Attaché program and what the chances were that Captain Baldwin's murderers would be caught. Bart passed on to him what he had been told: "The track record in general for finding and convicting the perpetrators of terrorist actions was not good, especially in Greece."

The plane-side ceremony was steeped in tradition and pride, as well as overflowing with sadness. Meriam Baldwin was every bit as courageous as Bart knew she would be, and she consoled her daughter Valerie who seemed numb with the heartbreak of losing her father.

After spending two hours with the family in the reception room, Bart and Admiral Ledney returned to Washington. Bart had also talked with the SAO and Mike Niceman and was satisfied that all possible assistance was being provided to the Baldwin family.

For Captain Baldwin's funeral the chapel at Fort Myer was overflowing with family and mourners. The flag covered coffin was escorted slowly into the chapel by an Honor Guard to the mournful processional music played by a military band. A moving eulogy was given by an officer who had been a close friend and shipmate of Chet Baldwin, and a military religious service was conducted by a Navy Chaplain.

Following the religious service the Honor Guard then moved the casket slowly to recessional music chords outside the chapel to an awaiting horse-drawn caisson. The caisson was pulled by a riderless horse with only one boot in the stirrup to symbolize the fallen warrior. When everyone in the chapel had moved outside, the caisson, the Honor Guard and a military procession with accompanying drum beat began its somber journey to the grave site.

Three volleys of rifle shots were fired, the mournful sound of taps played by a bugle, and the American flag draping the coffin was folded for its last time and presented to Meriam Baldwin. The green rolling hills of Arlington, that was the final resting place for so many American heroes, kept their solemn dignity as Chet Baldwin joined their ranks.

General Lowe directed the DAS Headquarters, except the Operations Center, to close for the afternoon so that the personnel could attend the funeral. After the funeral Bart thought about going back to the DAS office but decided against it. Tomorrow was time enough to look to future tasks.

CHAPTER 15

THE THINGS PEOPLE DO FOR THEIR COUNTRY

On Monday morning General Lowe came to work well rested with a renewed sense of purpose of about what had to be done in the DAS following the brutal slaying of Captain Baldwin. After a review of the weekend's cable traffic, his first action was to call in Colonel Martin and Mrs. Weber.

"George, Joan, the dead are buried and the living must go on. I want to return to a full schedule. I need two hours this morning to finish my memo to the Chairman, et al, and then I want to schedule two hours with Colonel Herrington and the Special Services Division crowd, and another one-hour session with Chuck Gregorios and the Congressional liaison folks. Also, squeeze in Nick Tortellie for thirty minutes. And Joan, I need you to arrange meetings for me this week with John Kitchen at the FBI and Art Cheek at CIA. Don't take no for an answer, and let's get calls made to Senator Bob Jones and Brian Corby at the SSCI."

"General, that's a lot of people!" Joan said, throwing up her hands.

As Bart began his final review of the memo he intended to send to the Chairman, the SEC DEF and others, he was satisfied he had taken adequate time to mull over the substance of what he was saying, and to recognize the possible consequences. Lowe was still on a learning curve when it came to the politics and repercussions of actions in the inner circles of the national security leadership in Washington. The bottom line of Bart's memo suggested that it was time to change U.S. policy, and the risk in doing so, he believed, was not only acceptable but prudent. Chuck Gregorios had suggested to Bart that he might want to circulate his memo in draft form to some of the experts around town and see what response it received before putting it on the street officially. At first Bart had thought that would be a good idea, but on reflection, he decided against it. He realized how persuasive some of the experts could be. That might cause him to rethink what he had said, and his boss might never have the benefit of Bart's independent view. However, rejecting Chuck's suggestion did not make Bart's agony over the memo any less strident.

Bart read the memo again. He then turned to the notes he had made on the trip and the first summary he had prepared on the Pan Am flight from Berlin. His notes said:

> Make these points to the Chairman:
> - Change is apparent everywhere in Eastern Europe.
> - Anti-Russian sentiment at all-time high in Warsaw Pact (WP) countries.
> - Defense costs vs. other economic costs of running WP countries including USSR at breaking point.
> - WP and USSR Military recognizes cost in basic needs for people due to 40 years of standoff between East and West. Civilian populations, particularly young people, want change.
> - WP countries and USSR are discreetly searching for ways to reach out to U.S., and ways for U.S. to reach out to them.
> - Military professionals in WP and USSR believe that military-to-military contact discussions and initiatives may offer a solution to the cold war stalemate.
>
> Conclusion: Multiple fissures exist in Iron Curtain and Kremlin wall.
>
> Recommendation: DOD should take the lead to establish increased contact with the USSR and WP and look for mutually agreeable initiatives that will lead to lessening of East-West tensions, reduced Russian military presence in the forward area, improved U.S., USSR relations, and ultimately an end to the Cold War.

> Caution: U.S. State Department and USSR and WP foreign ministries may oppose any major military-to-military contact as threatening to their turf and roles. Close coordination and understanding will be required.

After reviewing his notes, Bart was again sure that the memo was true to his original thoughts. He believed the memo captured the consensus of the views he had gleaned on his trip and was supported by the many specific examples he had included. While he had leaned heavily on the observations of his attachés and the first-hand information he had received from foreign and allied counterparts, he had also drawn from the comments of the many ambassadors, State Department personnel, CIA and other U.S. Government agency professionals, and the EUCOM military and civilian experts. After mulling all of this over in his mind Bart decided that it was time to fish or cut bait. With careful deliberation, he signed the memo. Then he pressed his intercom button and asked George to come into the office.

When George entered and walked over to his desk, Bart said, "Well George, here it is; the famous memo you and I have talked about so many times. I've signed it, and with it I may have sealed my fate."

George Martin was the only person in the DAS organization that Bart would confide in or reveal any self-doubts. From the times of the Roman Legions, military leaders realized it was essential to have a trusted aide or assistant with whom airing difficult decisions of command or responsibilities was possible. George was that person for Bart Lowe.

"I wouldn't worry about it, boss," said George. "You are just calling it as you see it and no one can challenge that. I'm betting you are right on the mark. And who should know better than I...because I was there."

"You've convinced me, George. Please ask Joan to make copies for Mr. Grant, the ASD ISA, General Reiley, the other Service Chiefs and Lieutenant General Murphy, the Director, DIA. And George can you arrange to have them all delivered by courier so that the copies arrive at the same time as the originals to the Chairman and SEC DEF?"

"Not a problem, boss. I'll take care of it."

Bart next summoned Colonel Bob Herrington and his SSD crew of Jensen Wong and Lieutenant Colonels Vaught and Berenger. He also asked his deputy, Pete Kalitka to sit in. He gave them a debrief of the visits he had made to Germany and Austria and the incidents and events that had taken place in Poland, Czechoslovakia, and Moscow. He told them he had been very impressed with the Army and Air Force HUMINT operations in Europe and the professionalism of the military's service operators. But he had detected less than enthusiastic support for their operations from the CIA Chief of Station in Bonn. Bart told them that he needed to talk to Art Cheek, the DDO at CIA, about that and the GREENFIELDS operation in Vienna. Bob Herrington told Bart there had been two additional compromises of service sensitive operations in Europe, and two more valuable agents had been lost.

"That probably explains Senator Thomas' renewed interest in calling a halt to our HUMINT operations," said Bart and told them of the call from General Reiley.

Herrington also said he had heard from his contacts at CIA that there had been more CIA compromises but that CIA wasn't saying anything official.

Then Bart handed Bob Herrington an envelope that he had received at his quarters, via European mail. The envelope contained a single white sheet of paper with the following handwritten note in block printing:

> A reliable contact of mine reports that the number two official of your embassy was seen in Vienna in a covert meeting with a known KGB officer. Briefcases were exchanged. In view of this development I can no longer risk any direct contact with anyone from U.S. Embassy. When you have proposal for safe meeting arrangements contact me at P.O. Box 71935.
>
> L.

After Herrington had read the note and passed it on to Captain Kalitka and the others, Bart said, "I intend to show this note to John Kitchen at the FBI and Art Cheek at CIA. Bob, when you have a proposal on how we can meet or contact GREENFIELDS safely, let me know; but let's not share the details of that with CIA just yet. Okay guys, any questions?"

"Wow, boss, you had some trip," commented Jensen Wong.

After a few more questions, all the staffers departed except Bob Herrington and Pete Kalitka.

"Bob, how much of this do you think is related to HEAT SEEKER?" Bart asked.

"Let's tick them off, boss. First, I believe all of the service operations that have been compromised in Europe are a result of HEAT SEEKER. Ditto for the GREENFIELDS problem, Czech officer in Prague and, clearly, the CIA agent compromises in Moscow. And probably the transfer or compromise of the DAO Moscow cooperating Soviet officers. Now as to the incident in Warsaw, I don't see any HEAT SEEKER connection there. I have to think you were just a target of opportunity for the Polish SA," answered Bob.

"Bob, do you think John Kitchen just wants to tell me about the new compromises?" asked Bart.

"I don't think so. He knows that I know about them and would inform you. I'm guessing he has some new development he wants to tell you about firsthand."

"O.K. That's enough for today. Bob, it goes without saying that this HEAT SEEKER business is bad, bad, bad, and you must work closely with the FBI, CIA and military services to try to bring it to closure. Let me know if there is something else you need that will help you."

"Just need some answers," Bob replied as he frowned in frustration.

"In the meantime, I need to think of some persuasive argument to convince Senator Thomas not to close down the service HUMINT operations. I know those commanders in Europe need them," Bart told Pete and Bob as they got out of their chairs and prepared to leave.

"Maybe that's your best argument: Field commanders need them," said Pete.

"Maybe you're right," answered Bart. "Maybe you're right."

When Chuck Gregorios and Robin Fitch came in they told Bart they had been as surprised as Bart by the push by Senator Thomas' staff to curtail or eliminate Military Service HUMINT operations. Robin saw the responsibility as chiefly that of Milt Cohen, Senator Thomas' principal staff assistant. She had conferred with the Army Congressional Liaison staff and learned from them that although Cohen was carrying out the Senator's direction, he was clearly carrying the ball. Robin surmised that Cohen had learned about the most recent compromises of service operations and saw an opportunity to put pressure on the Army. So far nothing was directed at the Air Force or Navy.

Cohen's reasoning, speculated Fitch, was that since the Army had the largest number of operations and people involved, if he could get the Army to cave in, the others would follow by default.

"Robin, can we reason with Cohen and convince him it's not really a good idea to cut the services out of these operations?" Bart asked.

"No, sir. I don't believe you can. My read of Milt is that he has selected this action, albeit with the Senator's blessing, as a cause celebre and sees it as an opportunity to make a name for himself. In order to stop it or even delay it, you must convince Senator Thomas."

"Senator Thomas, I believe, has a hang up with the military services conducting human intelligence operations," added Chuck. "What he may be missing is the importance of certain types of information to the battlefield commander and CIA's inability to provide that information."

"I agree," said Robin. "But I also believe if we can somehow convince Senator Thomas, we can get him to back off, even if he doesn't agree in principle."

"I read you and it makes sense. What we need now is a plan. Robin, you work on getting some face time with Senator Thomas to table the issue. Not immediately, but in the next thirty days. We need some time to get the rest of this together. Chuck, let's task Nick Tortellie and Bob Herrington to pull together some HUMINT operations examples that were big time payoffs to combat commanders and then I'll send a cable to the commanders asking them if they are willing to come to Washington and tell Senator Thomas how important this kind of support is to them. In the meantime, I plan to talk to Senator Bob Jones and Brian Corby, and if necessary, Senator Corbett to drum up support. Robin, you do the same with the key staffers and keep me informed on how it's going."

"Sounds like a plan, boss. We'll run with it," said Chuck.

When Colonel Nick Tortellie came in that afternoon, Bart was genuinely glad to see his hard working operations officer. Nick was the kind of officer you could always count on to look after the troops and make sure the DAS was not neglected.

"Nick, as you know, my attention has been focused almost exclusively on Eastern Europe and the Soviet Union for the last month. How is the rest of the world doing?"

"Well, as you would expect there has been considerable operational activity. But I think it is fair to say all crises are under control. I tried to keep you informed through the updates that we sent to George for you, and I think you are aware of the major activities that have taken place concerning our attachés."

"Yes, you did, and the updates were very helpful."

"At this Friday's operational update, I plan to tailor the briefings to emphasize the other parts of the world, particularly North Korea, China, the insurgencies in Central and Latin America, our contributions to the war on drugs, and activities in the Middle East and Africa."

"That's good, Nick. That's what I need."

"Also, we are on your calendar later this week to come back at you for a proposed Attaché Conference and travel schedule for the rest of 1987. I'm sure that the last thing you want to hear when you return from a long trip is details of the next trip. But word has spread now throughout the DAS on the conference in Garmisch and the rest of the attaché world is anxious to get their fair share of attention."

"I hear you, Nick. Also I need you to work closely with our DAS security people and the State Department on any security lessons we can learn from what happened in Greece. If counter terrorist measures need to be strengthened, then let's get out the word and let's do it. Any developments on the assassination investigation?" Bart asked.

"No sir. The FBI has it, but they are not hopeful in the near term."

"And the PNGs from Moscow?"

"All families returned and new assignments made. We are searching for qualified replacements that won't take too long to train. The reality is that General Alton will be short two attachés for longer than he would like."

"Okay, Nick, thanks for the information; I look forward to Friday and your worldwide update."

"Again, welcome back, boss. We all missed you."

The rest of the week went quickly. Joan was successful in getting meeting times for Bart at the FBI on Wednesday and CIA on Thursday. While at the FBI, Bart was able to talk to the FBI agents who were supervising the investigation in Athens. They provided Bart an overview of the 17 November terrorist organization and explained that 17 November had been ruthlessly skilled and successful at the terrorist actions and murders they carried out. If nothing could be found in the way of evidence at the bombing scene to link the attack to an individual or individuals, and none had been found at the Baldwin scene, then the Greek authorities and the FBI had little to go on. "Breakthroughs in terrorist attacks usually came as a result of an informer," they said. Often someone who became disgruntled with the terrorist organization or some of the individuals in it and was willing to give someone up." They assured Bart the investigation would remain open and active until such time as the perpetrators were caught. The FBI in this case was limited by the good offices and cooperation of the Greek authorities.

When Bart met with John Kitchen in his office, John said he had been so busy he hadn't played racquetball since Bart had left town. They corrected that by making a commitment to play at the Pentagon the following Tuesday.

John opened the meeting by saying, "I am sure Bob Herrington told you about the latest compromises of the service HUMINT operations, and unofficially I can tell you that there have been more, considerably more, CIA compromises. Protect me on that, Bart, that information should be really coming from CIA."

"I am going to see Art Cheek tomorrow, and I intend to discuss HEAT SEEKER with him. I am sure he will be candid with me."

"I wish I could say the same thing," John said, and laughed. "You know we have never talked about this Bart but the FBI and CIA are two different cultures. We, of course, work very closely with them in my field of foreign counterintelligence, but when dealing with them you never have complete confidence that they have told you everything. In fact your gut usually tells you that something very important is missing. And when we call them on it, they just fall back on their own unique charter and claim national security considerations won't allow us access to some sensitive compartment or operation that they are protecting. I don't mean to bad mouth CIA, but take this HEAT SEEKER investigation. This thing looks as though it may be the biggest espionage leak we have had since the Rosenberg case, and my guys are all busting their humps around the clock while our counterparts at CIA are treating this like business as usual. If I sound a bit frustrated it is because I am."

"Feel strongly do you, John?" Bart said tongue in cheek. They both laughed and John got up from his desk, went over to a water cooler and took a long drink.

When he returned to his desk, he relaxed, smiled at Bart and said, "The reason I wanted to meet with you, Bart, is that my guys have turned up a lead on a former military enlisted man, now in the CIA, who once served in Moscow although some time before HEAT SEEKER began. We don't think much of the lead, and I doubt that it is HEAT SEEKER-related, but we would like to check it out just in case and we need your help."

"He may have been attachéd to the DAS," replied Bart.

"He's with the CIA now. I think you could check records of his service. He speaks Russian, we know, and he served at CIA headquarters until recently when he was posted overseas. This is just for your ears right now."

"Sure, John, we'll be happy to assist, and when I return to the office I'll give you a point of contact in my SSD to help you. I assume that you will approach this as a national security investigation?"

"Yes, and if and when it turns into anything else we'll inform CIA and all the other necessary people." It's too early to do more than speculate."

"You mean you've not told CIA?" Bart asked.

John shook his head no. As I mentioned, we just turned up this lead."

"Well, I'll have a question or two for you later on that, but let me first show you an interesting note I received from our GREENFIELDS source in Vienna," Bart said, passing the note to John.

"Yes, very interesting. Do you mind if I make a copy of this?"

Bart replied, "I'd rather you just noted the first part of what it says. I am already very concerned for the security of this operation and would rather not have any unnecessary copies made."

"Fair enough. May I ask is this GREENFIELDS a reliable source?"

"Yes. Has been for years."

"Then this information is also probably reliable. We also have had an open investigation for a year on Felix Hoffman, the Deputy Chief of Mission in Vienna. A number of people in Vienna and Washington, including the CIA, reported him for what they considered suspicious activities. But nothing so blatant as your source suggests. This may give us sufficient basis for a 24-hour-a-day surveillance. This is very helpful, Bart. I appreciate it."

As Bart started to say something, John put up his hand and said, "Please let me anticipate your questions. Why didn't I tell you about these guys before? Do you see any HEAT SEEKER connection here? I certainly don't, but in view of your GREENFIELDS' concern that someone has blown the whistle, we clearly must factor the former GI's tour in Moscow or Hoffman's in Vienna as possible HEAT SEEKER connections, agents who may have sold out to the other side. But, have either now or in the past had access to the kind of information that HEAT SEEKER would have had to have. Hoffman could be the problem for your GREENFIELDS operation based on information he now acquires at the Embassy in Vienna."

"I see," said Bart, nodding.

"Your next question, General, would be what about any relationship between Vienna and Moscow? I still don't see a HEAT SEEKER connection."

"Does CIA agree with you on the Vienna possibility of compromise?"

"Yes, they do, and General, your last question is probably what about the COS's theory in Moscow that maybe the KGB had an inside man in the Embassy. Well we don't think so but based on our new Moscow lead and the COS's theory that maybe someone once got into CIA communications between Moscow and Langley and just dumped all that HEAT SEEKER information, we must continue to follow this trail. The weakness there is it would have to probably have involved more than one person. It couldn't just have been an attaché. He wouldn't have any CIA access. And if it was a CIA person in Moscow he or she shouldn't have had access to sensitive operations in other countries.

Bart laughed. "Well, I have to trust someone in this town. And I trust you. Having said all that, I have a practical problem. Senator Thomas of the SSCI wants to shut down our HUMINT operations. He doesn't think the military should be involved in the sensitive operations. He thinks that it should be the sole purview of CIA. My problem is that CIA does not do the military intelligence bit well, and my combat commanders need the support. Part of the ammunition Senator Thomas' staffers are using is the recent compromise of the service's operations. They think these compromises are caused by poor professionalism in a business we shouldn't be in anyway. If Senator Thomas could be briefed on HEAT SEEKER, he would know what the real cause of the compromises is and he might cut me some slack. So what do you think, Ace?"

"Jesus, Bart. Why didn't you pick something difficult?" John said with obvious chagrin. "Do you have any idea of our track record in trying to keep something closely held once we have shared it with any member of Congress? Although we have been working on this hummer since the end of 1985, HEAT SEEKER is still a wisp. It's only a suspicion. We don't have any hard evidence. And who knows, maybe the National Security Agency is right; they think it's a highly sophisticated technical penetration. And lastly, my friend, CIA is in the driver's seat on this. Their losses have been the greatest, and they have the most at stake. I'm confident that if you raise the question with Art Cheek, he will think you have taken leave of your senses. CIA is always loath to think of sharing things they don't have to with the Congress. And they know, as we know, that if word gets out to HEAT SEEKER that we are looking for him, or her, he may go to ground. In good conscience I don't think I can help you Bart."

"Well, professor, that brings me to my last question of the day. What is your gut feeling on HEAT SEEKER? Is it just a figment of our imagination? If not, who and where is it? Your many years in this business must tell you something."

"So, General, I must tell you hardly a week goes by that I don't ask myself that same question. And how do I feel? What do I believe? First, my logical lawyer's mind tells me not to rule out a technical penetration. It can do the most harm, and you may never know where you're losing it. Sometimes it's in places you least expect like an electronic switching station. As far as we know, this is all HUMINT type of information we are losing and there's only one place in our country that has the most of that, CIA. That doesn't necessarily rule out Langley as a technical target, but the information that we believe has leaked seems to only concern the USSR, Europe, and the United States. The KGB seems central in the loss of our agents, i.e., in every case we discern a connection to the KGB. So you might say that narrows down the places in CIA to look for any technical penetration. So what about people with access to the information? The DAS has had losses, as well as the military services, the FBI and the CIA. So is it somebody in the CIA, FBI or the DAS? I guess it could be, but neither the DAS nor the FBI have access to the CIA information, yet CIA has access to all of our HUMINT information. So my gut tells me if we are going to find someone doing this, it will probably be at CIA. But then, Bart, what do I know? If you ever read any of the classic espionage cases you know that Sergeant David Greenglas stole the technical secrets of the atomic bomb without access to any classified information. He simply was a good listener in the dining hall at Los Alamos. So maybe, just maybe, HEAT SEEKER is a food server in the cafeteria at Langley."

"Enough, John. My head is aching, and I haven't been worrying about this nearly as long as you have." Bart stood and readied himself to leave. "I'll see you on Tuesday."

Bart departed the FBI Headquarters and returned to his waiting sedan for the drive across the Potomac River to Rosslyn.

The next day Bart's meeting with Art Cheek at CIA Headquarters in Langley took place in CIA's Deputy Director of Operations' seventh floor office at half past twelve. Art Cheek met Bart at his office door. He was a short, stocky man in his mid-fifties with brown hair and horned rim glasses, he had his suit coat off and his tie loosened. Given both their busy schedules, they had agreed to meet at lunch. Art's administrative assistant, Mary Godwin, arranged for trays to be brought up to the DDO's office from the executive dining room for Art and General Lowe. Mary had called Bart that morning with a menu choice and he had selected the fresh fruit plate, iced tea and lime sherbet. Art Cheek was having a rainbow trout and parsley potatoes. The two, always busy men had adopted a routine. Small talk in the few minutes before lunch was served, and then a discussion of the issues.

"Okay Bart, what's on your mind?" offered Art.

"First I'd like to give you a run down on my trip to Eastern Europe and the Soviet Union, then raise some questions that came up on the trip and, finally, discuss HEAT SEEKER."

"Yeah, that," said Art with a scowl. Art Cheek was a man of few words.

Bart covered the highlights of his visits with the CIA Chiefs of Station in Bonn, Vienna, Prague, Warsaw, and Moscow. He voiced his concern for the DAS operations in Prague and Vienna and concluded with the problems he was having with the compromise of the military services' operations.

"What do you want me to do about any of that, Bart?" Cheek said, not too enthusiastically, in his New England nasal twang.

"First, I guess I want you to tell me why your guy in Bonn is slow-rolling the military people on their operations. Are we really that bad? Or is it that, like Senator Thomas, you don't think the military should be in a business that you consider your exclusive turf? I've looked at the military operations in Washington and in Europe and they look pretty damn professional to me, and the results they have obtained are what military commanders need."

Art was surprised at the outburst. "Whoa, Bart, I didn't mean to get your Irish up," Art said as he got up from the table and walked over to the window looking out over the brown oak winter skyline.

"Let me explain something to you. We have some old timers in CIA that have been around a long time. They tend to think we are in charge of the world. They think of military intelligence from the days after WWII and the Korean War. They imagine that the military intelligence types are a bunch of guys with crew cuts in civilian suits, wearing white socks, running around trying to do sensitive operations they don't understand. And sometimes these, let me call them old boys, whisper in other people's ears, like the Congressional staffers. You and I know that in today's world that impression is the furthest thing from the truth. You now have a wide range of capabilities and some outstanding individuals. I ought to know. We train them, and, in many situations around the world, work closely together. CIA neither has the time nor the resources to do your military mission. I am hard pressed to do our own, and the last thing I want is to assume responsibility for the military mission. You do that best and I am on record for telling Congress that."

"Okay, Art, I'll accept that but how does that treat my problem in Bonn?"

"It sounds to me like my guy in Bonn is fucking up. If you tell me you have a problem, I'll look into it and if he is fucking up, I'll burn his ass."

"Art, I'm more interested in working together as a team than I am in getting someone's ass burned."

"I know that Bart, and that's my intention also. Let me look into it, and I'll get back to you, okay?" With that he walked over to his desk and made a note. "What's next?"

"My problem with Congress. Any chance of getting you to brief Senator Thomas on HEAT SEEKER?"

Art was quick to respond. "No way, Bart. I'd like to be able to help you, but we don't have enough to go on. What we have is a problem, and we don't know enough about the problem to tell someone else about it, especially Congress. That place is like a sieve. Anything that goes in automatically comes out. And if word gets out we are pursuing it, we will be dead in the water for ever having a chance of catching the bastard."

"Art, level with me. Is there a HEAT SEEKER? Is it a person who works for me or for you, or is it a technical penetration as NSA suggests? Has the other side just got better at counterespionage? Where and how is the information being lost?"

"Christ, I wish I knew the answer to that! Look, I know you haven't been in this business long and haven't had to worry about these kinds of problems. But the thought of a mole buried deep in any organization is something you live in fear of all the time. It's our highest objective to get someone in the bad guy's organizations like the KGB and GRU, and we have obviously had some success over the years. So you can expect that our opposition over the years is trying to do the same thing, and in the case of the KGB with some success. That guy Howard that we lost to the Russians a couple of years ago for example. We are still trying to figure out the damage he did to us. It's enough to make you sick to your stomach. And now this HEAT SEEKER thing. Let me tell you something: I think we have been penetrated. The kinds of information that have been lost, the number of agents compromised, could only come from one place, here. None of you other guys have all of that information. Now the real question is, when you suspect or discover that you have been had, what do you do about it? You can't just shut down operations. The other side would really like that, and that would double their advantage. So what you do is press on with operations, transfer people around, and increase internal surveillance, hoping maybe you will come up with someone who will tell you who it is. That's how we got on to Howard. And the other thing you do is begin the search for the needle in the haystack like we and the FBI are doing now. And as you look at the hundreds of people that have access to the information that is being lost, you hope somehow you get lucky. And finally you re-look at all your security measures for handling sensitive information, see if you can tighten them, or perhaps change them to cut off the info to the mole. And again you must press on. Our customers are not interested in our problems. What they are interested in is the answers to their questions, and they want those answers today."

"Art, I appreciate your sharing that with me, and, of course, I won't discuss it with anyone else." Bart told Art.

"If you did, Bart, I would have to deny it."

"There is one thing in all of that Art: the security measures. My guys would like to compartmentalize the information we provide CIA concerning DAS sources and restrict access to that information to the smallest number of CIA people possible. That could possibly solve my GREENFIELDS problem. I am doing that in my own organizations and will ask the military services to do the same. Are you willing to cooperate with us on this?" Bart asked.

"Sure, Bart, I can support that. When I figure out who I want to handle that, I'll have Mary give you a call with the name of a point of contact." Then Art stood up, looked at his watch, realized they had already gone fifteen minutes over the allotted time and said, "I'll pop for lunch and the compartmentation thing, but that's all I am going to let you beat me out of today, General."

Driving down the quiet wooded road that leads from the CIA Headquarters back to the George Washington Parkway, Bart reflected on his conversation with Art. Although they came from very diverse backgrounds and professions, Art Cheek and Bart Lowe had hit it off immediately. Art had been very helpful to Bart as a newcomer to the big leagues in Washington, especially within the intelligence community. Bart liked Art and trusted him, but he did not envy Art his job. It was clearly one of the most powerful jobs in Washington, perhaps the world, but Bart believed it was also one of the most thankless.

By Friday Bart had received more than twenty calls concerning the memo he had sent to the Chairman, JCS.

The first call came from General Murphy who gave Bart an "attaboy" and said, "No one would ever accuse you of not taking risks."

From people in other agencies like CIA and State the reaction was split. More were against it than for it. Those against it said the memo was premature, based on insufficient information and evidence and jumped to flawed conclusions. The ISA, DOD people and the State Department people accused Bart of being out of his league and suggested he stick to straight attaché reporting and leave any policy changes to them. The hard-line Russian bashers wrote Bart off as someone who simply did not know the Russian track record, someone naive about Soviet intentions. Those who were for it told Bart "right on" and "it's about time someone was willing to call it." As best he could tell, those who supported the memo came from the younger defense analysts who had been worried about America's acceptance of the status quo for some time. The good news, Bart thought, was that no one had called him up to say he was fired.

Late Friday afternoon Joan came rushing in to Bart's office and said, "General Lowe, General Lowe. The Chairman is calling you; he is on the secure line."

Bart quickly picked up his phone and answered, "Bart Lowe."

"Bart, this is Jeremiah Johnson. I'm calling you to thank you for your memorandum on the Soviet Union and Warsaw Pact. It was very helpful and just what I was looking for. It's safe to say that the SEC DEF is also pleased. You won't be hearing from him, but he and I have discussed it, and we both are in agreement with your conclusions. As you might suspect, we have been getting signals for some time now from many directions suggesting that the Communist world, as we have known it, is changing dramatically. If we accept that, and the Secretary and I believe it to be inevitable, then the challenge to the United States is how to deal with that change. If we don't take the lead, then we may be forced to follow. As we implement our own changes the attaché reporting on what the other side is thinking and doing will be more important than ever. We still have a steep hill to climb. Tell all your folks for me we appreciate all that they have done."

"Yes, sir, I will be happy to do that."

At the end-of-day meeting, Bart told the assembled DAS leadership of the phone call that afternoon from the Chairman. Then he passed around a cable he had drafted to the U.S. attachés in the Warsaw Pact nations, the Soviet Union and the Eastern Europe Division commending them for their reporting.

That night as he went down the elevator, still buoyant from the Chairman's call and its potential impact for the future, Bart thought to himself, "Who ever said this was a tough job? I might even take tomorrow off."

One month earlier, Harold Sema also received a telephone call that should have been good news. Sema's personnel department called and informed him that he had been selected for a foreign posting. And, because this country was outside of his normal area of expertise, he would be receiving additional language training. Another feather in his cap, the personnel official had told him.

Sema's first reaction was shock.

The country sounded like a place in the backwaters of the world. "My God," he thought, "I'm not even sure I know where it is." When he asked the personnel official if there were any other choices, or whether he could decline the assignment, the personnel official, somewhat miffed, told him absolutely not. The decision had been made and was final unless Sema had some overriding personal reason that would keep him from accepting the assignment. The personnel officer then told Sema the language training, a six month course, began in less than thirty days and then rang off.

Sema was not very happy. He had become accustomed to the lifestyle that the money from the Russians had afforded him and what better place to live it than Washington. The last thing Sema wanted to do was to go off to some third rate country in the middle of nowhere.

Then the question came roaring to his mind: “what about access to the kinds of information the Russians wanted?” His present situation was ideal. He had access to everything. He certainly couldn’t duplicate that across the world in Nowheresville.

Harold Sema was not a happy camper.

CHAPTER 16

AND THE BEAT GOES ON

Driving up the road in Fort Myer Bart Lowe recalled the past two years of his job as Director of the Defense Attaché Service.

The rescue of Bill Kennedy in Syria had been one more in a never-ending string of crises around the world in places the United States was involved. This one, fortunately, was resolved without injury, unlike some of the others, such as Chet Baldwin's assassination in Greece.

In the winter of 1987, having returned from a month in Europe, Bart had his hands full; but, with a positive approach and a lot of hard work, he and the DAS staff had been able to work their way through most of the problems. Replacements had been found for the officers expelled by the Soviets from Moscow, another dedicated officer replaced Baldwin in Greece, and as the JCS Chairman had predicted, the Cold War had begun to thaw. The Chairman himself had accepted the invitation to visit the Romanians. A visit to the United States by the Chief of Staff of the Czech Army was in progress and a visit to the United States by the Soviet Defense Minister was being discussed in Washington and Moscow. A strong Secretary of Defense had carried the military-to-military contact initiative to the White House and convinced the President of its worth. Some Soviet reductions in the forward area had begun, with Hungary leading the way. Second-guessers to America's earlier hard-line approach to the USSR had come out of the woodwork in droves. General Alton and the attachés in Moscow had literally been working like Trojans as point men for the Chairman and the SecDef with the Russian military. Some high-level visits had taken place and others were scheduled.

Senator Thomas had been persuaded to leave the watchdog role over the HUMINT operations to General Lowe and called off the pressure by his staffer, Milt Cohen. The Senator did not have a change of heart, nor did Bart have to use the HEAT SEEKER card. He agreed to back off for the "time being," his words, because Bart's people, essentially Bob Herrington and Nick Tortellie, were able to convince him through several carefully crafted series of briefings that the compromises suffered were not due to any careless operational practices. The capper probably came when representatives from the key Unified and Specified Commands around the world testified that they needed the military HUMINT support and that CIA had neither the experience or resources to provide that support.

In a private session between Bart and Senator Thomas, the Senator had told Bart that he thought the time was coming when the military services would no longer be able to afford the resources to conduct their own individual HUMINT operations. At that time, if CIA couldn't do the job, there would be a need for a joint military effort similar to the DAS to conduct those sensitive operations. The Senator had extracted a promise from Bart that he would look into the feasibility of such an organization, think through the smart ways to establish it and come back to the senator within two years to re-address the issue. He thanked the Senator for his support and put Bob Herrington and Jensen Wong from SSD to work on the project.

Colonel Herrington and his people had been able to work out an arrangement with GREENFIELDS in Vienna whereby Countess Laressa mailed her information to a post office box in Bern, Switzerland. The P.O. box was controlled by the U.S. Defense Attaché there and he, in turn, forwarded this information to DAS Headquarters via diplomatic pouch. This was an agreeable arrangement for Countess Laressa because she already had a large amount of correspondence with a number of places in Switzerland. Once the details had been worked out, the very valuable information from GREENFIELDS resumed and had continued without interruption.

On the other hand, HEAT SEEKER still had not been resolved. The winter of 1987 was the last time any dramatic compromises or loss of agents without explanation occurred. The reasons for that were not clear. Bob Herrington and SSD, assisted by the Army and Air Force, made an in-depth analysis of all DAS and military service HUMINT compromises, personnel assignments and agent losses that could possibly be related to HEAT SEEKER. All of the DAS individuals involved were investigated with negative results. The cases were also cross referenced with the Navy's Walker and the Army's Conrad espionage cases to determine any HEAT SEEKER connections, again with negative results. The one common denominator that all the compromises had was that all seemed to involve someone who had been working for the military or the DAS sometime. And since the compromises involved DAS, Army, and Air Force operations, no single individual at either the Army, Navy, or Air Force ever had information concerning all of the operations.

Only a handful of people in the DAS, almost all in SSD, had sensitive information on most operations. Those individuals had undergone investigations and polygraph examinations with negative results. Even Bart had volunteered for the polygraph to set the right example. Bob Herrington's conclusions from the analysis were: 1) HEAT SEEKER was a technical penetration, its access apparently beginning in 1985 and continuing into the first part of 1987, or 2) if HEAT SEEKER was a mole, the period of access seemed to be 1985-87, or 3) that HEAT SEEKER was either a mole or a technical penetration that made a one-time access and acquisition of information in early 1985, or 4) that the KGB, for their own reasons, stretched out the closing down of the operations (1985-87) to support agent operations, and 5) CIA was the most likely place to find all of the information that was compromised. Herrington had shared his analysis first with the FBI and then the CIA. Neither could fault the analysis and assured him that their HEAT SEEKER investigations were continuing.

One other dimension in the HEAT SEEKER investigation was the results achieved in the better compartmenting of Defense

Department source information after Bart had gained agreement from Art Cheek at CIA to work together on this problem. Jensen Wong, a long time HUMINT operator, and Bart's ace computer and communications whiz, Lieutenant Colonel Jerry Kirsch, had designed and implemented in a Defense Source Registry that provided a much better cloak of security around sources, agents and operations and most importantly, strictly limited the number of individuals having access to the super sensitive information. There had been no unexplained compromises of agent operations since the implementation of the Defense Source Registry.

Bob Herrington would like to have taken credit for the halt to the compromises, but believed it was in reality HEAT SEEKER related. A much greater threat could exist, Herrington opined, if HEAT SEEKER still had access, but the recipient of HEAT SEEKER's information, believed to be the KGB, had made a decision not to use the information to roll up agents, as had been the case until 1987. The information could be used in a far more sophisticated way by feeding false information to the U.S. agents, thus misleading them and the United States on what the Russians were actually doing in their defense research, military doctrine and advance weapons systems development. So the mystery continued.

Nick Tortellie had recommended four additional Regional Attaché Conferences in 1987, which took Bart to each of the regions of the world and included visits to the major countries of that region. In March, Bart and some of the DAS staff had headed to the Far East and the Pacific Regional Attaché Conference, held at the U.S. Embassy in Seoul, Korea. Following that conference, Bart had gone on to Japan, Thailand, and the Philippines. The conference model that grew out of the Garmisch, Germany, conference contained briefings which included a perspective from the host country U.S. Ambassador, a regional overview from a Unified Command (in the Pacific, PACOM) and then a view from Washington, i.e., the DAS and other interested agencies.

In May, Bart had gone to Amman, Jordan and Abidjan, Ivory Coast for Middle East and Northern Africa conferences and had visited Israel, Egypt, Algeria and the Sudan. Both the EUCOM and CENTCOM Commands had participated. In September, the Western European Conference was held in the Hague, and Bart made visits to London, Paris, Brussels and Rome. December had taken him to the highest DAO in the world at La Paz, Bolivia, the South and Central America Regional Conference at Quito, Ecuador, and visits to Colombia, Peru, and Brazil. Following that conference Bart had taken leave and B.J. had flown down from Washington. They had spent a delightful Christmas in Belize as guests of the DATT and the U.S. Ambassador.

By 1988, in addition to the major adversaries of Russia, China, North Korea and Cuba, Bart Lowe had become knowledgeable about dozens of regional problems around the world. He and the DAS followed the often bloody argument between Israelis and Arabs, the war between Iran and Iraq, the fighting in Ireland, Angola, El Salvador, Somalia, Chad, Yemen, and Surinam, and the political/military struggles in Burma, Nicaragua, Chile, Cyprus, Algeria, Mozambique, Nambia, and the Philippines. He was able to quote chapter and verse on illicit drug activities in Colombia, Bolivia, Peru, Panama, Mexico, Burma, Laos, Thailand, the Netherlands, and Miami, New York and Los Angeles.

In many foreign countries, the government was a military government or the military was linked to the drug trade. That factor made the attaches some of the best observers on the U.S. country teams concerning foreign government or military involvement in illegal drugs. Reporting on drug activities became a major role for the attaches and the DAOs were of considerable assistance to the U.S. DEA teams serving abroad.

Bart had found that the Regional Attaché Conferences were a very useful command and management tool, not only for himself and the headquarters, but also for the attachés in the field. It gave them the feeling that they were a part of a larger organization with an important mission, and one that cared about them and their families. After the first two conferences, based on the feedback he received, Bart sensed that attachés and their families could easily lapse into feelings of isolation, depending on the conditions of the foreign countries where they were serving. Most important to them, he believed, was the understanding that the DAS Headquarters existed not only to task them, but also as an organization which would take on their problems and concerns and work to solve them.

Although Bart had always prided himself on planning ahead, his relationship with B.J. Ross was somehow suspended in time. They were both consummate professionals and their jobs demanded almost all of their time. But because they were both good managers of their time, they could normally squeeze in a few moments or hours. They were very comfortable together and completely relaxed with each other's situation. And they found it possible to be there for each other at difficult times. Theirs was a compatible relationship that was right for them both.

On a warm Sunday afternoon in 1988, as Bart drove into the garage behind his quarters at Fort Myer, his thoughts turned to having a cold beer. However, as he entered the back door, the phone was ringing and he moved quickly to answer it. The caller was General Lennie Murphy who said, "Bart, now that the Syrian crisis is over, how are you doing? Are you keeping all our other attachés and their ambassadors in line?"

"I certainly hope so, sir, but you never know what will happen tomorrow."

"Ambassador Pellicon from Tunisia was at the JCS the other day giving a briefing on the Palestine Liberation Organization, and he couldn't say enough about his attaché, his support from the DAS. You and your lads are doing a great job, Bart."

"Music to my ears, General Murphy. I'll pass along the word to the guys and gals in the trenches."

"After that briefing by the Chairman, your Chief, General Reiley and I had a little chat about you."

"Am I in trouble again?" Bart asked.

"No. No," Murphy replied. "It is just that the three of us are packing it in at the end of the summer, and we thought wouldn't it be great if old Bart Lowe, young fellow that he is, would be willing to hang around for another year or two just to give the new guys some continuity in their support. If you say yes, General Reiley will fix it with the Army, and the Chairman will approve it."

"What about the new guys? Maybe they won't want me on the team?" Bart asked.

"Don't sweat it, buddy. You have an excellent reputation in the community, even the State Department likes you, you must have a friend in court." Murphy was aware of Bart and B.J.'s relationship and said this tongue in cheek.

"Well, to tell you the truth, Lennie, I have been so busy I haven't even thought about it. I must do that soon, or I may not have another life to go to. But the DAS has been a dream come true for me, and I'll be happy to stay around a while longer."

"I'll pass along the word and see you at my retirement party, right?" and General Murphy hung up.

Lowe hung up his hat and got a Heineken from the fridge. He then went over to the tape deck and turned on some Montovani and plopped into the green leather chair in his study. As he sat listening to the relaxing music, his thoughts turned to his upcoming trip in September to China and Japan and other countries in the Pacific. In the past two years, Bart had been to Japan, but had been twice turned down by the Chinese for a visa to visit the DAO in Beijing. The DATT in China, an old Army service buddy of Bart's, Brigadier General Jack Fuller, had said it was because they liked to match up visiting VIPs with their own officials for visits and they weren't sure who to line Bart up with, their Defense Ministry or their Foreign Ministry. Jack had said to stay after them. They did finally agree to a September visit.

Bart's two earlier visits to Japan as Director of the DAS had been short and his schedule very tight. During the upcoming visit in September, however, Bart planned five days leave in Japan.

Fortuitously, on his most recent visit to Japan, Bart encountered a man at an embassy social that he had met in Japan more than thirty years ago while serving there as a young soldier. The man was a remarkable ethnic Japanese-American named Harry Banahara. In 1944 Banahara was a young lawyer who had just graduated from law school at USC, was drafted into the US Army, and sent to the Pacific to fight in the last days of World War II. After the war Banahara joined General MacArthur's staff and participated in the writing of the post-war Japanese constitution. Because of his legal brilliance, his flawless linguistic skills and his innate ability to instill confidence in both his Japanese contacts and his U.S. Army colleagues, Banahara rose quickly through the ranks and was promoted to full colonel at an early age. In fact, for many years he was known in both American and Japanese circles as the "boy Colonel." Because of his work on the constitution and his paternal friendship with the Japanese, the Japanese government offered him a splendid old residence in the Akasaka area of Tokyo. The house had belonged to a member of the Tojo family, long deceased, and had been seized by the Occupation Forces after the war. Because of the Occupation of Japan rules in effect, there was no problem with Banahara accepting the residence as his official quarters. With the quarters came a serving staff and a driver and car. Again, because of the need to employ as many Japanese as possible in post-war Japan, there was no objection from the U.S. Government. Harry Banahara remained in Japan for the rest of his 30 year Army career, first as part of the occupation force and then on the staff of the Headquarters, U.S. Forces, Far East. He became an indispensable part of the U.S. Government's civil affairs in dealing with the Japanese Government.

Bart Lowe had first met Banahara in 1955 at a lecture on post-war Japan Banahara was giving in English at Tokyo University. Banahara was an unforgettable personality, and Bart immediately recognized him last year at the embassy social he was attending. When Banahara retired from the military in 1974, he had been persuaded to stay on in Japan as a US Government civilian. Banahara had formed an office in downtown Tokyo called the Japanese-American Liaison Group. The office acted as an extension of the U.S. Embassy and the US Military Forces in

Japan. Harry Banahara gradually recruited about twenty-five individuals, either ethnic Japanese-American or Americans, with impeccable Japanese language skills, to work with him in the Liaison Group. Harry and his people got all the "too-hard-to-handle" problems. If the embassy or the U.S. military developed a difference of opinion with the Japanese, or a question somehow couldn't be answered, then it was given to the Banahara group because it was believed there was no member of the Japanese Government Harry did not know. No task was too difficult, it seemed, for Harry Banahara and his Liaison Group. And, of course, Harry had been of great service to the DAS and the DAO in Japan for many years.

Harry Banahara was a legend in his own time, and the Japanese insisted that Harry continue to live in the house on Minatoku Street. It was a landmark in Tokyo. Tourist guides would point it out as the home of Banahara-san, a great friend of the Japanese. When Bart Lowe encountered Harry Banahara at the embassy in 1987 and told Harry of his earlier time in Japan as a young man, Harry offered to revisit the places General Lowe had known and act as his guide.

As Bart sank lower and lower into the comfortable chair in the quiet study in his quarters at Fort Myer, the soft music and the beer acted as a soothing catalyst to Bart Lowe's tired mind and body. With thoughts of his youthful days in Japan gentle in his thoughts, he was soon asleep.

With less gentle thoughts, Harold Sema languished in his foreign assignment, more than ever convinced the U.S. government and those who ran its bureaucratic morass, had misused and mistreated him once again.

CHAPTER 17

THE FAR EAST

The long hot Washington summer of 1988 passed without further crisis. The Pacific Attaché Conference was to be held in Hawaii in mid-September and Bart was going from Honolulu to Jakarta, Indonesia, Singapore, Hong King, China and finally Japan. Bart planned only two official days in Tokyo and then he had leave for the rest of the week with Harry Banahara.

General Lowe, accompanied by George Martin, left Washington on Sunday morning via Northwest Airlines through Seattle to Honolulu. By traveling west into the earlier time zone, they arrived late in the afternoon, passing over one of the most unforgettable sights in the world, Diamond Head mountain on the southeastern end of Oahu, a dazzling bright green land rise against the dark blue waters of the Pacific.

Bart always enjoyed returning to Hawaii. He had served at PACOM Headquarters as a major in the early 1970s. Admiral John McCain, Commander in Chief, PACOM during the last years of the Vietnam War had visited Bart's unit, the 101st Airborne Division in Vietnam, and had been briefed by Lowe on the tactical situation in the 101st area of responsibility. Impressed with the young major the Admiral had invited Bart to be on McCain's staff in Hawaii when his tour in Vietnam was completed.

Six months later when Bart arrived at PACOM he was initially assigned to the J2/J3 briefing team to get his PACOM grounding and then moved up to the "bridge" to be one of Admiral McCain's aides. Serving with Admiral McCain had provided Bart the opportunity of traveling throughout the Pacific and gaining a unique perspective of the political, diplomatic, economic, and strategic elements of running a war.

The Attaché Conference went off without a hitch. PACOM, and the political/military advisor to PACOM, a State Department Ambassador presented excellent overviews of the U.S. foreign policy and political/military objectives in the Pacific. China, Russia and North Korea still posed the largest threats to stability in the region, but nationalistic struggles and political differences in Burma, Sri Lanka, India and Pakistan could erupt at any time. The Pacific attachés, particularly those from the hardship countries like Burma, Bangladesh, and Nepal relished the break in their tours.

On the last night of the conference, a dinner was arranged at the famous coastal artillery post, Fort Rugger, at the foot of Diamond Head Mountain. As Bart sat with an after dinner drink and watched the attachés and their spouses dance on the open air terrace he turned to George Martin who was sitting across the table and said, "George I think we can safely say that we have a happy group of campers to send back to their posts tomorrow."

"Yes, sir, I agree with you. Maybe there is a certain magic about Hawaii. I've heard nothing but good things about this conference. In fact I can't recall hearing a single complaint."

"By the way, what time are we off in the morning, George?"

"Our flight for Jakarta departs at 10:45. We need to be at the Honolulu International Airport at 10:00. The Northwest Airlines folks have confirmed our seats. Colonel and Mrs. Blaseman are on the same flight. You need to have your luggage ready for pick up in the morning at 9:00."

Northwest's non-stop flight from Honolulu to Jakarta departed Thursday morning on schedule. The flight was a long one, but by crossing the international date line the flight would lose a day and arrive late Friday afternoon. The time difference between Washington and Indonesia was 13 hours. Colonel John Blaseman, the current DAO in Jakarta, was on his third tour in the Far East. He had been the DATT in Burma before going to Indonesia.

General Lowe's purpose for going to Jakarta was twofold—a regular visit to the DAO as part of the Far East trip and, secondly, as head of a U.S. DOD delegation taking part in a Strategic

Defense Information Exchange Program with the Indonesian Armed Forces. The program was long standing between Indonesia and the U.S. and held annually in Washington or Jakarta. When the DOD people learned that Bart was traveling to the Far East on attaché matters they asked him to take on the Head of Delegation job. The Indonesian Head of Delegation also was a two-star Army officer.

The delegation, a group of political-military analysts from the Washington National Security community, had arrived in Jakarta the day before and were ready for the opening session on Saturday morning. The session in Jakarta, Bart had been told, would be similar to the one held in Washington last year. The first day and night were devoted to opening statements by the participants, a review of the conference schedule and the itinerary for social and travel events.

Indonesia's efforts to maintain economic and political stability and regional cooperation fit well with U.S. policy for the Pacific and formed a basis for good relations between the two countries. Because of some concern expressed in the United States over the Indonesian handling of human rights matters in the former Portuguese Colony of East Timor, the Indonesian government had approved a trip to Timor for the U.S. Delegation. The program was a friendly, non-contentious exchange between two allies and Bart anticipated no difficulties with his role.

On the plane ride from Honolulu, Bart had been able to go over the papers to be presented at the exchange program as well as his opening and tentative closing remarks. Most of the questions he had were answered by Colonel Blaseman, based on his own extensive knowledge of Indonesia and the long running exchange program. The few remaining questions that Blaseman could not answer Bart saved for his point of contact on the delegation. Bart had traveled in a light-weight running outfit to be as comfortable as possible on the long flight, but he had carried a hanging bag with a light weight suit, shirt and tie so he would be properly attired when met at the airfield by the Indonesian Head of Delegation.

Major General Saran Surot and a number of Indonesian officers from each of the military services were waiting at plane side when the Northwestern flight arrived in Jakarta.

"Distinguished General Lowe and party: Welcome to Indonesia," General Surot said as he greeted them. He then escorted Bart, George Martin and the Blasemans to a VIP lounge to await their luggage and process their passports. A separate car and escort was waiting for Colonel and Mrs. Blaseman. Bart and George were taken by General Surot into the city to the hotel where the American Delegation was staying. Upon arrival at the hotel, General Surot led the way up the elevator to the penthouse floor and then into an extra large reception room with a glassed terrace overlooking the sprawling city of Jakarta. Both the American and Indonesian delegations were there, already enjoying the warm Indonesian hospitality. The cocktail reception lasted approximately one hour; then General Surot said a few words of welcome and told everybody to get a good night's sleep because he intended to work them very hard the next day.

Before turning in that night, Bart decided to read awhile. As he sat, propped up with pillows, reading on the largest bed in the largest bedroom in the largest suite he had ever been in in his life, he was fascinated by a sign beside the bed. It said in English, "Push button for in-room massage." At first he ignored it but by the time he stopped reading curiosity had the better of him. He pushed the button and in less than two minutes, an oriental woman dressed in white massage garb was at his door. When he answered the door, he said to her, "Is it too late for the massage?"

She replied, "Of course not. It is available 24 hours a day."

She was certainly expert, and in the thirty minutes or so that it took her to finish the massage, Bart was completely relaxed, without a tense muscle in his body. As she readied herself to depart she smiled slightly and asked Bart, "Are there any other services that you require, sir?" Several tempting images passed through Bart's mind but he decided to leave the offer completely alone.

The first day of the exchange program went as scheduled and was held in a conference room at a nearby Indonesian government installation. That night the Indonesians hosted a traditional Indonesian dinner and entertainment affair that included much singing by both delegations. Without exception, the Indonesian delegation, including General Surot, were men of good voice. Bart could not say the same for the American delegation. Sunday was a free day for both delegations, and most of the men in the American delegation were going to use the free time for tours of Jakarta. In the interest of time, Colonel Blaseman suggested Bart visit the DAO at the U.S. Embassy. Blaseman promised some free time Sunday afternoon for a tour of the capital and a buffet dinner at the Blasemans where Bart would meet the ambassador and the other key embassy personnel.

The day spent at the DAO, and later at Colonel Blaseman's house, was filled with discussions of new methods and ideas on how to conduct the attaché business of the United States, on the social pleasure of meeting the dynamic ambassador, and in talking with an unusually adept group of Foreign Service Officers from the embassy staff. One message came across to Bart loud and clear. John Blaseman and the attachés were roundly respected by the Indonesians and the FSO professionals at the U.S. Embassy. Bart had made a mental check next to DAO Jakarta that said, "Here's one I don't have to worry too much about."

Monday was spent attending the Indonesian presentations, and Tuesday and Wednesday were spent on the day trips to East Timor, Bali and Kalimantan in the Indonesian interior. Thursday the U.S. presentations were made, and Friday was used for the free-wheeling exchange of views between the delegations and the program wrap-up that would bc written up by the Indonesian hosts for this years' program. The day was scheduled to end at 5:00, and Bart was confident General Surot would vigorously keep to the schedule as he had all week. Following the program, a farewell dinner was scheduled at 7:30.

Colonel Blaseman and George Martin had been attending most of the Exchange Program sessions in Jakarta, but Bart noticed that both were gone most of Friday afternoon. Just before the concluding remarks, Blaseman and Martin returned to their seats, and Bart received a high sign from George that meant they needed to see him right after the program broke up.

When Bart had completed his closing remarks, and as the delegations adjourned, Blaseman and Martin came over and Colonel Blaseman said, "General Lowe, I'm afraid something has come up that will require you meeting with the ambassador before you leave Jakarta. He and I discussed the matter this afternoon, and he is aware of your schedule this evening and your early departure in the morning. He suggests that you meet after the farewell dinner tonight no matter how late it is."

"Okay, John. I don't have any problem with that, but what about now? Can't we squeeze it in before dinner?"

"No, sir. There is not enough time, the matter may require extensive discussion."

"Can you at least give me the subject?" asked Bart.

"I'd rather not, not here," Blaseman said, looking around the still crowded delegation room. "But George has the information and he and Lieutenant Colonel Petroangelo can brief you when you get to a more secure place."

"Okay, John," Bart said, looking at George and receiving his nod.

"If you agree, General Lowe, I'll inform the ambassador that you will come to his residence as soon as the farewell dinner is concluded. I'll also be at the dinner and will accompany you to the ambassador's residence."

Bart shook a few more hands and then departed for the hotel with George Martin and Lieutenant Colonel Petroangelo. Riding back in the DAO sedan they did not mention the Blaseman matter in front of the Indonesian driver. When they reached the hotel and got out of the car, before Bart could enter the lobby, George said, "How about a short walk around the jogging trail before we go up, General?"

Bart nodded and followed George and Lieutenant Colonel Petroangelo around the side of the hotel into the plush, tropical grounds and onto the jogging trail. Once they were out of hearing distance from the hotel, and determined there was no one else on the trail, George, in a quiet voice said, "General Lowe, do you remember at the beginning of the summer in Rosslyn when you approved of Mike Petroangelo, the Assistant Army Attaché's periodic meetings with his Russian counterpart to see what might develop?"

"Vaguely," replied Lowe.

"Well," said George. "There was a dramatic development today. Let me turn it over to Mike"

"Sir," began Petroangelo, "I have been in Jakarta a little more than a year. Shortly after I arrived, I met a Lieutenant Colonel Andre Shashkin at a party given by the Soviet Embassy. Shashkin approached me and told me that he had served an attaché tour in the United States, the tour had been by far the best tour of his life, and he would like to talk with someone from the United States so he could maintain his English language skills. I reported this conversation and the DAS and CIA thought it would be a good idea to approve my contact with Shashkin and see where it would lead. For most of the time during my meetings with Shashkin, he did just what he said, make small talk about life in the U.S."

"I see," commented Lowe.

"However, last week on Friday when we met for lunch, the conversation took a decidedly different tack. In response to a question by Shashkin on what a U.S. military officer who has bought a house in Washington does with the house if he is transferred to some place like Jakarta, I explained that the officer could elect to sell the house and hope he was able to get back the money he had invested, or the officer could elect to rent the house in order to cover the cost of his mortgage payment. I also explained renters often left sooner than expected, and the officer could be left with a large house payment, which was the situation in which I now found myself. I told him I lost my tenants and had been unable to find another renter. Shashkin then asked sympathetically if I could sustain the financial hardship. And I told him, yes, but barely."

"Hmm." Lowe muttered.

officer. His friend, Shaskin said, was also military, but at the time, he was posing as a Soviet civilian diplomat. Shashkin had known Kapustin for many years, since the time they became Soviet Army officers. Georgi, Shashkin said, was a wild one—a heavy drinker and big spender. He was often in trouble with his superiors for being late for work because of hangovers and for using official operational money for personal reasons. Kapustin's superiors had threatened to send him home on more than one occasion if his conduct did not improve. Still, Georgi continued his wild ways, involved in so much trouble it was only a matter of time before he was returned in disgrace to the USSR. In fact, his lowest moment was when he had to ask Shashkin for money to help repay the money he had used from his official funds, as soon as the missing money was discovered by his superiors. Shashkin loaned him money, but had not seen Kapustin for more than a month and assumed he was lying low awaiting the inevitable return to Moscow.

Then one night Georgi Kapustin called in high spirits and invited Shashkin to dinner, assuring Shashkin that all expenses would be on him. Shashkin's first thought was that it was probably going to be a farewell occasion. When Shashkin accepted and met Kapustin in Georgetown at one of the more expensive restaurants, his friend already had several vodkas and was in the best of moods. He insisted on the best meals on the menu and was very generous with his tips. He informed Shashkin that he would be repaying his debt to him in full and he would not be going home in disgrace. Shashkin was astounded, and at first worried that Kapustin had finally done something completely outrageous like robbing the embassy. He was unsuccessful throughout the evening in getting Georgi to tell him where his new found affluence came from. Finally, in the last stop at the last bar when they were having the last drink at about 2:30 a.m., Shashkin pressed Kapustin one more time to explain his apparent good fortune. Through glassy eyes his KGB friend slurringly said to him, 'As the Americans say, I have hit the jackpot. I have found the pot of gold at the end of the rainbow. I have answered the 64,000 dollar question.'

"Not understanding any of this Shashkin said to Georgi, 'I don't understand you...you drunken lout...what the hell do you mean?'

Reaching over and grabbing Shashkin's head and pulling it toward him, Kapustin whispered in his ear, 'I have recruited a CIA agent. He is a gold mine. He is my drinking buddy. And my bosses have given me a huge bonus.'

"Shashkin's friend, Kapustin, passed out at the bar soon after his whispered remarks and Shashkin struggled to get him home. Shashkin did not know exactly what to make of Georgi's story. At first he thought it was just a fabrication to cover wherever he really got the money. On the other hand, there was the question of the money Georgi had? Where had it come from?

"In about two weeks Georgi contacted him and in a brief meeting he said to Shashkin, 'You know that story that I told you in the bar? Well, you must promise me that you will never mention that story to another person.'

"'Why? Is it true?' Shashkin had asked.

"'I can only tell you that if you should tell anyone else I would deny ever having said it,' Kapustin replied.

"From that day on Shashkin's friend changed," Mike Petroangelo said. "He seemed a new man and seemed to be a man of purpose. There were no longer any drinking bouts, and in fact Shashkin rarely saw Kapustin after that. We confirmed that Georgi left the Soviet Embassy in 1986 about the same time as Shashkin, but not in disgrace. Shashkin is no longer in touch with his friend who has disappeared in the KGB bureaucracy in Moscow. Was the story true? Shashkin could only believe it was," Petroangelo added.

"When I asked Shashkin if Georgi had ever mentioned the names of Americans he was in contact with Shashkin told me the only thing he could remember was Georgi saying 'that his American drinking buddy had served in Moscow and Washington and once even lived in Singapore, where Kapustin hoped to go someday.'

"That's where we stand now, General," concluded Petroangelo. "The problem with all of this is, should we pass this development on to the Jakarta COS and risk having everyone at CIA know about it? Colonel Blaseman immediately recognized the dilemma and went to the U.S. Ambassador with it this afternoon with the recommendation that you, General Lowe, and the ambassador meet tonight to make the appropriate decision."

"That's quite a cup full, Mike," Lowe said as they turned around at the end of the jogging path and headed back toward the hotel.

The first thought entering Bart's mind as he listened to Mike Petroangelo's story was HEAT SEEKER. But neither Mike nor George was cleared for HEAT SEEKER, and Bart couldn't think of any reason the U.S. Ambassador would be either.

"If true, boss, this could be a real disaster." George said.

"You're telling me." Bart replied.

"Colonel Blaseman also mentioned that the Russians could be trying to suck us into a deception, have us do a lot of work unnecessarily, only to find out it was just a hoax," added George.

"Yes, that's always a possibility," Lowe agreed.

"That's it, boss," George said, " Do you need me to go along with you and Colonel Blaseman to the Ambassador's tonight? Mike Petroangelo will be there."

"No. That won't be necessary, George. Thanks. Take the evening off and enjoy," answered Lowe as they reached the entrance to the hotel lobby. Lieutenant Colonel Petroangelo left them there and they went inside to their rooms.

The final dinner with the Indonesian delegation was an elaborate affair, replete with excellent food, much wine, many toasts, colorful entertainment and genuine hospitality, symbolizing friendship between two allies. The week-long experience had been very educational for Bart, and he had grown to like and admire his host, General Surot, and the other cordial members of the Indonesian delegation. When, in his concluding remarks, he thanked his hosts and said he hoped he would have the opportunity to return to Indonesia again, he meant it.

Lieutenant Colonel Petroangelo joined Colonel Blaseman and General Lowe for the trip to the ambassador's residence.

Ambassador Wilson greeted Bart Lowe and the other two attachés in shirt sleeves and invited them into the drawing room for coffee. After coffee was served, the Ambassador motioned to a door that led outside to a patio where a table, chairs and an umbrella sat alongside a small, well-stocked goldfish pond. The cool night air felt refreshing.

The ambassador offered seats around the table and then said, "General, because of the sensitivity of the matter we are about to discuss I didn't want to do it inside the residence." He then reached across the table to a small, black cube that was setting on the table and pressed a switch. The cube began to emit a low level sound akin to radio static. "The open air will be refreshing and this little buzzer will give us a modicum of security, provided we keep our voices low. What do you make of this thing that happened this afternoon?"

"Mr. Ambassador, I don't really know any more than you do. I've been thinking about it since I learned of it this afternoon. In comparing notes with John Blaseman and Lieutenant Colonel Petroangelo, we are satisfied Mike has reported it just as it happened; that is to say, I don't think there is any chance that what Shashkin said was misunderstood," Bart replied.

"If that is a given, what do you think we ought to do with the information?" the Ambassador asked.

"Well, I believe the potential damage to the United States, if what Shashkin says is true, is far too great to ignore the information, fully realizing that it may be some kind of ruse. I believe it needs to be checked out and investigated."

"And what are your thoughts about sharing this information with our COS Ruben Greene?" Turning to Colonel Blaseman, the Ambassador added, "I am sure he is anxious to know why our CIA representative here hasn't already heard from you, John, since the meeting was this afternoon."

"No doubt," said John Blaseman.

Responding to the ambassador, Bart said, "There is a legitimate way in which we can compartmentalize the results of the meeting today. As I'm sure you know, Ambassador Wilson, the rules governing these operations abroad are promulgated by the Director of Central Intelligence (DCI), and we all abide by them and, for the most part, follow the CIA lead. The guidelines, however, permit others subject to the rules, in this case the Defense Department, to ask for an exception and request a transfer of operational responsibility from CIA for any given source or operation. Since we began this operation with the Russian attaché, although with CIA cooperation, we can ask that we be given sole jurisdiction. For the time being, that would cut out your CIA Chief of Station Ruben Greene. He, of course, will be very curious, and probably pissed off, thinking he has been cut out of something good. But you can blame me, simply by saying that when I learned of it I wanted sole DAS operational responsibility and directed my guys to make it happen."

"If I would go along with that," the ambassador asked, "what happens to the explosive information about the recruitment of a CIA agent by the KGB?"

"Obviously, that is the most important part of this puzzle, Mr. Ambassador, and I suggest we must pass that information to the right, but limited, set of people in Washington. I believe that set of people to be the Deputy Director of Operations at CIA, Art Cheek, and an Assistant Director at the FBI who handles these kinds of things, John Kitchen, as well as someone you designate at the State Department. If you want my recommendation, I would say the Director of INR, Ambassador Ross. The plan I would suggest is that John and Mike draft a cable for me going to my SSD Chief in Washington, Colonel Bob Herrington, with instructions to show the cable to those individuals I mentioned, outlining the details of Colonel Petroangelo's meeting with Colonel Shashkin. If, after Art Cheek at CIA has seen the cable, he wants it shared with the COS here, then I have no objection. I believe sir, this would put the information in the hands of the people who can best judge if there is any substance to it and, if so, decide what has to be done."

The ambassador rolled his head back in thought for a moment and then said, "I like it."

When the ambassador walked his visitors to the front door of the residence he told Bart, “I hear that the Indonesians have been very pleased with the U.S. delegation this year and the exchange program. These people are good friends to have in this part of the world and deserve our best. Have a good trip to Singapore and come back and see us again.”

“I certainly hope to,” said Bart as he waved good night.

When the three officers were back inside Colonel Blaseman’s car they decided to go directly to the U.S. Embassy to prepare the cable to send to Colonel Herrington at the DAS. It was after midnight by the time they got to the embassy, and about 2:00 a.m. before the cable was completed. Bart and Colonel Blaseman then departed to take Bart back to his hotel while Lieutenant Colonel Petroangelo remained at the embassy to encrypt the cable and send it on to the SSD in Rosslyn. At 2:45 when Bart opened the door to his magnificent suite at the hotel, he found a note from George Martin saying that he had left a call for General Lowe for 6:30 in order to depart at 7:45 for the airport and their 9:00 flight to Singapore.

Preparing for landing in Singapore at the Paya Lebar Airport, Bart and George were treated to the awe inspiring sight of one of the largest, ship-laden, natural harbors in the world. Huge merchant ships awaited their turn to load or unload their maritime commerce. In keeping with its record as the world leader in on-time aircraft arrivals and departures, the Singapore Airport received Bart’s flight at its arrival gate precisely on time.

Lowe and Martin were met by the DATT, Navy Captain Lance Hargrove. Captain Hargrove was a naval aviator. The Singapore Navy consisted mainly of small craft and most of the Defense dollars went into maintaining a sophisticated Air Force with high performance aircraft. Captain Hargrove and the Air Force Attaché at the DAO in Singapore spent most of their time administering the U.S. security assistance package.

General Lowe's stay in Singapore was to be a short one—just Saturday and Sunday, and he would depart for Hong Kong on Monday. Accordingly, Captain Hargrove arranged a luncheon for Bart with the four-star Chief of Staff of the Singapore Air Force, 45-year-old General Winston Lee. Captain Hargrove planned to take General Lowe directly to the luncheon, and George would get checked in at their hotel and accompany the Air Attaché back to the DAO, linking up with Lowe and Hargrove after lunch.

On the way to the club where they were meeting General Lee, Captain Hargrove briefed Bart on the latest developments in a mutual agreement between the U.S. and Singapore to purchase a new fighter aircraft, together with the logistic train necessary to support it. The parties were still haggling over price, but Hargrove was confident the deal was going to be consummated.

The lunch was a delightful treat in a private room overlooking the 18th hole green at General Lee's Racquet and Golf Club. Bart found General Lee to be a gracious host, an impressive professional officer and a most capable representative of his country. In visiting countries in the Far East that had at one time been under British Colonial rule, Bart observed that the British had left behind at least three distinct characteristics: a desire that people and institutions be governed by law and order, that civility always be used in dealing with others, and the preference for clubs as a mark of success and social acceptance.

In the post colonial history of Singapore, its exceptionally gifted leader Lee Quan Yew had taken the best parts of British tradition and added to them the Chinese innate characteristics of family cohesion, commerce and ambition, his cfforts had made Singapore one of the most, if not the most, successful island nations in the world.

The afternoon was spent at the DAO where Bart found a stable, contented DAO family who considered themselves fortunate to be serving in such an urbane, sparkling clean, crime free country. Some free time was scheduled for the afternoon and Bart and George were taken to their hotel.

Dinner that night was at eight o'clock on the top floor of the hotel where the DAO members and their spouses joined General Lowe and Colonel Martin for a superb dinner of lobster bisque and beef Wellington; the dining room had a spectacular view of one thousand ships bobbing under their white anchor lights.

On Sunday morning, Bart and George, fresh from a good night's sleep, took a walking tour of downtown Singapore. Bart took the opportunity to pick up a few gifts for B.J. Ross, his mother and other family members. He and George arrived back at the hotel in time to swim for thirty minutes in the indoor pool and have a steam bath.

For many years the Singapore Government had allowed the DAO to maintain a large cabin cruiser, ostensibly for the purpose of training naval officers and to provide recreation for the DAO members and their families. Its real mission was to provide a means for the DAO to keep track of the many foreign flag vessels that transited the harbor at Singapore, particularly those flying the communist flags of the world.

Captain Lance Hargrove and his wife, Maddy, picked up Bart and George at 1:00 for a short drive to the marina where the DAO boat was kept; there they were joined by the rest of the DAO staff members and their families for a late lunch and three-hour cruise. Soon after boarding and getting underway Bart was presented with a skipper's hat that said "Commodore Lowe—DAS Fleet." On the business side of the cruise, Bart was amazed to find out how much could be learned about a merchant ship and its cargo, or a man-of-war, when observed closely by people who knew what they were doing—like his naval attachés.

For Bart's last night in Singapore, Captain Hargrove made arrangements for himself and General Lowe to have dinner with the head of the Singapore Security Service. The Singapore Security Service combined most of the functions of the CIA, FBI, NSA and Defense Department intelligence organizations in America. Simon Telford, of mixed Chinese and British parents, although relatively young (Bart guessed in his late forties), had been head of the service for ten years and worked directly for President Lee Quan Yew. Lance Hargrove told General Lowe that if one wanted to find out something in Singapore and was not sure where to go, the chances were always good that Simon Telford would know the answer. Telford had been very helpful to Hargrove during his time as the DATT, and Captain Hargrove wanted to repay that assistance by introducing Telford to General Lowe. Taking a long shot, Bart asked Captain Hargrove to ask Telford if he knew any Russians serving in Singapore named Kapustin.

Simon Telford turned out to be a fascinating dinner guest. He was a great admirer of the FBI, and made at least one trip a year to the United States in order to maintain his close contact with the bureau. Telford regaled Bart and Hargrove with one fascinating story after another. "Unfortunately," Telford said, he had, "no knowledge of any Russian named Kapustin in Singapore."

When he returned at 10:00 to the hotel, Bart thought about ringing George's room to double check on their departure time in the morning for Hong Kong. When he got to his room he realized his concern was for naught because the note with all the details from George was slipped under the door.

After Bart brushed his teeth and got ready for bed, he turned out the lights to savor the harbor view one more time. It was hard to imagine anything more spectacular than that great armada of ships representing the world's maritime fleet. But then, he thought, there's always Hong Kong.

CHAPTER 18

THE ORIENT EXPRESS

As the aircraft was pulling up to the arrival gate at the Hong Kong International Airport, Bart Lowe momentarily thought to himself: Now let's see, where are we? Laughing to himself, he turned to George and asked, "George how about going over the schedule before we deplane."

George Martin reaching into his briefcase and referred to a page he had clipped earlier and replied, "Sure, boss. We'll be here in Hong Kong for two days, Monday and Tuesday, then on to China for four days in Beijing, then to Tokyo next Sunday with one day of business at the DAO on Monday, and then on Tuesday I'll leave you and return home; you will depart for five days of leave with Mr. Banahara. Our Defense Liaison Officer (DLO) in Hong Kong, Monty Dillard, will be meeting us here at the airport."

"Thanks, George."

As Bart and George made their way through the passage way into the terminal area, Bart recognized the face of Army Colonel Dillard standing at the passport control desk. As Hong Kong was a British colony, the United States had a consulate instead of an embassy and a Defense Liaison Officer (DLO) rather than a Defense Attaché. The U.S. Consulate in Hong Kong was, in some ways, an extension of the U.S. Embassy in Beijing. Before the United States resumed diplomatic relationships with China, after the long break between the two countries stemming from the Korean War, Hong Kong had been the United States' key outpost for watching Red China. It was still an extremely valuable outpost. If Singapore was the Switzerland of the Far East, then Hong Kong was the Vienna.

The return of Hong Kong to China by the British in 1997 had been confirmed and the advance parties of mainland Chinese interests were already ensconced in Hong Kong. Often it was easier to get an answer to a tough Chinese defense question in Hong Kong than in China because of the freedom of movement and action in Hong Kong. Monty Dillard was an old China hand. He was a Chinese FAO who had served earlier in Beijing and also in Taiwan. Colonel Dillard, a blond, fair-skinned man with an infectious smile and habitual, relaxed good humor, had an excellent rapport with the British Customs authorities. General Lowe and Colonel Martin were out of the airport and on the way to their hotel in a matter of minutes.

Dillard had arranged for rooms on the 12th floor of the Hong Kong Hilton overlooking Hong Kong's historic Repulse Bay. The hotel was within walking distance of the American Consulate also close to Dillard's apartment where Bart and George Martin had been invited for dinner that evening. Colonel Dillard left General Lowe and Colonel Martin at the hotel with a promise to pick them up at 6:45.

The dinner for twenty people at the Dillard's included other officers from the DLO and their spouses, the American Consul General and his wife. The Dillards had a modern, three level apartment high up on Hong Kong Island. It was spacious and suitable for entertaining, with a breathtaking view of the sprawling Hong Kong city and harbor below it. Monty Dillard's wife Jewel was an ethnic Chinese-American born in California and educated at UCLA. She and Monty had met at UCLA, and she was responsible for getting him interested in Chinese language and culture. Monty and Jewel had no children, and she had a full-time job with an American precious stone dealer in Hong Kong who specialized in custom-designed Chinese gold pieces. Jewel was a bundle of energy and an ideal spouse for an attaché. She was as charming and entertaining as Monty was good humored. They were both extremely knowledgeable on China and great dinner hosts.

Bart's next day was spent at the consulate in the morning and in the afternoon visiting the Hong Kong Government offices and the UK Military Garrison. Bart knew the briefings he received at the DLO would give him a leg up on the briefings in China because the DAO in Beijing and the DLO in Hong Kong coordinated all of their information and operational requirements so they didn't duplicate each other's efforts. The DLO in Hong Kong had the luxury of coordinating efforts with their British colleagues and sharing in their results. It was a productive team effort.

Monty Dillard, because of his exceptional abilities with the spoken and written Chinese Mandarin language, had made unusual progress in making contacts in the Chinese Kowloon District and the new territories on the mainland side of Hong Kong. He was in regular contact with a group of Mainland Chinese businessmen who had enterprises in Kowloon, but were in reality part of the long standing communist vanguard established in Hong Kong until such time as the government in Beijing was given control of Hong Kong. Dillard, using information from both U.S. and British sources, had singled out individuals who had previous military service in China, whom Dillard believed were in current contact with the military on the mainland. He exchanged informal views with these individuals and was able to gain an additional perspective on Communist Chinese thinking beyond their official pronouncements. He was also able to use his Chinese contacts to pass information through them to Chinese military leaders that might not filter through their government.

Dillard suggested to General Lowe that he and George Martin accompany him and Jewel that night to a dinner he was having with some of his Chinese contacts at a restaurant in Kowloon. He had told his contacts that his boss was coming to Hong Kong and then traveling on to Beijing. They had indicated a high interest in meeting the American general and talking with him over dinner. Monty told Bart he believed the meeting would be useful to Lowe, and the Chinese guests would be willing to answer any questions he had about China, provided that their rules of informality and nonattribution were followed. Lowe agreed.

That evening the Dillards went to the Hilton Hotel and met Bart and George. Colonel Dillard suggested that they walk from the hotel to the nearby ferry that ran from Hong Kong Island to

Kowloon. The ferry ride was most pleasant in the early evening and the differences between the island and Kowloon side were apparent once the ferry docked. Kowloon was much more populated and commercial, and the buildings and apartment complexes were not nearly as grand as those on the Hong Kong side.

Colonel Dillard hailed a cab for the short ride to the restaurant where Bart had the distinct feeling of being part of a teeming crowd. The restaurant, called Fragrant Harbor, was several stories high and the clientele and the fare seemed to improve as one ascended. The Dillards' reservation was for the 4th floor and the other guests, eight Chinese men, all dressed in suits and ties were waiting at a round table. The table was in a large, open room with many other tables, but as soon as they were seated waiters put wooden screens around the table to provide privacy. Bart was seated between Monty on his left and Jewel on his right. George was to the right of Jewel and the Chinese gentlemen took the other seats. Monty explained that normally these meeting were done on a bachelor-basis, but that Jewel would help with the translations and in identifying the Chinese foods they were about to eat. It turned out to be a full and filling evening.

The ground rules Dillard set out were that everyone would enjoy the dinner, feel relaxed and not answer any questions with which they were not comfortable. Monty would act as moderator and Bart could simply give Monty a nod if he didn't want to discuss the subjects. The first order of business was to get the meal underway, accomplished simply by a signal from Monty to the head waiter. First, hot tea was served, and then soup. After the soup, small dishes of appetizers were served and quickly replaced with another as soon as one finished the delicacy. Items closer to what Bart would have considered main courses were served on slightly larger plates. None of the servings were large. A wonderful selection of foods was served one after the other with Jewel describing each food and its preparation to Bart and George, including descriptions of fish, shrimp, pork, ribs, pasta, rice, vegetables, sweet and sour chicken, beef, lobster, and some complex translations that Bart thought it would be better not to know too much about. As the food became hot and spicy, tall glasses of cold beer were served.

Once the chopsticks had been passed out and the meal was underway, the questions began. The questions seemed rapid, as they were spoken in Chinese, but Monty Dillard slowed them down through his translations and explanations. Bart would eat while the question was being asked and Monty would eat while Bart was answering. None of the Chinese men spoke English so Colonel Dillard was the key man in the proceedings. He controlled the questions masterfully. By the time the group was well into the dinner Monty had taken a question from each of the Chinese men and Bart had answered each one. Monty then suggested that Bart put questions to the group and he would get a volunteer to answer it. The questions and answers were related to the future of China and how China was viewed by the United States and the rest of the western world. If there was a central theme or interest to what the Chinese asked, it was what Bart called "Eco-Techno-Logical." There was high interest in understanding the U.S. economy and its possible application for China. They also wondered if the United States was willing to share its technology with China. As to military threats to China, it was clear that the USSR was their number one concern. When asked about Taiwan, they dismissed that as a territorial disagreement that would be peacefully resolved in time.

Bart was intensely interested in the discussion but was somewhat surprised that the Chinese food just kept coming. He thought they must have had somewhere between 15 to 20 servings and every time one was finished another immediately appeared. Each was more delicious than the last, and Bart was about to reach the point of being completely stuffed. Just at the moment a marinated fish dish was taken away, Bart turned to Jewel and whispered, "Jewel, how long before this meal ends? I'm not sure I can eat anymore. Everything has been delicious, but I'm about filled to the brim."

A shocked look appeared on Jewel's face, and she replied, "Oh, General! I am so embarrassed." As she said this, she immediately waved off the waiters and the next course that was just about to be served. "I forgot to tell you the custom. Since you are the guest of honor the courses are served until such time as you have had enough.

"Everything was so good, I guess I just kept shoveling it away," Bart said.

Jewel laughed. "I know. Some of the Chinese gentlemen at the table remarked that they were very impressed with how much you liked Chinese food and how large an appetite you had. Will you ever be able to forgive me, General Lowe?"

"Of course, Jewel. On the good side, it was certainly the best Chinese meal I have ever had in my life, and I wouldn't have wanted our Chinese friends to think that we were a bunch of wimps, right George?"

"Absolutely, boss, but I sure am glad someone called a halt to this food marathon."

Monty picked up on their conversation and shared it with the Chinese guests who all had a good laugh and congratulated Bart on his capacity for consuming Chinese food, one they all agreed exceeded their own. The serious mood side of the evening was broken and more hot tea was served and the conversation then was aimed toward the more normal questions of how Bart was enjoying his trip.

After dinner Monty and Jewel suggested a walk to a nearby Chinese market where in a space of three or four city blocks, the treasures of the western and eastern worlds were on sale for negotiable prices. Hong Kong was indeed both part of, and more than the fantastic world of Suzy Wong. George Martin could not resist the apparently flawless imitation Rolex watches. The late night ferry ride back from Kowloon to Hong Kong Island, with hundreds of Chinese junks anchored in the water and dimly lit, made for a pleasant memory.

If the airport in Hong Kong could be described as extravagant, then the airport near Beijing where Bart Lowe arrived in China would best be called lackluster. His first impression was similar to the one he experienced in Moscow: a uniformed presence presided over bureaucratic rows and rows of obstacles designed to slow the arriving passengers to a snail's pace in passing, hopefully, through the airport. The new arrivals were viewed with suspicion and delayed as long as possible. Even with the help of the DATT, Brigadier General Jack Fuller, who was an excellent Chinese linguist, it took Lowe and Martin one hour and twenty minutes to free themselves, their passports and their luggage from the airport.

"Bart, you old jumper, it's good to have you here. None of your predecessors were ever able to make it, you know. The Chinese would never agree to let them in," Jack Fuller said.

"I'm sure I can thank you for that, Jack. Not even the Chinese could turn down a smooth talking old paratrooper from the 82nd Airborne Division, right?"

Bart Lowe and Jack Fuller had met as majors when they were serving in the Army, in two fiercely competitive Airborne Divisions, the 101st and the 82nd.

"Bart, we have a great schedule planned for you while you are here. Most of it will have to be in Beijing, unfortunately, because the Chinese did not approve the trips to Shanghai and Guangzhou that I had in mind. The only excursion they would approve outside of Beijing is a road trip to the north to see the Great Wall of China. That will give you a good look at the Chinese countryside. We are also going to get you to the Old Imperial Palace—maybe you saw it in the movie *The Last Emperor*?"

"Yes, as a matter of fact, I did. That should be interesting," answered Bart.

"In addition we have tours at a Chinese rug factory, a porcelain plant, and the world's largest Kentucky Fried Chicken franchise, as well as a new franchise for delivering Peking Ducks to Chinese homes."

"Peking Ducks?" asked Bart and laughed.

"Yes, Peking Ducks. The duck is the favorite food of the Chinese, and the idea is to prepare the duck for eating and deliver the duck to the customer's house within 30 minutes of the order. It is like our Domino's Pizza. Bart, if all of this sounds like we are giving you the ladies' tour it is what is happening in China, and I believe it's the wave of the future. We can tell you all that we know about their strategic and nuclear capabilities, their military dispositions, and what we think their research efforts are trying to achieve in a couple of hours in the embassy. And, our people are working hard at that mission every day, but what is going to change their military posture in the future is what is now happening to their economy and in their cities. And I don't want you to miss that."

"Okay, Jack. I'm putty in your hands. Lead on."

"I don't believe that for a minute, but let me tell you what else we have in mind. The Chinese have agreed to have you call on the officer that is responsible for Military Affairs within the Chinese Foreign Ministry, General Kai. Kai is a Lieutenant General and a staunch member of the Old Guard. He will receive you in his office and after a few minutes of talk will invite you to lunch. I'll be included in the office call, but only you will go to the lunch; they will provide an interpreter. Kai has a deputy, a Brigadier General Ling, and I think he is a real comer. We will go to the Foreign Ministry a little early, and I will introduce you to Ling. He will accompany us when we call on Kai. Ling is really the guy who looks after the Chinese attachés around the world, and he served a tour as an attaché in the United States. I am having a reception for you on Friday night and both Kai and Ling are invited. Kai probably won't show, but Ling says he thinks he can make it and you will have a chance to talk with him informally."

Brigadier General Jack Fuller took Bart Lowe and George Martin straight to Fuller's quarters. He lived on the seventh floor of a multi-storied building in the Diplomatic Quarter. "The Chinese insisted that foreigners all live in one area so they could keep an eye on them." Jack said.

George Martin was staying with the Air Attaché, Colonel Bill Black. Colonel Black met the party at the apartment complex when they arrived from the airport, and George departed with him after they agreed that they would link up the next morning at the embassy.

Bart's first night in China was happily spent with the Fullers in their large apartment. Jack said that the apartment was actually quite comfortable for the two of them, since their children were in college in the United States, but that apartment maintenance was a problem. No air conditioning in the summer, the heat regularly broke down in the winter, and the elevator was often on the blink. An old paratrooper like Jack didn't mind climbing the stairs but it wasn't so easy for Anne because of her frequent trips, he said.

Jack told Bart many of the Chinese were still "thugs," but that there were many more who were determined to emulate life in the West and build a different China in the future. Jack did not think that change would take place as dramatically or rapidly in China as it apparently had in the Soviet Union. "There were too many hard-liners still in power, but change was out there," Jack said, "and like a great cloud on the horizon it was moving in."

Bart and Jack talked well into the night. Anne abandoned them at midnight, and they talked on until 1:00, satisfied they had caught up on five years of separation.

The traffic the next morning going into the U.S. Embassy was heavy, although nothing like Hong Kong. What the Chinese did not have in cars they made up for in bicycles. There were thousands of bikes on the streets of Beijing. Jack Fuller told Bart that he relished working with the U.S. Ambassador Dunston Howe. Howe, like Jack, was a Chinese foreign area specialist and had been somewhat of a visionary in the U.S. State Department concerning China. He had worked long, hard, and successfully on modifying the policy with China. He had argued that the security objectives for stability in the Far East could be shared by China and the U.S. regardless of the different forms of government. And he had been instrumental in increasing the dialogue between the

U.S. and China while enticing U.S. investors to take a chance there for the future. When they met, Bart understood Jack Fuller's admiration for Ambassador Howe; he was indeed an impressive individual, and Bart was pleased to learn that Howe's admiration for the work of Jack Fuller and the attachés was equally strong.

In the DAO spaces in the embassy, Jack's people had prepared an extensive set of briefings for Bart that dove-tailed nicely with the briefings he had in Hong Kong. DAO Beijing had been exceptionally successful in the last year in responding to their Chinese Defense Department's tasking requirements and Bart was curious why. Jack explained that he had an exceptionally apt and dedicated team of attaché professionals and their aggressiveness contributed in large measure to their success. Throughout the briefings Bart recognized also that there was a greater willingness on the part of the Chinese in all walks of life to seek out and talk to Americans and engage them in conversation. And the Chinese military, with notable exceptions from the Old Guard seemed willing to answer questions and discuss defense matters with the U.S. attachés. This factor motivated all of the DAO attachés and they had flooded the DAS Headquarters with information reports. General Fuller and his troops predicted that military-to-military contact requests and requests for visits to the United States by senior Chinese military officials were just over the horizon.

The next day, when they arrived at the Foreign Ministry, General Ling greeted them and took them to his office. He was as Jack Fuller had described, youthful, well appointed in his PLA uniform and articulate. He told Bart how much he had enjoyed and learned from his attaché tour in Washington and appreciated the assignment of an officer of General Fuller's caliber to Beijing. He unhesitatingly answered Bart's questions on the Chinese attaché system, but watched the clock carefully in order not to be late for General Lowe's visit with his boss.

General Ling accompanied Lowe and Fuller to General Kai's office, and although they arrived five minutes before the call was scheduled, General Kai kept them sitting in his outer office for ten minutes before he came out to greet Bart. When he did invite them into his office, he took a seat behind his desk and was very formal in his speech and demeanor. A short man, many years older than Bart, with heavy-lensed spectacles and short cropped black hair, he asked what Lowe's purpose was for visiting China. When Lowe responded that it was a routine visit to see how his attachés were performing—the same type visit he made to the other DAOs around the world—General Kai did not acknowledge his answer but went on to tell Bart what Kai's responsibilities were for the Chinese Foreign Ministry. He made it clear that if Lowe wanted to discuss attaché matters he would have to do so with his assistant, General Ling. The drift was that Kai was involved with far more important concerns and couldn't be bothered with small matters such as attaché affairs. Kai droned on for about 15 minutes about some issues the Foreign Ministry had with the U.S. Department of State, all translated by General Ling with an occasional aside from Jack Fuller.

Recognizing the uncomfortable situation, General Ling stood and gently interrupted his boss, reminding him it was time for lunch. General Kai apparently agreed, abruptly stood up and headed toward the door of his office with a hand motion to Lowe to accompany him. Bart's concern about being alone with General Kai because of the language barrier was somewhat eased when a Chinese colonel waiting outside Kai's door introduced himself as the official interpreter for the lunch and joined Lowe and General Kai on their walk to a nearby dining room. Jack Fuller and Ling broke off at this point to return to Ling's office.

Inside the small room a table with white linen and silver had been set for six. Three other Chinese officers were waiting and were briefly introduced to General Lowe as members of the Foreign Ministry staff. Bart's first thought was that the officers might speak English or were responsible for military actions with the United States but if that was the case it never became obvious. The three officers were silent parties throughout the lunch. Not so for General Kai. Almost immediately he began a second monologue aimed at Lowe who was seated across the table from him, with the interpreter at General Kai's left. Kai's onslaught this time was something along the line of—"if the United States wants to continue relations with China, it had better do a much better job of treating China like an equal. China is fed up with being treated like a third world lackey, and it is time that we receive some real respect."

The serving of lunch and General Kai's tirade coincided. The Chinese meal, consisting of several meat and rice courses, was served by military stewards in PLA uniforms, with white gloves. The first course was an egg drop soup. All at the table, with the exception of Kai, began to eat the soup when it was served. Kai was off to an early start in his speech and his words were coming so fast that the interpreter was having difficulty. To emphasize his points, General Kai started banging on the table with his hand. As he warmed to his subject the banging became more frequent, and Bart noticed that Kai's soup bowl, which he had not touched, was moving even closer to the edge of the table. Finally, with one particularly loud outburst and an equally hard push on the table the fragile soup bowl jumped out of its saucer and spilled over the table; a portion went into General Kai's lap. A stunned look appeared on the faces of the interpreter and the other officers. One officer, seated to Kai's right, immediately jumped up, retrieved the offending bowl and passed a napkin to Kai. Bart, who had been listening to and watching Kai deliver his words, could not help but laugh. The laugh was short, unintentional, certainly undiplomatic, and heard by all at the table. General Kai also heard the laugh and glared at Bart. It was, Bart noted, one of the few times during his meeting with General Kai that he made eye contact with Bart. The stewards quickly repaired the damage, and the lunch service continued. General Kai, having resisted the temptation to get up and leave the room after his embarrassment, gave lunch a little more attention, managed to eat most of it, and continued his insults of the United States. When the Chinese pastry and tea had been served and General Kai fell silent, Bart concluded the lunch was at an end. He placed his napkin on the table and addressed the interpreter.

"Please pass along my compliments to the people who prepared and served this excellent meal. It was delicious. Also my compliments to you, colonel, for a difficult job of translating. I thank you. And now please tell General Kai for me," and Bart looked directly at Kai, "I don't think I can remember ever being treated more rudely in any country I have visited, including the most underdeveloped countries of the world. I sincerely hope that you, sir, have the opportunity to visit the United States sometime so that we may show you the hospitality and dignity we extend to our visitors. If China truly wants to be treated as an equal in the world, it might start by treating its visitors with politeness and courtesy. Good day."

As soon as the Colonel had translated his words to General Kai, Bart rose and headed out the door with the interpreter fast behind him. The Chinese colonel led Bart downstairs to a lobby where General Fuller was waiting. Once they had picked up their uniform hats and were back in the DAO sedan, Jack asked. "Well, how did it go? Did they give you the Chinese water torture treatment?"

"Close," Bart said. "But I may have set Chinese-American relations back a few steps," and then related what had been said at the luncheon.

Jack listened, and then burst out laughing, saying, "Right on! It sounds like the only thing you didn't give him was a fuck you! Strong letter follows!" Then, in a more serious tone, he said, "You did exactly the right thing, Bart. Some of these guys are living in the past and they need to hear those words from us. The reality is that we can do far more for them than they can do for us, and we don't need to go to anyone hat in hand. I think you have struck another blow for freedom. Airborne!" Jack said, smiling broadly.

"All the way!" Bart replied.

At Jack's and Anne's cocktail party for Bart on Friday night, the guests included a broad spectrum of people—other country attachés, the U.S. Ambassador and embassy staffers, the rest of the DAO staff, General Ling and a number of other junior officers from the Foreign Ministry and Defense Department, the CIA COS, a number of academics from the University of Beijing, and several people from the United States and Chinese business communities. It was a group that was excited about what was happening in China and was very optimistic over China becoming a far more open member of the world community. General Ling told Bart that he had learned from the interpreter that General Kai had not been very hospitable to General Lowe at lunch. He apologized and tried to explain that General Kai was from the old school. He asked Bart to have patience in dealing with China and assured him that the wait would be worthwhile for both countries.

Bart thoroughly enjoyed the two days of tours Jack Fuller had organized. Jack sent a different group of people with Bart and George Martin for each tour. Bart was as impressed with the DAO Beijing team as he was with the cultural attractions and economic activities. The old Imperial Palace was a magnificent complex of buildings designed to last forever; once inside the walls of the former Forbidden City, it was easy to let one's imagination drift across the hundreds of years and imagine the Chinese Emperors who had lived there.

The trip to the Great Wall of China, and the trek along two miles or so of the wall left no doubt in Bart's mind of the vastness of China. A scale map at the entrance reflected the wonder that had been built around most of the land mass of ancient China. The width, height and just plain bulk of the Great Wall was well beyond anything Bart had imagined. The afternoon was warm and sunny, but breezy enough to require a light windbreaker.

As Bart walked along with the party of twenty people from the DAO he thought of Chinese history down through the ages. He also thought about the efforts of four U.S. Presidents, since the 1970s, to normalize relations with this nation of a billion people. He realized that while some aspects of Chinese society had changed, others would never change.

Bart's last afternoon in China was spent riding camels. On their way back to Beijing, Jack Fuller scheduled a stop at what was becoming a popular tourist attraction—the camel. For a small fee, any daring individual could take the loping animal for about a quarter mile ride and get a feel of what it might have been like to have been in one of Genghis Khan's camel brigades. In spite of the comfort and warmth between the two humps, Bart, as every infantry man would, was glad when the ride was over.

For his last surprise, Jack Fuller led the returning wall walkers and camel riders back to a neighborhood restaurant near the diplomatic quarter in Beijing for a treat of Peking Duck. No trip to China would be complete without, he told Bart, sampling the famous Chinese delicacy. It was a meal trip to be remembered. That night, after Anne had slipped away to bed, Bart and Jack had their last serious conversation about China.

"Bart, let me see if I can sum up my feelings about this huge, powerful and yet still backward country," Jack said. "I think China is like a giant that has been asleep and is now waking up." We have a great opportunity to assist and educate the giant. If we don't influence him in the right way, he will be a major contender. We should not make any mistake about that. Right now I believe we have a foot in the door with China, and we should continue to improve our position."

"Jack, that's a good analogy and while you haven't been able to show me the military capabilities of China, I have seen them in all of our intelligence holdings and I know we don't want to fight these guys in the future. I share your concerns. While you are here, keep your eye on the big picture, and if you see it going in the wrong direction, yell for help and we'll beat the bushes in Washington for whatever is needed."

The United Airlines flight from Beijing to Tokyo was forty-five minutes late leaving China and the flight took over four hours. Unfortunately, the drive into Tokyo from the Narita Airport would take another two hours and cost more than $50 in toll road fees. Japan surely had changed since the first time Bart went to Japan in 1954. The Japanese now had a saying: "the shortest distance between any two points is either under construction or filled with bumper-to-bumper traffic." And the saying was no exaggeration. If one wanted to be on time for any event in Tokyo one either had to take the Tokyo subway or plan on hours of travel time between destinations. Because of the huge numbers of cars and trucks on Japanese roads, most of the freeways had been double-decked, and some triple-decked, to accommodate the daily flow of traffic.

Navy Captain Carl Von Dalton, the DATT in Tokyo, met General Lowe and Colonel Martin at the airport and, with their black diplomatic passports, was able to move them quickly through the always-crowded international airport to the waiting DAO van. Von Dalton was a huge hulk of a man well over 6'5" and weighing 240 pounds, who caused heads to turn among the much smaller Japanese people. The heads usually turned a second time when they heard Captain Von Dalton speak flawless Japanese. He was a Navy brat born to Navy parents serving in Japan. He graduated from Annapolis, became a career Navy submarine officer and served three tours of duty with the U.S. Navy in Japan. When he was been nominated for the DATT job in Tokyo, Bart thought the nomination was too good to be true. His record and qualifications were that good. Carl Von Dalton had always wanted the job, sought it, got it, and was doing a great job with the Japanese. Lowe wished the DAS could be so lucky in obtaining such well-qualified DATTs everywhere in the world.

Once in the DAO van Bart was able to stretch out his legs, have a Diet Pepsi and relax. All of the DAO vans had been modified to serve as small offices because of the risk of getting caught for long periods in the traffic. It was not unheard of to have a 12-to-14 hour traffic snarl. The van contained two captain's chairs, two desks, a complete communications set, including a secure telephone, a small Sony TV, writing and recording materials, soft drinks and snacks, and two bench seats with pillows and blankets.

"General Lowe, we have you billeted at the New Sanno Hotel. I thought you might enjoy resting tonight, so I haven't made any plans for you." Turning to Colonel Martin, Von Dalton said,

"George, I have tickets for *The Mikado* if you are interested. Marki and I saw it last week, and it is superb. The tickets are not cheap, but I figured for a high flyer like you—no problem."

"Right up my alley, Carl, but maybe the boss would like to go? He requires no sleep, you know," George said, tongue-in-cheek.

"No, thank you. I like Carl's idea of a night off. I may just take dinner in my room tonight and relax in a marvelous Japanese sunken bathtub. But, George, I have seen *The Mikado* and as Carl says it is superb. You should go," replied Bart.

That settled, Von Dalton continued, "Now tomorrow, Monday, is a different matter. I would like to begin the day at 7:30 at the embassy, within walking distance of the hotel, where we'll plan a breakfast for all hands. Since this is a short visit, that will give you a chance to chat with everyone. After that, you'll spend two hours in the offices with the attachés for updates, followed by fifteen minute calls with the Ambassador, the DCM, and the COS. A helicopter will then pick you up for transit to Camp Zama in Yokohama for racquetball and lunch with your friend, Lieutenant General Barstow. The lunch will be a working one with updates from the U.S. Army. Then back on the helicopter for transit to Yokosuka, to call on the U.S. Forces, Japan Commander, General Upshaw, and to receive updates from the Navy and Air Force intelligence units based there.

I'll join you at Yokosuka for a flight to Ropunge, and we'll complete the day there at the Japanese Self-Defense Force Headquarters with a call on General Nogoyo, the Chief of Staff of the Japanese Army. All of this hell-bent-for-leather schedule is based on good weather for the helicopter flights; otherwise we would need a week to get you to all these places."

"Sounds like another Carl Von Dalton fast paced adventure to me," quipped Bart.

"Oh no, sir. I only follow your lead and that of your loyal horse holder, George Martin," responded Carl. The three men laughed.

"One footnote to all of that," added Captain Von Dalton, "I had hoped to have you over to my quarters for an informal dinner tomorrow night, but your friend and mine, Harry Banahara, contacted me with a request that you have dinner with him and the Chief of the Japanese National Police. I hesitated because you are going to be with him for your five days leave and I thought it could wait. But Harry says that it concerns something hot and I told him I would run it by you."

"I'll regret missing the time with you and Marki, but if Harry says it's important we better accept that. So tell him it's a go," Bart answered.

"Aye aye, sir, and incidentally I agree: Harry has never disappointed."

Captain Von Dalton used the rest of the time it took to get to the hotel briefing Bart on the unclassified items concerning DAO Tokyo. His chief problem was the high cost of living for attaché personnel in Japan. It was critical that they have access to U.S. Commissary and Exchange facilities or they would not otherwise be able to afford living in Japan. The problem was Congress wanted to close some of the facilities in Japan. All attachés in Japan required supplemental payments for their housing allowances, and the cost of living was particularly hard on the enlisted members of the DAO.

The New Sanno Hotel was an oasis for the American military member and his or her family in Tokyo. A stay at the New Sanno with affordable rates made a visit to Tokyo and Japan possible for many. Bart first stayed at the old Sanno Hotel in 1955 when it was used by American GIs in Japan for weekend leave. It had all the comforts of an American hotel, including a restaurant with hamburgers, milkshakes, ice cream and a good selection of other American foods. It was one of the original hotels taken from the Japanese after the war and scores of American visitors, either in the military or affiliated with the U.S. Government, had stayed there over the years. In the late 1970s when the old Sanno Hotel was plagued with maintenance problems, the Japanese Government offered to build the U.S. a new hotel in exchange for the very valuable property. An agreement was struck and the New Sanno was built about six blocks from where the old one had stood. The New Sanno was state of the art, had an attractive Oriental design, and contained every modern convenience. It became every bit the haven for the American military in the Far East as its predecessor had been.

After an excellent meal served in his suite, and a long soaking bath, Bart was ready for some light reading and a good night's sleep. Just before going to bed he used the secure phone in his room to call Chuck Gregorios. With the thirteen hour time difference Bart was able to catch Chuck at home with his Sunday morning papers and coffee. After about ten minutes of routine discussion over activities in the DAS, Chuck told him he thought the one country in the world that the DAS was the most concerned over at the present time was Panama.

Chuck said, "Panama is heating up again, but our DATT, Al Yale, is on top of it, and I don't look for anything to happen in the next few days that would require you to come home. If it plays out the way I think I'll send you an update cable for Carl Von Dalton to give you to read on your way home from Japan at the end of the week."

"Okay, Chuck. I am sending some things along for you with George on Tuesday and he will give you an update on all that we did on the road. I'll leave it in your capable hands. You know how to reach me if necessary, and if nothing else comes up, I'll see you next Monday." Bart hung up, climbed into the inviting king sized bed and was asleep in a few minutes.

The good weather held for the next day, and Bart was able to stick to his killer schedule thanks to the U.S. Army Flight Detachment from Camp Zama that provided him the helicopter transportation. It all seemed so easy above the miles and miles of cars that were steadily moving many of the 30 million or so people who resided in the Tokyo-Yokohama area.

A special treat took place on the midday trip from Tokyo to Camp Zama when the clouds over Japan cleared enough for Bart to see the white snows and peak of Japan's highest mountain, Mount Fujiyama.

At exactly 7:30 p.m. Harry Banahara walked through the hotel door. Bart, sitting in the lobby, would have recognized him anywhere. He was easily the best dressed and most distinguished looking man in the lobby. Harry was about 5'10" with clear brown eyes, sharp Oriental features, and a full, well-trimmed head of wavy gray hair. He was dressed in a dark blue three-piece business suit with a pale yellow tie and matching handkerchief. Bart knew Harry Banahara had to be close to 70 years old, but he didn't look a day over 50. He had a quick step, and when he spotted Bart he moved swiftly in his direction. As they drew close to one another he extended his hand and said, "General Lowe, so good to see you again."

Bart replied, "And you Mr. Banahara. I greatly appreciate you taking the time to go with me on this sabbatical."

"Not at all, General Lowe. I am looking forward to it. And please call me Harry. Everyone does."

"All right, Harry, I'm at your disposal."

In his car on the way to the restaurant, Harry informed Bart that they were going to meet Seyji Oharra, the National Police Chief, at a restaurant famous for Japanese Kobe beef.

"If you can forget the outrageous price you must pay when you are eating your steak, you will find it to be the best steak you have ever eaten. I want you to know, however, that I didn't insist upon this dinner just so I could impress you with Kobe beef. I have known Seyji Oharra since he was a very young man. He has always been a good friend to the Americans. Last week he called and asked to see me. General Lowe, as you know, Japan does not have a CIA or an FBI. The National Police is a little like both. The National Police is the largest security organization in Japan and has the most resources devoted to looking after the internal security of the nation. When I met Seyji for lunch last week, he told me he had learned some information of interest to the United States but he wasn't sure who to tell. He asked for my recommendation. After he told me what he knew, I asked him to let me think about it for a day or two. After thinking about it, I decided he should tell you."

"Are you going to tell me what it is, Harry?"

"No, sir. I want Seyji to tell you, and if you don't think you are the right one, I believe you will know who should have the information."

"Okay, Harry. Let's see how it goes," Bart said.

As Harry had promised, the Kobe beef steak was indescribably delicious and the service at the restaurant Harry had selected was five-star. Bart thought to himself while savoring a bite of the steak—"damn the price and full speed ahead!" Mr. Oharra was also uncommonly tall for a Japanese and appeared at first glance to be a much younger man. A closer look, however, at the gray around his temples and his features and mannerisms suggested that he had the maturity and experience to head up the world's largest Police Department. He was an interesting and well-informed dinner partner who spoke perfect English. After coffee was served, Mr. Oharra leaned across the table, and in a quiet voice began to relate a story to Bart.

"General Lowe, the National Police is responsible for the security of Japan in peacetime. As you can well imagine, because of the size of our country, the large population, and the threat of modern-day terrorism, we must call upon every source of information to keep us informed and prepared for any real or potential threat to Japan. I maintain a very close rapport with the security agencies of the other nations of the world and ask that they share their intelligence with us. Your country, has been most helpful to us. Your CIA, FBI and your Defense Department and military agencies regularly help us. For that we are forever grateful."

As he said this, he bowed his head in the Japanese custom and Bart nodded to acknowledge his compliment.

"Your chief competitors, the Russians, have also been helpful to us but for much more self-serving purposes. As I am sure you know, they maintain their largest KGB station in the world in Tokyo, chiefly for the purposes of stealing our technology. They also require my largest surveillance detail to keep an eye on them. In the course of this business I maintain regular contact with their KGB Resident, as I do with your CIA Chief of Station. The current KGB Resident has been in Tokyo about one year. He came here from their headquarters in Moscow. He is a very capable man, speaks excellent Japanese, much better than your CIA Chief, but he is a braggart, always bad mouthing the Americans and telling me how much better the KGB is than the CIA. At a dinner about two weeks ago we had a rather heated discussion on who had helped Japan the most, America or the Russians, and the case I made for the Americans was really compelling. As he grew more angry, he said to me, 'Mr. Oharra-san, if you only knew. We have penetrated the CIA, and they don't even know it.' After he cooled down he said to me, 'Oharra-san I was just joking.' But General Lowe, I know this man, and I don't think he was joking.

"Ordinarily, general, I would probably not pass something like this on to anyone. But in this business, who knows? It could be true, and certainly serious for the U.S. if it is. My friend Banahara-san says I should tell you, and I trust him. I wouldn't want this ever to get back to the U.S. Embassy, or for the source of the information to be identified. I must now ask you to consider this as a conversation that never took place."

Bart Lowe took a deep breath and slowly exhaled.

In the car riding back to the hotel that night, Bart told Harry that he wasn't sure that he was the logical one to receive the information from Mr. Oharra because of the extreme sensitivity of the matter, but he didn't know who would have been a better choice. Bart told Harry he did know, however, exactly the people in Washington who should receive the information.

Because of the sensitivity, Bart didn't want to risk spreading access to the information to others unnecessarily, and he believed it would be best to wait until he returned to Washington to pass it on verbally to those who had the need to know.

Back in his room at the New Sanno, Bart paced the floor for some time mulling over what he had learned and analyzing his decision not to share it with anyone at the U.S. Embassy in Tokyo. Bart knew that if somehow the information got back to the COS and the Ambassador, they would not take it kindly that a visitor to their turf carried something so important back to Washington without their knowledge. On the other hand, this HEAT SEEKER thing, if that's what this was, was so big and had already done so much damage that Bart had a responsibility to the DAS, as well as to John Kitchen at the FBI and Art Cheek at CIA that couldn't be ignored. Bart spent a troubled night but woke up the next morning convinced that he was doing the right thing. Mentally, he put HEAT SEEKER and what he had learned the previous night out of his mind until he was back in Washington.

CHAPTER 19

SOUTH OF THE BORDER

While Bart Lowe was on leave in Japan, Colonel Alan Yale, the DATT in Panama, was becoming increasingly worried about what General Manuel Noriega, the current Commander of the Panamanian Defense Force (PDF), might do to his old friend, the United States, or to Panama's most valuable asset, the Panama Canal. Al Yale had known "Tony" Noriega since Tony was a captain in the Panamanian National Guard.

When Al Yale was an aspiring young Captain of Armor, stationed at Fort Knox, Kentucky, he met a beautiful young lady of Guatemalan descent who was studying at the University of Kentucky at Lexington. Their chance meeting at a fraternity dance on a football weekend changed the course of their lives. Al Yale and Belinda Lopez fell in love and after several months of dating were married in the Chapel at Fort Knox. On their honeymoon they went to visit Belinda's family in Guatemala City, Guatemala, and Al was hooked. He was fascinated with the Central American culture and decided then and there if possible he wanted to serve and live in Central or South America. But what chances were there, he wondered for an Armor officer? When he looked into it, he found there was considerable opportunity in the military for varied assignments in Central and South America. All of the countries had military attaché offices and many of the countries had large Military Assistance Advisory Groups, or MAAGs. When Al found out about the Army's Foreign Area Officer Program he immediately applied for training as a Latin American FAO. He was accepted and excelled. Already fluent in Spanish, Al moved through FAO training with high honors.

His first assignment as a FAO was to the MAAG in Panama, where he was responsible for liaison with the Panamanian

National Guard Headquarters in Colon, Panama. Captain Tony Noriega in the G-2 Section was his point of contact. Al Yale knew from the time they first met that Tony Noriega was a man who was going someplace in Panama, not just because of his military skills, and he had those, but more for his strong determination to be a success and his willingness to do whatever necessary to achieve it.

Tony Noriega liked what he saw in his boss, General Omar Torrijos, the Commander of the National Guard. Torrijos had established a Military Junta in 1968, overthrowing the elected President and becoming the dominant power in Panamanian political life. Tony was a hustler. He was always doing something for somebody; he was always getting something for someone, particularly his seniors. And there were pay backs. Tony accumulated more favors than any other officer in the National Guard. Tony, like Al, had married early, but unlike Al, practiced the Latin American custom of taking a mistress. When Al left Panama the first time, he continued to follow Tony's career, and the two officers stayed in touch, corresponding from time to time.

Noriega was always promoted ahead of his contemporaries and rose quickly to the rank of Colonel and head of the powerful PDF G-2. In the years that Tony was head of the G-2 serving General Torrijos, rumors abounded that Tony was becoming a rich man by supporting the Americans, the Russians and the Cubans, playing the three off against each other. This was also the time when the rumors started that Tony was involved in illegal drugs, moving them through Panama to the United States.

By the time Al Yale was promoted to full Colonel and went back to Panama as the DATT, Tony Noriega had become "El Supremo," as he liked to call himself, and was the de facto ruler of Panama, although there was a figurehead president. Tony had warmly welcomed his old friend back to Panama and had even thrown a party for him at the PDF Headquarters where Al met many old acquaintances.

Noriega maintained their friendship. He always took Al's telephone calls, welcomed him as a visitor whenever Al asked to see him, and frequently asked Al to join him for private parties, just like the old days. Colonel Yale was embarrassed that his access to Tony was far greater than the U.S. Ambassador's or General Lyman's, the Commander-in-Chief of the U.S. Southern Command (SOUTHCOM) headquartered in Panama. They often asked Yale to get an answer for them from General Noriega when they could not.

On occasions Al would try and talk to Tony as a friend and ask about the rumors that were going around concerning Noriega's illegal activities. On these occasions Tony would either shrug off the allegations or just laugh at Yale. Clearly Tony Noriega was a changed man. He had a blond mistress who was often with him in public, and he was frequently seen with known drug figures. Then, too, he had begun attacking U.S. policies and openly supporting the Cubans and Russians in their economic endeavors in Panama. When Al pointed these affronts out in their private sessions, Tony radiated an attitude of being above all that and said, "Not to worry, I can deal with Uncle Sugar."

Al Yale concluded General Noriega had become so full of himself and so convinced of his invincibility that nothing short of a major confrontation between the United States and Panama would turn Tony Noriega around. The situation in Panama was growing more tense and the number of anti-U.S. incidents was on the increase. Colonel Yale had begun to send a weekly summary of activities in Panama to the DAS and other Defense Department customers. Al always coordinated his reports with the Embassy and SOUTHCOM, and since Colonel Yale was recognized as an expert with unique access to General Noriega, his reports were rarely challenged. Al Yale was the star reporter for many units and agencies and they were hounding him regularly for new information.

During the week that Bart Lowe was touring Japan with Harry Banahara, Al Yale reviewed his reports for the last six months concerning anti-American incidents in Panama. When he considered them in the aggregate, he believed he was seeing a disturbing pattern. What in the past had appeared to be routine, scattered, everyday happenings of Americans involved in isolated incidents with Panamanians, now appeared to be occurring regularly and on a wide front. American tourists, business people, dependents of the U.S. military forces in Panama and the U.S. military forces themselves were being subjected to various and continuing forms of harassment. For example, the PDF seemed bent on singling out Americans for a plethora of petty traffic fines and arrests of American G.I.s on trumped-up charges of drunk and disorderly conduct throughout the honky tonk entertainment areas that American military personnel frequented. And there seemed to be inordinate numbers of traffic or other altercations in front of U.S. military installations that succeeded in closing off base entrances and exits and backing up normal operations for hours. When the Panamanian authorities were asked to assist, they agreed, but did so only half-heartedly.

General Tony Noriega, Al was convinced, had made the decision to abandon his best friend, the United States. The question was how to expose Noriega's plan and thwart his efforts. Colonel Yale presented his analysis to the U.S. Ambassador and General Lyman, and while they were not as convinced as Al Yale of an orchestrated conspiracy by General Noriega, they endorsed Yale's initiative to incorporate his views into a special information report to be sent to a wide range of Panama watchers in Washington. It was this report that was forwarded to DAO Tokyo, to be passed to General Lowe to read on his Sunday evening return flight to Washington.

As Bart settled back into the comfortable seat of the first class cabin of Northwest Orient's 747 flight, he thought of the last five days. The flight attendant had already gone over the menu of the evening meal and had served him a Manhattan and a bowl of Macadamia nuts. As he sipped the Manhattan and chewed the tasty Hawaiian nuts he slowly and fondly recalled the highlights of the trip with Harry Banaharas.

When Bart, as a young soldier, had been transferred from Korea to Japan, he was assigned to a post north of Tokyo. Camp Drake was at one time home of the famous U.S. 1st Cavalry Division, but when Corporal Bart Lowe arrived in 1954 it was the

Headquarters for the IX Corps Artillery. Bart had been a sharp young soldier and after having been selected as soldier of the month three months in a row, he was selected to be a courier for the Commanding General.

For the next 18 months Bart's courier duties took him from one end to the other of Japan. He quickly discovered that his lack of Japanese language severely hampered his travels. English was rarely spoken at that time, particularly in the more remote areas.

On his own initiative, Bart enrolled in beginning Japanese classes three evenings a week at the Service Club at Camp Drake. The instructor was a young Japanese woman who worked at the Post Exchange. When Bart explained that he wanted to gain a familiarity with some Japanese technical terms, she agreed to help him with his research and to compile a glossary of terms that would be most helpful to him.

Bart and the Japanese language instructor became close friends. Her name was Cheriko, and she was four years older than Bart. Cheriko liked the Americans, but her family was a traditional Japanese family and they were uncomfortable with her employment at the base.

Cheriko offered to show Bart the historical and cultural side of Japan, and on the weekends when Bart was not on duty they would go sightseeing in Tokyo. Because of his regular study of the language and his use of it during his travels, Bart became proficient in Japanese.

During Bart's second year in Japan, he and Cheriko had become lovers. Bart, like so many young American men on the first visit to the Far East, was attracted by not only the natural beauty of the Oriental women but by their deference to men. Added to her education and knowledge of English, it made Cheriko an exceptionally attractive woman to Bart.

Cheriko's parents were shocked when they learned that Bart's and Cheriko's relationship had moved beyond professional teacher-pupil, and they forbade Cheriko to continue her intimate relationship with Bart. It was heartbreaking for the two of them, and Bart's first reaction was to convince Cheriko to ignore her parents' wishes and continue the affair with him. However, when he saw how deep Cheriko's concern was over breaking faith with her family, he decided not to unduly influence her. Ultimately, she made the decision to follow her parents' wishes and return to her traditional Japanese customs. She gave up her employment with the U.S. Army and obtained a job in Tokyo. It was a bitter-sweet ending for Bart Lowe as he completed his tour in Japan and returned to Florida to pursue his college education. Over the years he often thought of Cheriko and wondered what might have been.

When Bart sketched out his time spent in Japan as a youth to Harry Banahara, he had no idea the lengths Harry would take to make his revisit a memorable one. When Harry picked Bart up at the New Sanno Hotel they had gone to a nearby Japanese Self-Defense Force installation where a Japanese helicopter met them and flew them to Camp Drake. The Japanese Commanding General greeted Bart on his arrival and told him a special tour had been arranged to take him to and through all the places he had lived and worked so many years ago. The Japanese hadn't missed a trick. They took him to his old barracks, the room he shared with five others, the CG's old office, now located in an Imperial Military Shrine, the P.X., the Service Club, the old gym, the former Mess Hall, the library and the old movie house. Bart was astounded that while a new modern military post had been built around the old one, the old one had been preserved, largely intact as he remembered it. The Japanese CG hosted a lunch for Lowe and Banahara and allowed Bart to pontificate over the many happy days and nights he had enjoyed at Camp Drake.

Next came Harry's tour of old Tokyo—now swallowed up by one of the world's largest cities. It was amazing how Harry could find the places that young Americans frequented in those earlier days among the skyscrapers of modern Tokyo. The bathhouses, the coffee houses, the Japanese theaters, the Geisha houses, and dance halls. Harry knew them all, and Bart had been in each of them sometime during his years in Japan.

The next morning they set out on a three-day Bullet Train ride that took them north to the snows of Sapporo in Hokkaido, then south to the warm sea breezes of Osaka and then back to the central plain of Honshu. The nights were spent in simple rooms in the same Japanese military installations that had been under U.S. control during Bart's time in Japan. Harry even managed to get the Japanese to resurrect a vintage U.S. Army jeep for one of their jaunts up a mountain side in Sendai to a sequestered depot. The piece de resistance, Bart thought, was on the last night in Kyoto when Harry announced they would be having dinner with a Japanese family. The dinner was scheduled for 8:00 at the rooftop restaurant overlooking the Kyoto port. Harry and Bart arrived at the restaurant a little before eight and secured the reserved table. Soon thereafter an attractive Japanese woman who looked to be in her early fifties, dressed stylishly in western attire, and two young people, a man and a woman in their twenties, also tastefully dressed, joined Bart and Harry at their table. When introductions were made, the names were not familiar and Bart was not sure of the purpose of having dinner with this family. The woman did look vaguely familiar but Bart could not place the connection. Then suddenly it hit him. The woman sitting across the table from him was his friend of many years ago—Cheriko! Miracles of miracles, Harry had been able to find this one woman out of millions.

Cheriko told Bart that this nice gentleman, indicating Harry, had contacted her several weeks ago and had asked her if she would be willing to meet with an American friend from years ago. Cheriko said at first she was reluctant; she hadn't been in contact for many years with Americans and her English was now poor. But when she learned who the American was, she mentioned it to her children and they both agreed it would be a good idea. Both her son and daughter had studied in the United States and were very fond of Americans. Cheriko told Bart that shortly after he left Japan, her parents had arranged for her to marry an older, successful Japanese industrialist. They had moved from Tokyo to

Kyoto shortly after her marriage and had a happy life there. Her husband died four years ago. As the evening progressed, Cheriko's natural shyness receded and Bart recognized the same beauty and charm in the mature mother of two grown children that he had known so many years ago in the young woman it had been his privilege to love.

After dinner, Cheriko invited Bart and Harry back to her home, and they talked and recalled their time together until 2:00 a.m. in the morning. They promised to meet again either in Washington or Japan.

Back on the Northwest Orient jet flying at 39,000 feet above the Pacific Ocean, Bart's nostalgic thoughts were interrupted by the flight attendant who was ready to serve dinner. After dinner was served and a movie shown, Bart enjoyed five hours of uninterrupted sleep on the smooth flying aircraft.

The next morning after a breakfast of freshly squeezed orange juice, croissants, jam and a pot of coffee Bart broke out the report written by Colonel Yale. When he had finished reading, it was obvious things did not look good in Panama. After watching Al Yale perform as his attaché in Panama for the past two years, Bart had learned to place great confidence in Yale's reporting. He was one of the very best DATTs in the DAS and was probably the best Central and South American attaché serving in that part of the world. Bart was anxious to talk to Al personally and get his assessment on how fast things were moving in Panama.

Also on Bart's mind was the dinner he had in Tokyo with the National Police Chief and the information he had shared with Bart about the Tokyo KGB resident. Bart had not yet decided on exactly how or to whom he should pass the information, but whatever he was going to do, he would do it on Monday. The time saved in crossing the International Dateline would allow Bart to get a day's rest, recover from the jet lag that always followed Far East trips, perhaps spend a few hours with B.J. Ross, and report in Monday morning fresh and rested for duty.

Back in his office in Rosslyn on Monday, Bart decided that his first call would be to Art Cheek at CIA. Colonel Herrington had told Bart that when the information concerning the GRU officer in Jakarta was delivered by him to Mr. Cheek, Cheek received it without comment and had said only to pass his thanks along to General Lowe. John Kitchen at the FBI, on the other hand, was quite excited about the development and thought it would be very helpful in the investigation. Joan Weber was successful in getting Art Cheek on the secure phone her first try, and Bart heard the familiar New England accent.

"Hello, Bart. Welcome back."

"Thanks, Art. It's good to be back. Any problem, Art, with the way we handled the situation in Indonesia concerning my attaché Mike Petroangelo and the GRU officer who claims his associate recruited an American spy?"

"No. I think it was your only choice in the interest of security. My only concern is for my Chief of Station in Jakarta. He is a good guy, one of our best, and he doesn't know what the hell is going on. He figures he's being end runned about the Russian action down there, but he's not sure how or why. It may not make for the best relations between him and your guys. But my counterintelligence people say your decision to hold it close was the only way to go and of course our friends at the FBI are delighted," Art replied.

"Art, I hate to be the bearer of more bad news, but bad news never improves with age." Bart, without revealing the name of the source, related the information that had been passed to him and Harry Banahara in Tokyo by the National Police Chief concerning the KGB resident's claim that the KGB had penetrated the CIA.

"Jesus H. Christ," snarled Art. And then after a period of silence, "How reliable is your source? I mean this is the kind of bullshit you are always hearing in this business," Art said with no small degree of frustration.

"Harry Banahara says the source is a long standing friend of the U.S. with an impeccable track record for reliable information."

"Oh great." groaned Art. "And I suppose you didn't pass this along to my Station Chief in Tokyo either?"

"Under the circumstances and with HEAT SEEKER on my mind, I didn't think that would be prudent."

"Yeah. Yeah. I know."

"But, Art that's your call. If you think your man in Tokyo should know, be my guest. And while we are at it, I think I should also pass this along to John Kitchen at the FBI. Do you agree?"

"Oh yeah, sure. Anything to screw the agency," retorted Art Cheek.

Bart decided not to answer that salvo, and after more than a minute of strained silence Art said, "I'm sorry, I didn't mean that, Bart. I don't think you have any other choice but to pass it on to Kitchen, and I'm going to do the same thing with our counterintelligence people. It's just that this God damned thing has me so frustrated I get pissed off every time I hear something else about it."

"I hear you, Art, and I can appreciate your frustration. My only regret is that I seem to be a part of things that add to your frustration. But if somehow these things move us closer to solving this HEAT SEEKER mystery then all of the frustration will not have been in vain."

"Of course you're right, Bart," Art said, calmer now. "Let's get on with it and maybe these developments will move us closer to catching this bastard."

John Kitchen, at the FBI, not surprisingly, received the Tokyo information from Bart in a very positive manner. He immediately believed it to be related to HEAT SEEKER and, seasoned investigator that he was, he knew the more evidence he had, the more likely it was that the mystery could be solved. He also believed the counterintelligence people he was working with at CIA would agree. John promised Bart an update soon on the HEAT SEEKER investigation, particularly in view of the Jakarta and Tokyo developments.

When Bart got back into his routine at DAS Headquarters one of his first actions was to have a secure phone call conversation with Colonel Yale. Yale's assessment was that the tensions in Panama would likely continue unless the U.S. really got tough with General Noriega. Even then he wasn't sure Tony Noriega would back down. Al thought that the next six months in Panama would be critical. He asked General Lowe to assign two additional attachés to DAO Panama on a temporary basis to assist him in his coverage of the Panamanian Defense Forces and the events taking place in Panama. Colonel Yale said the Ambassador had no objection, as long as the assignments were temporary. Bart agreed and tasked the Central and Latin America Division Chief, Colonel Brian Lomb, to move two additional attachés to Panama within a week.

Colonels Tortelli and Lomb gave Lowe an update briefing his first day back that left no doubt in his mind that the U.S. Government was looking at Panama with a worried eye. Captain Pete Kalika, who had served in South America, agreed with Colonel Yale that things in Panama were going to get worse before they got better.

The tense situation in Panama continued through the fall of 1988, but eased up somewhat during the Christmas and New Year's holidays. Al Yale and the DAO, even with the help of the two additional attachés were swamped with monitoring the situations in Panama, reporting anti-U.S. incidents and responding to requests for information from a whole host of government agencies, not the least of which was the Joint Chiefs of Staff.

By January the JCS had appointed a new CINC, SOUTHCOM, General Maxwell Drummond, a hard nosed disciplinarian whose marching orders were to make sure the Panama Canal remained open to international commerce without interference from the Panamanian Government, and that the sovereignty of U.S. bases in Panama remained intact. The arrival of the new CINC at SOUTHCOM Headquarters garnered considerable media attention, and the U.S. Ambassador began a series of tough diplomatic notes to General Noriega, notifying him that the harassment of U.S. citizens and bases would not be tolerated.

These two events had an initial dampening effect on the number of incidents taking place in Panama, but the repose was short lived. By February, General Drummond had begun a strict program to keep U.S. military members and their families confined to their bases and off the Panamanian streets. The military police and security guards around the U.S. bases were doubled and the State Department's Travel Advisories to U.S. citizens warning against possible violence in Panama City and Colon, the two largest areas in Panama, greatly reduced the usually large number of free-spending American tourists.

General Noriega responded by refusing to meet with U.S. officials, rarely would he accept or return phone calls. He began a vitriolic media blitz, accusing the U.S. of gross mistreatment of its tiny ally and saying that Panama would not be intimidated. Anti-U.S. demonstrations were staged in the downtown Panama City business centers, cars were overturned and burned, and U.S. owned or sponsored business offices and buildings were stoned and vandalized. The PDF, in spite of U.S. protests, did little if anything to prevent or control these staged demonstrations. Anti-Noriega opposition to the PDF's economic and political power also began to grow. In May 1989, when national elections were held, Panamanians voted for the anti-Noriega candidates by a three-to-one margin. Noriega responded by annulling the election.

By the summer of 1989, Al Yale was confident that Panama and the United States were on a deadly collision course that could only spell disaster for Panama. In his discussions with SOUTHCOM, the CINC, General Drummond, and the DAS in Washington, Yale knew that the JCS had already developed a military contingency plan for dealing with Panama if the situation became intolerable, and it was getting close to that. Colonel Yale also knew that the President, DOD, and the State Department would rely heavily on the recommendations of General Drummond and the Ambassador as to the necessity and timing of any military contingency operation. He knew, too, that General Drummond was not a particularly patient man and General Noriega's technique of stonewalling him and refusing to talk and meet with him was quickly causing Drummond to lose the little patience he had left.

Colonel Yale, had been racking his brain to figure out how he might convince Tony Noriega of the no-win situation, and somehow persuade him to de-escalate the crisis. So far nothing brilliant had popped into Yale's mind, and he was not optimistic. On Wednesday afternoon of the third week of July, Al Yale was surprised when his secretary told him that Major Cordova from the PDF was on the telephone. Cordova was General Noriega's SGS, (Secretary to the General Staff), and Al Yale had not talked to him in weeks. Al picked up the phone and answered, "Colonel Yale."

"Hey, gringo. The 'El Supremo' is having a little private party tonight and he wants you to come. He says just like old times. Can you make it?"

Al Yale thought carefully before answering. Since the crisis had intensified, all U.S. personnel were instructed to keep any informal meetings with Panamanians to a minimum. But Al thought this might be an opportunity to reason with Noriega.

"Yeah, amigo. I can make it. What time?" Yale finally replied.

"Nine o'clock. I'll send a car for you. Are you still at the Rialto Apartments downtown?"

"Yes, that's the place. I'll be in the lobby at 9:00."

When he had finished the call, Al went up to the top story of the embassy and asked to see the ambassador. He told his secretary that it was something hot. The ambassador called for him about five minutes later, and after they discussed the invitation, he agreed with Colonel Yale that he had done the right thing by accepting the invitation to meet with General Noriega. As Yale left the ambassador's office, the ambassador said to him, "Watch yourself, Al. As you know, these guys can play rough."

That evening when Al told his wife, Belinda, of his plans, she was upset. "Al, you must be loco. You know you can't trust that bunch of cutthroats and you don't know what they have in mind."

"I know, Belinda. I thought about it a lot before deciding to go, but I feel I must if there is the slightest chance I could talk some sense into Tony's head."

"I don't like it, Al, and I wish you would reconsider. In fact, I wish now that we had never come back to Panama. This beautiful place has become a hell hole. You can't even walk on the streets anymore without feeling that someone will rob you or shoot you." And with that Belinda marched into her sewing room and slammed the door.

The black Chevrolet sedan arrived promptly at 9:00 and a PDF lieutenant opened the rear door for Colonel Yale. The sedan headed for the beach area. General Noriega liked to hold his private parties at houses that were either owned by him or other members of the PDF. He rarely held a party at the same place, so Al was convinced that this would be a house where he had never been. When the sedan reached the beach neighborhood, it was stopped at a PDF checkpoint. Whenever General Noriega was visiting an area, the PDF established a perimeter of security around the area to ensure that he was not surprised. After being cleared to proceed from the checkpoint, they drove only a short distance to a house set back among heavy trees facing the Pacific Ocean. The time was 9:30, and Colonel Yale was passed on by a uniformed PDF soldier standing at the front door.

Once inside, he adjusted his eyes to the dim light and smoke from many cigars. Yale estimated that there were approximately ten men and about a dozen women in the room. There was a three-piece Latin music group, two men and a female singer. Al recognized most of the men as senior PDF officers, although all were dressed in Guyaberra attire. He did not see General Noriega but recognized Colonel Gonzales, the Chief of Staff of the PDF who came over to greet him.

"Colonel Yale, my amigo, welcome. We are delighted you could join us for the evening. I know the 'El Supremo' will be pleased."

After a few moments of conversation with Colonel Gonzales, Al asked where General Noriega was and was told that he was around the house somewhere, perhaps in one of the bedrooms with a senorita. This was said with great laughter and gusto. The Panamanian men considered themselves great lovers and "El Supremo" always set the example for his men.

Al circulated and talked with the other officers. In the front room of the house was an open bar with two bartenders and a table well stocked with food, including freshly caught lobsters and cevetchi. Cevetchi, a Panamanian delicacy of bite-sized filets of white fish "cooked" with fresh lime juice was one of Al Yale's favorites. He washed the cevetchi down with a glass of beer.

Yale, who did not like to drink alcohol as a rule, had prepared himself for the evening by downing two large glasses of buttermilk before leaving his apartment. The buttermilk helped to absorb the alcohol. Al knew that if he didn't at least go through the motions of drinking with the PDF Officers, he would have no credibility with them. At the start, Al was able to stay away from the offers of hard liquor by saying he preferred beer with the food, and he was going to eat as much as possible to help absorb the alcohol.

About 30 minutes later, General Noriega came downstairs and went directly to Yale. He was obviously pleased to see his old friend and insisted that Al drink a toast with him. Al's first glass of scotch was thrust into his hand. As always, General Noriega liked to tell how the two were captains together and had been friends for years.

After recounting some good times together in earlier years with much laughter and bravado, General Noriega put his arm around Al Yale's shoulder and said. "Hey, my friend, how about sticking around for a while and maybe we can have a little talk, huh?"

Yale agreed, then Noriega said, "Okay, now I must see to my guests and the senoritas," and he walked off to mingle with the other people.

Al knew he was in for a long night. He had done this before. Noriega would drink, laugh, sing, dance and tease the women until the wee hours and then send everyone on their way. Finally he and Al would have their talk. But Al Yale was optimistic. It was, he thought, a good sign that Tony wanted to see him and maybe, just maybe, Tony was beginning to see the error of his ways and wanted to square things with the U.S. "Well, we will see," thought Al.

It was almost 1:30 a.m. when General Noriega bid goodnight to the last of his guests. Al had managed to keep his alcohol consumption to a minimum by using several subterfuges like pouring out drinks in the backyard, down the toilet and into the potted plants scattered throughout the house, but even so, Tony had frequently returned for toasts and Al had had no choice but to down several stiff drinks. In spite of the buttermilk and all the food, Al felt the effects of the alcohol and hoped he was up to purposeful conversation with Noriega.

When the last good-byes were said and the last person was out the door, Noriega grabbed a bottle of cognac and two glasses and motioned for Al to follow him out to the terrace. Noriega had Al hold the glasses while he poured double portions of cognac in both glasses.

Turning to look at the serene, moonlit Pacific Ocean, he said to Yale, "Hey amigo, why is your country treating me so badly?"

Yale was so surprised he almost dropped his glass of cognac. He hesitated a moment to make sure Tony hadn't made the statement in jest. But, with a glance at the intense look in Noriega's eyes, Al could tell he was very serious.

"General—Tony—my friend, I can't see how you can say that. The United States has bent over backwards over the years to be a friend to your country and you in particular." Al, having prepared for this moment carefully, summarized how patient the U.S. had been over the last few years, how the United States had taken certain actions to cut off assistance to Panama only after being provoked time and time again by Noriega and the PDF. Al concluded by saying that in spite of all that, it would not be too late to achieve some sort of rapprochement if General Noriega would be willing to approach the U.S. and offer to negotiate the current U.S./Panamanian differences.

"And how can you say that, my friend?" General Noriega replied, his voice rising. "What about all these bullshit notes and threats I am getting every day from the great Uncle Sam and his asshole representatives? Don't you people know this is our country, and no one is going to tell me how to run it?" Noriega then began a tirade of uncomplimentary slurs about the United States, partly spoken in English and partly in Spanish.

By this time Noriega was almost screaming, and two of his bodyguards came to the terrace entrance to see if "El Supremo" needed any help. Noriega finally stood up, waved the bodyguards back into the house and turned toward Yale.

"Listen to me, Colonel, the message you need to give to your ambassador, to General Drummond and to any other Americans is that I am in charge here and what I say goes. And that includes the Panama Canal. If you gringos don't like the way things are going, then you can just get the hell out of here. And you don't need to wait until the treaty ends. We can take care of ourselves, and Panama has other friends we can call upon if we need anything. You get the message, amigo? Yankee go home. We don't need you!" And with that General Noriega suddenly turned and threw his glass of cognac high in the air toward the water. Without another word, he returned to the house, quickly passed through it with his bodyguards scurrying behind and was out the door and into his waiting car.

When Al Yale re-entered the house he found Major Cordova waiting for him.

"So how did your little talk with the General go?" Cordova asked.

"Talk? That's what it was? He did most of the talking, and I did all the listening," answered Yale.

"Don't feel like the lone ranger, amigo. That happens to everyone. 'El Supremo' talks, and we all listen. He is a man with a larger purpose. He is going to free the Panamanians from the yoke of U.S. oppression."

"Come on Cordova. You know that's not true."

"Yes, amigo. I know that's not true. But 'El Supremo'—he thinks it's true, and so far no one on our side has had the balls to tell him he's wrong. And even if we did, I don't think he would listen. He thinks he is a man of destiny."

That night riding back to his apartment through the quiet and deserted streets of Panama City, Al Yale was sad. He knew now with a high degree of certainty that his one-time friend General Tony Noriega had fallen victim to the old axiom, power corrupts, and absolute power corrupts absolutely. He was almost certain that Noriega would not back down but continue on his disastrous collision course with the United States. And he was equally sure the United States was going to be left with no other recourse than to implement its military contingency plan and use force in order to ensure the safety of the Panama Canal and Americans in Panama. He didn't know it then, but the next time Al Yale would see General Tony Noriega would be as a prisoner of war in his own country.

CHAPTER 20

THE KINSHASA CONNECTION

Shortly after Colonel Alan Yale met with General Tony Noriega at Noriega's late night party in Panama, he sat down in his office at the U.S. Embassy and wrote a prophetic report on the thoughts of General Noriega and the future of Panama. Yale waited three days before writing his Defense Information Report on the outside chance that Tony Noriega might call him or have one of his minions call him to insist that what Noriega had said was expressed in a moment of anger and haste. But the call never came and Al knew he was duty bound to write the negative report. The "point of no return" report, as it later became known, hit Washington like a bombshell. As it was read by the DAS, JCS, Defense Department, State Department and the White House personnel, calls were immediately made to the U.S. Ambassador in Panama and to the CINC, SOUTHCOM, to see if they were aware of the report, and more importantly, if they agreed with it. Both the ambassador and the CINC confirmed they agreed with the negative conclusions of Colonel Yale's report.

In the report Al Yale covered the details of his late night meeting with General Noriega and painted a picture of a man who had completely lost his perspective and control. Yale believed that Noriega, in his quest for power as de facto dictator of Panama, had somehow lost his capability for rational thinking in his dealings with the United States. Noriega, Yale concluded, now believed himself to be invincible. The tense situation that existed in Panama would only grow worse, Yale believed, and diplomatic attempts to improve relationships between Panamanians and Americans would only be met by more bully-like tactics from Noriega and the Panamanian Defense Force. Yale was convinced that Noriega had passed the "point of no return" in his irrational scheme to throw the

Americans out of Panama and seize control of the Panama Canal. Colonel Yale firmly believed that only the application of overwhelming U.S. military force could turn around the disastrous circumstances taking place in Panama and stop General Noriega from carrying out his grandiose plans.

In Bart Lowe's mind, Colonel Yale's "point of no return" report marked the time in Washington when the contingency planning for military operations in Panama transitioned from tentative to definite. The military forces at Fort Bragg and other locations tapped for the "JUST CAUSE" contingency operation began their combat preparation and operational rehearsals in earnest. The question of the invasion of Panama was no longer if, but when.

In the ensuing months, to its credit, the U.S. Government demonstrated infinite patience with General Noriega and exhausted every diplomatic option, attempting to get him to back away from his destructive collision course with the United States, but all to no avail. Finally, as 1989 was growing to a close, dependents had been evacuated from Panama, and the embassy staff had been drawn down. Still Tony Noriega did not get it. Colonel Brian Lomb stopped by General Lowe's office at the end of the day and told Bart that he had just instructed the DAS Operations Center to be especially alert that evening and to inform General Lowe of any developments concerning Panama.

"Do you think 'JUST CAUSE' will go tonight, Brian?" Bart asked.

"It's difficult to say for sure, General, but I know they have been watching the weather closely and the forecast for the next three days for Central America is good. If I were a betting man, I would say the clock is about to run out on Tony Noriega," Colonel Lomb answered.

Brian Lomb, an old Latin American hand, was not a man given to hasty judgments. True to his prediction, Lowe was awakened in the early hours of the following morning by a call from the Operations Center advising him that all the major television networks were carrying live coverage of a press conference at the Pentagon announcing the "JUST CAUSE" invasion of Panama. Bart sat up in bed and reached for the remote on his bedside table and turned on the television. He was just in time to catch the beginning of a briefing by the Chairman, JCS, to the Pentagon press corps and the nation on Operation "JUST CAUSE" and the military objectives of the main invading force.

What happened from that point on in Panama quickly became history. The militarily superior U.S. forces encountered only minimal resistance in securing Panama and rendering the PDF ineffective. General Noriega eluded the invading U.S. forces for several days and hid out in the countryside, but he finally surrendered.

Colonel Al Yale played a key role following "JUST CAUSE" in assisting the CINC, and subsequently the State Department, in reconstituting a legitimate Panamanian Government with democratic institutions and elected officials. Colonel Yale was rewarded for his more than stressful three years in Panama with the Defense Attaché job in his wife's home country, Guatemala.

One of the areas of the world that Bart Lowe was concerned about was Africa. He believed he had not paid enough attention to the attaché staffs there. This was not deliberate, but because the other regions of the world had demanded more attention and clearly had higher priority U.S. interests. In his earlier visits to the African countries he had always come away with the impressions that the attachés and their families serving in that part of the world believed that their isolated posts were among the most hazardous and unappreciated in the world. These perceptions rose not just from the government instabilities in many of the nations, but also from the health hazards existing in most of the underdeveloped countries in Africa.

When the crisis in Panama had run its course, Bart tasked Colonel Nick Tortellie and George Martin to put together a trip for him that would take him to the DAOs in Africa he had not yet visited. Colonel Tortellie suggested that the trip take place the first of the year and include visits to Egypt, Chad, Zimbabwe, Zaire and South Africa. Nick recommended that the African trip begin with a stopover at EUCOM Headquarters in Stuttgart, Germany, and from there move south to Cairo, N'Djamena, Kinshasa, Harare, and return from Pretoria.

"You mean the State Department is finally going to let me into South Africa?" Bart asked.

"Yes and no. No, not for an official or overnight visit, but yes, for a pass through en route back to the United States," replied Tortellie. "As you know, the State Department and our Ambassador in South Africa have not approved any visits by high ranking U.S. military officers during the last three years because of the political situation there. But knowing your desire to visit all our attachés where they are stationed, our South African desk officer and State's desk officer did some innovative thinking and worked out a compromise. You can arrive in Pretoria on an early morning flight from Harare, Zimbabwe, be booked on an evening flight out of Pretoria and while you are waiting go into town, visit the U.S. Embassy and the DAO, have lunch and dinner with our group and their families, return to the Pretoria Airport and be on your way back home."

"Nick, that's brilliant. Why didn't we think of that before?"

"You've got me on that one, boss. I guess my only reply is that it was before my watch," answered Tortellie, always fast on his feet.

"Very well done, Nick. My compliments to the desk officer."

"If the trip is a go, George will accompany you and make arrangements for commercial air transportation from here to Europe and from Pretoria back to Europe and home. EUCOM will provide C-12 air transportation from Stuttgart to Cairo and then we'll use our DAO C-12 aircraft based in Zaire to get you to N'Djamena, Kinshasa and Harare. You need to fly commercial from Harare to Pretoria because the South Africans won't permit us to fly into Pretoria with the American C-12. Not even for a drop-off. Zimbabwe Air has a regular 8:00 a.m. Monday morning flight to Pretoria. The way we have the trip planned, you'll spend the last Friday, Saturday and Sunday in Zimbabwe, and according to our desk officer, Bobby Mitchell, one of the largest and best game parks in Africa is located just two hours south of Harare. Bobby highly recommends that you take the time to visit the game park."

"With pleasure, Nick, as long as it doesn't interfere with anything else that the DATT thinks I should do in Zimbabwe," Bart said.

"Quite the contrary, General. Our attachés are as proud of showing off the game park as the Zimbabweans. I went there last year on my visit to the African stations and was impressed with the number and variety of animals. It was better than a safari."

"I'm sold, Nick. Sign me up," Bart commented.

Bart spent his first Christmas in the States in more than three years. He flew to Miami Christmas Eve and spent Christmas Day with his mother and her neighborhood friends. The day after Christmas, he flew to Stowe, Vermont, and joined B.J. Ross for five days of skiing and winter fun. He returned to Washington on New Year's Day.

As the new year began, uncharacteristically, things in the DAS took a quieter turn and Bart found himself looking forward to the African trip. Africa, more than any other place in the world, had a certain mystique about it. Although Bart had attended three Regional Attaché Conferences in Africa and the Mid-East since he had joined the DAS, he still knew less about Africa than the other regions of the world.

Bart had not received any new information from SSD or John Kitchen at the FBI on HEAT SEEKER. Bart asked Joan Weber to call Mr. Kitchen's office and see if she could arrange racquetball and lunch with John before Bart left on the African trip.

Joan arranged for the two to meet at the Pentagon POAC the Friday before Bart and George's Sunday departure for Stuttgart.

After three very competitive racquetball games, Bart and John showered, dressed and picked up a light lunch in the POAC dining room. They moved to a vacant table in the corner of the room, and both having worked up a considerable appetite, wolfed their soup, salads and large lemonades. When both men had finished, Bart said, "John, would you like a cup of coffee before I interrogate you?"

"Interrogate me! I thought that was my job, general. Yes, I would relish a cup of that good black, extra strong military coffee."

Bart walked over to the large restaurant-type coffee urn and drew off two mugs of coffee. He picked a container of coffee cream and a sweetener for himself and two spoons and returned to the table. After Bart and John had stirred their coffee and taken their first swallows, Bart said, "John, the subject is HEAT SEEKER. I haven't heard anything from you, and I am more than curious. Are we still stalemated? Didn't that information coming out of Indonesia and Japan move this thing along? What can you tell me?"

John Kitchen rocked back in his chair, took another long swig of his coffee and looked around to be satisfied that the noise coming from the other tables in the room would not allow anything he said to be overheard. "No, Bart. By rights there isn't really anything I can tell you except that the investigation is continuing."

Before Bart could protest, John raised his hand and said, "I know, I know, you are about to tell me that won't cut it. And I know that all you and your people have put us onto deserves a better explanation," Kitchen conceded. "Actually, Bart, the information that was generated in Jakarta and Tokyo moved us considerably along the investigative path and greatly narrowed the scope of the problem. What I am about to tell you is really out of school, so you must protect me on this. Not a word of what I'm about to say to anyone, understood? We have narrowed a list of strong suspects down to six individuals. Only one of those individuals is not in the CIA, and I will be surprised if that individual doesn't fall off the list this week when some investigative activity is completed. I now firmly believe that HEAT SEEKER is one of the five CIA subjects we are investigating."

Bart leaned toward John, his interest obviously piqued and said, "Really. You have it down to five people, and you believe HEAT SEEKER is one of those?" Bart whispered.

Kitchen nodded.

"Well? Go on. What else can you tell me? Who are they? Where are they? And when are you going to arrest the right one?" Bart rapidly asked.

"Whoa!" John whispered back. "That is all I can and am going to say at this time. You have my word, Bart, when something breaks that I can talk about, you will be among the first to know." John finished his coffee, thanked Bart for the lunch and racquetball and was quickly gone, leaving Bart sitting at the table to ponder what he had heard.

The trip began on schedule. Lowe and Martin departed Dulles Airport on Sunday evening on a TWA flight to Stuttgart via Paris. A two-hour layover in Paris, waiting to make the Stuttgart connection, allowed for a brief meeting with the U.S. DATT in Paris, Rear Admiral Philip Devereau. Admiral Devereau had arranged for a private VIP lounge at the Orly Airport for the meeting and had brought along an officer from the French Foreign Ministry to provide Bart a briefing on the civil war in Chad. France had been involved in Chad since WWII and still had a contingent of French troops based there.

The twenty-minute briefing was a mini-history of the continuing tribal struggles in one of the most backward countries in North Africa. The French officer, a Major Fauk of the French Foreign Legion, had served two tours in Chad and spoke with experience and combat knowledge about the warring factions. The bottom line of the briefing was that the regime in power would continue to hold off the rebel factions who were backed by neighboring Libya if the French continued its considerable assistance to N'Djamena. Political support, unfortunately, was on the wane in France.

When the Chad briefing was completed, the lounge attendant served fresh croissants and rich French coffee. Bart and Phil Devereau used the remaining time to discuss DAO Paris operations and some budget shortfalls. George Martin was able to practice his excellent French with Major Fauk until the attendant signaled it was time to board the flight to Stuttgart.

As always the day and night spent at EUCOM Headquarters were worthwhile. A visiting officer's suite had been arranged at Patch Barracks, and the J2/J3 staff updates on Africa and the priority EUCOM information requirements were helpful to General Lowe. He finished the day on Monday with a call on the Deputy CINC and had a quiet dinner at the quarters of the EUCOM J1 who was a Naval War College classmate of Bart's.

An early morning departure from Stuttgart by military aircraft with a refueling stop in Athens, Greece, permitted an early afternoon arrival in Cairo. The DATT in Athens met Lowe at the Hellenikon Air Force Base during the one hour refueling stop to give Bart an update on the Greek investigation of the Baldwin assassination. Still no perpetrators had been apprehended, but the overall security situation in Greece had improved for Americans with the possibility of a new Greek-American defense agreement after the elections in May.

Landing at the Egyptian Air Base near Cairo was no problem. Given the monumental size of the U.S. Military Security Assistance package to Egypt, the Egyptian authorities were most hospitable. The Egyptian Air Base Commander personally welcomed General Lowe and Colonel Martin to Cairo.

The DATT in Cairo, Army Colonel David Apple, had crammed about as much business and entertainment possible into the three days and nights that Lowe would be in Egypt. The DAO staff in Cairo was an extremely busy and often frustrated set of people. The major distraction to duty in Cairo was the fact that all of the living quarters were a considerable distance from the downtown Cairo U.S. Embassy. The more than one-hour commute from any quarters was along boulevards jammed with thousands of commuters in small cars, scooters, trucks, buses, and other conveyances making their way at a snails' pace to and from the city sixteen hours a day. Added to this regular mass of humanity and machines was the Egyptian custom of motorists honking their horns at other motorists whenever one came in close proximity, which was constantly. Bart stayed at Colonel Apple's quarters during the visit, and in the several trips he made to and from the embassy, he marveled at how focused Dave Apple could be in spite of the non-stop Egyptian horn concert.

The itinerary that Colonel Apple arranged included ample time with the Egyptian General Staff and Egyptian Army Armored Corps so that they could demonstrate their application of the military assistance provided by the U.S.. The readiness of the Egyptian Army, the largest of the services, had greatly benefited from the M1 and M60 tanks, armored personnel carriers, Apache helicopters, and antiaircraft missile batteries and other equipment from the U.S. Military Assistance program.

Everywhere Bart went senior Egyptian officers assured him of their cooperation with the United States and of their reliance as an ally to the United States if conflict should arise in the Middle East. Colonel Apple and the DAO did not neglect Egyptian history or culture: Bart and George Martin were treated to a trip to the Pyramids, box seats at Cairo's opera house for Verdi's Aida, Egypt's favorite opera, and on their last night, a boat trip with the DAO families down the Nile River.

Near the end of the evening, Bart, momentarily alone, moved up to a vantage point on the bow of the old single sail sailboat and looked back across the Nile at the distant skyline of Cairo. He wondered to himself if somehow, someone had been keeping track over the years, since the beginning of time of how many soldiers or military men had been embarked on the Nile River.

On Thursday morning Bart and George said their good-byes to Dave Apple and the Cairo DAO, and joined Colonel Paul Talbot and Colonel Bob Stark on the C-12 aircraft that had arrived from Zaire. Colonel Talbot was the DATT at Kinshasa and Colonel Stark the Air Force Attaché or AIRA. They had flown the DAS aircraft to Cairo to take General Lowe and Colonel Martin to Chad and then on to Zaire. Their flight to Chad would take most of the day, but there would be a break when the aircraft stopped to refuel.

The C-12 aircraft had been in service for many years in the DAS and was known around the world for its reliability. It was a small, seven-passenger, twin engine, turbo assisted aircraft. The C-12 could be configured for either passenger or cargo lift, or a limited combination. The aircraft was normally only assigned to DAOs in countries where the distances were vast and transportation for moving about the country was limited. About one-third of the DAOs were assigned C-12 aircraft. At a DAO with a C-12, the requirement was for three pilots. The aircraft was flown by a crew of two but the third pilot was necessary for rotation of duties, leave, and other absences. Rated officers from all services were available, but the flying assignment was in addition to the professional attaché training and duties.

The DAS accepted only the most experienced flying officers from the services and as a result, the DAS's air fleet had the best safety record of any air force in the free world. The C-12 had comfortable side-by-side seating with room to stretch out, and pull out work tables that allowed Bart to get in several hours of "office time." As soon as the C-12 took off from Cairo, gained its cruising altitude, and headed south, Bart took off his shoes, made himself comfortable, pulled the work table down across his seat and settled into another day at the office—at 21,000 feet.

The weather in Cairo had been warm and Bart was traveling in a comfortable short sleeve shirt and light trousers. But nothing in Egypt had prepared him for the 129 degrees of heat that hit him when the C-12 door opened after landing in N'Djamena, Chad. It felt like the door to a blast furnace had been opened. A large portion of Chad is desert, and the country is hot and often plagued with burning winds and blowing sand. That day was no exception.

Bart was met at the aircraft door by the DATT, Lieutenant Colonel Mary Novak, a gutsy, bantam rooster of a woman with brown hair, dark features, and dressed in battle dress uniform. Mary Novak was an Army officer who had volunteered for the hardship attaché post in N'Djamena. The Army had been somewhat reluctant about nominating a woman for a post like Chad, with that nation's male dominated culture. But when the review board interviewed Mary, heard her proficiency in French and saw her determination to serve in Chad, they became convinced Mary was the right person for the job.

And Mary had not disappointed anyone. During her almost completed two year tour, Mary had become somewhat of a legend with the Chadian Military, the Chadian government leaders, the French forces in Chad, and the U.S. Embassy staff.

Shortly after Mary arrived at the small DAO in Chad, Bart, concerned for her safety, asked one of the most experienced DATTs in the region, a colonel serving in the Ivory Coast of Africa, to go over and see how Mary was doing. Some time later the Colonel sent a cable to Bart reporting that he had paid Mary a visit and had offered his assistance. His bottom line was that Lieutenant Colonel Novak was getting along just fine, and the Colonel would be surprised if Mary asked anyone for help.

Mary Novak took General Lowe and Colonel Martin back to her quarters in the DAO all terrain vehicle. The four-wheel drive vehicle was the only one suitable for Chad with its extremes of hot and monsoon weather. Shortly after Mary arrived in Chad, she had traded her smaller, modern and comfortable apartment in embassy housing in the center of N'Djamena for a larger, but run down old house, on the edge of the town. Mary persuaded the U.S. Embassy support people to design a generator support system to provide electricity and water to the house and obtained the generators on loan from the U.S. Army in Europe to drive the system. Mary scavenged, begged and bullied help to fix up the old house from a variety of people in the international community in N'Djamena and supplemented that assistance with support from the DAS. She repaid the help she received by turning the house into a refuge for visitors.

There was never enough space in the war torn capital to accommodate all of the foreign visitors. N'Djamena had only one or sometimes two currently open hotels, and few embassies in N'Djamena could accommodate visitors comfortably in their own limited quarters. Mary's quarters soon became known as Mary's "boarding house" and requests to put up overflow visitors came to Mary by the droves. She rarely turned anyone away. As a result, Mary became the best reporter on what was going on in N'Djamena and the rest of the country because of her wide set of contacts and sources. For General Lowe's visit she was able to provide rooms for Bart and George Martin and the C-12 pilots. Mary had a cook and two other people—Chadians—who looked after the "boarding house" and the visitors.

That night, after an excellent meal prepared by her cook, Mary regaled Bart and George and Colonels Talbot and Stark with stories of her time in Chad. The country was currently led by a popular warrior, President Habre, head of the dominant Gourane tribe. He spent most of his time running the war effort northeast of the capital where his army was engaged.

By far the largest assistance came from the French and their tactical air support, which had prevented opposing forces in the north, backed by the Libyans, from moving to the south and overrunning N'Djamena. Of late the CIA had offered considerable assistance in the forms of weapons and Toyota trucks that the Chadians used to carry 50-caliber machine guns and as a sort of mobile armor corps.

Mary Novak, administering a modest security assistance program for the U.S., was filling in the gaps between the French and CIA. The U.S. State Department was trying to assist the Chadians in running a government and found its work to be slow and only marginally successful. President Habre's most effective general, a French-educated officer named Deby, had defected to Sudan and was now attacking the Chad army. Mary was reporting to Washington on the progress of the civil war, and her reports had earned her high praise in National Security circles.

Because the Muslim religion was dominant in Chad, Mary at first had great difficulty in convincing her male counterparts she knew what she was doing. In any social situation, according to Mary, the men would gravitate to a separate room away from females, if any were present. Often Mary would be the only female. Her dogged persistence won out, and she was finally accepted in Chad. Mary said, "It still is no real thrill at informal meetings to always be the last person to be offered a drink of hot camel's milk out of the traditional one bowl that is circulated among the attendees."

The three days and nights that Bart Lowe spent on the ground with Lieutenant Colonel Mary Novak and the four other members of DAO N'Djamena, as well as the rest of the U.S. team, left no doubt in Bart's mind that they were really earning the money their country paid them to serve in this faraway, primitive and troubled land. He also left reassured that Colonel Novak could take care of herself and her people under any circumstances. She was one hell of a soldier and a superb attaché.

On Sunday morning, bags were packed early and the C-12 was scheduled for take off at daybreak to avoid the extreme heat that would come quickly after sunrise. Once airborne from N'Djamena, Colonel Paul Talbot passed the control of the C-12 to Colonel Bob Stark and went back to the main cabin to offer Bart and George freshly brewed coffee and begin the briefings on DAO Kinshasa.

Paul Talbot was a blond, blue-eyed, crew-cut Army officer of medium build who had flown every type of aircraft the Army owned. He had begun his career as a helicopter pilot and later moved to the fixed-wing birds. Paul had been the DATT in Zaire for most of the time Bart had served in the DAS. At the request of the U.S. Ambassador in Kinshasa, General Lowe had recently approved an extension for Paul that would extend his tour to four years. Extensions in Africa were rare. But Paul was a rare officer. At first blush he appeared rough around the edges with a tattoo on his left forearm. He had served a short tour in Zaire as a young captain attached to a Belgian aviation unit involved in a disaster relief operation. The six months he was in Zaire aroused an interest that would be with him for the rest of his life. He had caught what some call African wanderlust.

Over the years Talbot had tried unsuccessfully to get an assignment to Africa, but the jobs were limited and the timing didn't work out. He had spent many years in Germany and married a German girl, Ilse, who shared his interest in Africa. The two of them made many vacation trips to African countries. Then, when Paul was serving as a colonel in Berlin and had started to think about retirement, the Army's first nominee to be the DATT in Zaire fell out at the last minute due to illness. Paul learned of the opportunity, volunteered, flew back to Washington from his station in Germany, and was accepted by the DAS. From the moment he arrived on station in Kinshasa, if he wasn't the happiest officer in the DAS, he was convinced that he had to be in the top two.

Talbot had been born and raised in South Carolina. He had never completely lost his southern accent and he had a slow and easy way of talking that was a pleasure to hear. He added vignettes to his briefings that quickly piqued and held Bart's interest. Paul told Lowe that Zaire was a country that had not profited or advanced well under Belgian colonial rule. When the Belgians gave Zaire its independence in 1960, power in the country changed hands several times before the present ruler, President Mobuto, eliminated all competition and became a popular despot.

"The 'Heart of Darkness' still applies, General Lowe," Paul said. "Zaire is a country of more than thirty million people, only a few of whom have access to sanitation, safe water and health services. Buses don't run, telephones don't work, and it's a constant struggle to keep the bush from overgrowing whatever roads exist. The country is rich in natural resources—copper, diamonds and some other minerals—but the management of the resources is inefficient, and together with widespread corruption across the spectrum of government, the country has remained poor. Joe Mobutu has been the President for almost twenty-five years, and he has always been strongly anti-Communist. He threw out the Russians who were here in 1960 after independence. He has been a good ally to us and to NATO and has provided us base and landing rights in Zaire in the event of conflicts. This connection is also important, as I am sure you know, to EUCOM for their contingencies in this part of the world. We have insisted that the air bases we would use for contingency operations be maintained with the money, equipment and security assistance we have provided them, and they have done that pretty well.

Because of the excesses of government, his family and his tribe, Mobutu has been under increasing pressure from his own people and us to install a more democratic government and to hold free elections. But so far there have been only promises, and no real movement. Now, having said that, I still find Zaire a fascinating place. The challenges are so many, the country beneath the surface is so beautiful, and the people really need our help. I think you will find the morale of our DAO people to be sky high. Duty in Zaire is like no other place in the world."

"Sounds to me, Paul, like you should have been a missionary," Bart Lowe responded at the end of Talbot's briefings.

"Well, maybe so, General, and who knows what Ilse and I will do when my military service is completed. We may just stay in Africa. It certainly is still a frontier."

A refueling stop in Bangui in the Central African Republic gave everyone a chance for a break from the somewhat cramped spaces of the C-12. Flying weather continued good, George Martin kept Bart busy with paperwork, and the C-12 arrived that afternoon in Kinshasa on schedule. Paul Talbot's briefings had conditioned Bart not to be shocked at what he would find in Zaire.

Bart's first impression of Zaire at the Kinshasa Air Base where the DAO kept the C-12 was opposite to any sense of orderliness. In fact it was the absolute opposite of that old saying, "a place for everything and everything in its place." Aircraft of various ages, sizes and shapes were parked randomly around the base. Some were operational, but many were in the last stages of cannibalism. Many, many men were in uniform, but Bart could pick out only a few in the same uniform. Most wore hats, some not, some with shoes, most not, and all wore a mixture of shirts and trousers, military and non-military. Everyone, it seemed, had a weapon; some had two.

The greatest shock came when the DAO sedan, a four-wheel drive Ford Bronco with bulletproof glass that was waiting at the aircraft, departed the air base with Bart and George and Colonel Talbot. It began the drive across Kinshasa, making its way to the DATT's residence past throngs of wandering Africans. Bart's initial thought was, "It's a holiday and all the residents of Kinshasa have been given the day off." He had never seen so many people in one place who just seemed to be milling around.

The buildings they passed all seemed to be in disrepair, falling apart in several places. Lean-to type shacks lined both sides of the sometimes concrete, sometimes asphalt, sometimes dirt road leading into and across Kinshasa. An open-air vegetable market was on one side of the road, and Bart estimated that there must have been 2000 people standing around it. The crowds were so close to the streets that Bart was concerned that if someone fell in front of the Bronco, the vehicle would never be able to stop before hitting the person. Nevertheless, the DAO driver, a Zairian, drove confidently. He frequently turned to smile at Bart and George Martin in the back seat. Paul Talbot smiled and waved back at the people as the Bronco moved through the crowds as the people smiled and waved in a friendly way at the DAO vehicle. The drive was not covering any great distance because of the crowds. The barely moving two-way hodgepodge of traffic with a mix of trucks, old cars, scooters, bicycles and oxcarts seemed to be carrying gigantic loads or overloads of almost anything one could imagine. Paul explained that many of the trucks laden with people were, in fact, serving as buses.

"Is it always this way?" Bart asked as he flinched from each potential collision.

"Yes sir, pretty much so. But what is really fun is to stop, let the driver guard the vehicle and just walk out into the crowd and talk with the people. Although there is great poverty here, the people are friendly and always enjoy talking to a foreigner, particularly Americans. I recommend we try that while you are here, but on the first day that might be a bit much for you all," drawled Paul.

"You've got that right, Paul," replied Bart. "Maybe tomorrow." George seemed relieved.

The roads and crowds were finally mastered, and the vehicle turned off the main road and proceeded down a dirt road about a quarter of a mile. They were now in a neighborhood with larger homes, a mixture of European and African construction, many with walls built completely around the house.

"General, do you see that tower ahead of us?" asked Paul, pointing as he spoke toward a large tower-like structure standing several yards off the road.

"Yes, I do. What is it?"

"That's in my back yard, and after we have a drink and I show you around the house, I'll tell you a story about that tower."

Soon thereafter the vehicle pulled in front of a large, walled compound gate, blew the horn and a guard in bushjacket-type khaki uniform with a rifle over his shoulder opened the gate and waved them inside. Paul told him that the embassy provided 24-hour guard service to protect against theft.

The DATT residence was a sprawling single story with a combination of concrete, stone and wood, with a thatched African roof. The DATT's wife, Ilse, was a blond attractive woman in her early forties, dressed in a white sun-back dress and sandals. Bart and George had met Ilse previously at an African Regional Attaché Conference. She opened the double door entrance to the house and welcomed them.

"General Lowe. George. So good to see you again. Paul and I are thrilled that you have come to Kinshasa. Please come in, and I'll show you to your rooms," Ilse said as she led them to the rear of the house where several large bedrooms with private baths were located. After Bart settled in his room, unpacked, hung some clothes in the closet, and freshened up, he and George rejoined the Talbots who were sitting at the side of the house in a large sun porch overlooking a swimming pool, patio, and the large tower that Paul had referred to earlier.

Drinks were offered, accepted and quickly served by a smiling houseman in black pants and white shirt. Paul had covered the itinerary for the visit on the plane with Bart, and he knew they had some free time before getting ready for a dinner party.

The Talbot house was decorated in black and white—somewhat like a safari lodge—and brought to mind the kind of residence a white hunter, long in Africa, might live in. Bart was impressed and felt the surroundings instilled a sense of adventure. After cocktails, Ilse excused herself to get on with the preparation of the evening's dinner, and Paul invited Bart and George for a tour of the pool, patio, and tower.

Once out back, Paul led them over to the base of the tower; they could see that it had been built from a frame of steel with a wooden frame of stairs inside the steel frame leading upward, crisscrossing back and forth to a flat wooden observation deck. Paul invited General Lowe and Colonel Martin to climb the stairs with him to the top of the tower. There, a view of sprawling Kinshasa and its surrounding jungle was prominent and inspiring in a purple haze skyline. Sensing his guests' increasing curiosity, Colonel Talbot told them the history of the tower.

"Before I arrived in Zaire the tower was known for years as 'Smith's Folly.' Austin Smith was a Agency of International Development (AID) employee. He was a dedicated individual who served in Africa for many years and was devoted to improving the life of the Africans. He was the first occupant of this house after it was built, and in those days the house was close to the bush. Bush or jungle fires were a great threat to villages and towns in those days, as they still are today, and Austin saw the need for a fire watchtower to protect the area around his house. He was able to gain the financing to fund the materials and to hire an African construction team to do the job. When the question was posed by the African engineer on how high Smith wanted the tower to be, Smith told him he wasn't sure. He told them to get it started and he would check it to see how high it should be to monitor any distant jungle fire. The Africans made good progress and when the tower reached about 25 feet, Smith checked it, told them it was not yet high enough, and directed them to press on. Smith was suddenly called away to another part of Africa to consult on another project. Well, one delay led to another and Smith was gone for quite a time. When he returned, he found that the 30-or-35-foot tower he had originally planned had grown to 80 feet. The African engineer had his orders and he had pressed on. The tower, while Smith lived here, was used regularly and provided protective service to the Kinshasa community. As the town grew and the bush was pushed back, the need was less and the tower became neglected.

"The U.S. Embassy acquired the house, but it was not popular with the diplomats because of the oddity of the tower. When I arrived, I didn't care for my predecessor's quarters, located near the Embassy in the middle of Kinshasa. So, they offered me this house. I was fascinated by the tower, but it had been neglected for some time. I managed to scrounge some materials from the other AID projects in town and invited a battalion of Navy Seabees who were here on a road building exercise to come out for a couple of Sunday barbeques. Together we put the tower back in shape. I have the guards check for fires or any other problem that the vantage point will show. Among the Zairian Military, my quarters are known as the Talbot Tower and they look forward to coming here. It has made my job of keeping well informed much easier," Paul concluded.

"Quite a story, Paul, and you certainly have an impressive view from here. I am glad that it has practical applications," Bart remarked.

"I can see a spread in the Charleston, South Carolina, newspaper with a headline 'Favorite son Talbot's Tall Tale,' quipped George Martin. "I want to be sure we get a picture of this monument to attaché initiative, General," he added as the three officers headed down the tower steps.

Once down from the tower, Bart turned his attention to the swimming pool.

"Now this looks inviting, Paul, mind if I swim a few laps?"

"By all means, General. It's great for exercise, and we use it year round. I swim in the morning before going into the embassy and each night when I get home, no matter what the hour. I invite you to swim whenever you want. I only have one warning. The snakes from the nearby bush also enjoy the pool, and we usually pull out a bushmaster or cobra two or three times a month, so please always check before going in."

"General Lowe," George Martin announced. "I just changed my mind about swimming. I'll run in place in my room. I can conquer the wild blue yonder, but I'm going to leave any dealings with snakes to the ground pounders like Paul."

All laughing, the three men returned to the house. Bart changed into his swim suit, taking advantage of Paul's offer to use the pool.

That night Ilse hosted a sit-down dinner for 24 people. Although the weather was naturally warm, the dozen ceiling fans throughout the house kept the social rooms reasonably cool and comfortable. The guests were a cross section from the Zairian Senior Military, the U.S. Embassy and the allied attachés. The U.S. Ambassador, the Chief of the Zairian General Staff, and the French, British, Belgian, and German attachés were seated near Bart and were excellent dinner companions. All were upbeat about serving their duty tours in Zaire.

Bart was surprised by the quality and service of the meal. It was delicious French cuisine prepared flawlessly by Ilse's African cook and two serving assistants. From the wine, to the salad, to the entree, to the desert, everything was perfect. The French and Belgian attachés and their wives were lavish in their praise of the meal, and General Toponto, the Zairian Chief of Staff, told General Lowe in no uncertain terms that Mrs. Talbot was the best hostess in town. Ambassador Fargo added her endorsement. It was clear from all of the dinner guests, during cocktails, dinner, and desert and coffee that the Talbots were popular and well respected. It was obvious that the ambassador and Ilse Talbot had a close rapport and the two chatted comfortably throughout the evening. The time went by quickly, and Bart had to admit he was surprised at the sophisticated tone of his first evening in "The Heart of Darkness."

After the guests left, Bart, George, and the Talbots took coffee and cognac out to the sun porch.

"Ilse, thank you for a super evening and a really fine dinner. I can't remember having a better French meal anywhere. How do you do it? I must tell you I was really surprised. I know about the shortages of food items you regularly have here, and how long, and sometimes infrequent the supply lines are to Zaire. I was almost expecting to be eating MREs tonight and instead I enjoyed beef flambe and one of the best flans I have ever eaten," Bart commented. George Martin agreed.

Paul smiled and Ilse laughed.

"How kind of you to make such nice remarks. Are you sure you didn't think I was going to serve you wurst and beer tonight?" she added, continuing to laugh. "Seriously, general, I appreciate your thoughtful compliments, but don't forget we have been here almost three years, and we have learned how to get by and make the best of our circumstances. By no stretch of the imagination could I ever serve a meal like tonight's every night. Or even once a week. Now once a month, with the right kind of planning, saving, hoarding, and plenty of flexibility, such a meal is possible. And we have known you were coming for a while, so I was able to collect all the right things, but maybe such fortune won't happen for the next guest. That is all part of the challenge. That's what makes Africa interesting."

"Nonetheless, compliments are still in order," Bart interjected.

"Thank you again, but it has not always been so. Let me tell you a story to illustrate what I mean. When I first married my husband years ago, I knew in the military we would entertain a lot so I studied French cooking and how to prepare many meals and serve them. In the early years I did it all myself but when Paul became more senior, I was able to get help. Household help in

Zaire is very reasonable and many people need the work. The three people who helped with the dinner tonight were hired by me three years ago. I trained them and taught them everything I know. My favorite pupil has been our cook for this evening, I call him Pierre. He is now excellent, but we had some rough times along the way. Once he learned the basics of cooking, I began to teach him the finer points of meal presentation, how to make food more appetizing, and so forth. On one occasion I had just finished showing Pierre how to garnish food—you know—by adding greenery to the meat platter in order to make the meal look better. He got the idea and was doing pretty well in practice. We had a dinner party, and I told him to do the whole thing. He was a little nervous, but I was convinced he would pull it off. I was away the whole day and arrived home the same time as Paul and the guests. The cocktails and hors d'oeuvres were great. I didn't even go into the kitchen. The salad and bread course was a great success, and when the main entree was served, the meat dish was taken to the far end of the table and appeared to be tastefully garnished with something green. I couldn't tell what it was. But as the meat plate came nearer to me, I could make out the garnish and was horrified. Pierre, looking for something green, had decided on a box of green suppositories that he had found in the refrigerator and cut up into nice little pieces for his garnish. So you see things haven't always gone smoothly. After all, general," Ilse smiled and said, "this is Africa."

Driving into the Embassy the next morning, Bart was going over the schedule for the rest of his time in Zaire and remarked to Colonel Talbot, "Paul, I was curious about dinner with the ambassador Wednesday night since we just saw her at your quarters. Is that for a large group of people?"

"No, sir. That is just for you and her. Not even George is included," Paul said and looked over his shoulder to the rear seat and smiled at George Martin.

"What do you make of that, Paul? Does she have something on her mind? Any bad blood between you and her?"

"Again, no, sir. Not that I know of. She has been here now about a year. She is a real pro and a pleasure to work with. My guess is that she has something that she wants to share with you in private."

"Okay, Paul. We'll dine with the ambassador and see where that leads. One question for you. I guess I was surprised last night that the local CIA Station Chief wasn't among your guests for dinner, and I don't see a call on him or his office in my schedule. Isn't that unusual? Is he out of town or something?"

"Again, no, sir. He is here, and I am aware of your guidance that the DATT is supposed to work as closely as possible with the COS, but the current guy here is a real horse's ass as well as a loner, who has resisted all my efforts at any real rapport. For your information, I did invite him last night, and he declined. I also sent him a note letting him know you would be here and asked if he would like to see you. He said no. He arrived here shortly after I did. His predecessor was a prince of a man whom everyone liked. This guy has been a thorn in my side since day one. I have always prided myself on being able to get along with anyone, but he is the exception. To begin with, I think he is a drunk, and somewhat of a pompous drunk at that, not respected by anyone in the embassy. For my money he spends too much time with the Russians."

"Paul, I'm getting the feeling that if asked, you would not recommend the COS for a position of trust and responsibility with the U.S. Government?" Bart half jokingly asked.

"You're damn right I wouldn't," Paul replied, and then seeing the smile on General Lowe's face laughed in spite of himself. "Maybe I have lost my objectivity concerning this joker, General Lowe, but if the truth be known, I do worry about him and have this feeling that he is up to no good. He also seems to feel superior to the rest of us, Lord knows why. Oh, I know that the CIA people are different and often march to a different drum beat but I don't think this guy is even trusted by his own people. That is the scuttlebutt between our guys in the DAO and his people in the Station. And I know the Russians are his target but he is seen with them so often that even the Zairians are suspicious of him.

Incidentally, I believe he served an attaché tour in Moscow during his military days. Or, on the attaché staff as an enlisted man. I'm not sure which. I do know he has no love for me or my people here. He ignores us completely."

Bart's curiosity was aroused. "Well, Paul, why don't we push the envelope on this one a little further. How about getting back to his office and tell him I really need to see him while I'm here. Something to do with Washington business. Okay?" instructed Bart.

"Roger that, boss. I'll get on it as soon as we reach the embassy," Paul acknowledged. "I believe the CIA sent him here from his job at headquarters, Langley, operations section, I've been told."

Monday was spent at the DAO and the U.S. Embassy. At lunch Major Chris Watkins, the DATT from the two man Brazzaville DAO just across the Congo River from Kinshasa, came over to see General Lowe. Colonel Talbot and his people regularly assisted Major Watkins and his Operations Coordinator and their families with supplies and other items that the U.S. Embassy, in the rigidly communist Congo, could not obtain.

In his first year in Brazzaville, Major Watkins and Master Sergeant Orchard made regular vehicle trips back and forth across the bridge over the Congo river between Brazzaville and Kinshasa. The hard line Congo military, noting this, refused to allow U.S. Embassy officials, including Watkins and Orchard to exit the Congo and use the bridge. Watkins, using his initiative, bought a small boat and motor and negotiated the rough Congo River waters once a week between the two countries until the time when the Congolese lifted the bridge restriction.

General Lowe recognized the determined young Major and his DAO by presenting him a Defense Department Award. The Congolese had denied General Lowe a visa to go to Brazzaville during his visit so Lowe had responded by meeting with Watkins in Kinshasa. To sweeten the meeting General Lowe brought along a box for the Congo DAO containing twelve bags of Dorritos, an item particularly difficult to obtain in Africa. George Martin had somehow escorted the contraband through the custom authorities in four countries.

At the end of the day, Colonel Talbot told Bart that CIA's Chief of Station had agreed to see General Lowe for lunch on Wednesday, pleading a full schedule and prior commitments before then.

"A full schedule in Kinshasa? Can you believe that?" lamented Paul Talbot.

On Tuesday Colonel Talbot escorted General Lowe on his rounds of calls on the senior Zairian military at Army Headquarters. In the afternoon Talbot took Lowe and Colonel Martin in the C-12 to visit the main contingency air fields that would be used by U.S. and NATO forces in the event of crisis and concluded the day with stopovers at several Zairian Army posts along the Angolan border. The relations between Angola and Zaire had been historically tenuous because of the large number of Angolan refugees fleeing the conflict in Angola to Zaire. When Bart observed first-hand the density of the jungle between villages and towns and the small size of the unimproved airfield runways in Zaire, it drove home to him the importance of the small but rugged C-12 aircraft to the DAO's operations. This sole aircraft was also used to support six other DAOs and embassies in the region.

On Wednesday Bart and Colonel Talbot visited the separate U.S. Military Assistance Mission, or ZAMISH, that had been working with the Zairians for years. The Chief of the ZAMISH was an Air Force Colonel. In his briefings the colonel pointed out that the assistance program and the funding for the program had dwindled to next to nothing and the projection for the future was not good. He had recommended to his headquarters at EUCOM that the ZAMISH mission go to the DAO. Paul had concurred with that recommendation. Bart Lowe was in favor of combining the DAO and Military Assistance missions whenever possible as a cost-effective measure and had urged Defense to support ZAMISH, as well as other consolidations in as many countries as possible.

Paul dropped Bart Lowe off at the Continental Hotel at 12:00 for his lunch with CIA's COS. The Continental Hotel on Juin Boulevard, according to Paul Talbot, was the best hotel in Kinshasa and got most of the international business interest and visitors who came to Zaire. It was also the safest and best place to eat in Kinshasa, Paul said. Rumor had it that the hotel was actually owned by a member of Mr. Mobuto's family and enjoyed police and military protection.

Bart walked into the dining room, a large room with a safari motif and tables covered with white linen. The maître d' met Bart and when Bart mentioned he was meeting someone the maître d' said, "right this way," then led him to a corner table. There a tall middle-aged man with brown bushy hair and horn-rimmed glasses, dressed in a dark blue two-piece safari-type suit was already seated.

The maître d' approached the table and said, "Mr. Sema, your guest is here."

Sema did not get up from the table but extended his hand languidly across the table and said, "Harold Sema. You must be Lowe."

"Yes, I'm General Bart Lowe." Bart said. He shook the man's hand and took a seat next to him.

Sema reached for a glass in front of him, picked it up and drained the contents. He then said to the maître d', "Jeffrey, I'll have another one of these," and turning to Bart, said, "What will you have?" Sema never used General Lowe's title at any time.

Bart looked at the maître d' and said, "I'll have iced tea if you have it."

"Of course," replied the maître d', heading toward the bar.

A waiter quickly returned with Bart's iced tea and the drink Mr. Sema had ordered. Judging from the olives in the clear liquid in the short glass and Sema's slurred speech, Bart guessed that the drink was a Martini, and probably not Sema's first. The waiter had brought along two menus and hesitated a moment to see if the gentlemen wanted to order. Sema waved him off, and the waiter departed. Sema then reached for a pack of American cigarettes lying to his left on the table, took one out and lit it with a lighter that he had also taken off the table. The lighter, Bart noticed as Sema replaced it, was an inexpensive silver Zippo with the word Georgetown printed on it.

"Well, what brings you to Zaire?" Sema asked.

Bart explained the trip, the countries he was visiting and generally what he hoped to accomplish by his visits. Then he asked Sema a number of routine questions—how long had he been in Zaire; where did he come from, etc., to try and draw Sema out about himself. Sema answered the questions curtly, but didn't volunteer details.

Something about this man and Georgetown seemed vaguely familiar to Lowe, but he couldn't recall a connection. He took a sip from his iced tea when it was obvious to both men that the air between them was strained.

Sema then asked, "Specifically, why did you want to see me?"

"Intelligence operations," Bart replied. "The military services don't have any going here and while I know that is primarily the bailiwick of your agency, I wanted to know if you think it would be a good idea for the military to run some operations?"

With that Sema seemed to relax a bit and said, "Okay, let's order something to eat, and then I'll tell you what I think."

During the short time they had been talking, Sema had smoked two cigarettes and Bart noticed that the ashtray already contained the butts of three others.

As they opened their menus to make a selection, Sema held up his drink glass that was once again empty and signaled for a refill to the waiter who had been waiting nearby. When they had made their menu choices and the waiter had taken their orders Sema once again turned to Bart and said, "How about some wine? They have a pretty good selection here."

Not wishing to be too standoffish with Sema, and anxious for him to talk more about himself, Bart agreed and asked Sema to select something he considered good. Sema chose a South African white wine.

Lunch was served, and Sema had finished his first glass of wine by the time he and Bart had finished their soup. As a nonsmoker, Bart was grateful when the food was served, and Sema turned to eating. Bart was irritated that this man had not had the courtesy to ask if his smoking bothered Bart and was tempted to raise the subject, but decided against it so as not to alienate Sema. There was something familiar about Sema that Bart couldn't put his finger on, but the longer he could make him talk, the more confident Bart was that he would make the connection.

"Intelligence operations," Sema began, "no, I don't think it would be a good idea. The question is what for? Against who? The Zairians are an open book. You want anything from them, you just ask. And the only other game in town is the Russians and I have them covered," Sema said, as he munched his salad. "There really isn't any other significant target in Kinshasa. There are a few 'blockers' here, and the East Germans are across the river in the Congo, but these guys are all second teamers. There's no gold at the end of the rainbow for those guys in this part of Africa."

"Paul Talbot and my guys say you spend a good deal of time with the Russians, Mr. Sema, and assume they must be your main target," Bart interjected.

"And why not? They are the only game in town. The only worthwhile target anyway, so why wouldn't I spend my time with the Russians?" Sema continued, working on his main course and filling his wine glass for the third time.

"And you don't need any help with the Russians?" Bart asked.

"No, no. I told you, we have got them covered," Sema said, raising his voice somewhat. "And between you and me, you guys are amateurs when it comes to sensitive operations."

"Oh," Bart replied. "Why do you say that when we are not conducting any here?"

"Before I joined the CIA I was on the attaché staff at the embassy in Moscow for a time when I was in the Army. Your people in Russia couldn't find sensitive information with a map," Sema responded, grinning somewhat cruelly.

When I was in Washington at CIA Headquarters, I spent two years in the Soviet Branch, which incidently is my specialty, and one year in the Government and Military Liaison Branch. In liaison I also had access there to all of your sensitive operations, and I was not impressed. Most of your operations, it seemed to me, were only producing low level order of battle type results."

"And you don't think the military needs that kind of information?"

"No, to my mind that's just a waste of time." As soon as Sema said that, he noticed a man who had just arrived at the bar. He turned to Bart and said, "Excuse me, just a minute. I see someone I know at the bar. I'll be right back," and Sema got up and walked over to the bar.

Sitting now alone at the table, Bart realized he had been developing a slow burn as he listened to the arrogant man across the table from him. Bart had been about ready to give Sema a lecture on how important order of battle information was to U.S. Military forces when Sema left the table. But now, as he thought about it, he would probably, to use Sema's words, be "wasting his time." The thought also went through Bart's mind, "Here in this obscure post in Africa is a man who had access to the areas of greatest compromise, military service operations and other government operations, like the FBI and CIA operations against the Russians. No," Bart thought, "not HEAT SEEKER, that's too far a reach."

Bart noticed that Sema and the man he had gone to see at the bar seemed to be arguing over something, but Bart couldn't hear their conversation. And then the man Sema was talking to suddenly slammed his drink down on the bar and left the room. Sema looked quizzically after him for a moment, and then returned to the table. At the same time, the waiter arrived to see if they wanted coffee. Bart said yes, but Sema said he would stick to the wine, and then proceeded to pour the remaining wine from the bottle into his glass and lit another cigarette.

"Did you see that fellow at the bar?" Sema asked Bart.

"Yes." Bart replied.

"Well, he is the Russian KGB Resident, my counterpart at the Soviet Embassy."

"He didn't seem to be too happy to see you," Bart said.

"Oh, no, Boris is from the old school, and he is worried that if anyone sees us together they'll think we are trading secrets," Sema answered.

Bart was tempted to ask, "And are you?" but thought better of it and instead glanced at his watch, becoming relieved when he saw it was time for Paul Talbot to pick him up. He turned to Sema and said, "Mr. Sema, thanks for your time and comments. I enjoyed the lunch. When I get back to Washington, shall I give your regards to Art Cheek?"

Sema at first looked puzzled and then it seemed like a light went off in his head, and he realized that Bart was talking about his boss, the DDO at CIA.

"Sure, yeah, why not? Give old Art my best. Hell, he probably won't even remember me. I don't remember him fondly."

"But I sure as hell do," Bart thought to himself. He then rose and left a $20.00 bill on the table to cover his share of the lunch bill. Sema did not get up and gave no indication that he was leaving the restaurant.

In the car on the way back to the U.S. Embassy Bart turned to Colonel Talbot and said, "Paul, I believe my opinion of the Chief of Station is the same as yours. He was everything you said and more." Bart's curiosity was more than aroused by Sema's attitude, his previous assignments, and his local reputation for "being in bed with the Russians." He asked Paul a number of questions about Sema, hoping to find out as much as possible about the COS. In the back of his mind he was concerned that he might be jumping to conclusions about the man and thought if he learned more perhaps his suspicions could be assuaged.

Paul told Bart that his counterpart in the Soviet Embassy was a Soviet Army Colonel Pavlov, who had served in several posts in Africa during his military career. His biography said he was a GRU officer, and Paul gave him high marks on his collection of information efforts although he was a little rough around the edges in his treatment of the Zairians. According to Paul he saw his counterpart regularly at embassy social events and it was no secret that there was no love lost between Colonel Serge Pavlov and the Russian KGB Resident.

Paul said, "I was talking with Serge when the KGB man walked by and Sergei said, 'That one cannot be trusted. One of the crosses Russian military men must bear is serving with scum like that.' Shortly thereafter, he pointed across the room toward a group of people where Mr. Sema was standing and said, 'And if I were you tovaritsch Talbot, I would also watch out for that one,' pointing to Sema. I thought Serge was just trying to set me up to see if there was any bad feeling between us."

That afternoon Bart was so preoccupied thinking about Sema and a possible link with HEAT SEEKER that he could hardly follow the briefings he received at the political/military section of the embassy.

At 7:00 that evening, Colonel Talbot dropped Bart at Ambassador Fargo's residence for dinner.

Ambassador Kellie Fargo was a stately woman with gray hair, in her middle sixties. She was one of the most respected professionals in the U.S. Foreign Service and on her third ambassadorial tour in Africa. With piercing green eyes she had a commanding presence about her, whether she was discussing the Zairian economy or laughing at a funny story. She had been married for years to a prominent academic who spent three or four months of the year with her at her post. He was currently in the United States.

Bart was welcomed in the residence by a black major domo dressed in black trousers, black tie and a white jacket with a red sash across his shoulder. He introduced himself as Mr. Kiwoma and informed General Lowe that he had served with the U.S. Embassy for more than thirty years and had been on the personal staff of eight U.S. Ambassadors. He then took Bart to a small sitting room adjacent to the dining room where Ambassador Fargo was sitting in an easy chair, with a cocktail on the table beside her reading from a folder she held on her lap. When Mr. Kiwoma and General Lowe entered the room, she stood up, took off her reading glasses and put the glasses and the reading material on the table.

"General Lowe. Please come in. Thank you for joining me. I see you have met Mr. Kiwoma. Will you join me for a drink?"

"Yes. Thank you. If you have it, I would enjoy a Manhattan," replied Bart.

"Oh, certainly. You won't stump Mr. Kiwoma on a Manhattan. He is, among his many talents, an expert bartender. In fact, he's an expert in almost everything when it comes to running a residence. I don't know what I would do without him. Please, General Lowe, come sit beside me."

While they were having cocktails, Ambassador Fargo told Bart something about her experiences in Africa over the years and how much she had enjoyed her career in the Foreign Service. She told him that perhaps this would be her last tour; having said that she smiled at him and said, "But who knows? We'll just have to see what the future brings." This was said with a twinkle in her eye.

Bart was confident that he was not the first visitor to find Ambassador Fargo quite charming. After about thirty minutes, Mr. Kiwoma reappeared to announce that dinner was served. They exited the sitting room into the dining room and took chairs facing each other across the middle of the table. The ambassador had not been jesting, bragging about the talents of Mr. Kiwoma. He supervised and assisted in the serving of a delicious meal. The main course was an African fowl and wild rice complemented with an excellent white Chablis from neighboring Zimbabwe. Conversation during the meal was casual, and no sensitive subject was surfaced by the ambassador. Bart began to think she had no agenda and was merely being gracious. But after desert was over and the coffee had been poured, Ambassador Fargo said, "Mr. Kiwoma, please leave the coffee pot and close the dining room door. We are not to be disturbed."

Turning to Bart she said, "I have two matters that I want to discuss with you in private. The first is easy. It is a good news item. I didn't want to embarrass him in front of you when you and Colonel Talbot came around for your office call the other day. Although I told you he was doing a great job, it goes well beyond that. I can't say enough about Paul and Ilse Talbot. They are by far the strongest members of my embassy team. Although life here can be really tough sometimes, I never hear a bitch or complaint from those two. They are real team players. I think he should be a general officer. If there is anything I can do to toot his horn, career-wise, please let me know. I don't know what you are doing in the DAS, but in all my tours the attachés have been top notch. Please keep it up."

"Ambassador Fargo, that is excellent feedback and I am delighted to know that you feel the same way we do about Colonel Talbot." Bart replied, obviously pleased. "I wish I could say that it was in my authority to promote Paul Talbot and others like him to brigadier general, but as I am sure you know, our promotion systems in all the military services are very competitive. Your evaluation of him will be helpful and I will ensure that your opinion is noted in his efficiency reports."

"The second subject is not very pleasant and quite frankly it is neither your business nor your responsibility. I am perplexed and hope you may be able to offer some advice. The problem I am concerned about is my Chief of Station, Mr. Harold Sema. First of all, my predecessor told me that Sema was an odd duck and suggested I keep an eye on him. I have done that and I suspect he has a drinking problem. In fact, it was reported to me that he had so much to drink at my 4th of July reception last summer that he passed out and had to be carried home by his people. I didn't see it, but I believe the Zairians did. I do know they don't like him. Although he is an excellent Lingala and French linguist his name never appears on any of their guests lists. I had him in after the 4th of July reception and blessed him out. He denied it. Said he was sick from something else. I also offered him help if he needed it. I have dealt with alcohol problems before. Again he denied any

problem. The Zairians mentioned to me that they are concerned that he spends too much time with the Russians. I had him in again, and he says that they are his prime target and he is just doing his job.

I can't fault Mr. Sema for the work his CIA staff does as part of the embassy team. He has some good people, and he is smart enough to let them do the weekly staff briefings. And the final thing is he has the reputation for having a lot of money and being a big spender. I don't know if that is true, if it is his money or CIA money. His people say he has a wife that comes from money. He is here unaccompanied, but she has reportedly been out to see him and my deputy says she dropped a bundle. The bottom line is I don't trust the man, and I am not sure what to do about it. I've mentioned the subject to our desk officer at the State Department and asked him to check Mr. Sema out discreetly with CIA. Our guy could find out nothing from CIA headquarters. The desk officer did report that CIA headquarters seemed particularly alert, but also reticent to respond to questions when he pursued inquiries about Mr. Sema. I am considering sending a cable to the CIA Director. Do you think that would be a good idea?"

Bart took a long sip of his coffee and then answered. "Ambassador, obviously I'm reluctant to discuss a matter on which I really know very little; yet, I can appreciate your dilemma. If I may, let me think out loud a bit and see if it makes any sense. At most embassies around the world it is important for the Defense Department's attaché to work closely with CIA's COS because of our mutual interest in threats to the United States. It is one of the areas I regularly check on during my visits. The COS and the DATT here are not working together, and from what I can tell that is the COS's choice. Paul Talbot is not an admirer of Mr. Sema, and he tells me he has been stonewalled in every attempt to work closely with him. I met Mr. Sema for the first time today, and I must admit many of the concerns that Paul has expressed were evident to me, and I was not comfortable with Mr. Sema's behavior.

Having said that, I have learned through experience in my own job that the CIA has a multitude of exceptionally smart and dedicated people working a wide-range of very sensitive missions. The importance of their operations or the methods employed sometimes appear strange, but when the objective of the operation and the security safeguards surrounding the operation are known, their actions and intentions are clear. And who knows? Maybe Mr. Sema and his seemingly odd, even obnoxious ways, are part of some strategically critical scheme. Rather than sending a cable to the CIA Director at this time, I would recommend that you consider sending a cable or initiating a secure phone call to Ambassador Ross, the ASD, INR at State. B.J. Ross is really a good head with a lot of CIA coordination experience and I think she would be the logical one to take up a matter like this with CIA headquarters. I work closely with B.J. on DAS matters and she has been very helpful to us. I feel sure she would be able to assist you."

"Of course!" Ambassador Fargo said, slamming her hand down on the table, "Why didn't I think of that? Well, general, I know you have an early departure in the morning, so I don't want to keep you too late. Thanks for having dinner with me and being such a good listener. And thanks for the advice. I intend to take it."

When they left the dining room and went out into the large foyer, Colonel Paul Talbot was waiting to return Bart to their quarters. Not surprisingly, Mr. Kiwoma had called the colonel when he had served the coffee and told Paul he thought the general would be leaving soon.

Riding back in the DAO vehicle, Bart knew that Paul was curious as to what took place at the dinner with the Ambassador, but of course he didn't ask. Bart told Paul exactly what happened and added that he would also follow up his conversation with Ambassador Ross in Washington, and if he learned anything he could pass on concerning Sema he would let Paul know as soon as possible.

Paul then said. "Are you ready for a surprise?"

"Sure." Bart said. "I have found this business is full of surprises."

"Harold Sema called the quarters tonight and asked when you were leaving. He wants to invite you on a crocodile hunt Sunday night."

"Interesting." What do you make of that Paul?"

"I'm not sure boss," Paul said and shrugged, "He's never invited me!"

Bart finally went to bed after sharing nightcaps and coffee with the Talbots and George. He was troubled over the information he had heard and now even more suspicious of Harold Sema. He continued to wonder why the man seemed strangely familiar to him. And now the crocodile hunt invitation. The question was what should he do, if anything, about it. He had been tempted to tell Ambassador Fargo about HEAT SEEKER and the coincidence of Sema's access and times in Washington to the disastrous leaks of information. Of course he couldn't do that, and he hoped he wasn't jumping to faulty conclusions. Could he go to Zimbabwe and South Africa and come back Sunday night to Zaire? He was restless that night and a phrase kept going through his mind. "HEAT SEEKER in the Heart of Darkness." Finally, he drifted off to sleep.

Ilse Talbot was up early Thursday and prepared a continental breakfast for the group. She had been a delightful hostess and Bart presented her a crystal bud vase memento of his appreciation that George always carried for such occasions. Bart and George said their good-byes and Colonel Talbot drove the general and Colonel Martin to the waiting C-12 at the Kinshasa Air Base for their trip that morning on to Harare, Zimbabwe. The same crowds were lining the street, with the same waves and smiles, but Bart hardly noticed. He had too much on his mind. Colonel Talbot remained in Zaire and Colonel Bob Stark and Commander Wes Truecoat were flying Bart and George that day. The two officers had come out early that morning and loaded the C-12 with some supplies for DAO Harare and some other packages for the U.S. Embassy. At the last minute, Bart told Paul Talbot to contact Sema and tell him if at all possible he would try to make it back Sunday night for the crocodile hunt.

When the aircraft was airborne, and Colonel Stark had passed around fresh coffee, George Martin observed that General Lowe seemed preoccupied. He was sure of it when the general waved away the stack of work that George had accumulated in Kinshasa and was about to pass to Bart. Instead Bart asked George for a pad of paper and quickly fell into deep thought beginning suddenly and quickly to make what looked to George like cryptic notes.

What Bart was actually doing was going over and over all of the facts of the HEAT SEEKER case that he could remember—the dates, the operations, the compromises, then comparing those against the time when Harold Sema worked at CIA Headquarters. And the foremost thought in his mind was, "Is it possible that Sema is one of the five names on John Kitchen's list of FBI suspects?" Bart's first thought that morning had been just to wait until he got back to Washington and then pass his suspicions on to John Kitchen. But based on what he could recall, his gut told him it was more than just a coincidence. The clincher came, however, when Bart suddenly remembered why Harold Sema had seemed familiar to him. Bart was sure that Sema was one of two men who were at the next table at Clyde's in Georgetown more than three years ago when Bart and B.J. Ross had met for a late dinner. Bart vividly remembered the occasion because they were seated in the no-smoking section enjoying their cocktails when two men came in, took the table next to theirs, ordered drinks and immediately started smoking cigars. The smoke coming over to Bart and B.J.'s table was so heavy and annoying that Bart had no choice but to complain. The waiter who took the complaint then asked the two men to stop or move to a table in the smoking section. The two men had at first taken umbrage at the waiter's request and had accosted him in loud voices, particularly the younger one who had a heavy accent. Then the older one, the man Bart believed was Sema, calmed the younger one down, and they moved without incident to another table.

Bolstered by his recollection, Bart organized his thoughts and wrote out an "EYES ONLY" message for Colonel Bob

Herrington at SSD at DAS Headquarters with instructions to pass the information on immediately to John Kitchen at the FBI. The problem now was the message transmission. Because no one else on the trip, not even George Martin, was cleared for HEAT SEEKER, Bart would have to do the encryption himself. Once he had reduced the message to its shortest possible length, Bart turned to George and said, "George, three things. One, as soon as we get to Harare we need to tell the DATT, Lieutenant Colonel Brooks, that I need a break in the planned schedule as soon as possible and the necessary code materials to prepare and send an encrypted message back to the headquarters. Two, I am going to draft a second OPIMMEDIATE message for you to send to Captain Hargrove in Singapore. Three, alert the DAO in Pretoria that we may be a day late if we return to Kinshasa on Sunday. If we do George, can you work your magic on our return flights to the States?"

"Yes, sir. I'll get right on it as soon as we land," Colonel Martin replied. George Martin knew what had been bothering the old man. One of those very few things that George was not cleared for. "But believe me," George thought to himself," who needs it. I've got enough to worry about as it is."

The DAO team in Harare reacted to the unscheduled drill like champs, and Bart struggled through the encrypted message preparation alone in the DATT's office in the embassy. He then released the Herrington and the Hargrove messages that George had typed. The rest of the visit in Zimbabwe went off as planned and the trip to the game park was an experience that Bart and George wouldn't soon forget. Shades of *Out of Africa* were strong in the men's minds. Bart had instructed Colonel Herrington and Captain Hargrove to reply to his cables by Sunday morning, Zimbabwe time. Nothing had arrived when George checked on them Saturday night. Bart spent a near sleepless night not knowing whether or not to press on to South Africa or to return to Kinshasa for the Sunday night crocodile hunt.

On Sunday morning while General Lowe was having breakfast with Lieutenant Colonel Brooks, George walked the three blocks from their hotel to the U.S. Embassy to check on the cable traffic. At 9:15 he came running into the dining room out of breath and red-faced. He had two messages to show Bart. The first was a short message from Colonel Herrington. It referenced his earlier message and contained only two sentences.

"John Kitchen said to tell you BINGO! Our people also confirm that subject served in Moscow during a three year hitch in the Army, 1957-1960."

Bart could hardly believe his eyes.

The second message from Captain Hargrove stated:

"Simon Telford reports that the individual mentioned in your cable served briefly in Singapore, noting that the Singaporian Foreign Office records reflect that a white, male individual named Harold Sema with a U.S. Diplomatic passport was assigned to the U.S. Embassy from 1971-72. Hope this helps. Simon sends warm regards. Very respectfully, Lance."

Bart bolted out of his seat and said, "George, we are going back to Kinshasa."

CHAPTER 21

THE CROCODILE HUNT

Most of the day on Sunday was spent on the C-12 flight back to Kinshasa. Bart had told George to simply advise the operations center at Rosslyn and DAO Pretoria that his visit and return to the United States would be delayed by one day.

Bart had no idea what to expect from the crocodile hunt, or even why Harold Sema had suggested it. He did know he felt compelled to accept Sema's invitation, since he believed the pieces of the long standing HEAT SEEKER puzzle were falling into place and that Harold Sema held the remaining answers. Bart also realized that what he was about to do, given the latest information he had learned about Sema, was well beyond his authority and really should be a matter for the CIA and FBI.

He knew for certain that if he had queried John Kitchen on the advisability of any further contact with Sema, his FBI friend would not have only said no; he would have said, hell no! Yet, Bart's gut told him he had a role to play in HEAT SEEKER, so he decided to press on.

Paul Talbot met Bart and George at plane-side when they arrived back in Kinshasa. He suggested that they return to his quarters for a swim, refreshments and a couple of hours of rest before departing on the crocodile hunt. Once in the sedan and underway, Bart could sense a feeling of tension from Paul. He put it to him.

"What's on your mind Paul?"

"General, I don't think that this crocodile hunt is a good idea. Frankly, I'm surprised you would come all the way back to Kinshasa just for the opportunity of spending a few hours in a miserably hot jungle with a shithead like Sema. I must be missing something!"

Paul's plain spoken perplexity broke the tension, brought a smile to George's face, and caused Bart to laugh. It was the first time Bart had relaxed all day.

Paul looked even more confused and said, "I don't get it."

Bart attempted to ease Colonel Talbot's discomfort by explaining what he could. "I hear you, Paul, and you need to know that you are not alone. I suspect that the same thought has crossed George's mind. Am I right, George?

"Roger that, boss," George confirmed. Bart could see a wrinkle of concern across George Martin's forehead.

"You both need to accept that I have good reasons for returning and that I haven't completely taken leave of my senses. Suffice it to say that I am hoping to find out more about the man Harold Sema during the few hours we'll have together. The crocodile hunt is unimportant. It is the opportunity to spend some more time with Sema. As to why? For the time being you'll just have to take my word that it's something I need to do."

Paul took a deep breath and turning his head to face the general said, "Yes, sir, I can live with that. Now let me cover the details. When I got the word this morning that you were coming back, I immediately called Sema. He seemed pleased that you could go with him. I took the liberty of telling him that you wanted me and George included on the hunt. He balked, pleading not enough room in the boats. I went out on a limb, General Lowe, and told him absolutely that you could not go unless I accompanied you. DAS regulations for official VIP visitors, etc.. He caved in reluctantly, but wouldn't go for George. Sorry George."

"You were stretching the truth, Paul."

"Maybe so, general, but there was no way I was going to let you go on that hunt alone with Sema. I don't know what he is up to but crocodile hunting is a dangerous sport."

Paul then told Bart that Sema and his assistant, Rob Joiner, would meet them at 9:00 that evening at his quarters. They would travel in two Land Rovers, heading north out of Kinshasa, up the Zaire—formally the Congo—River, approximately two hours to a location on the river where they would meet with Zairian Park

Rangers and depart by flatboat for the crocodile hunt. The best time for finding the crocodiles on the river was shortly after midnight. The hunt would last three or more hours, the objective being to get a dozen or so crocs. With luck, they would be back to Kinshasa by dawn.

Paul explained that the flatboats contained large searchlights for blinding the crocodiles so that they could be shot and then lifted into the boats by the accompanying park rangers. An accurate shot between the eyes would kill a crocodile instantly and it could then be safely brought into the boat. The real danger came if the shot failed to kill the crocodile and the wounded reptile was mistakenly brought into the boat, pissed, to say the least, at his tormentors.

Finally, Paul said, that the elements along the river, being so close to the equator, were often brutal: tropical heat, monsoon rain, and mosquitoes the size of quarters.

"Sounds like a fun evening, huh, general?"

Bart, serious again, swallowed, half smiled, and muttered, "sounds like."

Harold Sema and his assistant arrived promptly at 9:00. Bart was asked to ride in the lead Land Rover, with Sema driving and Paul and Rob Joiner riding in the trail vehicle.

Sema was dressed in a khaki safari suit and brown, above the ankle, leather boots. Bart had purchased a similar outfit from the safari supply store at the hotel in Harare that morning.

The back of the Land Rover was filled with a variety of outdoor equipment and four high powered hunting rifles. Bart could make out ponchos, two sleeping bags, tarps, water containers, folding chairs, mosquito nets, a case of tinned food, a flare pistol and a large first aid kit.

"Looks like a lot of gear for just one night's hunt Mr. Sema," Bart said.

"Why don't we knock off the Mr. Sema and the general bit? You call me Harold and I'll call you Bart, okay?"

"Fine by me," Bart replied. "I want you to know, I greatly appreciate the invite and am looking forward to the crocodile hunt," Bart added, hoping to establish an early rapport with Sema—to get him talking.

"Yeah, well we'll see. Probably by 1:00 or 2:00 a.m. you'll be cursing me. It can get miserable on the river that time of night," Sema said, looking dubiously at Bart. "At any rate, it will give you an idea of what life is really like in this God forsaken country. I can't wait to get back to the world."

Bart had difficulty in getting Sema to say very much. He seemed sullen. It was very dark outside and the lighting in the Land Rover was dim, making it difficult for Bart to make out Sema's facial expressions. He sensed more than saw that Sema's eyes were glassy and although he could detect no smell of alcohol, Bart suspected that Sema had been drinking.

It did not take long to get out of Kinshasa and once they were on the open road Sema really stepped on it. So much so that Bart checked his seat belt three times. Sema seemed like a man on the edge, more than anxious to get where he was going.

The trail Land Rover was having a hard time keeping up with Sema, given the pot holes and poor condition of the road. Noting the flashing lights in the rear view mirror Bart called it to Sema's attention.

"Goddamn wimps," snarled Sema but grudgingly slowed down.

Failing to draw Sema out, Bart tried a different tact. He began to tell Sema how much he had enjoyed his earlier trips to the Far East and how impressed he was with certain countries. For example, Hong Kong and Singapore. He then asked Sema if he had ever served in that part of the world.

"Yeah, I served a hitch in Singapore and a few months in Jakarta."

"That must have been a great place to live."

"CIA potholes on the roads to promotion," Sema snarled.

What Bart Lowe didn't know as he was trying to get Harold Sema to talk about himself was that Sema was thinking as much about Bart as Bart was thinking about him. And beneath Sema's thoughts was a seething anger.

When Harold Sema returned from his last overseas assignment to CIA Headquarters in 1984, he had been assigned to the Government and Military Liaison Office. A nothing job. His buddies and classmates were all serving in important jobs and Harold Sema, with 24 years service was still a nobody in the eyes of his colleagues. Also, he had no friends. His anger had been building for years. Admittedly, he was different than others and he knew he rubbed people the wrong way, particularly his bosses. But he was smarter than them. So smart, in fact, he wasn't going to have to take their shit—CIA's shit—much longer. Since he had met KGB officer, Kasputin, in Washington, his financial outlook had brightened considerably.

After a year in the liaison job, strictly small potatoes, he asked to be transferred to his area of expertise, the Soviet Branch. It worked out. The job was no great shakes, but it got him out of the building to keep his contacts with the Russians. He enjoyed the many embassy parties and what others in CIA thought of as arm wrestling with the Sovs.

It was inevitable and obvious that while he was pitching to the Russians, his increasing anger with CIA was clouding his judgment. Then he made a decision. He wasn't just getting angrier over how he had been treated by CIA, he decided to get even.

He had access to everything the Russians wanted and the money was great. It began to make up for all the years of frustration. Then, because the Russians overreacted and misused the information he gavc them, the agency suspected that there was a leak getting to the Russians. He almost closed the Russians down, but then they agreed to be more discreet with the information and things returned to normal. More money.

But wouldn't you know it. A task force was formed at CIA Headquarters to find the leak and Harold Sema was selected to be on the HEAT SEEKER Task Force. Ironically, Soviet Branch had to come up with a representative and they didn't want to lose anyone important so they gave the task force Sema. Sema worked out of the Counter Intelligence Branch but still had access to the Soviet Branch. The best of both worlds. More money.

Then Sema got the word he was going to Africa. At first he thought it would screw everything up. He didn't have much time. He almost panicked. Then he found out that the language training in French and Lingala was right there in Washington at the State Department's Foreign Service Institute. He could continue his access and help the HEAT SEEKER Task Force in his spare time. And the task force had carte blanche on any files and information at Langley. That was where he first learned of General Bart Lowe.

Lowe's name kept appearing as he picked up tidbits of information around the world. The HEAT SEEKER task force thought Lowe was great. Sema thought he was a military jerk putting his nose where it didn't belong. He also believed the task force had engineered the transfer of him and two others to remote posts as a panicky "cleansing operation" at headquarters. Well, he had a surprise for the military jerk. Before the night was over, Lowe would wish he had never heard of HEAT SEEKER.

Sema had no idea what Lowe was doing in Africa. He thought it might just be a coincidence, but when Lowe insisted on seeing him, and after they had met, Sema decided on arranging a little surprise for him. Sema figured Lowe would find out he had been in the attaché office in Moscow years ago, spoke Russian fluently, and had served in the Far East and Washington in Soviet related assignments.

Because he was smarter than anyone else and knew computers like the back of his hand, Sema was still able to access the Soviet Branch files through the secure communications in his embassy office. He had put that software capability in place before he left Langley. HEAT SEEKER information was different. The task force had changed; a bunch of new people and all their secret codes had been changed. Sema still had one close contact on the task force. She had been pretty closed mouthed lately, but she had told him that Lowe was still providing helpful information to Washington's CIA operations deputy, Art Cheek.

The two hour trip north along the Zaire River had taken them through several downpours but when they reached the clearing where the Zairian Game Park Rangers were waiting in a hut shelter, the rain had stopped. The thatched roof of the shelter stood about eight feet from the ground and rested on four wooden poles and a center brace. Two smoke pots sat beside the shelter to keep the insects away and a lantern had been hung inside the hut for light. A small fire had been made and a pot of coffee was on the fire. The four rangers, native Zairians, dressed in the green shirt and shorts of the park uniform greeted the party as they got out of the Land Rovers. Introductions were made all around and Bart learned that two of the rangers, frequent guides on the crocodile hunts, spoke English, the other two, French and Lingala. Communication was not a problem. Coffee was offered and accepted by all except Sema. As they stretched their legs around the fire, Sema extracted a flask from one of his pockets, removed the cap and took a long pull. He then offered it to Bart and Paul and his assistant Rob. All declined.

"This will do you more good than that coffee. A little alcohol in the blood will help keep the mosquitoes away," Sema volunteered, and again, getting no takers, took another swig from the flask before putting it back in his pocket.

In spite of the smoke, the mosquitoes were beginning to swarm in strength around the newly arrived hunters. The park rangers offered a foul smelling oil in small bottles without a label with instructions to douse it on any exposed part of the body. The oil, as rank as it was, met with instant success. The dive bomber attacks ceased but the swarming continued. Bart hoped that the effect of the oil didn't wear off too soon lest he be carried off bodily by the cannibal-like mosquitoes.

When they had finished their coffee, the rifles were taken out of the Land Rovers and the party moved across the clearing to an old but still sturdy tree where the rangers had placed a large square target with the drawing of a crocodile's head at the center. A small white dot between the croc's eyes was the bulls eye of the target. The lead ranger explained that the flatboat's searchlight would locate the crocodiles by their two orange eyes, visible along the shallows of the river bank. The light would blind the croc's while the boat silently approached to within a distance of approximately ten feet, affording the hunter a direct shot. The well aimed shot, if it struck the crocodile between the eyes, would enter the crocodile's brain, killing it instantly, without pain or suffering. At the time of death the lifeless reptile would begin to sink back into the river. At that time, the rangers would catch the croc with large gaffing hooks and pull the trophy onto the boat. Two flat-boats would be used for the hunt tonight, each capable of holding six crocodiles. Hunting crocodiles was permitted only under park ranger supervision although the rangers admitted poaching was a problem. The take from the hunt, the crocodile skins and meat, would end up in the government's stores.

Sometimes, the ranger pointed out, a near miss shot would take place, stun the croc temporarily and the croc, when it found itself in the flatboat, would strike out with mouth and tail at anyone in its way. A decision would have to be made then whether or not to risk a second shot, possibly making a hole in the boat, or to try and use the gaffs to force the wounded crocodile back in the water. In the unlikely event that this should occur, the rangers, he said, would make the decision—so not to worry.

Bart looked at Paul and Paul rolled his eyes.

Then, Sema leaned over and whispered in Bart's ear, "That's bull shit. When in doubt, shoot."

Bart began to think that Paul was right. The crocodile hunt was not such a good idea.

When the ranger's briefing was over, they each took six shots at the target to familiarize themselves with the rifles and the distance at which they would encounter the crocodiles. The rifles were old 30-06's, single shot, bolt action pieces. They had apparently received very good care over the years, were immaculately clean, and the sights were in excellent condition. As a result, at 10 feet, they were remarkably accurate.

Sema led off with a rifle he was obviously familiar with and made six straight bulls eyes.

Paul was next and he also made six bulls eyes, having done this before.

Bart, also a competent marksman made four bulls eyes, slightly missing the first two shots while he got the feel for the rifle.

Rob was the least familiar with the weapons and asked for a second set of six practice shots to improve his marksmanship.

"All qualify for the hunt," the ranger reported.

The flatboats were tied up just behind the clearing at a small dock that belonged to the Game Park. The vehicles were secured, the equipment to be taken aboard was parceled out among the eight individuals and the boats were loaded by the light of the lantern. Sema indicated that he and Bart and two of the rangers would be in one boat, Paul and Rob and the other two rangers in the second boat. The flatboats were as the name suggested, boats with a flat bottom and square ends, about 20 feet long and 5 feet wide.

The water, ammunition, ponchos, and first aid kit were stowed in the rear of the flat-boats. In front of that, there was a bench for the rangers, an open area of approximately 12 feet, and then two swivel chair seats in the front for Sema, on the left, Bart, on the right, and a small storage area forward for a radio that could be used to contact the Park Headquarters, and the six foot high platform that held the battery supplied searchlight. Beside the seats that Bart and Harold Sema occupied were wooden holders for the rifles. A small outboard motor on the rear of the boat would be used initially, the rangers said, to move them to the hunting location and then wooden poles and paddles would be used for movement in the shallow waters near the river banks.

When all was ready, the lantern was extinguished, the motors started, and the flat-boats pulled smoothly away from the dock. The rangers had informed them that they would be moving up river for about thirty minutes before coming to an area where they would find crocodiles. The searchlights would not be used until the reached the crocodile area.

As they started up river, Bart looked down at the luminous dial of his Seiko watch and saw the time was 12:05. The night was as dark as ink and he knew it would take time for his eyes to adjust to the darkness. He was surprised at how very dark it was. He could not see either shore line and only sensed Harold Sema sitting next to him. As the sounds of the jungle magnified and the overwhelming heat of the humid equatorial night fell on him like a hot blanket, he thought to himself, "What the hell am I doing here? I must be out of my mind!" A kind of penetrating fear, similar to the hot, wet, rain that started falling, permeated Bart Lowe's body.

When the ponchos had been broken out, Bart quickly got into his. The torrents of rain suspended the swarming mosquitoes, but the heat inside the poncho was almost unbearable. The rain fell so hard and in such quantities that one of the rangers gave Sema and Bart bailing cans. There was so much water coming down, Bart thought they would have to turn back. But as quickly as it started, it stopped. Off came the ponchos and the ranger informed them they would be heading into the river shore line, the motors would be cut and the hunt for the crocodiles would soon begin.

Bart had gained his night vision and now could make out both shore lines; he estimated they were a quarter mile apart. Paul's boat was about 200 meters behind them and Bart could barely make out their profile on the horizon. The two boats would stay about 100 meters apart for the hunt. The rangers exchanged hand signals, turned the flatboats toward the far shore and switched the searchlights on.

The light made the approaching jungle seem even more alive. The already steady chorus of jungle animal, bird, and insect noises increased and then, suddenly, orange eyes appeared by the score along the river bank.

Sema indicated he would take the first shot and quietly readied his rifle. When the boat reached within ten feet of four sets of orange eyes Sema picked one on his side of the boat and slowly pulled the trigger of his rifle. The sound of the rifle that had seemed like a mild backfire back in the clearing, now sounded like a cannon.

Bart was conscious of three things happening simultaneously. The noise of the jungle momentarily ceased; the rangers poled the boat forward along side the shot crocodile; and, all the other orange eyes disappeared. Before he knew it, the two rangers had gaffed the crocodile, and placed all eight feet of it within a foot of where he was sitting. He had swiveled around to watch the croc being brought into the boat. Once it was lying on the floor of the boat he unconsciously drew both feet back and braced himself for a possible crocodile attack.

Sema laughed, and the two rangers put their fingers to their mouth asking for quiet. As soon as they had examined the crocodile and determined that it was dead, the rangers turned the searchlight off and the flatboat began to move further up the river.

Bart looked back over his shoulder, and soon saw the light of the second boat, heard a shot, and then saw the light go off. As his boat continued to move up river, Bart began to think about his upcoming turn, and began to steel his nerves for the shot he would need to make. He would not embarrass himself in front of Sema. Bart did not have long to wait. When the flatboat again turned in toward the shore and the searchlight came on, they found themselves in the middle of even more orange eyes than the first time. In fact, Bart was within six or eight feet of several crocodiles.

He had no problem with his shot and the rangers brought an even larger crocodile into the boat.

"Like shooting clay ducks in a shooting gallery," Sema remarked, and reached into his side pocket for his flask.

After taking a drink, he again offered the flask to Bart. Bart was tempted this time, but didn't want Sema thinking he needed a drink. Instead, Bart reached for the container of water and drank about a pint without stopping. While he was drinking the water Bart felt a rush of adrenaline move through his body. Slowly the tension that had been building up began to recede.

By 2:55, there were five crocodiles in the boat and Bart assumed the same amount in the second flatboat.

After Sema shot his third crocodile Bart turned to him, saying, "Harold, as far as I'm concerned, I've got the hang of crocodile hunting and we can call it a night whenever you're ready."

Bart was hot, wet, tired, and increasingly uneasy with the growing mound of reptiles piled in front of him. He had learned that Sema was an expert marksman and apparently not disturbed by the dangers of crocodile hunting. He could think of nothing more to be learned about Harold Sema in the middle of the night and was now anxious to return.

But Sema was not ready to call it a night. "No, I want to get one more. We don't have a really big one yet, and there is a place a little further up river where the big ones hang out."

With that he signaled the ranger to move on up river, and the boat began its stealthy movement. They hadn't been underway more than five minutes when the torrential rains returned and they had to put on the ponchos once again. Bart thought that the rain might cause Sema to change his mind about one more crocodile, but Sema just stared ahead like a man determined to finish what he had set his mind on. Bart tried to relax, feeling as if he was in a steam bath. If Bart had known what was on Sema's mind, he certainly would not even attempted to relax.

An inner rage had slowly been building within Harold Sema during the six hours he had been with Bart Lowe. Bart had become, for Harold Sema, a symbol of all the things that had gone wrong for him in his life and the biggest threat to changing the life that was now both right and profitable for Sema. "Just a few more minutes and this military meddler will get his. A tasty meal for our slimy friends," Sema thought, "And no one will be the wiser. I was and am smarter than all that attaché bunch put together in Moscow who disapproved my application for officer training when I was in the Army."

The rain stopped just as they were pulling into the far shore line again. Bart could not make out the second boat yet.

Sema slipped out of his poncho, and Bart started to do the same, but then, feeling a kind of numbness, thought, "Oh, the hell with it, it will probably start again in a few minutes." Bart had no idea how important keeping his poncho on would prove to be.

When the searchlight came on, it was clear that Sema had been right. The size and number of orange eyes that could be seen was by far the largest group and biggest crocodiles seen that night. There must have been a hundred crocodiles.

Sema looked over the choices very deliberately and carefully picked out his target. Bart watched him slowly pull the trigger and grin with satisfaction as the round struck a perfect bulls eye. The rangers were on it quickly, but struggled getting the crocodile in the boat because of its size. Both he and Sema swiveled around to watch the big croc. When it was finally in the boat Bart estimated that it must be twelve feet because it stretched the full length between the seats and practically covered all the other crocodiles.

The searchlight then went off and Bart momentarily relaxed in the darkness, sleep pulling on his tired mind and body.

Suddenly, Harold Sema stood up and shouted, "The croc's alive! Move back!" As he shouted he attempted to reach under Bart's right arm to lift Bart to his feet, but instead got a hold of Bart's poncho and started pulling on it. Bart, in alarm, cooperated with Sema, rising quickly to his feet, beginning to turn to step forward in the boat. As he was doing so, swaying a bit, he felt Sema pushing him toward the water. Already off balance, Bart could not reverse his direction and felt himself falling backwards toward the river.

In his desperation, he reached out toward Sema's left shoulder, barely getting his hand out of the poncho and into the epaulet of Sema's safari suit and pulled as hard as he could. As he fell, he could feel Sema pulling back the other way, the epaulet tearing and coming off in his hand. Sema, losing his balance, toppled over the other side of the boat into the river.

When Bart hit the water he went heels over head into the wet darkness tangled inside his poncho. It felt as if he had fallen against a large bank of mud. Bart struggled to right himself and get to the surface of the water, but whatever it was, seemed to shift on top of him with a great weight. He could see nothing and he could not free himself from the poncho. It seemed like a blanket around him. His lungs felt as though they were going to burst as the blackness clouded his mind. While he held his breath, consciousness slipped slowly away.

On the other side of the boat Harold Sema's shouts for help had turned to screams. One ranger was firing his rifle wildly into the water around Sema while the other was trying to reach him with the gaffing hook. Both rangers were panicking because they could not locate Lowe. The other boat, hearing the commotion, was moving rapidly toward them.

The next thing Bart Lowe remembered was waking to someone blowing air into his mouth. Could it be B.J.? No, it was a man! What the hell was Paul doing?

"General, General! Can you hear me?" Paul Talbot shouted.

"Of course I can hear you, Paul. What the hell is going on?" Bart asked, still groggy as his disorientation slowly began to fade away.

Then Bart noticed that Paul was kneeling beside him and Bart realized he was laying on the pile of dead crocodiles in the bottom of the flatboat. As he struggled to sit up, still covered by the poncho, Bart saw that Harold Sema was lying beside him. But something was different about Sema. Bart then realized that where Sema's right arm and leg had been, now was only a great wad of blood soaked gauze and two tourniquets tied to the stumps of what was left of his arm and leg. Bart now saw in the light of the boat's searchlight that blood was everywhere. Bart felt like he was going to vomit but all that came up was water and mud grit from the river's bottom.

Bart's memory leading up to when he went into the water began to return, but he was not clear as to what had happened after that. He noticed that the two flatboats had been lashed side by side and the outboard motors were moving the boats down the river as fast as possible with both searchlights on.

"What's going on now, Paul?"

"We have radioed the Park Headquarters and they have requested a medivac helicopter from the MAAG. The chopper will meet us at the clearing where we left the Land Rovers. But it will take us about forty minutes to get there. It's the best we can do," Paul answered, looking worried and tired.

Rob Joiner, riding in the adjacent boat, kept watching intently as Paul ministered to Bart while Rob reworked the bandages on Harold Sema.

"Is Sema still alive? Did the crocodiles get him? Why didn't they get me too? Weren't we both in the water?" Bart asked, looking at Paul and Rob.

"Yes, general. Sema is still alive but barely. I don't think he is going to make it. He lost too much blood and is in deep shock. I don't know the answer to the second question. What I know is that as soon as we heard you yell and the sound of someone falling in the river we turned on our searchlight and hauled ass for your boat. It took us about two minutes to get there. When we arrived the rangers were just pulling Sema into the boat. They used the boat hooks and literally pulled him out of the mouth of a crocodile. The crocs evidently got him as soon as he hit the water," Paul explained. "Rob and the rangers immediately tried to stop the bleeding but he lost a lot of blood. I looked around and you were nowhere to be seen. I first thought you had swam ashore, but you didn't answer my calls. I poled and poked all around the boat worried that a croc had you and was holding you under water. General, I hate to say it, but I thought you were a goner. Christ, I think I was in shock. Running around yelling for you and poling like a madman. Then after about another minute, it seemed like an hour, you just floated up sort of caught on a log, about six feet from the boat. Rob was the first to spot your poncho. It was snagged on a rotten tree. You were face down. I feared the worse, but when we got you into the boat you still had a pulse and so I started mouth to mouth resuscitation. You had half the Zaire River in your stomach." This last comment by Paul was with a sigh of relief.

"By the way." Paul asked. "How did you and Sema fall in the river?"

"We didn't, Paul. Sema pushed me, and he must have lost his balance when I tried to grab hold of him."

"What!" Paul and Rob said in unison, expressing surprise and wondering if Bart was delirious from the loss of oxygen when he was under the water.

Just then, miraculously, Harold Sema, stirred and opened his eyes and looked at the three men around him.

"The crocs got me huh?" Sema faintly murmured and attempted to raise his head, but was unsuccessful. He looked at Rob and said, "How bad is it?"

"Pretty bad, Harold. You've lost an arm and a leg and a lot of blood. But we are getting you to a medivac helicopter. It won't be much longer."

Then Sema turned his gaze toward Bart. "What are you doing here? How did the crocs get me and not you?"

"I'm not sure, Sema, but it certainly wasn't any fault of yours that they didn't get me. You tried your best to make that happen," replied Bart.

This comment brought frowns from Paul and Rob thinking that something was definitely wrong with Bart to accuse Sema of the unthinkable.

Bart then raised himself up on one elbow and looked Sema directly in the eyes. "Harold. Let me level with you. You are not going to make it. You've lost too much blood. I'm surprised you even regained consciousness. But, since you did, isn't there something you would like to tell us before you die? And I don't mean that you tried to push me in the river. I already know that. I'm not sure why. Why me?"

By this time Paul and Rob didn't know what to say or do. Paul thought to himself, "Christ, I'm confused."

Sema's breathing was irregular and his eyes kept opening and closing. He stared back at Bart and whispered, "You mean about HEAT SEEKER ?"

Bart was taken aback for a moment. How did Sema know the code name for the security leak? But he quickly responded, "Yes, tell us what you know about that."

With the slightest of smiles, Sema slowly told the sordid story. It was difficult to hear his faint voice over the sound of the outboard motors so the three men pressed close to his face.

"I know everything about that. I am HEAT SEEKER. And they put me on the task force to try and catch myself. What a laugh. Tell Art Cheek that the whole story is on my computer at my house in Alexandria. I kept a record of everything I passed to the Russians. To the KGB. They were the highest bidders for my services. I outsmarted the whole Goddamn agency."

Sema's words were more and more labored; they could barely hear him. Bart knew he was close to death.

"But why, Harold," Bart asked. "Why did you do it?"

Bart knew Sema had heard his question but wasn't sure Sema would or even could answer it as his strength continued to fade, but Sema gained a brief surge of breath, grinned and whispered, "Why did I do it? For money of course. Why else? And I deserved it."

Bart quickly pressed for one more question.

"Were there others involved?"

He couldn't tell, as Sema stared back at him, whether or not Sema decided not to answer that last question, or if the life had just gone out of him. At any rate Harold Sema was dead, and the question of an accomplice died with him.

How tragic, Bart thought, for an American with all the advantages to betray his country.

He turned to Paul and Rob and could see the bewilderment on their faces. No matter, he thought. I can explain it all when we get back to Kinshasa. He was bone tired and sore all over. He felt like his chest had been crushed. He was glad when the rain began again.

CHAPTER 22

DESERT WIND

General Lowe and Colonel Martin arrived back at Dulles Airport in Washington shortly before noon on Friday. The long overnight flight from Pretoria to Frankfurt and the eight hour connecting flight from Frankfurt to Dulles had been tiring in spite of the first class comfort, service, and considerable care on British Airways and TWA. Bart had been able to grab a couple of hours of sleep on the flight out of Pretoria, but the Frankfurt-Washington leg was during daylight hours, and he and George spent most of the time comparing notes on the trip and writing after-trip reports. Once they were in Lewis Ridge's Lincoln limo heading toward Washington on the Dulles Access Road, Bart used the mobile phone to talk to Chuck Gregorios. Bart intended to go directly to his quarters at Fort Myer unless his presence was required immediately at DAS Headquarters in Rosslyn. Chuck said it was not. He had been able to put off the onslaught of people who wanted to talk to Bart until Monday. Chuck told Bart that he would leave a file of important cable traffic and other items in the DAS Operations Center for him in the event that Bart wanted to come in over the weekend.

☆ ☆ ☆

Zaire was still fresh on Bart's mind. When the flatboats reached the clearing where the Land Rovers were left, the medivac helicopter was waiting. An officer from the ZAMISH was there to escort him and Sema to the hospital in Kinshasa where they were met by the embassy physician. Harold Sema was confirmed as DOA when they arrived. Bart had suffered three cracked ribs in the river, probably when he struck the tree log as he fell, and he was kept overnight at the hospital Monday for rest and observation.

The embassy and Sema's assistant Chief of Station, Rob Joiner, sent out the preliminary reports on Sema's death on Monday, and George and Paul informed DAS Headquarters of the incident involving General Lowe without mentioning HEAT SEEKER. Given the unusual circumstances, Bart made the decision to inform the ambassador, Colonel Talbot, Mr. Joiner, and George Martin of HEAT SEEKER. Between them they spent Tuesday and Wednesday preparing the necessary "EYES ONLY" cables to officials in Washington at Defense, State, CIA and the FBI. Bart also talked on the secure line to John Kitchen, Art Cheek, Bob Herrington, and B.J. Ross.

Paul Talbot's theory on why Sema was attacked by the crocodiles, but not Lowe, was that when Bart entered the water he fell against the huge log and his poncho was snagged. When the log settled against the boat, pinning Bart underneath, it held him down until he passed out. Fortunately for Bart, the log shifted again allowing his motionless body, covered by the poncho, to partially appear at the surface.

Sema's cries for help and his flailing about trying to get back to the boat had only served to excite the crocodiles, and their feeding frenzy had begun before the rangers could get him back into the flatboat. Bart had no way of knowing if his inert body, the mud-covered log, dark poncho and Sema's frenzied movements combined to distract the crocs. He was just thankful and happy to be alive. The discomfort of the cracked ribs would be gone in a few weeks.

For the first time since the ride began, Bart noticed the heavy patches of snow on the Virginia countryside visible from the Dulles Access Road. January, Bart thought, is not one of the better months in Washington, but it was a welcome change from the hot, humid, and wet weather of equatorial Africa.

When the limo pulled up in front of Bart's quarters at Fort Myer, Sam Wild came out, and welcomed his boss home and took charge of the baggage and briefcases. Bart resisted Sam's efforts to feed him something as soon as he walked in but agreed he would enjoy a 6:30 dinner. He then went upstairs and climbed into bed.

He slept soundly until 5:30 and before jumping into the shower he convinced Sam that the meal he would like best for dinner—actually the one he missed the most—was Sam Wild's SOS, that is creamed beef on toast, with scrambled eggs and crisp bacon on the side. The long shower, first hot and then cold, brought Bart out of the lethargic feeling that came over him after a long flight and changing time zones. He dressed in casual slacks, turtleneck and sweater. He went downstairs in time to enjoy a waiting Manhattan—no one made them any better than Sam—not even Hans in Berlin, and his first look at a *Washington Post* in almost three weeks. He sat at the far end of the dining room table as he ate his dinner, so he could watch the ABC evening news on the television in the adjoining study. Sam's evening breakfast was sinfully delicious—way too much fat but absolutely irresistible and perfectly satisfying.

After dinner Bart tackled his mail and social invitations—making notes for Joan—and finally called B.J. Ross. They chatted for almost thirty minutes and made a date to get together on Saturday. Bart was in bed and asleep again by 11:15, having turned off the evening news on the television in his bedroom after his third nod.

Bart spent two hours in the Operations Center on Saturday and then went to B.J.'s for the rest of the weekend. He regaled her with his African adventures, and gratefully accepted B.J.'s hospitality and concern for his safety and physical well being. The convalescing hero found that sensual pleasures for the wounded, were possible if the wounded had an aggressive partner willing to exercise initiatives. She was. They did. "Convalescing wasn't so bad after all," he thought.

Bart woke early Monday. Joan and George and Chuck Gregarios were already at their desks when he arrived at the office at 6:45. Although he had been gone only three weeks Bart was very happy to see his official family and realized then how much he relished working with this group of competent and dedicated people. His near tragedy in Zaire had driven that point home to him.

As he settled in his office with a mug of coffee and chatted a few moments with Joan Weber he realized that he had now been with the DAS more than three and a half years. It was hard to believe. If anyone had told him four years ago that he would be taking on a job that would immerse him in what he was doing to the point that he would ignore what he wanted to do in life after military service, he would have laughed and said "No way." It was the people, he guessed, and so many missions to accomplish, and problems to be solved that fascinated him. Unlike any other job he had experienced in the military, his job in the DAS was a never-ending one. And Bart liked it. This morning, he couldn't wait to get to work and he was even looking forward to getting into the stacks of paper on his desk to discover what new topics were waiting in his never dull DAS world. In the blink of an eye he was totally engaged.

At 7:45 Joan buzzed Bart on his intercom and said, "General, Mr. Kitchen from the FBI is on the secure line for you."

"Thank you, Joan," Bart said, picking up his secure line. "Is this the famous FBI counterspy?"

"I don't know about famous. It's John Kitchen. Welcome back. But more importantly, how are you, my friend? I'm so pleased you survived the dark continent."

"Not as much as I am, believe me. I have fought in three wars, but never faced crocodiles before."

"How are the ribs?"

"The ribs are mending nicely, thanks. I assume this call concerns our favorite conversation piece: HEAT SEEKER. Am I right?" Bart inquired.

"Please note the time," John replied. "I knew that yours would probably be the first call I'd receive this morning after 8:00, and I wanted to be Johnny-on-the-spot and beat you to it. When we received your first message from Zimbabwe we already had Harold Sema on our list of prime suspects. Based on your input we convened a special meeting of the HEAT SEEKER Task Force and, after the information already in our investigative files was rehashed, we voted unanimously to consider him our number one suspect. Hence my BINGO message."

"Thanks a lot for warning me." Bart said.

"Whoa. I didn't have any idea you were going off in the jungle with him."

"Yeah. You're right. And I guess if I had told you, you wouldn't have been very happy about it, right?"

"Right again. You bet your ass I wouldn't have been happy. That could have cost you your life, and almost did."

"I hear you, and I know you are right, but—well, where are you now?" Bart asked.

"Still busting our humps 24 hours a day. Last Wednesday, after your call, the cables from Kinshasa, and the corroborative statements from Colonel Talbot and Rod Joiner, the assistant COS, we were able to obtain a federal warrant to enter Sema's home in Alexandria, Virginia and seize his computer and a number of discs. From what our technicians, working with the CIA guys can tell, all the details from day one are there, including how he was able to continue to tap the Langley data bases from his communications in Zaire."

"Is Sema's wife involved, or any others?" Bart asked.

"We don't think so. Their marriage wasn't very close the last few years and he apparently kept work-related things pretty much to himself. With him in Africa, and her at their home in Alexandria, they didn't have much opportunity for regular contact. She is cooperating with us and has been very helpful so far. We may have to hold her as a material witness. It is a very difficult time for her. The body was returned on Thursday and a quick funeral was held on Saturday for just the immediate family and a handful of people from CIA," John recounted.

"I didn't realize it had all been handled so fast."

"It moved right along, Bart. From all we can tell, it appears Sema was the only one involved. We won't know that with absolute certainty until the investigation is complete, and that won't be a complete wrap for several months, maybe longer."

"John, what about the Russians and their role in it?"

"We'll confront them in time. We always do. And they may or may not admit it. They will probably make Sema a hero of the Soviet Union at some point. At least that's what the old Russians would do. Who knows with the new Russians?"

"Is this thing going to get into the press? Bart asked.

"Glad you asked. We and the CIA are briefing the congressional committees this afternoon and the Attorney General will make a statement to the press at four o'clock. You can bet the story of HEAT SEEKER will make all the network's evening news."

Now it was Bart's turn to say whoa. "John, am I going to be mentioned in that? Do I need to give my bosses a heads up?"

"No, general. Your role and identity have been protected. And the press release has been coordinated with all concerned agencies, including the Defense Department. When the circus begins, and believe me, it will, it usually starts in Congress and then snowballs with the media fanning the fire. The pertinent questions will not be how we caught the bad guy, but how could it have happened? What took so long to catch him? Who can be blamed? Believe me, the HEAT SEEKER beat will go on for some time."

"John, you sound like a man who's been there before."

"Many times, Bart, and I am sure this will not be the last."

"One other question for you, John. I hope Art Cheek doesn't think I'm some kind of fink who looked everywhere in the world for one of his guys to rat on?"

"No, I don't think that's the case. I know you talked to him, and I believe he knows you only did what you had to do. The same as any of us. Art is sickened by all of this, particularly since one of his own CIA guys was the culprit. But I know he wanted to catch the bastard as much as any of us," John said.

"All right, my friend. Thanks for bringing me up to date."

"And a special thanks to you, Bart Lowe. The bureau and CIA owe you a debt of gratitude so don't be surprised, one day, when the FBI Director and the DCI summon you for recognition."

"I got all the recognition I needed, John, when they pulled me out of that African river with all my fingers and toes."

"Right on buddy," John agreed, ending the call.

On Monday night the HEAT SEEKER missile blast hit Washington D.C. and within 24 hours the story appeared in the media around the globe. It began to unravel pretty much the way John Kitchen predicted, with new heat waves coming out each day. By the following week a steady stream of informed government and military officials had talked to Bart about his role in HEAT SEEKER. He suspected that it was only a matter of time before someone in the media would get wind of his involvement. But Bart believed the worst was over. He was ready to get back to DAS business as usual.

Bart spent the next two weeks at his desk reading the various action summaries, cables and reports that the DAS's worldwide operations generated. The amount of paper and information flowing up, down, and laterally throughout the Defense Department and the U.S. Government was, as always, mind boggling. By the end of the second week Lowe had drastically reduced the neatly placed stacks on his desk, and enjoyed, for the moment, a feeling of accomplishment.

One item that had captured his attention was a cable from Colonel James Poreman, the Defense Attaché in Iraq. The cable was Jim Poreman's initial assessment of what was going on in Iraq with the Iraqi Military. Following the Iran-Iraq war, the civilian leadership at the U.S. State Department and at DOD was nervous about Iraq's future. The United States had discreetly assisted Iraq during the war, not wanting to see Iran make further fundamentalist gains in the Mid-East. However, some of the methods of fighting used by Iraq during the war alarmed the United States, particularly Iraq's use of chemical weapons. State and Defense advisors wanted to keep a close eye on Iraq and see where Iraq might be going with its development of weapons of mass destruction and its manufacture of chemical and biological warfare arms.

A new U.S. Ambassador was selected and sent to Baghdad, a woman with impressive diplomatic credentials in the Arab world. The Defense Attaché in Baghdad had been in place during most of the war and was anxious to return to the United States. Arab specialists and linguists are not easy to come by in any of the military services but the DAS was fortunate when the Army nominated Colonel James Poreman. Poreman was serving at that time as the Mid East-Africa Division Chief in the DAS. Bart hated to lose him at the headquarters but Poreman was certainly the best officer for the job. He had served previous tours in Damascus, Beirut, and Amman, Jordan. When Bart returned to Washington from Africa, Colonel Poreman had been in Iraq just over thirty days.

Jim Poreman pulled no punches in his information report on Iraq and its military. He and his NATO attaché colleagues were convinced that the Iraqi military was continuing its pursuit of chemical and biological warfare and weapons of mass destruction through research and development and would attempt to acquire these weapons for use on future battlefields.

Also covered in Poreman's assessment cable was an item that Poreman estimated was fast becoming the number one political-military issue in Baghdad. The issue was based on the great economic cost of the war to Iraq. The war had reversed Iraq's foreign trade balance from a large surplus into a severe deficit by the war's end. In the last few years of the war Iraq had been forced to borrow money and accept assistance from many quarters, many of those in the Arab world. One major benefactor had been Kuwait, and at the war's end, Kuwait had been the first to demand an early return of the money it had loaned Iraq to prosecute the war. In the eyes of the Iraqis, particularly Saddam Hussein, Chief of State and supreme commander of the armed forces, this was an affront. In Saddam's and the Iraqi military's minds, they saw themselves as the savior of the Arab world. The Iraqis had paid for the war with

Iran in blood and lives, and Hussein believed the costs should be shared by all, never to be repaid.

The Kuwaities did not see it that way. The bottom line was that the Iraqis wanted to ignore the debt and the Kuwaities were banging on the table for their money. Poreman had concluded his cable by saying, "There is bad blood blowing in the desert wind."

After digesting Colonel Poreman's cable Bart Lowe knew that Jim Poreman was the right man on the ground to keep an eye on the Iraqis. He had a gut feeling that, with HEAT SEEKER turned off, that wind in the desert just might be the DAS's and its Director's next major challenge.